W9-CND-040

Other books by Simone de Beauvoir from Norton

The Coming of Age
The Mandarins
She Came to Stay

TRANSLATED BY LEONARD M. FRIEDMAN

ALL

NEW YORK · LONDON

a novel by SIMONE DE BEAUVOIR

MEN ARE MORTAL

W·W·NORTON & COMPANY

Copyright © 1946 by Éditions Gallimard
First English edition published in the United States in 1955.
Originally published in France under the title,
Tous Les Hommes Sont Mortels.
All rights reserved
First published as a Norton paperback, 1992.
Translated by Leonard M. Friedman
Printed in the United States of America

Library of Congress Cataloging-in-Publication Data

Beauvoir, Simone de, 1908–
[Tous les hommes sont mortels. English]
All men are mortal : a novel / by Simone de Beauvoir ; translated
by Leonard M. Friedman.
p.   cm.
Translation of: Tous les hommes sont mortels.
ISBN 0-393-30845-6
I. Title.
PQ2603.E362T613   1992
843'.914–dc20   92-6620

ISBN 0-393-30845-6 (pa)

W.W. Norton & Company, Inc.
500 Fifth Avenue, New York, N.Y. 10110
www.wwnorton.com
W.W. Norton & Company, Ltd.
Castle House, 75/76 Wells Street London WIT 3QT

6 7 8 9 0

TO

JEAN-PAUL SARTRE

PROLOGUE

"It doesn't mean much. They applauded Florence just as long."

She sat down at her dressing table and began combing her hair while Annie unbuttoned her dress. *Florence doesn't give a damn about me*, she thought. *Why should I worry over her?* But she did worry and there was a bitter taste in her mouth.

"Is Sanier really here?" she asked.

"Yes. He got in from Paris on the eight o'clock train," Roger answered. "He's going to spend the weekend with Florence."

"She has him pretty well hooked, hasn't she?"

"That's the way it looks."

She stood up and let her dress fall to her feet. Sanier did not interest her in the least, and she even thought him rather ridiculous. But still, she was pained by what Roger had told her.

"I wonder what Mauscot will have to say about it."

"He lets Florence get away with a lot," Roger said.

"But doesn't Sanier mind Mauscot?"

"It's my guess he doesn't know about him."

"Yes, I suppose so," Regina said.

"They're waiting for us at the Royal to have a drink. Shall we go?"

"By all means! Let's go!"

A fresh river breeze was blowing in the direction of the cathedral, the notched towers of which were just barely visible. Regina shivered.

"If *As You Like It* is a hit I'll never go on tour again."

"It's going to be a hit," Roger assured her. He squeezed Regina's arm. "You'll be a great actress."

"She *is* a great actress," Annie declared indignantly.

"Really, it's very nice of you to say so, but . . ."

"Why? Don't you believe it?" Roger interrupted.

"What would that prove?" She pulled her scarf tightly around her neck. "There has to be some sort of sign, like a halo suddenly appearing over your head, and then you'd really know you're Rachel or La Duse or Sarah Bernhardt."

"There'll be plenty of signs," Roger said gayly.

"But none of them will really be certain. You're lucky not to be ambitious."

He laughed. "What's to stop you from imitating me?"

Regina laughed, too, but mirthlessly. "Myself," she replied.

A red cavern opened at the end of the darkened street—the Royal. They went in and she caught sight of them immediately, seated at a

CHAPTER 1 ❧ The curtain went up again. Regina bowed and smiled. Pink spots from the glare of the brilliant lights flickered above the multicolored dresses and dark suits. In every face there were eyes, and reflected in each pair of eyes was Regina, bowing and smiling. The roaring of cataracts and the rumbling of avalanches filled the old theater, and then an impetuous force ripped her from earth and sent her soaring toward heaven. She bowed again. As the curtain came down, she felt Florence's hand in hers. Quickly, she dropped it and walked toward the wings.

"Five curtain calls! Not bad!" the stage manager remarked.

"Well, not bad for a city like Rouen."

She went down the stairs which led to the lobby, and they were there, waiting for her with flowers. Suddenly she fell back to earth. When they were seated in the shadows, invisible, anonymous, it was impossible to tell who they were—she might very well have been performing before a gathering of gods. But now, seeing them in the light, one at a time, she found herself confronted by mortal beings of no special importance. They spoke the proper words of course—"A work of genius! An overpowering performance!"—and their eyes glowed with enthusiasm, a little flame that lit up at the right time and was thriftily snuffed out the moment it was no longer needed. They surrounded Florence, too, and brought her flowers. And when they spoke to her they turned on that little flame in their eyes. As if they could like both of us! Regina peevishly thought. The one was blonde, the other brunette, completely different. Florence was smiling. Nothing in the world could stop her from believing that she had just as much talent, that she was just as beautiful as Regina.

Roger was waiting for Regina in her dressing room. He took her in his arms. "You were never better than tonight!" he said.

"Too good for that kind of an audience," Regina replied.

"Did you hear that applause!" Annie exclaimed.

table with the rest of the troupe. Sanier had his arm around Florence's shoulder. He held himself stiffly in his well-cut suit of English cloth and he was looking at her with the expression that Regina knew well, having seen it so often in Roger's eyes. Florence was smiling, revealing her beautiful, childlike teeth. In her mind she was turning over the words he had just said—or was about to say: "You'll be a great actress. You're not like other women." Regina sat down next to Roger. "Sanier is wrong," she thought, "and so is Florence. She's nothing but a talented child without any real genius. No woman in the world can compare with me. But how can I prove it? And she doesn't worry about me, but in my heart she's an acid wound. I *will* prove it," she fervently said to herself.

She took a small mirror from her purse and pretended to arrange the arc of her lips—she had to see herself. She loved her face, the lively shade of her blonde hair, the noble austerity of her high forehead and her nose, the ardor of her mouth, the audacity in her blue eyes. She was beautiful, with a beauty so severe and so solitary that at first it was startling. "Ah! if only there were two of me," she thought, "one who spoke and the other who listened, one who lived and the other who watched, how I would love myself! I'd envy no one." She closed her purse. At that very moment there were thousands of women who were complacently smiling at their reflections in thousands of little mirrors.

"Shall we dance?" Roger asked.

"No, I don't feel like dancing."

Florence and Sanier had gotten up; they were dancing. They danced badly, but they were unaware of it, and they were happy. Love was in their eyes, only love. The great human drama was unfolding between them, as if no one on earth had ever loved before, as if Regina had never loved. For the first time, in anguish and in tenderness, a man desired a woman; for the first time a woman felt herself become an idol of flesh in the arms of a man. Springtime blossomed anew, unique as every springtime, and Regina was already dead. She dug her pointed fingernails into the palm of her hand. It was undeniable: no amount of success, no triumph could, in that instant, prevent Florence from shining with sovereign glory in Sanier's heart. *I can't stand it, I won't stand it.*

"Do you want to leave?" Roger asked.

"No."

She wanted to stay there, wanted to watch them. She watched them and she thought, *Florence is lying to Sanier and Sanier is deceiving himself about Florence; their love is nothing but a misunderstanding.* But when they were alone together, their love was indistinguishable from a true and great love, for Sanier was unaware of Florence's duplicity and Florence buried all thought of it. *Why am I like that? When people are living, when I see them in love and happy, I feel as if someone were twisting a knife in me.*

"You look unhappy this evening," Sanier remarked.

Regina winced. They had laughed, danced, emptied several bottles of wine. It was late and the cabaret was almost empty, but she had not noticed the time passing.

"I always have a letdown after giving a performance." She forced herself to smile. "You're lucky to be a writer—books live on. The rest of us won't be here very long."

"What's the difference?" Sanier said. "The important thing is to succeed in what you're doing."

"What for?" she asked. "For whom?"

He was slightly drunk but his face remained impassive. Except for the jutting veins of his temples, it seemed to be carved of wood.

"I'm sure that both of you will have exceptional careers," he said warmly.

"But there are so many exceptional careers!"

He laughed, "You're very demanding."

"Yes, it's my worst vice."

"On the contrary, it's the chief virtue."

He looked at her tenderly and it was worse than if he had scorned her completely. He saw her, appreciated her, and yet it was Florence whom he loved. True, he was Roger's friend; true, Regina had never attempted to seduce him. Nevertheless, he knew her and he loved Florence.

"I'm tired," Florence said.

The musicians were putting away their instruments for the night; some had already gone home. Florence and Sanier, arm in arm, were leaving. Regina took Roger's arm. They walked down a little street with freshly plastered façades, decorated with signs painted in stained-glass colors: The Green Mill, The Blue Monkey, The Black Cat. Old women seated in front of their doors greeted them as they passed. Then they turned off into a street of middle-class houses; the closed shutters all had heart-shaped vents. The sun had already risen, but the whole city was still asleep. The hotel was asleep. Roger stretched and yawned. "God, am I tired!"

Regina went to a window overlooking the hotel's little garden; she raised the Venetian blind. "That man!" she exclaimed. "He's already up! I wonder why on earth he gets up so early?"

He was there, stretched out on a deck chair, as immobile as a Hindu ascetic. He was there every morning. He never read, he never slept, he spoke to no one; he did nothing but gaze at the sky with his wide open eyes. From dawn to dusk he lay there in the middle of the lawn without moving.

"Aren't you coming to bed?" Roger asked.

She closed the window and lowered the blind. Roger was smiling at her. She would slip in between the sheets, lay her head on the swollen pillow, and he would take her in his arms. In all the world only he and she would exist. And in another bed, Florence and Sanier. She walked toward the door.

"No, I'm going to get some air."

She crossed the hall and went down the silent stairs, where shiny copper warming pans were hanging from the wall. She hated to go to sleep; while she slept there were others who were awake, and she no longer exerted any control over them. She pushed open the door to the garden—a green lawn surrounded by gravel walks and closed in by four walls on which thin virgin vines were climbing. The man did not blink an eye; he seemed to see nothing and hear nothing. "I envy him. He doesn't realize that the earth is so vast and life so short; he doesn't know that other people exist. He's perfectly satisfied with that patch of sky above his head. As for me, I want to cherish each thing I have as though it alone were all that mattered in the world. But I want everything, and my hands are empty. I envy him. I'm sure he doesn't know what boredom is."

She threw her head back and looked up at the sky. She tried to concentrate: "I'm here and the sky's above me. That's all; that's enough." But it didn't work. She was unable to prevent herself from thinking of Florence lying in Sanier's arms . . . Florence, who wasn't thinking of her. She looked down at the lawn. It was a very old pain. She was lying on a similar lawn, her cheek against the ground. Insects were scurrying about in the shade cast by the grass, and the lawn was a huge, monotonous forest of thousands of little green blades, all equal, all alike, hiding the world from each other. Anguished, she had thought, "I don't want to be just another blade of grass." She turned her head. The man was not thinking of her either; he hardly distinguished her from the trees and chairs scattered about on the lawn—just another stage prop. He irritated her; she had a sudden desire to upset his tranquillity, to exist for him. She had only to speak; it was always so easy—they answered and the mystery was dissipated, they became transparent and hollow, and were then cast aside with complete indifference. It was so easy, and yet the game hardly ever amused her any more—she was certain in advance of winning. But that imperturbable man intrigued her. She studied him. He was rather handsome, with his large, hooked nose. He seemed very tall and athletic looking. He was young, especially his skin, his smooth, youthful skin. He seemed not to feel the presence of people or things about him. His face was calm as death, his eyes empty. As she watched him, a sort of fear overtook her. She got up without saying a word.

But he must have heard something, for he looked at her; at least he looked in her direction. The trace of a smile crossed his face and his eyes fixed her so insistently that it should have seemed insolent. But he did not see her. She did not know what he saw, and for a moment she thought, "Is it possible that I don't exist? Is this not I?" Once before she had seen eyes like those, when her father held her hand while he was lying in bed, the rattle of death in his throat. He held her hand and she no longer had a hand. She was frozen to the spot, without voice or face or life—an illusion. And then she regained consciousness; she took a step forward. The man closed his eyes. If she had not moved, it seemed to her that they would have remained face to face through all eternity.

"What a strange man!" Annie said. "He didn't even go in to eat."

"Yes, he's strange, all right," Regina said.

She offered a cup of coffee to Sanier. Through the window of the veranda she could see the garden, the stormy sky, the man lying on a chair, his black hair, his white shirt, his flannel trousers. He was still staring at the same square of sky with eyes that did not see. Regina had not forgotten that look; she would have liked to have known how the world appeared through such eyes.

"He's neurotic," Roger declared.

"That doesn't explain anything," Regina said.

"To me he's a man who's had an unhappy love affair," Annie said. "Don't you think so, Princess?"

"Perhaps," Regina answered.

Perhaps a picture was glued to his eyes and covered them like a film. But what kind of face did she have? Why was she so lucky? Regina passed her hand across her forehead; it was a stifling day. She could feel the weight of the air against her temples.

"More coffee?"

"No, thanks," Sanier replied. "I promised to meet Florence at three o'clock."

He got up and Regina thought, *It's now or never.*

"Why don't you try to convince Florence that the role is not for her," she said. "Really, it won't do her any good, you know."

"I'll try, but she's stubborn."

Regina coughed. There was a lump in her throat. *Now or never. I mustn't look at Roger. I mustn't think of the future. Just think of nothing and plunge.* She placed her cup on the saucer.

"You have to keep her away from Mauscot's influence. He's forever giving her bad advice. If she stays with him long enough, she'll ruin her career."

"Mauscot?" Sanier said. He curled his upper lip, revealing his teeth; it was his way of smiling. But his face grew red and the veins in his forehead jutted out.

"What! You mean you didn't know!" Regina exclaimed.

"No," Sanier answered.

"Why, I thought everyone knew about it," Regina said. "They've been going together for more than two years now. He's been very useful to Florence, you know."

Sanier tugged at the edges of his coat. "I didn't know," he said absently. He held out his hand to Regina. "See you soon."

His hand was warm. He walked slowly toward the door in his stiff, calm gait. He seemed terribly embarrassed by his anger. There was a long silence. It was done and it could not be undone. Regina knew that she would never forget the tinkle of her cup against the saucer, the circle of black coffee on the yellow porcelain.

"Regina! How on earth could you do a thing like that?" Roger asked.

His voice trembled; his tenderness, the familiar gaiety in his eyes were gone. He was a stranger, a judge, and Regina was alone in the world. She blushed and hated herself for having blushed.

"You know very well that I'm no do-gooder," she said slowly.

"But what you just did is really low."

"Call it low if you like," she retorted.

"What have you got against Florence? What happened between you two?"

"Not a thing."

Roger stared at her with a pained expression on his face. "I don't understand."

"There's nothing to understand."

"At least try to explain it to me," he said. "Don't let me think that it was an act of pure malice."

"Think whatever you like!" she said violently.

Annie was looking at her in dismay. Regina suddenly turned on her and seized her by the wrists. "And don't you criticize me, either!" she said.

She quickly left the room. Outside, an opaque sky was crushing the city; not a breath of air was stirring. Tears gathered in Regina's eyes. "As if malice were ever pure! As if there were pleasure in being malicious. They would never understand, not even Roger could understand. They were easygoing and insensitive; no bitterness burned in their hearts. I'm not their kind." She walked rapidly down a narrow street; water was flowing in the gutter. Two small boys were laughing and chasing each other around a public toilet; a woolly-haired little girl was bouncing a ball against a wall. No one bothered about her, a passer-by. "How can they be so passive? I refuse to be passive." The blood rushed to her face. "Florence must know by now, and tonight at the theater everyone will know." She would read their thoughts in their eyes: envious, treacherous, mean. "I gave them an opening and now they'll be only too happy to hate me." She could find no comfort even in Roger. He stared at her with desolate eyes: treacherous, envious, mean.

She sat down on a stone parapet. A violin squeaked in one of the run-down houses. She wished she could fall asleep and wake up much later, very far away; she sat there for a long while. Suddenly, she felt drops of water on her brow; the stream in the gutter became ruffled. It was raining. She began walking again. She did not want to go into a café with her eyes all bloodshot, and neither did she want to return to the hotel.

The street led into a square dominated by a cold gothic church. When she was a child, she had loved churches, and she still had fond remembrances of her childhood. She entered the church, kneeled before the high altar and sank her head in her hands. "Dear God who sees into the depths of my heart . . ." In times past, she had often uttered that prayer when deeply distressed. And God heard her, always agreed with her. At that time she had dreamed of becoming a saint. She practiced flagellation, and at night slept on a board. But there were too many chosen ones in Heaven, too many saints. God loved everyone; she could never be satisfied with such undiscriminating benevolence. She stopped believing in Him. "I don't need Him," she thought as she lifted her head. "Blamed, disgraced, reproached, what does it matter, if only I remain true to myself. And I *shall* be true to myself; I shall never lie to myself. I'll force them to admire me so passionately that every one of my gestures will be sacred to them. Someday, I'll feel the halo above my head."

She left the church and hailed a taxi. It was still raining. In her heart, there was a great, peaceful freshness. She had conquered shame! "I'm alone, I'm strong, I've done what I wanted to do," she said to herself. "I proved that their love was nothing but a lie; I proved to Florence that I exist. Let them hate me, let them scorn me—I won!"

Night had almost fallen when she entered the lobby of the hotel. She wiped her feet on the door mat and glanced through the window; an oblique rain was lashing the lawn and the gravel walks. The man was still lying on his deck chair; he had not budged. Regina turned toward the chambermaid, who was carrying a tray to the dining room.

"Did you see that, Blanche?"

"What?" the maid asked.

"One of your guests is sleeping out in the rain. He'll catch pneumonia if you don't get him inside."

"Him! Try talking to that one!" Blanche said. "You'd think he was deaf. I tried shaking him because the chair'll get ruined. With the water and all. But he didn't even look at me." She shook her head and added, "He's peculiar, that one."

She wanted to continue talking, but Regina no longer felt like listening. She pushed open the door to the garden and walked over to the man. "You ought to go inside," she said gently. "Don't you feel the rain?"

He turned his head; he looked at her, and this time she knew that he saw her.

"You ought to go inside," she repeated.

He looked at the black sky and then at Regina. His eyes squinted as though dazzled by the little light still left on earth; he seemed to be in pain.

"Go inside. You're going to get sick," she said.

He did not move. She had stopped speaking, but he was still listening as if her words were coming from very far off and he had to make a great effort to hear them. His lips moved.

"Oh, there's no danger," he said.

¥

Regina turned over on her right side. She was no longer sleepy, but she had no desire to get up. It was only eleven o'clock and she did not know how she would kill the long day that separated her from evening. Through her window she could see a patch of sky, scrubbed and gleaming—after the storm, fair weather. Florence had not reproached her (she was the kind of person who did not care for scenes) and Roger began to smile again. It seemed as though nothing had happened, and in fact, nothing ever did happen. A sudden knocking on the door made her start.

"Who is it?"

"It's the chambermaid to get the tray," Annie replied.

The woman entered; she took the tray from the coffee table and in her rasping voice, said, "Nice morning, isn't it?"

"It seems to be."

"You know that crackpot in fifty-two stayed outside till it was pitch black," the woman remarked. "And this morning he showed up with his clothes all soaked. Didn't even change."

Annie went over to the window and looked outside.

"How long has he been in this hotel?"

"About a month now. Soon as the sun comes up, he goes down to the garden and stays there till nighttime. Doesn't even turn down his bed when he goes to sleep."

"How does he eat?" Annie asked. "Do you bring his meals to him in his room?"

"Never," the chambermaid answered. "He hasn't put a foot outside this hotel since he's here, and nobody ever comes to see him. It seems like he just doesn't eat."

"Maybe he's a fakir; you know, one of those Hindu ascetics," Annie ventured.

"He must keep food in his room," Regina said.

"I never saw any," the woman claimed.

"He hides it . . ."

"Maybe."

The maid smiled and walked toward the door. Annie leaned out the window for a moment longer and then turned around.

"I wonder if he really does have food in his room."

"Probably."

"I'd like to know for sure," Annie said.

She left the room abruptly; Regina stretched and yawned. With a look of disgust, she glanced at the rustic furniture, the pastel-colored cretonne hanging from the walls. She hated these anonymous hotel rooms where so many people came and went without leaving a trace of themselves, where she would leave no trace of *herself*. "Everything will be exactly the same, except that I won't be here any more. That's what death is," she thought. "If only you were able to leave an impression of yourself in the air, where the wind, howling, would rush in. But no! Not a ripple, not a rift. Another woman will lie on this bed . . ." She threw off the covers. Her days had been avariciously planned, not a moment to be wasted; and yet there she was, cloistered in this sad and insignificant city where she could do nothing but kill time, time which died so fast. "These days here shouldn't be counted," she thought. "The fact that I haven't lived them ought to be taken into account. That would give me twenty-four times eight, a stock of one hundred ninety-two hours to draw from at times when the days are too short."

"Regina," Annie called. She was standing in the doorway, an air of mystery about her.

"What is it?"

"I said that I left my key in my room and I asked for a pass-key at the desk," Annie said. "Come on to the fakir's room with me and we'll see whether or not he has any food stored there."

"You certainly are curious," Regina declared.

"Aren't *you* any more?" Annie asked.

Regina went to the window and glanced in the direction of the motionless man. She was not concerned about whether he ate or did not eat. The only thing she would have liked to discover was the secret of his stare.

"Come on," Annie said. "Don't you remember the fun we had when we robbed Rosay's little house?"

"I'm coming," Regina answered.

"It's room fifty-two."

She followed Annie down the deserted corridor. Annie turned the key in the lock and the door opened. The room was furnished in rustic style; light-colored drapes hung in front of the windows. The blinds were lowered, the shutters closed.

"Are you sure this is his room?" Regina asked. "It doesn't appear to be occupied."

"Room fifty-two, I'm sure," Annie replied.

Regina slowly pivoted around. Not a single sign of human habitation was visible; not a book, not a paper, not a cigarette butt. Annie opened the closet; it was empty.

"Well, where does he keep the food?" Annie asked.

"Perhaps in the bathroom," Regina said.

There was no doubt it was his room. Above the washbowl were a razor, a shaving brush, a toothbrush and a bar of soap; the razor was no different from all other razors, the soap was real soap—solid, reassuring objects. Regina pulled open a closet door. She saw clean linen on one of the shelves and a flannel jacket on a hanger. She slipped her hand into one of the pockets.

"This is becoming interesting," she said. She withdrew her hand; it was filled with gold coins.

"My God!" Annie exclaimed.

In the other pocket there was a scrap of paper. It was a certificate from the Seine-Inférieure Asylum. The man had amnesia. He went by the name of Raymond Fosca, but neither his birthplace nor his age were given. He had been released from the asylum a month before, but the length of his stay was nowhere stated.

"Oh!" Annie said, disappointedly. "Monsieur Roger was right after all. He's crazy."

"Naturally, he's crazy," Regina said. She put the paper back in the pocket. "I'd like to know why they put him away, though."

"Anyway, there's no food here," Annie said. "He doesn't eat." With a perplexed look on her face, she surveyed the room once more. "Maybe he's really a fakir," she said. "A fakir can be crazy, too."

❧

Regina sat down in a wicker chair next to the immobile man and called softly, "Raymond Fosca!"

He drew himself up and looked at Regina. "How do you know my name?" he asked.

"Ah! I'm sort of a sorceress," Regina answered. "But that shouldn't surprise you. You're a sorcerer yourself. You manage to live without food."

"You know that too," he said.

"I know a lot of things."

He let himself fall back in the chair. "Leave me alone," he said. "Go away. You haven't any right to follow me here."

"No one is following you," she said. "I live in this hotel and I've been watching you for the past few days. I'd like you to teach me your secret."

"What secret? I haven't any secret."

"I'd like you to teach me how you manage never to be bored."

He did not answer. He closed his eyes. She called to him again, softly. "Raymond Fosca! Do you hear me?"

"Yes," he replied.

"I get terribly bored," she said.

"How old are you?" Fosca asked.

"Twenty-eight."

"You have, at most, fifty more years to live," he said. "They'll pass quickly."

She grabbed him by the shoulders and shook him violently. "What!" she cried out. "You're young, you're strong, and yet you prefer to live like a dead man."

"I haven't found anything better to do."

"Search," she said. "Would you like it if we searched together?"

"No."

"You say 'no' without even looking at me. Look at me."

"It's not worth the trouble," he said. "I've seen you a hundred times."

"But from far away . . ."

"From both far and near."

"When?"

"In all ages," he said. "Everywhere."

"But it wasn't I." She leaned toward him. "You must look at me. Now tell me, have you ever seen me before?"

"Perhaps not."

"I knew it!"

"For the love of God, go away!" he pleaded. "Go away, or else everything will begin again."

"And what if everything did begin again?"

❧

"Do you really want to take that lunatic back to Paris with you?" Roger asked.

"Yes, I want to cure him," Regina answered. She carefully placed her black velvet dress in her valise.

"Why?"

"It's amusing," she said. "You can't imagine the progress he's made in four days. Now when I speak to him, I know he hears me, even if he doesn't answer. And often he does."

"And after you've cured him?"

"Then I'll drop him," she said gayly.

Roger put down his pen and looked at Regina. "You frighten me," he said. "You're a real vampire."

She leaned against him and put her arms around his neck. "A vampire who never really made you suffer."

"You haven't had your final say yet," he replied guardedly.

She liked his thoughtful tenderness, his intelligent devotion; he belonged to her body and soul, and she loved him as much as she could love any being other than herself.

"How is your work going?"

"I think I have a good idea for the forest setting."

"I'll leave you alone then. I'm going to see my patient." She went down the corridor and knocked at the door of room 52.

"Come in."

She pushed open the door and he walked toward her from the back of the room.

"May I turn the light on?" she asked.

"Go right ahead."

She pushed the switch. On the table next to the bed she noticed a package of cigarettes and an ashtray full of butts. "Well! You smoke!" she said.

"I bought some cigarettes this morning." He offered her the package. "I guess you're satisfied."

"Me? Why?"

"Time is beginning to flow again."

She sat down in a chair and lit a cigarette. "You know, we're leaving tomorrow morning."

He was standing by the window looking at the starry sky. "Always the same stars."

"We're leaving tomorrow morning," she repeated. "Are you ready?"

He sat down in front of Regina. "Why do you bother with me?"

"I've decided to cure you."

"But I'm not sick."

"You refuse to live."

He observed her with a cold, worried eye. "Tell me, do you love me?"

She laughed. "That's my business," she said in an ambiguous tone of voice.

"Because you mustn't."

"I don't need your advice."

"But this is something very special," he said.

"I know," she haughtily declared.

"What exactly *do* you know?" he said slowly.

She looked at him steadily. "I know that you've just come out of an asylum and that you have amnesia."

He smiled. "Ah, me!" he sighed.

"What do you mean, 'Ah, me!'?"

"If only I were lucky enough to have amnesia!"

"Lucky enough!" she said. "You must never deny your past."

"If I had amnesia, I'd be almost like other men. Perhaps I'd even be able to love you."

"You have my dispensation," she said. "But you can be sure of one thing, I don't love you."

"You're beautiful. See what rapid progress I'm making. Now I know you're beautiful."

She leaned toward him and placed her hand on his wrist. "Come to Paris with me."

He hesitated. "Why not?" he said sadly. "In any case, the wheel of life is turning again."

"Does that really make you sorry?"

"Oh, I don't hold it against you. Even without you, it would have happened sooner or later. Once I was able to hold my breath for sixty years. But as soon as someone tapped me on the shoulder . . ."

"Sixty years!"

"Sixty seconds, if you like," he said. "What's the difference? There are moments when time stands still." He looked at his hands for what seemed a long while. "Moments when you're beyond life and yet still see. And then time begins flowing again, your heart beats, you stretch out your arms, you take a step forward. You still know, but you no longer see."

"Yes," she said. "You suddenly find yourself back in your room combing your hair."

"You have to comb your hair, of course. Every day." He lowered his head, his face was drawn.

She watched him silently for a long moment. "Tell me, how long were you in the asylum?"

"Thirty years."

"Thirty years! How old are you then?"

He did not answer.

———

CHAPTER 2 🖋 "Well, what's happened to your fakir?" Laforêt asked.

Regina, smiling, filled the port glasses. "He goes to restaurants twice a day, he wears chain-store suits and he's as boring as an office clerk. I think I over-cured him."

Roger leaned toward Dulac. "There was a crackpot in our hotel in Rouen who thought he was a fakir. Regina decided to bring him back to his senses."

"Did you succeed?" Dulac asked, turning toward Regina.

"No matter what she does, she's always successful at it," Roger answered for her. "She's an extraordinary woman!"

Regina smiled. "Excuse me a moment. I'm going to see how the dinner's coming along."

Crossing the living room, she had the uneasy feeling that Dulac was studying her. With the well-trained eye of a connoisseur, he appraised the shape of her calf, the curves of her body, the suppleness of her walk. *A horsetrader!* She opened the door to the kitchen.

"Everything all right?"

"Everything's all right," Annie replied. "But what shall I do with the soufflé?"

"Put it in the oven as soon as Madame Laforêt comes. She'll be here soon." She stuck her finger in the sauce of the duck à l'orange. It had never turned out better. "How do I look?" she asked Annie.

Annie examined her with a critical eye. "I like your hair better in plaits."

"I know," Regina said. "But Roger wants me to tone down all my distinctive features. He only appreciates ordinary beauty."

"It's a shame," Annie said.

"Don't worry. As soon as I've made two or three films, I'll make them accept my real face."

"Does Dulac seem interested in you?"

"That kind is never easy to interest." Then, between her teeth, she muttered, "I hate those horsetraders!"

"Be sure not to make any scenes," Annie worriedly advised. "Don't drink too much and don't lose your temper."

"I'll be an angel. I'll laugh at all of Dulac's little jokes. And if I have to sleep with him, I'll sleep with him."

"He won't ask for *that* much!" Annie laughed.

"What's the difference. I'd just as soon sell myself wholesale as retail." She looked at her reflection in the mirror hanging above the sink. "I can't afford to wait much longer," she said, half to herself.

The doorbell rang. Annie walked quickly to the door while Regina continued to study her face. She hated that hair-do and the movie-star makeup. She hated the false smile that was even now forming on her lips, and the mundane intonations of her voice. *It's degrading*, she angrily thought, *but I'll have my revenge later.*

"It's not Madame Laforêt." Annie stood at the kitchen door with a dismayed look on her face.

"Who is it?"

"It's the fakir."

"Fosca? What does he want here now? You didn't let him in, I hope?"

"No. He's waiting in the hall."

Regina closed the door of the kitchen behind her and went out to
the hall. "My dear Fosca," she said coldly, "I'm very sorry, but I
absolutely cannot see you this evening. I distinctly asked you not to
come here."

"I just wanted to find out if you were sick. It's been three days since
I last saw you."

She looked at him irritably. He was wearing a gabardine suit and
he held his hat in his hand. His appearance was outlandish.

"You could at least have phoned me," she said dryly.

"I wanted to *find out*."

"Well, now you've found out. Excuse me, but I'm giving a dinner
this evening and it's very important. I'll stop by to see you as soon as
I have a few minutes to spare."

He smiled. "A dinner isn't very important."

"My whole career is at stake tonight. I have a chance of making
a sensational debut in the movies."

"The movies aren't very important, either."

"And I suppose what you have to tell me is of the world's greatest
importance," she retorted with unconcealed annoyance.

"Ah! don't forget it's you who wanted it this way. Before, nothing
seemed important."

The doorbell rang again.

"Go in there." Regina pushed him into the kitchen. "Annie, say
that I'm coming right away."

Fosca smiled. "Smells good!"

He took a mauve-colored petit four from a platter and stuck it in
his mouth.

"If you have something to tell me, talk, but hurry up," she said.

He looked at her gently. "You made me come to Paris. You pestered
me to start living again. Well, now it's up to you to make my life
livable. You mustn't let three whole days go by without coming to
see me."

"Three days isn't long."

"For me, it's long. Remember, I have nothing else to do but wait for
you."

"That's just where you've made your mistake," she said. "You may
have nothing to do, but I've got a thousand things to keep me busy. I
can't take up all my days with you from morning till night."

"You asked for it. You wanted me to take notice of you. Now nothing else matters to me. I know you're alive and I feel an emptiness inside me when you're away."

"Shall I start the soufflé?" Annie asked.

"Yes, we'll eat right away," Regina answered. "Listen," she said, turning to Fosca, "we can discuss this later, I'll come to see you soon."

"Tomorrow?"

"All right, tomorrow."

"What time?"

"About three o'clock." She edged him gently toward the door.

"I'd have preferred seeing you now." He smiled. "I'm going, but you must come to see me."

"I'll come," she promised.

She slammed the door violently behind her. "What nerve! He'll wait a long time before he sees me again! If he ever comes back, don't let him in."

"Poor fellow, he's crazy," Annie said.

"He doesn't look it any more."

"His eyes are so strange."

"Well, I'm not a sister of charity," Regina protested.

She went into the living room and, smiling, walked toward Madame Laforêt. "Excuse me," she said. "Can you imagine! My fakir was just here bothering me to death."

"You should have invited him to stay," Dulac said.

Everyone burst out laughing.

"Some more brandy?" Annie asked.

"Please."

Regina downed the brandy and sat herself comfortably in front of the fireplace. She felt warm and cozy. The radio was softly playing a jazz melody. Annie had lit a small lamp and was peeling cards off a deck, trying to read her fortune. Regina simply sat there quietly and did nothing. She looked at the flames and then at the walls, on which misshapen shadows were nimbly dancing. And she felt happy. The rehearsal had gone very well. Laforêt, always so stingy with compliments, had praised her highly. *As You Like It* was going to be a success, and after that anything could be hoped for. "I'm getting there," she thought with a self-satisfied smile on her face. Lying before the fire in Rosay's house, how often had she sworn to herself that one day she would be loved, would be famous! She felt like taking that ardent little girl by the hand, leading her into the room and saying to her, "I've kept your promises. Look who you've become!"

"Someone's ringing," Annie said.

"Go see who it is."

Annie ran off to the kitchen. By climbing on a chair, the whole length of the hallway could be seen through a small transom.

"It's the fakir."

"I thought so. Don't open."

The bell rang a second time.

"He's going to ring all night," Annie said.

"He'll get tired soon."

For a moment there was silence, then a series of prolonged, insistent rings, then silence again.

"You see, he's gone," Regina said.

She pulled the skirts of her dressing gown around her legs and rolled herself up again on the rug. But the ringing of the bell had been enough to spoil the perfection of that happy moment. On the other side of the door, the rest of the world existed again; Regina was no longer alone with herself. She looked at the parchment lamp shades, the Japanese masks, all the little things she had carefully chosen one by one and which now brought back memories of precious moments. But the things grew silent, the memories faded, and this moment, like the others, would fade, too. The ardent little girl was dead, the avid young woman was going to die, and the great actress she hoped so passionately to become, would also die one day. Perhaps her name would be remembered for a while. But there would be no one to remember that singular taste of life on her lips, the passion burning in her heart, the beauty of the red flames and their phantasmagorial secrets.

"Listen!" Annie said, raising her head. There was a frightened look on her face. "I heard a noise in your room."

Regina looked at the door. The knob was turning.

"Don't be frightened," Fosca said. "I'm sorry, but you didn't seem to hear the doorbell."

"Ah! It's the devil!" Annie exclaimed.

"No, not at all. I just came in through the window, that's all."

Regina stood up. "I'm sorry the window wasn't locked."

"I'd have broken the pane." He smiled and Regina returned the smile.

"Wouldn't you be afraid to do a thing like that?" she asked.

"No. I'm never afraid. But in my case it's nothing to be proud of."

She pointed to a chair and filled two glasses. "Sit down."

He sat down. He had scaled three stories at the risk of breaking his neck and had caught her by surprise with her hair in disarray, her cheeks shiny and wearing a pale pink terry-cloth robe. He distinctly had the advantage.

"You can go to bed, Annie."

Annie leaned over Regina and kissed her on the cheek. "If you need me, just call."

"Uh-huh. Don't have any bad dreams." The door closed and she looked at Fosca. "Well?"

"You see, you won't get away from me so easily. If you stop coming to see me, I'll come to you. If you shut your door to me, I'll get in through the window."

"You'll simply force me to barricade the windows," she said coldly.

"I'll wait for you at the door, I'll follow you through the streets . . ."

"And what will you gain by all that?"

"I'll see you, I'll hear your voice." He got up and went over to her chair. "I'll hold you in my arms," he said, seizing her by the shoulders.

"You don't have to squeeze so hard," she said, wriggling herself free. "I suppose it's all the same to you that you're making yourself repulsive?"

"How could that possibly bother me?" He looked at her compassionately. "Soon you'll be dead and all your thoughts with you."

She stood up and recoiled a few steps. "Right now, I'm alive."

"Yes, and I can see you."

"Well then, don't you see that you're annoying me?"

"Of course. But your eyes are so beautiful when you're angry."

"Then my feelings mean nothing to you?"

"You'll be the first to forget them," he said.

"Ah!" she exclaimed in exasperation. "You're forever talking about the time when I'll be dead! But even if you were to kill me just one minute from now, it wouldn't change a thing. Your presence is disagreeable to me—now!"

His face broke into a smile. "I certainly don't want to kill you."

"I should hope not." She sat down again, not entirely reassured.

"Why are you giving me up?" he asked. "Why do you spend your time with those insects and never with me?"

"What insects?"

"Those ephemeral little men with whom you're always laughing."

"Can I ever laugh with you?" she said irritably. "All you know how to do is look at me and not say anything. You refuse to live. But *I* love life. Can you understand that?"

"What a shame!"

"Why?"

"It will all be over so soon."

"Again?"

"Again. Always."

"Can't you talk about anything else?"

"But how can you think of anything else?" he asked. "How on earth can you feel so permanently settled in the world when you've just hardly come into it and when you're going to leave it again in so few years?"

"At least when I die, *I'll* have lived," she retorted. "You, you're already a corpse."

He lowered his head and looked at his hands. *Beatrice had said that, too. A corpse!* He lifted his head again. "After all, you're right, I suppose. Why should you think of death when you're going to die whether you want to or not. It will be so simple for you; you won't have to bother yourself about it at all."

"And you?"

"Me?" He looked at her with a look so desperate that she was afraid of what he was going to say. But he said only, "It's different."

"Why?"

"I can't explain it."

"You can if you want to."

"I don't want to, then."

"But I'd like to hear about it."

"No," he said flatly. "It would change everything between us."

"That would be just fine. Maybe you'd seem less boring."

He gazed into the fire. Above his large, hooked nose, his eyes beamed. And then the momentary light quickly died. "No."

She got up. "All right, then. Go back to your room if you have nothing interesting to tell me."

He stood up, too. "When will you come to see me?"

"When you decide to tell me your secret," she answered.

Fosca's face hardened. "All right. Come tomorrow."

She was sprawled out on the iron-framed bed, the hideous iron bed with its scaly bars. Turning her head aside, she could see a patch of the yellow bedspread, the false marble top of a night-table and a corner of the dusty tile floor. Nothing affected her any longer, neither the strong smell of ammonia, nor the screeching children on the other side of the wall. All of it, everything, was completely indifferent to her, neither near nor far, simply *elsewhere*. Nine strokes echoed in the night. She remained motionless. There were no more hours or days, no more time, no more place. Somewhere, they had been waiting for her and the soup had grown cold. Somewhere, on a stage, *As You Like It* was being rehearsed and no one knew where the heroine was. Somewhere, a man was standing on a rampart and triumphantly stretching out his arms toward a large, red sun.

"Do you really believe all that?" she asked.

"It's the truth," Fosca answered. He shrugged his shoulders. "Years ago, it didn't seem so extraordinary."

"There must be places where you're still remembered, then."

"Yes, there are places where people still speak of me, but as if I were a legend."

"What would happen if you threw yourself out that window?"

He turned his head and looked at the window. "I'd probably hurt myself very badly and be laid up for a long while. I'm not invulnerable, you know, but no matter what may happen to me, I always heal up perfectly."

She stood up and looked at him fixedly. "Do you really believe you'll never die?"

"Even if I wanted to, I couldn't," he answered.

"Ah!" she sighed. "If only I were immortal!"

"What then?"

"The world would be mine."

"That's what *I* thought, a very long time ago."

"Why don't you think so now?"

"It would be impossible for you to imagine. Year after endless year I'll be here. I'll always be here." He buried his head in his hands.

She stared at the ceiling and repeated to herself, "I'll always be here,

I'll always be here." There was a man who dared think that, a man arrogant enough and free enough to believe himself immortal. Silently she thought, *I might say I'm completely free. I might say I've never met a man or woman who could compare to me. But never would I have the audacity to say, "I am immortal."*

"Oh, how I'd like to believe that I'll never rot in a grave!"

"On the contrary, immortality is a terrible curse." He looked at her mournfully. "I'm alive and yet I'm not living. I'll never die and yet I have no future. I'm no one. I'm without a past, faceless."

"No," she said gently, "*I* see you."

"You see me?" He passed his hand over his face. "If only it were possible to be absolutely nothing. But there are always other people on earth and they see you. They speak and you can't prevent yourself from hearing them, and you answer them, and you begin to live again, knowing that you don't really exist. Endlessly."

"But you do exist," she protested.

"I exist for you, at this moment. But do *you* really exist?"

"Of course," she answered. "And so do you." She grabbed him by the arm. "Don't you feel my hand on your arm?"

He looked at her hand. "That hand, yes, but what does it mean?"

"It's my hand, that's all," Regina replied.

"Your hand . . ." He was silent for a moment. "You have to love me and I have to love you. Then you'd be there, and I would be where you are."

"My poor Fosca," she said tenderly, "I'm sorry, but I don't love you."

He looked attentively in her eyes and slowly said, "You don't love me." He shook his head. "No. It's no good. You've got to say, 'I love you.'"

"But you don't love *me*."

"I'm not sure." He bent over her. "I know that your mouth exists," he said abruptly.

He crushed his lips against Regina's. She closed her eyes. The night exploded. It had begun centuries ago and would never end. From the depths of time, a wild, burning desire had come to place its lips on hers, and she abandoned herself to that kiss—the kiss of a madman in a room rank with the smell of ammonia.

"Let me go," she said, rising. "I have to leave."

He made no effort to stop her.

No sooner had she opened the door to her apartment than Roger and Annie surged forth from the living room.

"Where have you been?" Roger asked. "Why weren't you here for dinner? Why did you miss the rehearsal?"

"I forgot what time it was," Regina answered.

"Forgot what time it was? With whom?"

"You can't always have your eyes glued to a clock," she said impatiently. "As if every hour were exactly equal! As if it made any sense at all to measure time!"

"What's happened to you?" Roger asked. "Where were you?"

"I made such a wonderful dinner," Annie said. "There was turtle soup to begin with . . ."

"Turtle soup!" Regina laughed scornfully.

At seven o'clock, turtle soup, and at eight o'clock Shakespeare. A time for everything and everything in its place. Minutes must not be wasted; soon they would all be used up. She sat down and slowly took off her gloves. Out there, in a room with a dusty tile floor, was a man who believed himself immortal.

"Whom were you with?" Roger repeated.

"Fosca."

"You missed the rehearsal for Fosca?" Roger asked incredulously.

"One rehearsal isn't so important."

"Regina, tell me the truth." He looked in her eyes and in his straight-forward way asked again, "What happened to you?"

"I was with Fosca and I didn't notice the time."

"Then you too must be going crazy."

"To tell the truth, I wouldn't mind it at all," she snapped back.

She looked around her and thought, *My room. My things. He's lying on the yellow bedspread, where I was just lying, and he believes he saw Dürer's smile, the eyes of Charles V. He has the audacity to believe it.*

"He's a very extraordinary man," Regina said.

"He's a lunatic."

"No. It goes deeper than that. He just told me he's immortal." She glanced at Roger and Annie disdainfully; they looked stupid.

"Immortal?" Annie said.

"He was born in the thirteenth century," Regina stated matter-offactly. "In 1848 he went to sleep in a forest for sixty years. Then he spent thirty years in an asylum."

"Enough of that nonsense," Roger said.

"Why couldn't he be immortal?" she asked defiantly. "It doesn't seem to be any greater miracle than to be born and die."

"Oh, please!" Roger exclaimed.

"And even if he's not immortal, he *believes* he's immortal."

"It's a classic case of delusions of grandeur. He's no more interesting that a man who thinks he's Charlemagne."

"What makes you think that someone who believes he's Charlemagne isn't interesting?" Suddenly Regina's face burned with anger. "Do you think you're so interesting, you two?"

"That's not very nice of you," Annie protested vexedly.

"You want me to be like you," Regina said. "And to think! I actually started to become like you!"

She got up, walked toward her room and slammed the door behind her. "I'm like them!" she said furiously to herself. "Little men, little lives. Why didn't I stay there on his bed? Why was I afraid? Am I a coward? *He* walks in the street, a picture of modesty in his felt hat and his gabardine suit, and all the while he's thinking, 'I'm immortal.' The world is his, time is his, and I'm nothing but an insect." With the tips of her fingers, she gently stroked a narcissus in a vase on the table. "And if I, too, believed I were immortal? The perfume of the narcissus is immortal—and the fever that's swelling my lips. I *am* immortal." She crushed the flower in her hand. It was useless—death was in her. She knew it, and even now she awaited it expectantly. To be beautiful for ten more years, to play Phèdre and Cleopatra, to leave a faint remembrance in the hearts of mortal men, who, little by little, would crumble to dust—once she was able to satisfy herself with these modest ambitions. She removed the pins which held back her hair and the heavy tresses fell to her shoulders. "One day I'll be old, dead, forgotten. And at this very moment, while I'm sitting here thinking these things, a man in a dingy hotel room is thinking, 'I will always be here.'"

"What a triumph!" Dulac exclaimed.

"I especially like the subtle way your Rosalind displays so much coquettishness, so much . . . so much *ambiguous grace* under her man's clothes," Frénaud remarked.

"Let's not talk about Rosalind," Regina said. "She's dead."

The curtain had come down and Rosalind was dead. She died every night, and there would come a day when she would not be born again. Regina lifted her champagne glass and emptied it. Her hand was trembling. From the moment she left the stage, she had not stopped trembling.

"I'd like to have some fun," she said plaintively.

"Let's dance together," Annie suggested.

"No. I'm going to make Sylvia dance."

Sylvia cast a quick glance at the respectable people seated around the room. "Don't you think we'll make too much of a spectacle of ourselves?"

"And when you're playing a role, don't you make a spectacle of yourself?" Regina said.

She took hold of Sylvia. She was rather shaky on her feet, but she was able to dance even when she could no longer walk straight. The orchestra was playing a rumba and she began to wiggle obscenely, like a Negress she had once seen. Sylvia seemed very embarrassed. She moved about in front of Regina, not knowing what to do with her body, and she was smiling with an expression of polite good will. All of them had the same smile on their faces. That evening Regina could have done anything she pleased and everyone would have applauded her. She abruptly stopped dancing.

"You'll never be able to dance," she said to Sylvia. "You're too damned sensible."

She fell back into her seat. "Give me a cigar, Roger."

"You'll get sick," he warned.

"So what! I'll vomit. It'll be distracting at least."

Roger handed her a cigar. She lit it carefully and drew a long puff. A bitter taste filled her mouth. That, at least, seemed real, thick, tangible. Everything else seemed so far off—the music, the voices, the laughter, the strange and familiar faces whose shimmering images were infinitely reflected in the cabaret's mirrors.

"You must be worn out," Merlin said.

"More than that, I'm thirsty."

She emptied another glass of champagne. Drink, always drink. But despite the wine, her heart was cold. A little while before, she was burning. They were standing up, shouting and clapping their hands. Now they were sleeping or chatting, and she was cold. Was he sleeping, too?

He had not applauded, he had remained seated, but he had looked at her steadily. From the depths of eternity he had looked at her and Rosalind became immortal. *If I could believe him,* she thought, *if only I could believe him!* She hiccupped and her mouth became pasty.

"Why doesn't anyone sing? When you're happy, you sing. You're happy, aren't you?"

"We're happy about your triumph," Sanier said in his grave, intimate manner.

"Well, sing then!"

Sanier smiled and in a restrained voice began to sing an American song.

"Louder," she said.

He did not raise his voice. She put her hand over his mouth and angrily said, "Shut up. *I'm* going to sing."

"Don't start a scandal," Roger said anxiously.

"It's not scandalous to sing."

She burst out vigorously with:

"The daughters of Camaret say that they are virgins . . ."

But her voice did not obey her. She coughed and began again.

"The daughters of Camaret say that they are virgins . . .
But when they're in bed . . ."

She hiccupped again and felt the blood draining from her face. "Excuse me," she said in a mundane tone of voice. "I'm going to vomit."

She walked to the back of the room, staggering a little. They were all looking at her—her friends, strangers, the waiters, the maître d'hôtel— but she passed through their gazes as easily as a phantom through a wall. She glanced at the mirror in the ladies' room. Her face was pale, her nose pinched and there were splotches of caked powder on her cheeks.

"There's all that remains of Rosalind." She leaned over a toilet and threw up. "What now?" she asked herself.

She flushed the toilet, wiped her mouth and sat down. The floor was tiled, the walls bare. It looked like an operating room or a monk's or lunatic's cell. She had no desire to rejoin them; they could do nothing for her, not even distract her for a single evening. She would rather have stayed where she was, in that antiseptic cubicle, all night long, all her life, walled in by whiteness and solitude, walled in, buried, forgotten. She stood up. She had not stopped thinking of him for a single moment all evening, he who had not applauded, but who had devoured her with his ageless gaze. *It's my last chance, my only chance!*

She took her coat from the cloakroom and called to them as she walked toward the door, "I'm going to get some air."

She left the cabaret and hailed a taxi. "Hotel de la Havane, rue Saint-André-des-Arts." She closed her eyes, leaned back and succeeded in calming herself for a few minutes. But then she thought wearily, "It's all an act. I don't believe it." She vacillated. She could have knocked at the window and had herself driven back to the *Mille et Une Nuits*. And then what? To believe or not to believe? But what meaning after all did those words have? She needed him.

She crossed the dingy courtyard, climbed the stairs and knocked at his door. No one answered. She sat down on the cold stone steps. Where was he at this time of night? What visions—visions that would never die—passed through his mind? She buried her head in her hands. "Believe in him? Believe that the Rosalind I created is immortal, became immortal in his heart?"

"Regina!" Fosca exclaimed.

"I've been waiting for you. I've been waiting for you for hours." She stood up. "Take me with you."

"Where?"

"Anywhere. I want to be with you tonight, that's all."

He opened the door to his room. "Go on in."

She entered the room. Yes. Why not here, surrounded by those cracked and peeling walls? When he looked at her, she was beyond space, beyond time; the setting had no importance.

"Where have you been?" she asked.

"Just walking in the night." He touched Regina's shoulder. "And you've been waiting for me! You're here!"

"You didn't applaud me," she said, half smiling.

"I wanted to cry. Maybe another time I'll be able to cry."

"Fosca, tell me the truth. You mustn't lie to me tonight. Is it really true?"

"I never lied to you," he said.

"Are you sure it's not all just a dream?"

"Do I look like I'm crazy?" He placed his hands on Regina's shoulders. "Dare to believe me. Dare!"

"Can't you prove it to me somehow?"

"Yes, I think I can." He walked over to the wash basin, and when he returned he was holding a razor in his hand. "Don't be frightened," he said.

Before she could stop him, a stream of blood gushed from Fosca's throat.

"Fosca!" she cried out.

He staggered over to the bed and lay there with his eyes closed, pale as a corpse. The blood continued to flow from his slashed throat. His shirt and the sheets became sticky with it and it dripped onto the tiles. All the blood in his body, it seemed, escaped through the gaping lips of the deep gash. Regina grabbed a towel, dipped it in some water and placed it against the wound. Her whole body was trembling. Horrified, she stared at the wrinkleless, youthless face, the face perhaps of a corpse. Foam gathered at the sides of his mouth and formed into beads; he seemed to have stopped breathing.

She called to him: "Fosca! Fosca!"

He half opened his eyes and breathed deeply. "Don't be afraid."

Gently, he removed her hand and pushed away the bloody towel. The blood had stopped flowing, the lips of the gash had drawn together. Above his crimson shirt, only a long pink scar remained on his neck.

"It's impossible!" she exclaimed. She hid her face in her hands and began to cry.

"Regina! Do you believe me now?" He got up and took her in his arms. She felt the sticky dampness of his shirt against her breast.

"I believe you."

For a long while, she stood there motionless, pressed against that overpowering and mysterious body, that living body on which time showed no effect. And then she raised her eyes and looked at him in horror, in hope.

"Save me," she pleaded. "Save me from death."

"Ah!" he said fervently. "It's *you* who must save *me!*" He took Regina's face in his hands. He looked at her so intensely that it seemed as if he wanted to tear her soul from her body. "Save me from the night and from apathy," he said. "Make me love you and know that you alone exist among all other women. Then the world will fall back into shape. There will be tears, smiles, expectations, fears. I'll be a living man again."

"You *are* a living man," she said, offering him her mouth.

Fosca's hand was resting on the varnished table and Regina was looking at it. "That hand . . . that hand which caressed me, how old is it?"

she asked herself. "How can I know the flesh won't rot from one moment to the next, fall off and leave nothing but a few white bones?" She raised her head. "Is Roger right? Am I going mad?" The noonday light poured into the quiet bar where mysteryless men were comfortably sunk in leather chairs, drinking their apéritifs. It was Paris, the twentieth century. Regina's eyes turned back to the hand. The fingers were strong and fine, with nails a bit too long. "His nails grow, and so does his hair." She looked up at his neck, his smooth neck, with no trace of a scar. "There must be some explanation," she thought. "Maybe he really is a fakir, knows tricks, secrets . . ." She brought her glass of mineral water to her lips. She had a dull pain in her head and her mouth was pasty. "I need a cold shower and a nap. Then maybe I'll be able to see things clearly," she said to herself.

"I'm going home."

"Ah! Of course," he said, and then added angrily, "After the day, the night. After the night, the day. Never an exception!"

They were silent. She took her purse and he remained silent. She took her gloves and still he remained silent. Finally she asked, "When will we see each other again?"

"See each other again?" He looked absently at the platinum blonde hair of a young woman seated at a corner table.

Suddenly the nightmarish thought occurred to Regina that he might vanish into thin air from one moment to the next, and she felt as if she were falling dizzily down a deep chasm, through layer and layer of dense fog. And she imagined that when she reached the bottom of that immense gorge, she would turn into a blade of grass, which the coming winter would forever blight.

"You're not going to leave me, are you?" she asked in anguish.

"Me? But you're the one who's leaving."

"I'll be back. Don't be angry. I have to let Roger and Annie know that I'm all right—they must be worried." She placed her hand on Fosca's. "I'd rather stay, you know."

"Then stay."

She threw her gloves on the table and put down her purse. She strongly needed to feel his eyes upon her. *Dare to believe me . . . Dare!* What was she to believe? He looked neither like a charlatan nor a madman.

"Why are you looking at me like that?" he asked. "Do I frighten you?"

"No."

"Do I look different from anyone else?"

She hesitated. "No, not right now."

"Regina!" he said in a prayerful tone of voice. "Do you think you'll ever be able to love me?"

"Let me have a little time." She silently watched him for a moment. "I hardly know anything about you. You'll have to tell me about yourself."

"It's not a very interesting story."

"I'm sure it must be," she protested. "Have you loved many women?"

"A few."

"What were they like?"

"Let's not talk about the past, Regina," he said abruptly. "If I'm to become a man amongst men again, I have to forget the past. My life begins here, today, beside you."

"Yes, you're right."

The young woman with the platinum blonde hair walked to the door of the bar, followed by a rather ripe old gentleman. They were going to lunch. Life's daily routine continued in a world tamely submissive to all the natural laws. "What am I doing here?" Regina asked herself. She could find nothing more to say to Fosca.

With a determined look on his face, he rested his chin on his fist and reflected. Finally he said: "You have to think of something for me to do."

"Something to do?"

"Yes. All normal men have things to do."

"Well, what would interest you?" she asked.

"You don't understand," he said. "You have to tell me what interests *you* and how I can help you."

"But how could you help me? You can't play my roles for me."

"No, I suppose not." He began to reflect again. "I'll have to find some kind of work, then."

"That seems like a good idea. What can you do?"

"As far as something useful goes, very little, I'm afraid," he said with a smile.

"Do you have any money?"

"Not much."

"And you never worked before?"

"I used to do coloring work."

"That won't get you very far," Regina said.

"Oh, I don't care about getting far." Disappointedly, he added, "I would have really liked to do something for you."

She touched his hand. "Stay near me, Fosca. Look at me and remember everything about me."

He smiled. "That's not difficult. I have a very good memory." His face darkened again. "Much too good."

She nervously squeezed his hand. He spoke and she answered, as if everything they were saying were true. *If it's true, he'll remember me forever. If it's true, I'm loved by an immortal man!* Her eyes surveyed the room. An ordinary crowd; mysteryless men. But did she not always know she was different? Did she not always feel herself a stranger among the rest, reserved for a destiny that was not theirs? Ever since she was a child, there was something special, something unique about her. She looked at Fosca. *It's he. He's my destiny. From the depths of time he came to me, and he'll bear me in his memory until the end of time.* Her heart pounded heavily. *And if it's all a lie?* She studied Fosca's hand, his neck, his face, and she thought irately, *Am I like they? Must I have absolute proof?* He had said, "Dare! Dare!" and she wanted to take the dare. If it were an illusion, a dream, there was more grandeur in that folly than in all their wisdom.

She smiled at Fosca. "Do you know what you ought to do?" she said. "You ought to write your memoirs. It would make a remarkable book."

"There are more than enough books as it is," he objected.

"But this one would be completely different from all the others." She leaned toward him. "Didn't you ever try to write?"

He smiled. "I did some writing in the asylum. In fact, I spent about twenty years writing."

"You must let me read it."

"I tore it all up."

"Why? It might have been very good."

He laughed. "I wrote for twenty years and then one day I realized that it was always the same book."

"But now you're a different man," she said with conviction. "You must try again."

"A different man?"

"A man who loves me and who's living in this century. Won't you try to start writing again?"

He looked at her and his face brightened. "If that's what you want, I'll do it," he said devotedly.

He looked at her and she thought, *He loves me. I'm loved by an immortal man.* She smiled, but she did not want to smile, for she was afraid. She looked around at the four walls. She would no longer be able to expect any help from the familiar world surrounding her; she was entering a strange universe where she would be alone with an unknown man. *What lies ahead for me now?*

⌁

"It's time now," Regina said gently.

"Time for what?"

"To leave."

Through the window of her dressing room, they had been watching the snowflakes falling steadily under the light of a lamppost. The sidewalks were covered with white, a soft stillness hung over the city. Rosalind's dress was lying on a chair.

"Let's just imagine that time has stopped," Fosca said.

"But where I'm supposed to be tonight, it hasn't stopped."

He stood up. She was always astonished by his tallness—a man from another age.

"Why do you have to go?" he asked.

"Because it helps."

"Helps what? Whom?"

"My career. An actress has to meet a lot of people and be seen everywhere, otherwise it wouldn't be long before she's buried and forgotten." She smiled. "I want to become famous. Won't you be proud of me when I'm famous?"

"I like you just the way you are," he said in his low-sounding voice. He drew her against him and kissed her long and passionately on the mouth. "You're very lovely tonight."

He gazed at her and she felt warm under his gaze. It was insufferable for her to think that there would be a time when his eyes would no longer look at her, when her life would sink into indifference, oblivion. She thought for a moment and then said, "You can come along with me if you like."

"You know very well I'd like to," he said.

Florence's living room was filled with chatting men and women. Regina stopped for a moment at the door; she felt a sharp bite in her heart. Every woman in the room preferred herself to all others, and for each of them there was at least one man who preferred *her* above the rest. *How can anyone have the audacity to believe that she alone is right in preferring herself?* Regina thought.

She turned toward Fosca. "There are quite a few pretty women here."

"Yes."

"So! You're beginning to notice *that* already!"

"Looking at you, I learned to see."

"Tell me, who do you think is the prettiest?"

"From what point of view?"

"Now that's a strange question."

"To have a preference, one must have a point of view."

"Well, don't you have one?"

He hesitated for a moment and then a smile lit up his face. "Yes, I suppose I do, after all. I'm a man who loves you."

"Well?"

"Well, you're the most beautiful, then. Who could look more like you than yourself?"

She looked at him a trifle mistrustfully. "Do you really think I'm the most beautiful?"

"You alone exist," he ardently whispered.

She walked over to Florence. Ordinarily, she disliked being greeted as a guest in someone else's home, in someone else's life, but she felt Fosca following behind her, looking awkward and timid, and she drew courage from the knowledge that she alone existed in his immortal heart. She smiled at Florence.

"I didn't think you'd mind if I brought a friend along."

"He's more than welcome."

She circled the room, shaking everyone's hand. Florence's friends disliked her; she could feel the malevolence hidden behind their hypocritical smiles. But that evening, their opinions did not bother her in the least. *Soon they'll all be dead and their thoughts with them. Insects!* She felt invulnerable.

"Are you going to drag that man around with you wherever you go?" Roger asked. He seemed very displeased.

"He didn't want to leave me," she replied indifferently. She took a cocktail Sanier offered her. "Florence is ravishing this evening."

"Yes, isn't she," he said.

He and Florence had broken up for a while, but finally they were reconciled and now Sanier appeared more taken with her than ever. Regina had followed them with her eyes while they danced, tightly pressed against each other. There was nothing but love in their eyes, but it was only an ordinary, mortal love.

"We'll have to have a serious talk together," Roger said.

"Whenever you like."

She was weightless, free; that bitter taste in her mouth had disappeared. She was a great oak whose branches touched the sky and which looked down at the restless motion of the grass in the fields below.

"I'm going to ask you a favor," Sanier said.

"Go right ahead."

"Would you recite a few poems for us?"

"You know that she never likes to recite," Florence said.

Regina's eyes circled the room. Fosca was leaning against a wall, his arms hanging loosely at his sides. His eyes seemed glued to her. She stood up.

"All right, if you like. I'll recite *Les Regrets de la Belle Haumière*." As she walked to the center of the room, everyone fell silent. "Fosca," she murmured to herself, "listen carefully. I'm reciting these lines for you."

He lowered his head and avidly contemplated her with eyes that had looked upon so many women who were famous for their beauty, their talents. For him, all those diverse destinies made up one single history, and Regina had now become a part of that history. Now she could vie for his eternal affection with her dead rivals and those who were not yet born. "I'll triumph over all of them and I'll have won the contest in both the past and future." Her lips moved and every inflection in her voice reverberated through centuries and centuries.

"Regina, if you don't mind, I'd like to take you home now," Roger said when she returned to her seat amid much applause.

"I'm not tired," she protested.

"But I am. Please . . ." His half-pleading, half-imperious voice irritated her.

"Very well," she said dryly. "Let's leave."

Silently, they walked through the streets. She was thinking of Fosca, whom she had left standing in the middle of the room and who was looking at other women. She had stopped existing for him and eternity was lost. The world around her was as hollow as a tinkling bell. *He must always stay with me,* she thought.

"I'm sorry," Roger said as they entered the apartment, "but I had to speak to you alone."

Burning embers were aglow in the fireplace. The drapes had been drawn and the lamps, shielded by parchment shades, cast an amber light on the statuettes and Japanese masks. And all these things seemed only to be waiting for someone to look at them to make them spring to life.

"Well, speak," she said.

"When is it going to come to an end?"

"What?"

"That ridiculous affair of yours."

"It's not going to end," she said with finality.

"What do you mean?"

She looked at him and it suddenly occurred to her that this was Roger. *We love each other. I don't want to make him suffer,* she thought. But her thoughts seemed like remembrances from another world.

"I need him," she said.

Roger sat down beside her and said persuasively, "You're just playing a part. You know very well he's sick."

"You didn't see that gash in his throat."

Roger shrugged his shoulders. "And what if he is immortal?"

"Ten thousand years from now, someone will still remember me."

"He'll forget you."

"He says that he never forgets anything."

"Then you'll be there, pinned in his memory like a butterfly in a collection."

"I want him to love me like he never loved before, like he'll never love again."

"Believe me," Roger said, "it's better to be loved by someone who's mortal, but who loves only you." His voice trembled. "You're alone in my heart, Regina. Why isn't my love enough for you?"

In the depths of Roger's eyes, she saw her tiny image; a fur hat was perched on her blonde hair. *Nothing but my reflection in a mirror,* she thought.

"Nothing's enough for me."

"Then you don't really love him, either?" Roger said.

He looked at her anxiously. His mouth was quivering and he found it difficult to speak. He was suffering, a small, sad suffering which was throbbing very far off, in the midst of a dense fog. *He'll have loved me, he'll have suffered, and one day he'll be dead—one life among countless millions.* She knew what her decision would be from the moment she left her dressing room.

"I want to live with him," she said.

———

CHAPTER 3 ✉ For a moment Regina stood motionless at the entrance to the room. In a single sweep, her eyes embraced the red drapes, the beams of the ceiling, the narrow bed, the dark furniture, the books ranged on shelves. Then she closed the door and went back to the living room.

"I wonder how Fosca is going to like living in that room," she said.

Annie shrugged her shoulders. "What's the good of going to all that trouble for a man who looks at people like they were clouds! He won't notice a thing."

"That's just it. He has to be taught to notice things."

With the skirt of her apron, Annie was rubbing a port glass which she placed on the coffee table. "It might have been easier if you'd at least bought him light-colored furniture."

"You don't understand anything," Regina said.

"I understand very well," Annie protested. "When you've finished paying the furniture store and the painters, you won't have a sou left. And it's not with those four old pieces of gold he has in his pocket that you'll be able to feed him."

"Please! Don't begin again."

"You don't imagine he'll be able to make any money, do you?"

"If you're afraid of starving to death, you can quit and start looking for another job."

"How can you be so mean!" Annie exclaimed.

Regina shrugged her shoulders without answering. She had made out a budget and decided that, with a few small deprivations, it would be possible for the three of them to live on what she was earning. But she, too, had her misgivings: he would be there night and day.

"Pour the port in a decanter," Regina said, "the old port."

"But there's only one bottle left."

"Well?"

"Well, what will you offer Monsieur Dulac and Monsieur Laforêt?"

"Pour the old port in a decanter," Regina said impatiently.

Suddenly she gave a start. Even before he had rung the bell, she had recognized his step on the stairway. She went quickly to the door. He was standing there wearing his felt hat and gabardine suit, holding a small valise in his hand, and like every other time her eyes met his, she wondered who, exactly, he saw.

"Come in," she said. She took him by the hand and led him into the room. "Do you think you'll like living here?"

"With you near me, I'd be happy anywhere." He had a benign and somewhat stupid smile on his face. She took his valise from him.

"But this isn't just anywhere." She was silent a moment and then added, "Take off your coat, sit down. You're not just visiting, you know."

He took off his coat, but he remained standing. He looked around him with all the good will he could muster for the occasion. "Did you furnish this room yourself?"

"Of course."

"You chose those chairs, those decorations?"

"Yes. Why?"

He slowly turned around. "Every one of these things speaks for you, and you collected them together so that they would tell your whole life's story."

"And I also bought olives and shrimps," Regina said a little impatiently. "And I made potato chips with my own hands. Come and try them."

"Do you get hungry sometimes?" Annie asked.

"Yes, indeed! Since I began eating again, I get hungry regularly." He smiled. "Three times a day!"

He sat down and took an olive from an oval dish. Regina poured some port in her glass.

"It's not the old port," she said angrily.

"No, it's not," Annie confessed.

Regina grabbed the glass and emptied it into the fireplace. She walked deliberately over to the cabinet and took out a dusty bottle.

"Can you tell an old port from an ordinary port?" Annie asked Fosca.

"I don't know," he replied apologetically.

"There! You see!" Annie exclaimed.

Regina slowly tilted the old bottle and filled Fosca's glass. "Drink it up," she said. Then, turning to Annie, "How on earth can you be so stingy! I detest stinginess!"

"Do you?" Fosca asked. "Why?"

"Why?" Regina laughed weakly. "Are *you* stingy?"

"There was a time when I was."

"I'm not stingy," Annie protested with a wounded expression on her face. "But I think it's a shame to be wasteful."

"I remember the joy of seeing everything in its place, every second, every gesture," he said. "Sacks of wheat were piled up in attics. Even the smallest grain felt heavy."

Annie listened to him with a stupid, flattered look, and the blood rushed to Regina's cheeks.

"I can understand thriftiness but not miserliness. You can want something with all your heart, but as soon as you have it, you ought to be free with it."

"Oh! But you're not free at all with *your* things," Annie said.

"Me? Well, just look." She took hold of the old bottle of port and emptied it in the fireplace.

"Sure," Annie sneered. "Port! But the day I broke one of your ugly masks, did you tear into me!"

Fosca watched the scene with interest.

"Because it was you who broke it!" Regina's voice trembled with anger. "But I can break them all to pieces. Right this moment!" She grabbed one of the masks that was hanging on the wall. Fosca, who had gotten up, went over to her and gently took hold of her wrist.

"What good would it do?" He smiled. "I knew that, too—the will to destroy."

Regina breathed deeply and composed herself. "According to you, then, whether you're this or whether you're that, it's neither good nor bad."

"Why should it be good or bad?"

"If I were stingy or cowardly, you'd like me just as much, I suppose?"

"I like you just the way you are." He smiled at her tenderly, but an unpleasant constriction remained in Regina's throat. Was it possible that he placed no value on those virtues in which she took so much pride?

She abruptly stood up. "Let's go see your room."

Fosca followed her. He examined the room, showing no sign of either approval or disapproval. Regina pointed to a table on which a ream of white paper had been stacked. "That's where you'll work," she said.

"What will I work at?"

"Didn't we agree that you'd start writing again?"

"Did we agree to that?" he said playfully. He touched the red blotter, the virgin paper. "I used to like to write. It'll help me pass the time while I'm waiting for you."

"You mustn't write just to make the time pass."

"I mustn't?"

"You asked me once to give you something to do, something to do for me." She looked at him fervently. "Try to write a good play that I could star in."

With a perplexed look on his face, he touched the paper. "A play that you could star in?"

"Who knows? Maybe you'll write a masterpiece. And then we'll both be famous."

"Is fame so important to you?"

"Nothing else counts," she answered.

He looked at her and suddenly took her in his arms. "Why shouldn't I be able to do what mortal men do?" he said, half angrily. "I'll help you. I *want* to help you."

Furiously, he pressed her against him. In his eyes there was love and something akin to pity.

Regina made her way through the chattering crowd that had gathered in the lobby of the theater. "We've been invited to have champagne with Florence, but I don't suppose you want to, do you?"

"No, I don't think so," Fosca said.

"Neither do I." She was wearing a new suit and she knew she was looking her best, but she had no desire to parade herself before those ephemeral men. "What did you think of Florence?" she anxiously asked.

"She didn't move me at all."

Regina smiled. "That's just it! She can't seem to get any feeling into the part."

At the exit of the stuffy theater, she joyfully breathed in the warm street air. It was a lovely February day and the smell of spring was already discernible.

"I'm thirsty."

"So am I," Fosca said. "Where shall we go?"

She reflected. She had taken him to the little bar in Montmartre where she had first met Annie, and the café near the Place de l'Opéra where she used to have sandwiches before going to Berthier's courses, and that place in Montparnasse where she lived when she was playing her first role. Then she thought of the restaurant along the Seine which she had discovered a few days after arriving in Paris.

"I know a charming spot out towards Bercy."

"Let's go."

He was always ready to agree to anything she proposed. She hailed a taxi, they got in and he put his arm around her shoulders. He looked young in the well-cut suit she had chosen for him, and he no longer appeared the least bit outlandish—a man no different from all other men. Now he ate, drank and slept regularly; he made love; he looked and listened like a normal human being. Only, on fleeting occasions, there was a faint, disquieting glimmer in the depths of his eyes. The taxi stopped and they got out.

"Have you ever been here before?" she asked.

"Perhaps," he replied. "Everything has changed so much. Long ago, this wasn't even Paris."

They went into a sort of chalet and sat down at a table on a wooden terrace overlooking the river. A barge was tied up to the bank and on it, a woman was washing laundry and a dog was barking. On the other side of the water, low houses with green, yellow and red façades were grouped together. Further downstream, a series of bridges could be seen, and in the distance, the tall chimneys jutting from Paris rooftops.

"It's nice here, isn't it?" Regina said.

"Yes, I like rivers."

"I used to come here often. I would sit at this very table and study parts and dream of playing them one day. I drank lemonade—wine was too expensive for me then." She broke off and then asked, "Fosca, are you listening to me?" It was never possible to be completely certain he was really listening.

"Of course," he said. "Wine was too expensive, you drank lemonade." He stopped abruptly and sat up stiffly with his mouth agape, as if a great idea had suddenly struck him. "Are you rich now?" he asked.

"I'll become rich."

"You're not rich and I'm costing you money. You'll have to find me a job. Fast!"

"There's no hurry." She smiled at·him. She had no desire to have him spend his days in an office or a factory; she needed to keep him near her and share every moment of his life with him. He was sitting there, contemplating the water, the barge, the low houses. And all those things Regina loved so well, were entering eternity along with her.

"But I'd like to have a job," he insisted.

"Try first to write that play you promised me. Have you thought about it at all?"

"Of course."

"Do you have an idea?"

"I have quite a few, in fact."

"I knew you would!" she said gayly. She gestured to the proprietor who was standing by the door. "A bottle of champagne." Turning back to Fosca, she said, "You'll see, we'll do great things together."

Fosca's face darkened; a disagreeable remembrance seemed to have passed through his mind. "A lot of people have told me that."

"But I'm not like the others," she said ardently.

"That's true," he quickly agreed. "You're not like the others."

Regina filled the glasses. "To our plans!"

"To our plans!"

As she drank the wine, she studied him somewhat anxiously. She could never tell exactly what he was thinking. "Fosca, if you hadn't met me, what would you have done?"

"I might have been able to fall asleep again. But that's not very likely; it would take a really exceptional stroke of luck."

"A stroke of luck?" she said reproachfully. "Are you sorry you're living again?"

"No."

"It's wonderful to be alive!"

"Yes, it's wonderful."

They smiled at each other. From the barge, the shouting voices of children could be heard, and on another barge or in one of the small, colorful houses, someone was playing a guitar. Evening was fast falling, but a stubborn ray of sunlight still clung to the glasses filled with clear wine. Regina's hand was resting on the table; Fosca gently took hold of it.

"Regina, I feel happy this evening."

"Only this evening?"

"Ah! You can't imagine how new this is for me. There were times when I rediscovered hope, boredom, desire, but never this illusion of plenitude."

"Is it only an illusion?" she asked.

"What's the difference? The point is, I *want* to believe in it."

He leaned over her and under his immortal mouth she felt her lips swell, the lips of a proud child, of a young, solitary girl, of a gratified woman. And that kiss, along with the image of all these things she loved, was engraving itself eternally in Fosca's heart. *A man with hands and with eyes, my companion, my lover,* she thought. *And yet he's immortal, like a god.* The sun was now sinking rapidly in the sky. *But the sun is no different for him than it is for me.* The smell of water rose from the river and the guitar was softly singing in the distance. Suddenly, neither glory nor death, nothing except the violence of that moment, had any importance for her.

"Fosca," she said, "do you love me?"

"Yes."

"Will you remember this moment?"

"Yes, I'll remember it, Regina."

"Always?"

His hand tightened about hers.

"Say it: always."

"This moment is ours, it exists. Let's not think of anything else."

🐝

Regina turned off to the right. It was not the shortest way to her apartment, but she was fond of this narrow street with its black gutters and its stout wooden beams which shored up the walls of ancient houses. She liked the warm, damp spring night and the big yellow moon laughing in the sky. Annie would be lying in bed, waiting only for Regina's kiss before going to sleep, and Fosca would be writing. From time to time, he would look up at the clock. Regina should have been home from the theater by now, but she wanted to prolong her walk through those streets she loved, streets where one day she would no longer walk.

She turned again to the right. There were so many men, so many women who had breathed with equal fervor the sweetness of spring nights and for whom the world was now obliterated. Was there really no recourse against death? Could they never, for just one hour, be brought to life again? She had forgotten her name, her past, her face. There was only the sky, the humid breeze and that indefinable bitterness in the tender evening. *I am not I, nor am I they. And yet . . . and yet I am as much they as I.*

Regina turned to the left. *But I AM I. The moon shines in the sky for everyone, but in every heart it's unique, unshared . . . Fosca will walk the streets thinking of me, but it won't be me. . . . Oh, God! Why can't we break that hard, transparent shell that keeps us, all of us, shut in alone with ourselves? . . . Only one moon in only one heart. But which one? Fosca's or mine? . . . I would stop being myself . . . To win all, you must lose all. Who made that law?*

She pushed open the street door of the old building and crossed the court. Annie's window was lit up; all the others were darkened. Was Fosca already asleep? She quickly climbed the stairs and noiselessly turned her key in the lock. As she entered the apartment, she heard laughter coming from behind Annie's door—Annie's laughter and Fosca's. The blood rushed to Regina's cheeks and she felt as though claws were clutching at her throat. She had not experienced that torn feeling for a long time. She silently went over to the door.

"And every evening," Annie was saying, "I would take my seat in the balcony. I couldn't stand the idea of her acting for others and me not seeing her."

Regina shrugged her shoulders. *Why does she always have to be putting on airs,* she thought irritably. She knocked and opened the door. Fosca was sitting in front of a plate full of pancakes and a bottle of white wine. Annie was wearing her black dressing gown and a pair of earrings; her cheeks were flushed with animation. *It's a parody!* Regina thought with a sudden surge of anger.

"Nice to see you so gay," she said in an icy voice.

"Look at the wonderful pancakes we made, Princess," Annie said. "He's good, you know. He flipped them over without ruining a single one." Smiling, she offered the plate to Regina. "They're still nice and hot."

"No, thanks, I'm not hungry." She looked at the two of them with hate in her eyes. *Is there no way of preventing them from existing without me? How can they dare? It's pure insolence!* There are moments when one stands proudly atop the summit of a solitary mountain and the eye, in one sweep, embraces a uniform earth, the lines and colors of which blend into a single, unbroken landscape. And at other moments, one is down below, where every patch of ground can be seen to exist for itself, separately, with its humps and hollows and its sloping terraces. Annie pouring out her remembrances to Fosca, and he listening!

"What were you talking about?"

"I was telling Fosca how I met you."

"Again?" Regina picked up a glass and tasted the wine. The pancakes looked warm and appetizing and she felt like eating one, which only served to increase her anger. "That's her standard recital. She has to spill it out to all my friends or else she's not satisfied. Anyhow, there isn't a thing that's remarkable in the whole story. Annie is a romantic; you shouldn't believe everything she makes up."

Tears came to Annie's eyes, but Regina pretended not to notice them. With satisfaction, she thought, *I'm going to make you cry, but good!*

"I walked all the way home," Regina said nonchalantly. "It was so nice out! Do you know what I decided we'd do, Fosca? We can take a little trip out into the country between performances."

"Wonderful idea!" Fosca said. He was calmly eating one pancake after another.

"You'll take me along, won't you?" Annie pleaded.

It was the question for which Regina was waiting. "No. I want to spend a few days alone with Fosca. I have a few stories to tell him myself."

"Why?" Annie asked in desperation. "I won't be in your way. I used to go everywhere with you and you never thought I was any trouble."

"That may have been so up till now."

"But what did I do?" Annie asked, bursting into tears. "Why are you so mean to me? Why are you punishing me?"

"Don't talk like a child. You're too old; it's not becoming any more. I'm not punishing you. I just don't feel like taking you with us, that's all."

"You're mean!" Annie cried out. "Mean!"

"You certainly won't get me to change my mind by crying. And besides, you're horribly ugly when you cry." Regina cast a regretful glance at the pancakes and yawned. "I'm going to bed."

"Mean! Mean!" Annie slumped down on the table; tears were streaming from her eyes.

Regina went to her room, took off her coat and began to let down her hair. *He's staying with her! He's consoling her!* She felt like crushing Annie under her heels.

She was already in bed when he knocked. "Come in," she called out. Smiling, he walked over to her.

"You didn't have to hurry so," she said sarcastically. "Did you at least have time to finish the pancakes?"

"I'm sorry, but I couldn't leave Annie alone. She was really very upset."

"She cries easily," Regina said with a derisive laugh. "Of course, she told you everything, I suppose. How she was a cashier at the little bar in the theater, and me suddenly appearing out of nowhere, dressed like a gypsy with a patch over my eye."

Fosca sat down at the foot of the bed. "You shouldn't take it out on her like that. Don't forget, she's trying to exist, too."

"She, too?"

"All of us are trying."

And for a brief moment she saw that look in his eyes again, the look that had frightened her in the garden of the hotel.

"I guess you'll hold that against me," she said.

"I could never hold anything against you."

"You must think I'm terribly mean." She looked defiantly at Fosca. "It's true. I hate seeing other people happy and I enjoy making them bow to my will. Annie wouldn't be in the way. I'm not taking her along out of pure meanness."

"I understand," he said gently.

She would have preferred him to look at her in horror, like Roger. "And yet you're good," she said.

He shrugged his shoulders and there was a look of uncertainty on his face. She threw a rapid glance at him. What could be said of him?

Neither miserly nor generous, neither courageous nor fearful, neither bad nor good. With him, these words lost all meaning. It even seemed strange that his hair and eyes had color.

"It's not worthy of you to spend an evening frying pancakes with Annie," she said.

He smiled. "But the pancakes were good."

"You have more important things to do than that."

"What, for instance?"

"You haven't even written the first scene of my play yet."

"Oh, I wasn't inspired this evening," he said.

"You could always read. All those books I bought for you . . ."

"But they always tell the stame story."

She looked at him anxiously. "Fosca! You're not going to go back to sleep, I hope!"

"No," he replied. "No."

"You promised to help me, remember? You said to me, 'Whatever a mortal man can do, I can do.' "

"Ah! That's the whole question!"

Regina jumped out of the taxi and raced up the stairs; it was the first time Fosca had missed an appointment. She opened the door to her apartment and stood there with her mouth agape. Fosca, perched on a ladder, was washing the windows and singing.

"Fosca!"

He smiled. "I washed all the windows."

"What's got into you?"

"You told Annie this morning that the windows had to be washed." With a rag in his hand, he climbed down the ladder. "Look, isn't it a good job?"

"You were supposed to meet me at four o'clock in the lobby of the Pleyel. Did you forget?"

"Yes, I seem to have forgotten," he said in a confused voice. He wrung out the rag over a bucket. "I got so absorbed in my work that I forgot all about it."

"Well, now we've missed the concert," Regina said irritably.

"There'll be others."

She shrugged her shoulders. "But I wanted to go to *that* one."

"That one and that one only?"

"That one only." She looked at him for a moment and added, "Go get dressed. I don't like to see you in those old, worn-out clothes."

"I wanted to dust the ceiling, too. It's not very clean."

"What kind of a crazy notion is this, anyhow?"

"I just felt like helping you."

"That's not the kind of help I need."

Fosca walked docilely toward his room while Regina lit a cigarette. *He forgot about me*, she thought. *I alone existed for him and now he's beginning to forget me. Has he changed so fast? What goes on in his head?* She felt uneasy and paced back and forth across the room.

When Fosca reappeared in the living room, she laughingly asked, "Does keeping house make you happy?"

"As a matter of fact, it does. When they made me sweep out the dormitories at the asylum, I was very happy."

"But why?"

"It keeps one busy."

"There are other things to occupy your time with," she said.

He looked up at the ceiling; there was a sorrowful expression on his face. "What I really need is for you to find me a job."

Regina winced. "Is it getting that boring?"

"I have to have something to do."

"Didn't I suggest . . ."

"I want to do work that doesn't make me think." Longingly, he looked at the transparent windows.

"Well, I hope you don't have any intention of becoming a window washer."

"Why not?"

In silence, she took a few steps across the room. *Why not, after all?* she thought. *What else does he have to do with himself?*

"If you take a job, we'll be separated all day long."

"That's how people live," he said. "They're apart and then they see each other again."

"But we're not like other people."

Fosca's face darkened. "You're right, of course. No matter what I did, I could never be like everyone else."

Regina looked at him uneasily. She loved *him* because he was immortal. And he loved *her* in the hope that he would once again be able to share the feelings of a mortal. *We'll never make a happy couple,* she thought.

"The trouble is, you don't try to take an interest in things that are happening *now*, in this day and age. Read, go to art galleries, come with me to concerts."

"That wouldn't help in the least."

She put her hands on his shoulders. "I'm not enough for you any more. Is that it?"

"I can't make your life mine."

"You used to look at me, you used to say that I was all . . ."

"When you're alive, you're not satisfied with just looking."

She thought a moment and said, "Well, why don't you go to school and become something interesting? An engineer or a doctor."

"No, it takes too long."

"Too long? My God! don't you have enough time?"

"I have to have something to do *right now*," he said. "I don't want to do anything that makes me question myself." He looked prayerfully at Regina. "Tell me to peel potatoes or to wash the curtains . . ."

"No."

"Why not?"

"It would only be a way of putting you back to sleep again and I want you to stay awake." She took him by the hand. "Come and take a walk with me."

He followed her obediently, but he stopped a moment at the door. "The ceiling still needs a cleaning," he said regretfully.

"Here we are," Regina said.

"Already?"

"Of course. Trains go fast—faster than coaches."

"The thing I'd like very much to know is what people do with all the time they now save," Fosca said.

"You have to admit that they've invented a lot of things in the last hundred years."

"Yes, but they're always inventing the same things."

He was sullen. As of late, he often grew sullen. They walked along the platform in silence, went through the gate of the little station and started off down the road. Fosca was walking with his head lowered, kicking a stone with his foot. Regina took his arm.

"Look around," she said. "I was raised here; I love this place. Take a good look."

Irises were blooming on the thatched roofs and roses were climbing against the walls of the low houses. In orchards, closed in by wooden fences, chickens were pecking away under flowering apple trees. The past swelled up in Regina's heart like a bouquet of faded flowers coming to life again. She remembered the climbing ivy, the peacock's feathers, the smell of phlox in the moonlit garden and the many impassioned tears—*I will be beautiful, I will be famous.* At the foot of the hill, beyond the fields of golden wheat, there was a village with slate roofs which gleamed in the sun around a small church. The bells were ringing. A horse was climbing the hill, pulling a cart, and a peasant, walking alongside it, was holding a whip in his hand.

"Nothing has changed," Regina said. "What peacefulness! You see, Fosca, for me, this is eternity. Those calm houses, the bells that will ring till the end of the world, that old horse climbing the hill like his grandsire climbed it in my childhood."

Fosca shook his head. "No, that's not eternity."

"Why not?"

"There won't always be villages, or carts, or old horses."

"That's true," she said, gripped by the thought. With a single glance, her eyes embraced the serene landscape lying under the blue sky, immobile as a painting, as a poem. "What will take their place?" Regina asked.

"Large-scale cultivation, perhaps, with tractors and geometrical fields. Maybe even a new city, lumberyards, factories."

"Factories . . ."

It was impossible to imagine. One thing only was certain: that this countryside, older than any living memory, would one day disappear. Regina felt a wrench in her heart. An immobile eternity. She might have had her share of it, but suddenly the world was nothing but a parade of fleeting visions, and her hands were empty. She looked at Fosca. Could anyone's hands be emptier than his?

"I think I'm beginning to understand," she said.

"Understand what?"

"The curse."

They were walking side by side, but each was alone. *What can I do to make him learn to see the world through my eyes?* She had not imagined that it would be so difficult; instead of growing closer to her, it seemed that from day to day he drew further away. She pointed to a road to their right, which was shaded by tall oak trees, and said, "It's there."

With deep feeling she recognized the blossoming fields, the barbed wire under which she used to creep on her stomach, the fishing pond with its mossy water. It was all there, so near—her childhood, her departure for Paris, her enraptured return. Slowly, she circled the garden, surrounded by a white fence. The gate was closed and the little entrance door locked. She jumped over the fence. *Only one childhood, only one life—my life.* For her, time would stop one day, had already stopped, breaking itself against the impenetrable wall of death. Her life was a large lake in which the world was reflected in pure, motionless images. The red beech trees would forever tremble in the wind, the phlox would exhale its sweet odor, the waters of the river would murmur; and in the rustling of the leaves, in the blue of the tall cedars, in the perfume of the flowers, the whole universe was held prisoner.

There was still time. She had to cry out to Fosca, "Leave me alone! Leave me alone with my memories, with my brief destiny! Let me be resigned to be myself, and one day, to die!" For a moment she stood motionless in front of the house with its closed shutters—alone, mortal and eternal. And then she turned her eyes toward him. He was leaning against the white fence, looking at the beech trees and cedars with that look which would never die, and again time resumed its flight into infinity, the pure images clouded over. Regina was carried away by the torrent; it was impossible for her to stop or withdraw. All that could be hoped for was to stay afloat a little longer before being transformed into foam.

"Come," she said.

He leaped over the wooden crossbars. She placed her hand on his arm. "This is where I was born," she said. "See that window? . . . Over there . . . above the laurel bushes. That was my room. I could hear the water running in the fountain in my sleep, and the smell of magnolias used to seep in through the window."

They sat down on the steps leading to the front door. The stone was warm and insects were buzzing around their heads. And as Regina talked on, the garden become peopled with phantoms. A little girl in a long dress with a train was walking down the gravel paths; a grown girl, too thin, was declaiming the imprecations of Camille in the shadow of the weeping willow. The sun was sinking in the sky and Regina continued to talk, eager to bring back to life for a brief instant the little, transparent beings in whom her own heart had once beat.

Night had already fallen when she finished speaking. She turned to Fosca. "Fosca, were you listening to me?"

"Of course."

"Do you remember everything I said?"

He shrugged his shoulders. "It's a story I've heard a hundred times."

She jumped up. "No! It's not the same!"

"The same one, the only one."

"It's not true!"

"Always the same efforts, the same defeats," he said wearily. "They always begin all over again, one after the other. And I begin over again, like the others. It will never end."

"But I'm *different*," she said. "If I weren't different, why would you love me? You do love me, don't you?"

"Yes."

"And there's no one else like me?"

"Yes," he replied again. "You're unique like all other women."

"But this is me, Fosca! Don't you see me any more?"

"I see you. You're blonde, generous and ambitious. You're horrified of death." He shook his head. "Poor Regina!"

"Don't feel sorry for me!" she shouted. "I forbid you to feel sorry for me."

She turned and ran from the garden.

💅

"I have to be going now," Regina said.

She wearily looked at the door of the bar. On the other side of that door was a street which led to the Seine, and across the river, her apartment, where Fosca was sitting at a table and not writing. He would ask, "Did the rehearsal go well?" and she would answer, "Yes." Then there would be silence again.

She stretched out her hand to Florence. "So long."

"Have another drink," Sanier said. "You have plenty of time."

"Time? Yes, I've got all the time in the world," she murmured. Fosca did not watch clocks.

"I'm sorry the rehearsal went so badly," she said.

"On the contrary, it's wonderful to watch you work," Florence protested.

"You made some splendid innovations," Sanier remarked.

They spoke to her gently, pushed the plate of sandwiches toward her, thoughtfully offered her cigarettes, and their eyes were full of solicitude. *They don't bear any grudges*, she thought. And for once, she did not feel the pleasant crackling of contempt in her heart; she could no longer feel contempt for anyone.

"Have you really decided? You're definitely leaving Friday?" Regina asked.

"Yes, happily," Florence replied. "I can't take any more."

"It's your own fault," Sanier said reproachfully. He turned to Regina. "She doesn't spare herself in her everyday life any more than she does on the stage."

Regina smiled understandingly. *He looks at her in the same way Roger used to look at me*, she thought. He measured Florence's weariness, shared her joys, her sorrows, advised her. In his heart there was a warm place reserved for no one but her. *A couple!*

Regina got up. "I really must leave now."

She was not made for those easy smiles, the tender chitchat and simple human understanding. She pushed open the door and was plunged into solitude. Alone, she crossed the Seine and walked toward the red building where Fosca was patiently waiting. But it was no longer the proud solitude she used to know; now she was just another woman, another woman lost under the sky.

Annie had gone out and Fosca's door was closed. Regina took off her gloves and stood motionless in the center of the room. The big table, the curtains, the masks, the statuettes on their shelves, all seemed asleep. It was as though there had been a death in the house and everything, intimidated, had withdrawn itself from existence. Hesitantly, she took a step; the slightest movement seemed out of place. She took out a package of cigarettes and put it back in her purse. She had no desire to smoke, no desire to do anything. In the mirror, even her face appeared to be asleep. She put a lock of hair in place, walked toward Fosca's room and knocked on the door.

"Come in."

He was sitting on the edge of his bed, knitting a long band of green wool with an air of stubborn diligence.

"How did it go?" he asked.

"Lousy," she said dryly.

"Well, it'll go better tomorrow," he said in a comforting voice.

"No, it won't."

"Don't worry, I'm sure it will work out all right."

She shrugged her shoulders. "Can't you stop working on that thing for just a few moments?"

"If you like." With a regretful look, he laid the scarf down beside him.

"What have you been doing?" she asked.

"Just what you saw me doing."

"And what about that play you promised me?"

"Ah! The play!" he said, and in an apologetic tone added, "I was hoping that things would turn out differently."

"What things? What prevents you from working on it?"

"I can't."

"You mean you don't want to."

"I can't. I wanted to help you but I can't. What have I got to say to people?"

"Writing a play isn't so terribly difficult," she said impatiently.

"It seems easy to you because you're part of that world."

"Try! You haven't even set a single word down on paper."

"I'm trying," he said. "For a brief moment one of my characters begins to breathe, but then he fades out. They're born, they live, they die. That's all I can say about them."

"But you've loved women. You've had friends, enemies."

"Yes, I have recollections. That's true. But it's not enough." He closed his eyes. He seemed to be desperately searching his mind for some lost remembrance. "It takes a lot of strength, a lot of pride, or a lot of love to believe that a man's acts have any importance, that life outweighs death."

She drew near to him. "Fosca, is my life really unimportant in your eyes?" In her throat, there was a painful tightness; she was afraid of the answer he might give.

"You shouldn't ask me that question."

"Why not?"

"You shouldn't worry about what I think. That's a weakness."

"A weakness?" she said, perplexed. "Would you consider me more courageous if I buried my head in the sand?"

"I once knew a man," Fosca said. "He didn't bury his head in the sand. He looked me in the face, listened to what I had to say. But he made his own decisions."

"You speak of him with a great deal of respect." The thought of this unknown man caused a sudden pang of jealousy to sweep over her. "Wasn't he also just another man trying in vain to exist?" she asked.

"He did exactly what he wanted and he hoped for nothing."

"Is that what's important, then—to do what you want to do?"

"It was important for him."

"And for you?"

"He didn't worry about me."

"But was he right or wrong?"

"I can't answer for him."

"It sounds as though you admire him."

He shook his head. "I'm incapable of feeling admiration."

Regina took a few steps across the room. She did not know what to do with herself. "And me?" she asked.

"You?"

"Am I just another woman to you?"

"You think too much about yourself. That's not good."

"What should I think about?"

"Ah! that I don't know," he said.

❧

Regina walked off the stage. Fosca was sitting in the shadows in the rear of the empty theater, and as she went to meet him, a familiar voice stopped her: "Regina!" She turned around and saw that it was Roger.

"I hope you don't mind my coming," he said. "Laforêt invited me and I was really so anxious to see your Bérénice . . ."

"Why should I mind?" She looked at him in astonishment. She had imagined that seeing him again would have moved her—lately, everything that touched on her past, unsettled her. But Roger seemed a familiar, indifferent object.

"Regina," he said, "you're a marvelous Bérénice. You can do tragedy just as well as you do comedy. I'm positive now that soon you'll be the best actress in Paris."

His voice trembled slightly and a corner of his mouth quivered nervously. He was deeply moved. She looked toward the rear of the theater, at the seat which Fosca had just left. He who would remember, had he seen? Did he at last understand that she was different from all other women?

"It's really nice of you to think so," she said. She realized that they had been looking at each other for a long moment without speaking.

Roger studied her with an attentive, anxious air. "Are you happy?" he asked in a muffled voice.

"Of course," she answered.

"You look tired . . ."

"It's all these rehearsals," she said. His prolonged gaze embarrassed her; she was no longer accustomed to being scrutinized so carefully.

"Have I become ugly?"

"No, of course not. But you *have* changed."

"Perhaps."

"There was a time when you'd have thrown a fit if I said that you've changed. You're greatest desire was to always stay the same."

"Well, I guess that's because I've changed." She forced herself to smile. "I have to say goodbye now. Someone's waiting for me."

He held her hand for an instant. "Will we see each other again? When?"

"Whenever you want. Just call me up," she said indifferently.

Fosca was now waiting for her in front of the theater.

"Excuse me," she said, walking up to him. "I was held up."

"You don't have to excuse yourself. I like to wait." He smiled. "What a lovely evening! Would you like to walk home?"

"No, I'm tired."

They climbed into a taxi. She was silent. She wanted him to speak spontaneously, but for the whole length of the ride he said nothing. Upon arriving at the apartment, they went directly to her room and she began to undress. Still he said nothing.

"Well, Fosca," she said, breaking the silence, "what did you think of me this evening?"

"I always like to watch you act."

"But did I act *well?*"

"I suppose so," he answered.

"You suppose so, but you're not sure?"

He did not answer.

"Fosca," she said, "you saw Rachel act, didn't you?"

"Yes."

"Was she any better than I? *Much* better than I?"

He shrugged his shoulders. "I don't know."

"But you *must* know."

"Act well, act badly—I haven't the least idea what meaning those words have," he said impatiently.

There was an empty feeling in Regina's heart. "Wake up, Fosca! Please! Don't you remember? You used to come to watch me every evening. You seemed fascinated. Once you told me you felt like crying."

"Yes," Fosca said. He smiled gently. "I do like to see you act."

"But why? Isn't it because I'm a good actress?"

Fosca looked at her tenderly. "When you act, you believe in your existence with such deep faith! I've seen that same thing in two or three women—at the asylum. But they believed only in themselves. For you, other people exist, too, and there were times when you succeeded in making even me exist."

"What!" Regina exclaimed. "That's all you saw in Rosalind, in Bérénice? That's all the talent you give me credit for?" She bit her lip; she felt like bursting into tears.

"That's not bad, you know. Not everyone can be successful at pretending to exist."

"But it's not pretense," she said disconsolately. "It's true. I do exist!"

"Oh! you're not so sure of it as you'd like to believe. If you were, you wouldn't have insisted so much on taking me to the theater with you."

"I *am* sure!" she said furiously. "I exist, I have talent, I'll be a great actress. You're blind!"

He smiled and said nothing further.

¤

"How does it look?" Annie asked. She was carefully arranging a scaly pineapple in a large bowl filled with crushed ice. Regina quickly surveyed the table. Everything was in its place: the flowers, the crystal glasses, the hors d'oeuvres, the sandwiches.

"It looks very nice to me," she replied.

With a fork, Regina began whipping a mixture of raw egg yolks and melted chocolate. Florence's gatherings were always carefully planned, but it was much too easy to fix a numerical value to the famous wines and pedigreed petits fours which she invariably served—

expensive, impersonal, assembly-line articles. Regina wanted to make this party a masterpiece, one impossible to duplicate. She liked to entertain. For an entire evening, the furnishings among which she spent so much of her life would be reflected in their eyes; they would eat the delicacies she so painstakingly prepared, and listen to the records she had chosen for them. All evening long, she would reign over their pleasures. She energetically beat the eggs and in the bottom of the bowl, the custard began to thicken.

From the living room came the sound of a monotonous, relentless pacing. "God! How he irritates me!" she exclaimed.

"Do you want me to tell him?"

"No . . . Don't bother."

For more than an hour he had been pacing the floor like a bear in a cage, the cage of eternity. She was beating eggs while he paced back and forth in the living room. Drop by drop, every second accumulated in the bottom of the bowl, black, rich and savory, while every one of his steps, every movement of his legs, every swing of his arms, vanished in the air without leaving a trace. *As You Like It*, *Bérénice*, the contract for *The Tempest*—day after day, she patiently built her future. And he came and went, undoing the steps he had just taken. For her, everything would crash to earth in one single stroke.

"Finished," she said. "I'm going to get dressed."

She slipped into her long, black taffeta dress and chose a necklace from her jewel box. "Tonight I'll wear my hair in plaits," she said aloud. As of late, she had developed the habit of speaking aloud to herself. The doorbell rang; the guests were beginning to arrive. She slowly braided her hair. "Tonight I'll show them my real face." She looked in the mirror and smiled at herself; the smile gelled. The face she used to love so much now seemed like a mask; it no longer belonged to her. Her body, too, had become a stranger to her—a shop-window mannequin. She smiled again, and again it was the mannequin who smiled back from the mirror. She turned around; a moment longer and she would have begun making faces at herself.

She pushed open the door. In the room, the little lamps were lit, and sitting about in chairs and on the couch were Sanier, Florence, Dulac and Laforêt. Fosca, seated among them, was speaking gayly, while Annie served cocktails. Everything seemed real. Smiling, she offered them her hand and they smiled politely back.

"My! How beautiful you look in that dress!" Florence said.

"You're the one who's ravishing tonight."

"These cocktails are wonderful."

"They're a concoction of my own."

They drank their cocktails and looked at Regina. The doorbell rang again, and again she smiled, they smiled, and all looked and listened. In their benevolent, malevolent, captivated eyes, her dress, her face, the furnishings in the room, glowed like a thousand little flames. And everything still seemed real. A brilliant party! If only she had been able to avoid looking at Fosca . . .

She turned her head away. His eyes, those eyes full of pity which stripped her bare, were fixed on her—she was sure of it. He saw the mannequin, he saw the comedy.

She took a plate of pastry from the table and passed it around. "Help yourself."

Dulac bit into a cream puff and his mouth filled up with the thick, black custard. *A second of my life*, Regina thought, *a precious second of my life in Dulac's mouth. They're devouring my life with their mouths, with their eyes. Well, so what!*

"What's wrong?" said an affectionate voice. It was Sanier.

"Everything," Regina answered.

"Tomorrow you're signing the contract to do *The Tempest*; *Bérénice* is a triumph; and you say that everything is wrong."

"I have a perverse character."

Sanier's face became grave. "On the contrary."

"On the contrary?"

"I don't like contented people."

He looked at her so tenderly that a small hope was rekindled in her heart. She was suffocating from the desire to speak a few sincere words and to make this moment, at least, true.

"After what I did, I thought you'd despise me," she said.

"Me? Despise you?"

"Don't you remember? When I told you about Mauscot and Florence . . . That was pretty low."

"I can't believe you capable of doing anything low."

She smiled and a new flame rose up in her. *If I wanted . . .* She had a sudden desire to feel herself burning in that scrupulous, passionate heart.

"I was always under the impression that you were critical of me."

"You were mistaken."

She looked him straight in the face. "What *do* you think of me?"

He reflected a moment and then replied. "There's something tragic about you."

"What?"

"You're craving for the absolute. You were made to believe in God and to spend your life in a convent."

"There are too many chosen ones," she protested, "too many saints. God would have had to love only me."

All at once the flame died out. He was just a few feet away from her, watching her. He saw her looking at Sanier, looking into his eyes, trying to set his heart afire. He saw the give and take of words and glances, the play of mirrors, empty mirrors, reflecting only each other's emptiness. Abruptly, she reached for a glass of champagne.

"I'm thirsty," she said.

She emptied the glass, filled it again. Roger would have said, "Don't drink so much," and she would have drunk and smoked, and her head would have buzzed with revulsion, rebellion, noise. But he said nothing, only watched, thought. *She's trying, she's trying.* And it was true; she *was* trying. The game of mistress of the house, the game of glory, the game of seduction—all of them were only one single game, the game of existence.

"I see you're enjoying yourself," she said to Fosca.

"The time is passing."

"I know you're laughing at me, but you don't intimidate me."

She looked at him defiantly. In spite of him, in spite of his compassionate smile, she wanted once more just to feel the hot fire of life. She felt like tearing off her clothes and dancing naked; she felt like murdering Florence. What happened afterwards had no importance. Were it only for a minute, only a second, she wanted to blaze into a flame that would rip through the night. She suddenly burst out laughing. If, in a single instant, she destroyed both the past and the future, she would be certain at least that that instant existed. She jumped up on the couch, raised her glass and said in a loud voice, "My dear friends . . ."

They all turned their faces toward her.

". . . the moment has come for me to tell you why we're gathered here this evening. It's not to celebrate the signing of the contract to do *The Tempest* . . ." She smiled at Dulac. "I'm sorry, Monsieur Dulac, but I'm not going to sign the contract."

Dulac's face hardened and Regina smiled triumphantly. A stupefied expression appeared in every pair of eyes.

"I'm not going to make *that* film or any other film. And I'm dropping out of *Bérénice*. I'm retiring from the theater. I drink to the end of my career!"

One minute, no more than a minute, but during that minute she existed. They looked at her uncomprehendingly, and they were afraid. She was the lightning, the torrent, the avalanche, the chasm which suddenly opened under their feet and from which great anguish arose. She existed.

"Regina! Have you gone crazy?" Annie asked, startled.

Everyone was speaking, speaking to her—"Why? . . . Is it possible? . . . It's not true! . . ." And Annie, overwhelmed, clung to Regina's arm.

"Drink with me!" Regina cried out. "Drink to the end of my career!" She swallowed her drink and burst into a loud laugh. "A beautiful ending!"

She looked at Fosca, defied him. She was burning, existing. She threw down the glass; it shattered into a thousand pieces against the floor. He was smiling and she was naked to her very bones. He tore away all her masks, saw through all her gestures, words, smiles. She was nothing but the beating of wings in the middle of a vast emptiness. *She's trying, she's trying.* And he knew, too, for whom she was trying. Behind all the words, the gestures, the smiles, lurked the fundamental deceit, the emptiness.

"What a comedy!" she laughed.

"Regina, you've had too much to drink," Sanier said gently. "Why don't you rest up for a while?"

"I'm not drunk," she said gayly. "I see everything clear as day." Still laughing, she pointed to Fosca. "I see everything through his eyes."

She stopped laughing. With his eyes, she even saw through this new comedy, the comedy of lucid laughter and hopeless words. The words caught in her throat. Everything was dying out. The room grew silent.

"Come and lie down awhile," said Annie.

"Come," Sanier said.

She followed them. "Make them leave," she said to Annie. "Make them all leave!" And angrily, she added, "And the two of you, leave me alone!"

She stood motionless in the center of the room and then, in a frenzy, spun rapidly around. She looked at the Japanese masks on the wall, the statuettes on their shelves, the old marionettes in the tiny theater. And in those precious objects, she saw her whole past, her long years of self-love. But now they seemed to her nothing but cheap trash.

She threw the masks to the floor. "Cheap trash!" she repeated aloud, trampling with her feet. She threw down the statuettes and the marionettes and stamped on them, crushing all the old lies.

Someone touched her shoulder. "Regina," Fosca said, "where will that get you?"

"I don't want any more lies." She fell into a chair and buried her head in her hands. She was completely exhausted. "My whole life is a lie," she muttered.

There was a long silence and then he said softly, "I'm going to leave."

"Going to leave? Where? Why?"

"Far away from you. You'll forget me and then you'll be able to live again."

Terrified she looked at him. She was nothing now. He had to stay near her. "No! It's too late. I'll never forget you. I'll never forget anything."

"Poor Regina! What can I say?"

"Don't go away, that's all I ask."

"All right, I won't go."

"Never," she said. "You must never leave me."

She threw her arms around his neck and crushed her lips against his; her tongue darted into his mouth. Fosca's hands pressed her close to him, and she shuddered. With other men, she felt only their caresses, never their hands. But Fosca's hands existed, and in them she felt herself an object of prey. Feverishly, he threw off his clothes, as if time, even for him, were slipping too rapidly away, as if every second were a treasure which must not be wasted. He clasped her in his arms and a hot wind rose inside her, sweeping away words, images. They were fused together in the act of love and the bed, except for a great black shudder, seemed empty. She was the prey of a desire as ancient as the earth, a wild, new desire which only she could satisfy, and which was a desire not for her alone, but for everything. The moment blazed; eternity was conquered. Tensed and tingling with an expectant, anguished passion, she panted heavily in rhythm with Fosca. He groaned and she dug her nails into his flesh. She was torn open by the triumphant spasm in which everything found completion and everything fell apart; she was left without hope, rudely ripped from the burning silence, suddenly thrown back into herself—Regina, futile and betrayed. She wiped her sweating brow with her hand; her teeth were chattering.

"Regina," he said gently. He kissed her hair, caressed her cheeks. "Sleep, Regina, sleep. We're allowed sleep, at least."

His voice was so full of sadness that she wanted to open her eyes, to speak to him. Was there no way out? But she remained silent, for she knew that he had already read her thoughts. There had been too many other nights for him, too many other women. She turned over and pressed her cheek against the pillow.

Regina opened her eyes to the dull, half-light of early morning. She stretched out her arms across the bed. No one was next to her.

"Annie!" she called out.

"Yes, Regina."

"Where's Fosca?"

"He went out," Annie replied.

"Went out? At this time of day? Where did he go?"

Annie avoided her eyes. "He left a note for you."

She took the note, a scrap of paper folded in half.

"*Goodbye darling Regina. Forget I ever lived. After all, it is you who are alive and I count for nothing.*"

"Where is he?" She jumped out of bed and hastily began to dress. "It can't be! I told him not to leave."

"He left during the night," Annie said.

"Why did you let him go? Why didn't you wake me up?" Regina said, seizing Annie by the arm. "Are you a complete idiot? Why?"

"I didn't know."

"What do you mean you didn't know? He gave you this note. You read it, didn't you?" She looked angrily at Annie. "You let him leave on purpose. You knew and you let him go. Idiot! Idiot!"

"Yes," Annie said. "I admit it. He had to leave for your own good."

"For my own good! So the two of you were scheming for *my* good!" She shook Annie violently. "Where is he?"

"I don't know."

"You don't know!" Regina stared intensely at Annie and thought, *If she really doesn't know, there's nothing left for me but to die.* She sprang over to the window.

"Tell me or I'll jump."

"Regina!"

"Don't move or I'll jump. Where is Fosca?"

"In Lyons, in the hotel where we spent a few days together."

"Are you telling me the truth?" Regina asked distrustfully. "Why should he have told you?"

"I wanted to know. I . . . I was afraid of you."

"So he asked your advice!" She put on her coat. "I'm going to get him."

"I'll go get him for you. You have to be at the theater tonight." •

"Didn't you hear me last night? I said I was through with the theater."

"But you were drinking. Let me go. I promise I'll bring him back."

"I'll bring him back myself," Regina said. She opened the door. "And if I don't find him, you'll never see me again."

Fosca was sitting at a little table on the terrace of the hotel. He was smoking and in front of him was a bottle of white wine. When he saw Regina, he smiled. There was no trace of astonishment on his face.

"Ah! Here already!" he said. "Poor Annie! She didn't hold out very long."

"Fosca, why did you leave?" she asked.

"Annie asked me to."

"She asked you!" Regina sat down at the table and angrily said, "But *I* asked you to stay."

He smiled. "Is there any reason why I should obey you rather than her?"

Regina poured herself a glass of wine and gulped it down. Her hands were trembling. "Don't you love me any more?" she asked.

"I love her, too," he said gently.

"But not the same way."

"How can I make any distinction? Poor Annie!"

Regina felt a horrible nausea in the pit of her stomach. *In the fields, millions of blades of grass, all equal, all alike* . . .

"There was a time when only I existed for you . . ."

"Yes, and then you opened my eyes."

She hid her face in her hands. A blade of grass, nothing but a blade of grass. Everyone believed himself different, preferred himself above others. And all of them were wrong, she no less than the rest.

"Come back with me," she pleaded.

"No. It won't work. I thought I could become a man again—it happened to me before, after other long sleeps—but this time I just couldn't. I can't any more."

"Try! Just once more."

"I'm too tired."

"Then there's nothing left for me," she said dejectedly.

"Yes, I realize that. It's unfortunate for you." He leaned toward her. "I'm sorry. I made a mistake. I shouldn't make mistakes any more," he said with a little laugh. "I'm old enough to know better. But I don't suppose they can ever be completely avoided. When I'm ten thousand years old, I'll still make mistakes. You never really learn."

She grabbed Fosca's hands. "All I ask is twenty years of your life. Twenty years! What's twenty years to you?"

"You don't understand," he said sadly.

"No, I don't understand! If I were in your place, I'd try to help people; in your place . . ."

He cut her off. "But you're not in my place." He shrugged his shoulders. "No one can imagine what it's like. I told you once that immortality is a curse."

"You make it a curse."

"No. I fought to make something good of it. You don't know how I fought!"

"What do you mean? Tell me about it."

"Impossible. I'd have to tell you everything."

"Well, why not?" she said. "We have time, don't we? All the time in the world."

"What good would it do?"

"Do it for me, Fosca. Maybe it will be less terrible when I understand."

"It's always the same story. It will never change. I'll live it again and again, countless times, forever." He looked around him. "All right, I'll tell it to you."

BOOK I

I was born in Italy on the 17th of May 1279 in a castle in the city of Carmona. My mother died shortly after my birth and I was raised by my father who taught me to ride horseback and shoot a bow and arrow. The monk in charge of my education tried to instill the fear of God in me. But ever since my childhood, I've thought only of what happens here on earth and I've feared nothing.

My father was handsome and strong; I admired him. When I saw Francesco Rienzi, with his scrawny, knock-kneed legs, passing by on his black horse, I used to ask in astonishment, "Why is he the ruler of Carmona?"

My father would look at me gravely. "Never wish to be in his place," he would say.

The people hated Francesco Rienzi. It was said that he wore a thick coat of mail under his clothes, and there were always ten guards surrounding him. In his room, at the foot of his bed, lay a large chest secured by three padlocks, and this chest was filled with gold. One after the other, he accused the noblemen of the city of treason and confiscated their wealth. In the main square stood a scaffold, and several times each month the rope would strain to a body. He took money from the poor as well as from the rich. Whenever I strolled in the city with my old nurse, she would point out the hovels where the weavers lived, children with scabby buttocks, beggars seated on the steps of the cathedral, and she would say to me, "The duke has caused all this misery."

Carmona was built atop an arid rock; there were no fountains in the squares. Men would go by foot to the surrounding plains to fill their goatskin bags, and water cost as much as bread.

One morning the bells of the cathedral sounded the death-knell and the façades of all the houses were covered with black drapes. Astride a horse, alongside my father, I rode in the procession which was accompanying the remains of Francesco Rienzi to his final resting place. Bertrando Rienzi, dressed entirely in black, led the funeral cortege of his brother. The rumor spread that he had poisoned him.

The streets of Carmona were filled with the clamor of festivity. The scaffold standing in front of the palace was torn down; the lords, dressed in silks and brocades, rode in cavalcade with their retinues; tournaments took place in the main square. Across the plains echoed the sounds of hunting horns, the joyous barking of dogs, and in the evening, the ducal palace glowed with a thousand lights.

But Bertrando soon began confiscating the wealth of the rich merchants and noblemen, and threw them in dungeons where they slowly rotted away. The chest with the three padlocks was always empty; new taxes were constantly being levied against the miserable artisans. In alleys rank with the odor of pestilence, children fought over scraps of bread. The people grew to hate Bertrando Rienzi.

Friends of Pietro d'Abruzzi often gathered at night in my father's house and whispered together by torchlight. Scuffles broke out every day between his partisans and Rienzi's. Even the children of Carmona were divided into two camps, and below the ramparts, among the brushwood and rocks, we battled with stones, some shouting, "Long live the duke!" and others, "Down with the tyrant!" We fought viciously, but I was never satisfied with this game—the fallen enemy rose again, the dead came to life. The day after a battle, victors and vanquished both found themselves unharmed. It was no more than a game, and I kept asking myself impatiently, "How much longer am I going to be a child?"

I was fifteen years old when joyous fires were lit at every crossroad. Pietro d'Abruzzi had stabbed Bertrando Rienzi on the steps of the ducal palace. The crowd carried him aloft triumphantly. He spoke to the people from a balcony, promising them relief from their sufferings. The doors of the prisons were opened, the old magistrates were dismissed, the Rienzi faction driven from the city. For several weeks there was dancing in the squares and laughing faces everywhere. In my father's house we began to speak in normal tones again. I looked in wonder at Pietro d'Abruzzi who had plunged a real dagger into a man's heart and delivered his city.

One year later the noblemen of Carmona donned their heavy armor and raced across the plains at a gallop. The Genoese, spurred on by the exile faction, had invaded our lands. They tore our army to shreds and Pietro d'Abruzzi was killed by a lance. Under Orlando Rienzi's reign Carmona became Genoa's vassal. At the beginning of every season, wagons laden with gold passed through the main square and, our hearts seething with rage, we watched as they disappeared on the road to the sea. In somber workshops, the weavers' looms hummed day and night, and yet the townspeople walked about with bare feet, dressed in tattered clothing.

"Can't anything be done?" I asked.

My father and Gaetano d'Agnolo would silently shake their heads. For three years, day after day, I asked the same question, and they only shook their heads. At last one day Gaetano d'Agnolo smiled.

"Perhaps," he said, "perhaps something can be done."

Orlando Rienzi wore a coat of mail under his doublet and practically all of his days were spent behind a barred window in his palace. When he went out, twenty guards surrounded him. Servants tasted the wine in his glass, the meats on his plate. And yet, one Sunday morning while he was in the cathedral attending mass, the soldiers of his escort having been bought off, four young men sprang upon him and slit his throat. They were Giacomo d'Agnolo, Leonardo Vezzani, Ludovico Pallaio and myself. His body was dragged through the court in front of the church and thrown to the crowd, which ripped it to pieces while the tocsin rang. Suddenly, all of Carmona's townsmen appeared in the streets carrying arms. The Genoese and their partisans were brutally massacred.

My father turned down an offer to rule the city and we made Gaetano d'Agnolo our chief. He was an upright and prudent man. He had negotiated secretly with Pietro Faenza, the condottiere, whose armies came immediately and stationed themselves at the foot of our walls. Supported by these mercenary troops, we firmly awaited the Genoese. For the first time in my life, I took part in a real battle between men. The dead did not come to life again, the vanquished fled in disorder; every thrust of my lance helped save Carmona. That day, I would have died with a smile on my lips, certain of having contributed to a triumphant future for my city.

For days, joyous fires blazed at all the crossroads, there was dancing in the squares and processions circled the ramparts chanting *Te Deums*. And then the weavers began to weave again, the beggars to beg, and the water bearers to trudge through the streets, bent under the weight of their loads. The wheat grew poorly in the devastated plains and the bread the populace ate was black. The townspeople now wore shoes and their clothing was made of new goods; the old magistrates were removed from office. But otherwise, Carmona remained unchanged.

"Gaetano d'Agnolo is too old," Leonardo Vezzani often told me impatiently.

Leonardo was my friend; he excelled in all physical activities and I felt in him a bit of that fire which was devouring me. One night, during a banquet to which he had invited us, we seized old Gaetano and compelled him to abdicate. He and his son were both exiled and Leonardo took power.

The people had no longer expected anything from Gaetano and they greeted the birth of a new hope with joy. The old magistrates were replaced by new men and there was merrymaking in the squares. It was springtime. The almond trees were flowering in the plains and the sky never seemed bluer. Astride a horse, I often clambered to the tops of the hills which blotted out the horizon, and I gazed upon the vast expanse of green and pink which stretched out to the foot of another line of blue hills. *Beyond those hills are other plains and other hills,* I thought. And then I looked toward Carmona perched on her rock, bristling with her eight proud towers. *Here is where the heart of this vast world beats, and soon my city will fulfill its destiny.*

The seasons passed and the almond trees blossomed anew. Festivals took place under the blue sky, but no fountains spouted in the squares, the old hovels were still standing, and wide, smooth streets, white palaces, existed only in my dreams. I questioned Vezzani.

"What are you waiting for?"

He looked at me in astonishment. "I'm not waiting for anything."

"Why don't you act?"

"Haven't I acted?" he asked.

"Why did you take power if you weren't going to do anything with it?"

"I took it; I have it. That's enough for me."

"Ah," I said fervently, "if only I were in your place!"

"Well?"

"I would form powerful alliances for Carmona, I would undertake wars, I would enlarge our territory, I would build palaces . . ."

"All that would require a great deal of time," Vezzani remarked.

"You have planty of time."

His face suddenly became grave. "You know full well I don't."

"The people love you."

"They won't love me for long." He put his hand on my shoulder. "These great enterprises of which you speak, how many years it would take to see them through! And how many sacrifices they would require! In no time at all, I would be hated and killed."

"You can defend yourself."

"I don't want to be like Francesco Rienzi," he said. "Besides, you should know that all precautions are useless." He smiled with that smile I liked so well. "I'm not afraid of death. But at least I will have lived for a few years."

He was right; he was a condemned man. Two years later, Geoffredo Massigli had him strangled by his devoted henchmen. He was a crafty man who conciliated Carmona's noblemen by according them great privileges; he governed neither better nor worse than another. In any event, what hope was there that one single man could keep the city in his hands long enough to bring about prosperity and glory?

My father, who was growing old, asked me to find a wife so that he might smile upon his grandchildren during his last days on earth. I married Catherina d'Alonzo, a noble, beautiful and pious young girl, whose hair gleamed like pure gold. She bore me a son whom we called Tancredo. Not long after, my father died. He was buried in the cemetery which dominated Carmona and I watched as the coffin was lowered into the grave, the coffin in which I felt my own desiccated body lay, where my useless past was buried, and my heart felt as though it were caught in a vise. *Will I die like him, without having accomplished anything?* During the days that followed, when I saw Geoffredo Massigli pass by on his horse, my hand tightened around the handle of my sword. But I thought, what good would it do, since they would only kill me, too.

At the beginning of the year 1311, the Genoese moved against Florence. They were rich, powerful and devoured by ambition. They had conquered Pisa, they wanted to become the rulers of all northern Italy, and perhaps their arrogant plans went even further than that. They sought an alliance with us in order to crush Florence more easily and then subdue us in turn; they asked for men, horses, provisions, fodder and free passage through out territory. With great pomp, Geoffredo Massigli received their ambassador. It was said that the Genoese were prepared to buy his assistance with gold, and he was a greedy man.

On the twelfth of February at two o'clock in the afternoon, while a magnificent procession escorted the Genoese emissary toward the plains, Geoffredo Massigli, passing under my window on horseback,

was struck directly in the heart by an arrow. I was the best archer in
Carmona. At the same moment my men raced through the city, shouting "Death to the Genoese!" and the townsmen, whom I had secretly
alerted, invaded the ducal palace. That evening I was Carmona's prince.

I saw to it that every man was armed. The peasants abandoned the
plains and entrenched themselves behind the ramparts, bringing their
wheat and livestock with them. I sent messengers to Carlo Malatesta,
the condottiere, to call him to our aid. And I closed Carmona's gates.

"Send them back to their homes," Catherina pleaded. "For the love
of God, for the sake of your love for me and for our child, send them
back to their homes."

She fell to her knees before me, tears streaming down her cheeks
which were marbled with red splotches. I placed my hand on her head.
Her hair was dull and stringy, her eyes colorless, her body thin and
grey under the coarse cloth of her dress.

"Catherina, you know very well that the granaries are empty."

"You can't do it! It's inhuman!" she said in a bewildered voice.

I turned my head away. Through the slightly open window, the
cold air from the streets entered the palace—and the silence. In silence,
the black procession advanced along the main street, and men standing
in the doorways of their houses and leaning out of windows, silently
watched it pass. Only the docile shuffling of the crowd and the metallic
click of horses hoofs could be heard.

"Send them back to their homes," she said.

I looked at Giovanni, then Ruggiero. "Is there any other solution?"

"No," said Giovanni.

Ruggiero shook his head. "No."

"Then why don't you chase me out, too?" Catherina asked.

"You're my wife," I replied.

"I'm another useless mouth. My place is with them. Ah, what a
coward I am!" She buried her face in her hands. "Dear God, forgive us!
Dear God, forgive us!"

They came down from the market place, they climbed up from the
lowlands.

A cold sun glazed the red-tile roofs which were separated at intervals
by wide, dark crevices. Through each crevice they advanced in little
groups, surrounded by mounted guards.

"Dear God, forgive us! Dear God, forgive us!"

"Enough of that litany," I said. "I know that God is protecting us."

Catherina rose and went to the window. "All those men!" she cried out. "They just watch and say nothing!"

"They want to save Carmona," I said. "They love their city."

"Don't they know what the Genoese will do to their wives?"

The procession emerged in the square: women, children, old men, the sickly. They came from the high roads and the low, carrying small bundles in their hands—they had not yet lost all hope. Some of the women were bent under heavy loads, as if blankets, pots and happy souvenirs of times gone by would still be of use on the other side of the ramparts. The guards brought their horses to a halt, and behind this barrier the great pink basin slowly filled up with a black and silent crowd.

"Raimondo, send them back to their homes," Catherina pleaded again. "The Genoese won't let them pass. They'll all die of cold and hunger in dirt ditches."

"What did the soldiers get to eat this morning?" I asked.

"Boiled bran and grass soup," Ruggiero answered.

"And this is the first day of winter! Can I worry about women and old men?"

I looked out the window. A shout ripped through the silence. "Maria! Maria!" The shouting came from a young man. He crossed the square, dashed under the horses' bellies and burst through the crowd. "Maria!" Two soldiers seized him and dragged him to the other side of the barrier. He struggled in vain under their grasp.

"Raimondo!" Catherina cried. "Raimondo, it would be better to surrender the city." With both hands, she clung to the bars of the windows. She looked as if she were about to fall, crushed by a heavy weight.

"Do you know what they did to Pisa?" I asked. "The walls razed, all the men in slavery. It's better to cut off an arm than to die completely." I looked at the high, white stone towers which rose proudly above the red roofs. *If I refuse to surrender Carmona, they'll never be able to take her.*

The soldiers had released the young man and he stood motionless under the palace windows. He raised his head and shouted, "Death to the tyrant!" No one budged. The cathedral bells began to ring; they tolled the death-knell.

Catherina turned toward me. "One of them will kill you," she said vehemently.

"I know."

I pressed my brow against the pane. *They will kill me.* I felt the coldness of the coat of mail against my chest. They had all worn a coat of mail and none of them reigned more than five years. Upstairs, in the icy attic, shut in among their flasks and filters, doctors had been searching for months for an antidote to poisons. But they found nothing. I was a condemned man.

"Catherina," I said, "swear to me that if I die you'll never surrender the city."

"No," she retorted, "I will *not* swear to it!"

I walked over to the fireplace. Tancredo was lying on a rug in front of the thin fire of vine branches. He was playing with his dog; I picked him up in my arms. He was pink and blond; he looked like his mother. He was a very small child. I put him back on the floor without saying anything. I was alone.

"Father," Tancredo said, "I'm afraid that Kounak is sick. He looks sad."

"Poor Kounak, he's very old."

"If Kounak dies, will you give me another dog?"

"There's not a single dog left in Carmona," I answered.

I went back to the window. The bells were still tolling and the black mob began to move forward. Without a word, without a gesture, the men watched as their fathers and mothers, their wives and children, shuffled by. The resigned herd slowly descended toward the ramparts. *As long as I'm here, they won't weaken,* I thought. An icy coldness penetrated my heart. Will I be here long enough?

"The service is going to begin," I announced.

"Ah, now you're going to pray for them," Catherina said. "The men will pray while the Genoese rape their wives!"

"What I've done had to be done." I drew near to her. "Catherina . . ."

"Don't touch me."

I gestured to Giovanni and Ruggiero. "Let's go."

Atop the main street, the cathedral gleamed—white, red, green, golden, joyous as a peaceful morning. The bells continued to toll the death-knell and the men, somberly dressed, climbed silently to the church. Even their faces were mute; they looked at me with eyes in which there was neither hate nor hope. Above the closed shops the rusty signs squeaked in the wind. Not a blade of grass was left in the cracks of the pavement, not a nettle at the base of the walls. I climbed the marble steps and turned around.

At the foot of the bramble-covered rock on which Carmona stood, the red tents of the Genoese could be seen among the gray olive trees. A black column flowed from the city, descended the hill and straggled toward the camp.

"Do you think the Genoese will take them in?"

"No," I replied.

I went through the cathedral door and the clicking of arms mingled with the funeral hymn reverberating under the vaulted stone ceiling. When Leonardo Vezzani walked past the flowers and the scarlet tapestry, there were no guards surrounding him and he was smiling. He was not thinking of death. Yet here he was, dead, strangled. I kneeled down. They were all stretched out under the flagstone of the choir: Francesco Rienzi, poisoned; Bertrando Rienzi, stabbed; Pietro d'Abruzzi, killed by a lance; and Orlando Rienzi, Leonardo Vezzani, Geoffredo Massigli, and old Gaetano d'Agnolo who died of old age in exile . . . There was an empty space next to them. I bowed my head. *How much longer will it be?*

On bended knee at the foot of the altar, the priest prayed softly and grave voices ascended toward the arched ceiling. I pressed my gloved hands against my brow. *A year? A month?* My guards were standing behind me, but behind them was a void. Only men—feeble, traitorous beings between me and the void. *It will happen from behind.* My hands pressed harder. I could not turn my head. It was all important that the people not know. *Miserere nobis . . . Miserere nobis . . . There will be the same monotonous rumbling of prayers, and the black catafalque, with its silver tear drops, will stand exactly on this spot. And this three-year struggle will have served no purpose whatever . . . If I turn my head, they'll think me a coward . . . I don't want to die without accomplishing anything."*

"Dear God!" I muttered. "Let me live!"

The murmur of the prayers swelled and diminished like the sound of the tide. Did it reach as high as God? Was it true that the dead lived again in heaven? *Up there I will have neither hands nor voice. I will see the gates of Carmona opened, I will see the Genoese raze our towers, and I will be helpless. Ah! I hope that the priests lie and that I die completely.*

The voices were stilled. A halberd pounded the flagstones and I left the church; the light dazzled me. For a moment I stood motionless atop the main stairway. No invalids were begging, no children playing on the steps. The polished marble glistened under the sun. Out there, the slope of the hill was deserted. A confused swarming could be seen around the red tents. I turned my eyes away. What went on in the plains, what went on in the heavens, did not concern me. It was for women and children to question themselves—"What are they doing? Will they hold out much longer? Will Carlo Malatesta arrive by springtime? Will God save us?" As for me, I counted on nothing. I kept Carmona's gates closed and I counted on nothing.

Slowly I went back down to the palace. A heavy silence hung over the city like a malediction, and I thought, *I'm here now, but someday I'll no longer be here. I'll be nowhere . . . It will happen from behind and I won't even know it happened.*" Then, fervently, I said to myself, *No, it's impossible. It can't happen to me, not to me!*

I turned toward Ruggiero. "I'm going up to the attic."

I climbed up the winding staircase, took a key from my belt and opened the door. A rancid, bitter odor gripped me by the throat. The room was strewn with rotten herbs; pots and retorts were cooking on a stove amid a thick vapor. Bent over a table covered with phials and beakers, Petrucchio was grinding a yellow paste in a mortar.

"Where are the others?"

Petrucchio raised his head. "They're sleeping."

"At this time of day?"

The door to the living quarters was slightly ajar; I pushed it open with my foot. The eight doctors were lying on beds which had been installed against the walls for them. Some were sleeping and the others were absently staring at the great beams of the ceiling. I closed the door.

"They're working too hard! They'll die at the task!" he said.

I leaned over Petrucchio's shoulder. "Is that an antidote?"

"No. Its a salve for chilblain."

I took the mortar in my hand and threw it violently to the floor.

Petrucchio looked at me coldly. "I'm trying to do *useful* work." He bent down and picked up the heavy marble mortar.

I walked toward the stove. "I'm certain it can be found," I said. "Everything has its opposite. If there are poisons, there must be antidotes."

"Maybe a thousand years from now it will be discovered."

"Then it exists! Why can't it be discovered right now?"

Petrucchio shrugged his shoulders.

"I need it right now," I said.

I looked around me. The solution was there, hidden in those herbs, in those red and blue powders, and I was unable to see it. I stood before the beakers and phials like a blind man before a rainbow, and Petrucchio was blind, too. The antidote was there and no one in the world was able to see it.

"Oh, God!" I exclaimed.

I slammed the door behind me.

The wind was whistling around the sentry posts. I leaned my elbows on the stone parapet and watched the crackling flames which rose from the bottoms of the ditches surrounding the ramparts. In the distance, fires were glowing in the Genoese camp, and in the shadows behind them were the plains, immense and useless like the sea, with their deserted roads and abandoned houses. Alone on her rock, Carmona was an isle in the middle of that sea. In gusts, the wind carried the smell of burned brambles to my nose and red sparks flew off into the black air. *They're burning the brushwood from the hill, but it won't last more than two days,* I thought.

The sound of steps, the click of heels, made me raise my head. They were moving along one by one behind a guard who was carrying a torch; their hands were tied behind their backs. The guard passed in front of me, then a woman with large red cheeks, then an old woman, and a young one who looked at the ground and whose face I could not make out, another who appeared to be pretty. Behind them came an old bearded man and another old man. They had hidden themselves to save their lives, and now they were going to die.

"Where are you taking them?" I asked.

"To the west rampart. It's the steepest side."

"There aren't very many."

"They're the only ones we found," the guard said. He turned toward the prisoners. "Let's go. Move on."

"Fosca!" cried one of the men in a strident voice. "Let me talk to you. Don't let me die!"

I recognized him. It was Bartolomeo, the oldest and most miserable of all the beggars who held out their hands under the porch of the cathedral. The guard struck him lightly. "Move along."

"I know the cure," cried the old man. "Let me talk to you."

"The cure?" I walked over to him. The others had already disappeared into the night. "What cure?"

"The cure. It's hidden in my house."

I stared at the beggar; he was surely lying. His lips were trembling and despite the icy wind there were beads of sweat on his yellow brow. He had lived for more than eighty years and he was still struggling to preserve his life.

"You lie," I said.

"I swear on the Gospel that I'm not lying. My father's father brought it with him from Egypt. If I lie, you can kill me tomorrow."

I turned toward Ruggiero. "Have this man brought to the palace with his cure."

I leaned over the battlements and cast one last glance at the forlorn fires which were writhing in the night. A piercing cry ripped through the silence; it came from the west rampart.

"Let's go back," I said.

Catherina was seated by the fireplace, wrapped in a blanket; she was sewing by the light of a torch. When I entered the room, she did not raise her eyes.

"Father," Tancredo said, "Kounak doesn't move any more."

"He's sleeping," I said. "Let him sleep."

"But he doesn't move at all."

I leaned over and touched the old dog's listless hair. "He's dead."

"He's dead!" Tancredo exclaimed. His pink face screwed up, and tears came to his eyes.

"Don't cry now," I said. "Be a man."

The tears streamed down his cheeks. *Thirty years of caution, thirty years of fear, and yet one day I'll be stretched out, stiff, and nothing will depend upon me any more. Carmona will be left to these feeble hands. Ah, how the longest life is short! What good are antidotes, spies, coats of mail? What good all these murders?*

I sat down next to Catherina. She was darning a tattered piece of cloth with hands covered with chilblains. I called softly to her. "Catherina . . ." She turned a deathly face in my direction. "Catherina, it's easy to blame me, but just for a moment, try to put yourself in my place."

"May God save me from ever having to be there." She leaned over her work again and remarked, "It's going to freeze over tonight."

"Yes." I watched the pale, shifting shadows which were trembling on the wall tapestry and suddenly I grew very tired.

"Children," she said, "with a whole long life before them."

"Ah! be quiet!"

They will all die, but Carmona will be saved. And then what? I will die and the city I saved will fall into the hands of Florence or Milan. I will have saved Carmona and I will have done nothing.

"Raimondo, let them come back into the city."

"Then all of us will die," I replied.

She lowered her head and pushed the needle with her red, swollen fingers. I felt like laying my head in her lap, caressing her legs, smiling at her. But I no longer knew how to smile.

"The siege has lasted a long time," she continued. "The Genoese are tired. Why not try to negotiate with them?"

I felt as if I had been struck a dull blow in the hollow of my chest. "Is that really the way you think?" I asked.

"Yes."

"You want me to open the gates to the Genoese?"

"Yes."

I passed my hand across my face. They all thought the same way; I knew it. For whom was I struggling, then? What was Carmona? Unfeeling stones and men who were horrified of death. In all of us, the same horror. If I had delivered Carmona to the Genoese, perhaps they would have spared us; we might have lived a few more years. A year of life, a night of life. For one night, the old beggar pleaded with me. *One night, a whole life . . . Children with their whole lives before them . . .* Suddenly, I felt like giving it all up.

"My Lord," Ruggiero said, "here is your man and his cure."

He was clutching Bartolomeo by the shoulder and he held out to me a dusty bottle filled with a greenish liquid. I looked at the beggar, with his wrinkled face, his dirty beard, his blinking eyes. *If I escape sickness, poison and swords, one day I'll be like him.*

"What is this cure?" I asked.

"I'd like to speak to you alone," Bartolomeo answered.

I gestured to Ruggiero. "Leave us alone."

Catherina started to rise, but I placed my hand on her wrist. "I keep no secrets from you." And turning to the beggar, I said, "Well, speak."

He looked at me with a strange smile on his face. "In this bottle," he began, "is the elixir of immortality."

"Is that all!"

"You don't believe me?"

The coarseness of his ruse made me smile in turn. "But if you're immortal, why are you so afraid of being thrown off the ramparts?"

"But I'm not immortal," replied the old man. "The bottle is full."

"And why haven't you drunk any?"

"Would *you* dare to drink it?"

I took the bottle in my hand; the liquid was cloudy. "You drink first."

He shook his head. "Is there a living animal in this place? A small animal?"

"Tancredo has a white mouse."

"Have her get it," said the old man.

"Raimondo, he's fond of that mouse," Catherina said.

"Go get it, Catherina," I ordered.

She got up.

"The elixir of immortality!" I said in a mocking tone of voice. "Why didn't you think of selling it to me sooner. You'd never have had to beg again."

Bartolomeo brushed his finger across the dusty neck of the bottle. "It's this cursed bottle that made me a beggar."

"How did that come about?"

"My father was wise. He hid the bottle in his attic and forgot about it. When he was dying, he told me of its secret, but he advised me to forget it, too. I was twenty years old and I was made a present of eternal youth. What did I have to worry about? I sold my father's shop and squandered his fortune. Each day I said to myself, 'I'll drink it tomorrow.'"

"And you never drank?"

"Poverty struck me and I didn't dare drink. Old age came, and infirmities. I would say, 'I'll drink the moment I'm about to die.' A little while ago, when the guards discovered me inside the hut where I was hiding, I didn't drink."

"There is still time," I observed.

He shook his head. "I'm afraid to die, but an eternal life—how long it must be!"

Catherina placed a little wooden cage on the table and silently sat down again in her chair.

"Watch carefully," the old man said. He uncorked the bottle, poured a few drops in the palm of his hand and grabbed the mouse. It let out a squeal and plunged its snout into the green liquid.

"It's poison," I said.

The mouse appeared thunderstruck and lay inert in the old man's hand.

"Wait."

We waited. Suddenly the motionless body moved.

"It was sleeping," I said.

"Now," Bartolomeo instructed, "twist it's neck."

"No!" Catherina cried.

He placed the mouse in my palm. It was alive and warm.

"Twist it's neck."

I violently tightened my grip; the little bones cracked. I threw the lifeless body on the table. "There."

"Watch, watch!" Bartolomeo said excitedly.

For a moment the mouse remained motionless, lying on its side. Then it rose again and began to scamper about on the table.

"It was dead," I said.

"It will never die again."

"Raimondo, make him leave. He's a sorcerer," Catherina said.

I seized the old man by the shoulder. "Must I drink the whole bottle?"

"Yes."

"Will I ever grow old?"

"No."

"Make him leave," Catherina repeated.

I looked at the old man distrustfully. "If you've lied to me, you know what will happen to you?"

He lowered his head. "But if I haven't lied, will you let me live?"

"Ah, your fortune is made," I answered. I called for Ruggiero.

"My Lord?"

"Keep a close watch on this man."

I closed the door and went toward the table. I reached for the bottle.

"Raimondo, you're not going to drink it?" Catherina said.

"He's not lying," I reassured her. "Why would he lie?"

"Ah! that's just it," she said.

I looked at her and my hand fell back to my side.

"When Christ wanted to punish the Jew who laughed in his face, he condemned him to live forever," she said ardently.

I did not answer. *The things I'll be able to do!* I thought, and I grabbed the bottle. Catherina hid her face in her hands.

"Catherina . . ." I looked all about me. Never again would I see this room with the same eyes. "Catherina, if I die, open the gates of the city."

"Don't drink," she pleaded.

"If I die, you can do anything you like."

I brought the bottle to my lips.

When I opened my eyes, it was broad daylight and the room was filled with people. "What's the matter?" I said. I raised myself to one elbow; my head was heavy. Catherina, standing by my bedside, was looking at me through petrified eyes. "What's the matter?" I repeated.

"You've been lying on that bed for four days now, cold as a corpse," Ruggiero answered. He, too, seemed frightened.

"Four days!" I leaped up. "Where's Bartolomeo?"

"Here." The old man drew near and looked at me bitterly. "You gave me a bad fright!"

I took him by the arm and led him to an alcove near the door. "Has it happened?"

"Without doubt."

"I'll never die?"

"No. Not even if you want to." He began to laugh and wave his hands wildly. "So much time!" he cried out. "So much time!"

I raised my hand to my throat; I was suffocating. "My coat, quickly."

"Are you going out?" Giovanni asked. "I'll alert the guards."

"No. No guards."

"It's unwise," Ruggiero warned. "The city isn't calm." He shifted his eyes. "It's not easy to get used to hearing that wailing coming from the ditches day and night."

I stopped at the door. "Were there any disturbances?"

"Not exactly. But every night someone or other tries to throw provisions over the ramparts. Sacks of wheat have been stolen from the storehouse. And the people are grumbling."

"Anyone heard complaining will be given twenty lashes" I ordered. "And any man caught at night on the ramparts will be hung."

The expression on Catherina's face suddenly changed; she took a step toward me. "Don't you want to let them return?"

"Ah! don't begin again," I said impatiently.

"You said to me, 'If I die, open the gates.'"

"But I'm not dead."

I looked at her swollen eyes, her sunken cheeks. *Why is she so sad? Why are they all so sad?* As for myself, I was bursting with joy.

I crossed the pink square. Nothing had changed—the same silence, the same shops behind their heavy wooden shutters. And yet everything was new as dawn, the gray, mute dawn of a radiant day. I looked at the red sun suspended in the cottony sky and I smiled; it seemed as though I could have plucked that great joyous ball right from the clouds. The sky was within my grasp, and I felt the whole future inside my heart.

"Everything all right? Nothing to report?"

"Nothing to report," replied the sentry.

I made the rounds of the sentry posts. The rocky hill was bare; not a fire was left in the ditches, not a blade of grass. *They will all die.* I pressed my hand against the stone battlement; I felt harder than the stone. What had I deprived them of? Ten years? Half a century? What was a year? A century? *They were born to die,* I thought. I leaned over. The Genoese would also die, those little black ants that were scurrying about their tents. But Carmona would never die. She would stand forever under the sun, guarded by her eight high towers, and she would grow bigger and more beautiful every day; her armies would sweep across the plains, dominate the whole of Tuscany. I gazed at the undulating hills which obliterated the horizon. Beyond those hills, there's a world I thought, and something exploded in my heart.

The winter passed. In the ditches the fires had long since gone out and the moaning had ceased. With the first warmth of spring, gusts of wind carried the putrid odor of carrion into Carmona. I inhaled it without disgust. I knew that the mortal miasma which drifted from the ditches was infecting the Genoese camp. They were losing their hair, their limbs became swollen, their blood was purple, and they were dying. When Carlo Malatesta appeared on the ridge of the hills, the Genoese hastily broke camp and fled without joining battle.

Wagons laden with sacks of flour, sides of meat and casks filled with wine followed the condottiere's troops into the city. Great fires were lit in the squares and triumphant songs broke out everywhere. Men kissed each other in the streets. Catherina squeezed Tancredo tightly in her arms, and for the first time in four years, she smiled. In the evening an immense feast was held. Malatesta, seated to the right of Catherina, drank and laughed like a man who had achieved his heart's desire. I, too, felt the warmth of the wine coursing through my veins, and I was filled with joy. But it was unlike the joy of the others; it was hard and dark, it weighed on my heart like a heavy stone. *This is only the beginning!*

When the meal was over, I took Malatesta to the treasure room and paid him the sum of money that had been agreed upon.

"And now," I proposed, "would you be willing to pursue the Genoese and lay hold of the castles and cities that border on my lands?"

He smiled. "Your chest is empty."

"It will be full tomorrow."

At the break of dawn, I sent heralds through the city. Under pain of death, every citizen had to surrender, before nightfall, all the gold, all the silver, all the precious stones he possessed. I was told that several men had grumbled but none had dared disobey. When the sun had set, heaps of jewels were piled high in the chests. I divided these riches into three parts. One was entrusted to the provost in charge of provisions for the purchasing of wheat; another was given to the weavers for the procurement of wool. The third chest, I showed to Malatesta.

"How many months will this keep your troops in my service?"

He plunged his hand into the sparkling jewels. "Several months."

"How many?"

"That will depend upon the profits of war," he said. Then he smiled. "And also on my own good pleasure."

He let the precious stones slip carelessly through his fingers while I impatiently watched him. Every pearl, every diamond was seed for future harvests, a fortress defending our frontiers, a piece of ground wrested from the Genoese. I summoned experts who spent the night evaluating the exact amount of my fortune, and I reached an agreement with Malatesta calling for a fixed pay per day and per man.

Then I had all of Carmona's men brought together in the palace square and I spoke to them ardently.

"There are no women in your homes," I said, "nor wheat in your attics. Let us go reap the wheat of the Genoese and bring back their daughters to our houses."

I added that the Holy Virgin had appeared to me in a dream and had promised that not a single hair of my head would fall until Carmona became the equal of Genoa and Florence.

The young people donned their armor. All had sunken cheeks, sallow complexions, black circles under their eyes, but the famine which had sapped their bodies had also tempered their spirits, and they followed me without complaint. To rouse their courage, I pointed out the purple bodies of the Genoese sprawled out dead in ditches all along the way. Malatesta's soldier's with their florid complexions, their full cheeks, their robust shoulders, seemed to us as though they belonged to some superhuman race. The condottiere led them as his fancy willed, now prolonging a halt more than was necessary to give them a rest, now continuing on without respite simply because he felt like riding horseback by the light of the moon.

Instead of pressing hard upon the fleeing Genoese, he wanted to take the castle of Monteferti by storm, explaining that he was bored with encountering only enemies who were dead or dying. The escapade cost us a full day and several of his captains. When I reproached him for this waste, he answered haughtily, "I make war for my own pleasure."

Thanks to the breathing spell we had given them, the Genoese were able to avoid an encounter by taking refuge in Villana, a fortified city protected by impregnable ramparts. In view of this, Malatesta declared that we would have to give up our venture. I asked him to remain patient for just one night. On the westerly approach to Villana, an aqueduct led into the city, bringing a stream of water which rushed beneath the ramparts through a subterranean canal. No man could have passed through that conduit without drowning. I told no one of my plan; I simply ordered my lieutenants to lie in wait before the west postern and, after stripping off my armor, I disappeared into the dark tunnel. At first, I was able to breath the stale air stagnating under the vaults, then the ceiling became lower and I could see that the space between the stones and the water soon vanished completely. I hesitated; the current was violent. If I had gone in any further, I would not have had the strength to turn back toward the light. *And if the old man lied?* A dense blackness closed in on me from all sides, and the only sound I heard was the gushing of water. But if the old man had lied, if I were mortal, what difference would it make if my life ended that day or the next? *Now I'll know,* I thought, and I plunged.

He had lied. My head buzzed, a vise was squeezing my chest. I was going to die and the Genoese would throw my bloated body to the dogs. How could I have believed that insane fairy tale? I was suffocating from rage as much as from the icy water; I wished only that the agony would be over quickly. There seemed no end to my dying. And suddenly it dawned on me that I had been swimming for a very long time and that I wasn't going to die. I swam to the opening at the end of the tunnel. There was no longer any possible doubt—I was really immortal! I wanted to fall to my knees and thank the devil or God, but no sign of their presence appeared around me. As I stood in chilly silence, I saw only a crescent moon embedded in the sky.

The streets were deserted. I made my way to the west postern where I slipped behind the sentry and felled him with a single thrust of my sword. In the sentry post, two soldiers were sleeping; I killed the first while he was still asleep, and the second after a brief fight. I opened the gate. My men silently entered the city and, taking the garrison by surprise, massacred every last soldier. At dawn, the terrified inhabitants discovered that they had changed masters.

Half of the men were sent to Carmona as prisoners to work our lands, and a large number of young, marriageable girls, who were to assure our posterity, were led away with them. From Villana, our troops dominated the plains and we seized several small towns without difficulty. I led the assaults through hails of arrows and my men called me the Invincible.

I wanted to follow up my successes and lay hold of the port of Rivella, vassal of Genoa, which would have given Carmona an outlet to the sea. But Malatesta, abruptly deciding that he was tired of fighting, told me he was going to withdraw with his troops. I had no alternative but to head back to Carmona. For some distance, I rode alongside this man who had no ultimate objective in life and who disposed of himself with the reckless abandon of mortals. We parted at a crossroads and as he went off in the direction of Rome in search

of new adventures, I followed him for a long while with my eyes.
Then I spurred my horse and galloped toward Carmona.

I did not want the fate of my city ever again to rest in the hands
of mercenaries, and I resolved to build an army for Carmona. I
needed a great deal of money. I levied heavy taxes; I decreed a law
against luxury, prohibiting all men and women from wearing jewelry
and from owning more than two coarse cloth outfits. Even the noblemen were obliged to eat only from earthenware or wooden dishes.
Those who rebelled were thrown into dungeons or thrashed in public,
and I confiscated their wealth. I forced all the men to marry before
the age of twenty-five, and the women to bear numerous children
for their city. Laborers, weavers, merchants and noblemen—I made
soldiers of them all. I, myself, kept watch over the training of re-
cruits. Soon, I had formed a company, then two, then ten. At the same
time, in order to increase our wealth, I encouraged the growth of
agriculture and commerce, and every year a great fair drew hundreds
of foreign merchants to Carmona who came to buy our wheat and
goods.

"How much longer must we go on living like this?" Tancredo
asked. He had his mother's blond hair and a greedy mouth. He hated
me. He did not know I was immortal, but believed I was protected
against sickness and old age by some mysterious drug.

"Just as long as it serves a purpose," I answered.

"Serves a purpose!" he exclaimed. "What purpose? For whom?"
A hopeless rage hardened his eyes. "We're as rich as Siena and Pisa
and yet the only time we ever celebrate is for a wedding or a baptism.
We dress like monks and live in convents. I'm your son, but every
morning and night I have to drill under the orders of a boor of a
captain. My friends and I will grow old without having had a youth."

"The future will reward us for our pains," I said.

"And who'll give us back the years you're robbing us of?" he asked.
He looked me straight in the face. "Me, I have only one life."

I shrugged my shoulders. What was one life?

At the end of thirty years, I had in my service the largest and best-
equipped army in all Italy. I had begun preparations for an expedition against Genoa when a great storm broke out over the plains.
For a whole day and night, a torrential rain poured down from the
skies. The rivers swelled, the streets of the low town were transformed

into streams of mud which seeped into the houses. In the morning, while the women were cleaning their soiled floors, the men looked in dismay at the squares invaded by a yellowish slime, the torn-up roads, and the young shoots of wheat bent over by the violence of the downpour. The sky remained a leaden gray. In the evening the rain began falling again and the peril with which we were menaced suddenly occurred to me. Without losing a moment, I sent merchants to Genoa for the purpose of buying up wheat in Sicily, Sardinia and all the barbarian lands to the north.

The rains fell all during the spring and summer. All over Italy, crops were drowned, fruit trees slashed to pieces, fodder lost. But before the end of autumn, Carmona's granaries were filled with sacks of grain which ships, equipped at our expense, had brought from overseas. With an avaricious passion, I breathed in the dusty odor; the slightest grain weighed heavily. I had public ovens constructed and each morning I, myself, doled out the hundred measures of wheat which were distributed to the bakers to make loaves of bran and flour, the weights of which I had regulated. The indigent were provided food without having to pay. Throughout all Italy there was a shortage of wheat; its price rose to thirty-six pounds the hundredweight, and bran cost almost as much. In the course of the winter, four thousand men died in Florence. In Carmona, however, neither the poor, nor the sickly, nor strangers were driven from the city, and there was enough grain left over for planting. During the first days of spring of the year 1348, when all the fields in Italy were barren, the crops rippled in our plains and a fair was opened in Carmona's main square. Leaning over the ramparts, I watched the caravans which ascended the hill and I thought, *I have vanquished famine!*

The blue sky and the clamor of festivity poured in through the open window. Catherina was sitting next to Louisa, Tancredo's wife; they were both embroidering. I had perched my grandson, Sigismondo, on my shoulders and I galloped about the room which was full of blossoming almond-tree branches.

"Giddy-up, giddy-up!" cried the child.

I loved him; he was closer to me than any other being. He was unaware that his days were numbered; he knew nothing of years, months, weeks. He was lost in the heart a resplendent day, without tomorrows and without end, an eternal beginning, an eternal present. His joy was as infinite as the sky. "Giddy-up, giddy-up!" he shouted. And I ran, thinking, *The blue of the sky will never fade, and there will be more springtimes for me than almond flowers. My happiness will last forever!*

"But why do you want to leave so soon?" Catherina asked. "Wait until Pentecost. It's still cold up there."

"I want to leave," Louisa replied. "I want to leave tomorrow."

"Tomorrow? How can you think of it? It will take at least a week to get the house in order."

"I want to leave," Louisa repeated with finality.

I approached her and looked with curiosity upon her obstinate little face. "Would you mind telling me why?"

Louisa stuck her needle in the canvas of the tapestry. "The children need air."

"But they seem to me to be in wonderful health!" I remarked. I pinched Sigismondo's calf and smiled at the two little girls seated on a rug in a ray of sunlight. "Springtime is so beautiful in Carmona!"

"I still want to leave," Louisa insisted.

Tancredo smiled coldly. "She's afraid."

"Afraid?" I said. "Oh what?"

"She's afraid of the plague," Tancredo replied. "And she's right. You should never have let those foreign merchants inside the city."

"What foolishness!" I exclaimed. "Rome and Naples are far away."

"I heard that at Assisi there fell a rain of big black, eight-footed insects with claws," Louisa said.

"And near Siena, the earth split open and began to spit fire!" I said mockingly. I shrugged my shoulders. "If you start believing all the rumors that are being spread . . ."

Catherina turned toward Ruggiero who was dozing in a chair with both hands on his belly; lately he slept almost constantly. He was growing heavy.

"Ruggiero!" Catherina called to him. "Ruggiero, what have you heard about the plague?"

"A Genoese merchant told me that it's already reached Assisi," he replied indifferently.

"Even if what you say is true, it could never reach up here," I assured them. "The air is as pure as in the mountains."

"Of course, *you* have nothing to worry about," Louisa said.

"Did your doctors think of the plague, too?" Tancredo asked.

"Alas! my dear son, they thought of everything," I answered. I looked at him venomously. "I promise you that in twenty years it will be Sigismondo who'll rule alongside me."

He arose and violently slammed the door behind him.

"You shouldn't go so far with him," Catherina admonished.

I did not answer.

She looked at me hesitantly. "Aren't you going to see those monks who asked to speak to you?"

"I refuse to allow their hordes to enter Carmona," I replied.

"But you can't very well refuse to hear them out," Catherina said.

"Perhaps they can tell us something about the plague," Louisa ventured.

I gestured to Ruggiero. "Very well. Tell them to come in."

Throughout Italy's famine-ravaged cities, fanatics fervently preaching penitence had arisen. At the sound of their voices, merchants abandoned their businesses, artisans their workshops, laborers their fields. They wore white robes and hid their faces under hoods; the poorest among them wrapped themselves in sheets. Barefooted, they wandered from city to city, singing canticles and exhorting the inhabitants to join their troupes. That morning they had arrived at the walls of Carmona and I had forbidden them to pass through our gates. The monks who led them were, however, allowed to come up to the palace. They entered behind Ruggiero; they were dressed in white robes.

"Sit down, brothers," I offered.

The smaller of the two monks took a step toward a damask-covered chair, but the other stopped him with a sharp gesture. "That's not necessary," he said.

I cast an unfriendly glance at the tall, tan-faced monk who stood before me with his hands hidden in his sleeves. *That man is passing judgment on me*, I thought.

"Where have you come from?"

"From Florence," the little monk replied. "We've been traveling for twenty days."

"Have you heard anything about the plague reaching as far as Tuscany?"

"My God! No!" the little monk exclaimed.

I turned toward Louisa. "You see!"

"Is it true, Father, that the famine caused more than four thousand deaths in Florence?" Catherina asked.

The little monk shook his head. "More than four thousand," he affirmed. "We ate bread made of frozen grass."

"We here once lived through such a thing," I said. "Have you ever been to Carmona before?"

"Once. Almost ten years ago."

"Isn't it a beautiful city?"

"It's a city that needs to hear the word of God," the tall monk burst forth.

Everyone turned his head toward him. I frowned.

"We have priests here who deliver excellent sermons every Sunday," I said dryly. "Besides, the people of Carmona are pious and their life is austere; there are neither heretics nor libertines among them."

"But pride is corrupting their hearts," the monk fervently said. "They no longer care about their eternal salvation. You think only of dispensing the blessings of the earth, and these blessings are nothing but vanity. You have protected them from famine, but man does not live by bread alone. You believe you have accomplished great things, but you have done nothing."

"Nothing?" I said. I began to laugh. "Thirty years ago there were twenty thousand men in Carmona. Now there are fifty thousand."

"And how many will die saved?" the monk asked.

"We are at peace with God," I angrily replied. "We have no need of discourses, nor processions." Turning to Ruggiero, I said, "Have these monks led outside of our walls and have the penitents chased into the plains."

The monks left in silence; Louisa and Catherina said nothing. I was not sure then that the heavens were empty, but I did not worry about heaven. And the earth in any case did not belong to God; the earth was *my* domain.

"Grandfather, take me to see the monkeys," Sigismondo said, pulling me by the arm.

"Me too! I want to see the monkeys too," said one of the little girls.

"No," Louisa protested. "I forbid you to go outside. If you go out, you'll be struck down by the plague. You'll get all black and die."

"Don't fill them with nonsense," I said impatiently. I put my hand on Catherina's shoulder. "Come down with us to the fairgrounds."

"If I go down, I'll have to climb back up again."

"Well?"

"You forget that I'm an old woman."

"Don't be silly," I said, "you're not old."

Her face was still the same; the same timid eyes, the same smile. But I had noticed for some time now that she always seemed tired; her cheeks were puffed and yellow, there were wrinkles around her mouth.

"We'll walk slowly," I said. "Come."

We went down the old Via dei Tintori. The children walked in front of us. On both sides of the street, workers with blue fingernails plunked skeins of wool into vats filled with azure and blood-colored dyes. A violet liquid seeped between the cobblestones.

"Ah!" I sighed. "When will I ever be able to tear down these old hovels."

"What will you do with all these poor people?"

"Yes, I know," I answered. "They'll have to die first."

The street led directly to the fairgrounds where the air smelled of cloves and honey. The rattling of tambours and the tinny sound of a brassband could be heard above the shouting merchants. Crowds of people pressed against the stands which were loaded down with woolen goods, bolts of linen, colorful fruits, spices and cakes. The women longingly held heavy yarns and delicate laces in their hands, children were biting into honey-covered wafers, and wine flowed from large pitchers set on wooden counters. There was warmth in both their stomachs and their hearts. As I strode across the square, a great cheer filled the air. "Long live Count Fosca! Long live Countess Fosca!" A bouquet of roses fell at my feet; a man took off his coat and threw it on the ground before me. I had vanquished famine and all this happiness was my doing.

The children shrieked with joy. I stopped obediently in front of the trained monkeys, I applauded the dancing bear and the acrobats walking on their hands. Sigismondo excitedly pulled me to the right, then the left.

"This way, grandfather! This way!" he cried out, pointing to a knot of spectators who were intensely watching a sight we were unable to see. I approached and tried to make my way through the crowd.

"Don't go any closer, my Lord," shouted one of the men, looking up at me with a terrified expression on his face.

"What's going on?"

I broke through the crowd. A man, no doubt a foreign merchant, was stretched out on the ground, his eyes closed.

"Well, what are you waiting for? Why don't you get him to the hospital?" I said impatiently.

They silently looked at me; no one budged.

"What are you waiting for?" I asked. "Take this man away."

"We're afraid," one of the men answered. He stuck his arm in front of me to bar the way. "Don't go any nearer."

I pushed him aside and knelt down beside the motionless body. I took hold of the foreigner's wrist and rolled up his wide sleeve. His arm was covered with black spots.

¥

"The priests are downstairs," Ruggiero said.

"Already?" I passed my hand across my face. "Is Tancredo here?"

"No," Ruggiero replied.

"Is *anyone* here?"

"No. I had to hire four men and promise them a fortune, at that."

"No one!" I exclaimed.

I looked all about me. The candles were almost burned out; a grayish light penetrated the room. I would have said, "Catherina, no one is here." And she would have replied, "They're afraid. It's only natural." Or perhaps she would have blushed and said, "They're too cowardly." I couldn't think of how she would have said it. I reached out my hand and touched the wooden coffin.

"There are only two priests," Ruggiero said. "And they say the cathedral is too far away. They want to hold the service in the chapel."

"As they wish."

I let my arm fall back to my side. The four men, big, red-faced peasants, tramped into the room. They walked toward the bier without looking at me and heaved it onto their shoulders with a brutish movement. They hated the frail body lying inside the coffin, the white body splotched with black. Above all, they hated me. When the plague broke out, it was rumored that I owed my youth to a pact with the devil.

The two priests were standing at the foot of the altar; a few servants and several guards were ranged against the walls. The bearers set the coffin down in the middle of the empty nave and the priests hurriedly muttered their prayers. One of them traced a large sign of the cross in the air and then they both walked rapidly to the door. The bearers followed with the bier. Behind me were Ruggiero and several soldiers. Day was breaking, the air was warm and pink. Inside their homes, people were waking up and discovering in horror that their arms were covered with black spots. Those who had died during the night were taken from their rooms; corpses, still warm, lined the streets. The pestilential odor hanging over the city was so strong that I was astonished the sky remained visible.

Two men carrying a plank on which a corpse was lying stepped out of a doorway. They fell in behind the soldiers in order to profit from the prayers the priests were murmuring.

"My Lord," Ruggiero said.

"Let them be."

A mule loaded down with bundles emerged from a side street. A man and woman were trudging along behind it; they were fleeing. Many people had fled during the first days, but the plague followed them wherever they went. It spread in every direction like wildfire; they came upon it in the plains and in the mountains. No place was left where one could safely take refuge. Nevertheless, these two were attempting to escape. As she passed by me, the woman spat on the ground. Further on, a band of young men and dishevelled women were coming down the street, singing and reeling drunkenly. They had spent the night in revelry in one of the large abandoned palaces. Laughing, they crossed in front of us and a voice cried out, "Son of the devil!"

Ruggiero started toward them.

"Never mind, let them alone," I said.

I looked at the pallbearers' thick necks, at their large hands planted on the wooden coffin. "Son of the devil!" they repeated and spat on the ground. But their words and acts had no importance: they were all condemned to death. Some fled, some prayed, others revelled. All would die.

We finally reached the cemetery. There were four coffins behind

Catherina's. Along every street, funeral processions climbed toward the holy burial grounds. A canvas-covered cart passed through the gate and drew up before a pit in which bodies were piled high. On the paths grown over with weeds, priests and gravediggers hurried to and fro amid a welter of confusion. Not for an instant did the sounds of picks and shovels cease. All of Carmona's life had taken refuge in this place of death. Catherina's grave was dug at the foot of a cypress tree. The bearers lowered the coffin into the hole and threw a few shovels of earth on the cover. The priest made a sign of the cross and quickly went off in the direction of another grave.

I raised my head and for the first time since arriving at the cemetery, became aware of the foul odor which hung heavily in the air. I pressed my hand against my mouth and walked toward the gate. A cart was slowly making its way up the street, and into it, men were heaving dead bodies which had been lying against the walls. I stopped. What was the use of going back to the palace? No one was left in the palace. Where was she? Under a cypress tree lay an old, mean-looking woman, and in Heaven drifted a formless soul, unhearing and speechless, like God.

"Come, my Lord," said Ruggiero.

I followed him. In front of the palace, standing on one of the counters abandoned by the merchants, the dark-faced monk was preaching and waving his arms wildly. When the plague broke out, he re-entered the city and I did not dare chase him. The populace listened to him devotedly; too few guards were left in my entourage for me to defy him sacrilegiously. He saw me and cried out in a strident voice, "Count Fosca! Now do you understand?"

I did not answer.

"You built new houses for the people of Carmona, and now they are buried in the earth. You clothed them in handsome robes, and now they lie naked in shrouds. You filled their stomachs, and now they are food for worms. In the plains, herds without shepherds are trampling down the useless crops. Yes, you vanquished famine. But God has sent the plague and the plague has vanquished you!"

"That only proves we must learn to vanquish the plague, too," I angrily shouted back.

I went into the palace and stopped abruptly at the door. I was surprised to see Tancredo standing by a window; he seemed to be waiting for me. I walked over to him.

"How can anyone be such a sniveling coward?" I said. "A son who hasn't courage to accompany his mother to her last resting place!"

"I'll prove my courage in other ways," he replied disdainfully. He blocked my way. "Wait," he said.

"What do you want?"

"As long as my mother was alive, I restrained myself. But now I've had enough." He stared at me with menacing eyes. "You've ruled long enough. It's my turn now."

"No," I said. "It will never be your turn."

"It's my turn!" he said violently.

He drew his sword and struck me directly in the chest. A dozen confederates surged forth from an adjacent room shouting, "Death to the tyrant!" Ruggiero threw himself in front of me. He fell. I thrust my sword and Tancredo fell. There was a sharp pain between my ribs. I spun around, striking out in every direction. Seeing Tancredo on the floor, several of his confederates fled, and soon my guards came running into the room. Three men were sprawled out on the floor. The others were subdued after a short fight.

I knelt down beside Ruggiero. He was gazing at the ceiling; a frightened look was frozen on his face. His heart had stopped beating. Tancredo's eyes were shut. He was dead.

"You're wounded, my Lord," a guard said.

"It's nothing."

I got up, slipped my hand under my shirt and drew it out wet with blood. I looked at the blood and began to laugh. I went over to the window and breathed deeply. The air filled my lungs and swelled my chest. The monk was still preaching and the mortal mob silently listened to him. My wife was dead, and her son and my grandchildren; all my friends were dead. I alone lived on, and there were no others like me. My past was buried; there was nothing now to hold me back, neither remembrances, nor love, nor duty. I was above all laws, my own master, and I could dispose of puny human lives as I pleased, lives destined only for death. Under the formless sky, I drew myself up erect, felt myself alive and free, knew that I would forever be alone.

I leaned out the window and smiled. A strange army! There were at least three thousand of them in the square, wrapped in long, sheetlike garments which hid even their faces. Every man was holding a horse by the reins. Under the flowing cassocks, they had donned their armor and strapped on their swords. I went over to the Venetian mirror. Beneath my white woolen hood, my face seemed as dark as a Moor's; my eyes were not those of a pious man. I pulled my cloak over my face and went down to the square. Toward the end of the epidemic the populace, distraught by the horror of the catastrophe from which they had just escaped and bewildered by the preachings of the monks, gave themselves up to all the extremes of an exalted piety. Pretending to have been won over to their fanatical beliefs, I exhorted all able-bodied men to accompany me on a long pilgrimage; we were armed, presumably, only in order to defend ourselves against the brigands who were overrunning the countryside. Most of my companions believed in the sincerity of my aims, but some of them followed along only because they had grave doubts.

We left the city by way of the old Via dei Tintori; nothing was left of the houses along the miserable street but heaps of rubble. The devil had no doubt heard my prayers: all the inhabitants in this section were dead of the plague and workers had just finished razing their hovels. They were dead; other men would be born. Through it all, Carmona lived on, standing proudly atop her rock, surrounded by her eight high towers, devastated but intact.

The first city we came to was Villana, whose streets we traversed chanting canticles. The townspeople joined our troupe in great numbers. Then we passed into Genoese territory. At each city along the route I would seek out the governor and ask him to make us welcome. His permission granted, we would form a procession and march through the streets, preaching penitence and gathering up alms. When we were deep into the heart of the country, I pretended that the Genoese officials refused to receive us. The surrounding countryside, devastated by famine and pestilence, provided almost no food. Soon, we began to suffer from hunger. A few penitents proposed returning to Carmona, but I objected that it was too far, that we would die of starvation before reaching our homes. I suggested that the best we could do under the circumstances was to continue on to Rivella, a large, prosperous port where we would certainly not be refused assistance.

The governor of Rivella did, in fact, agree to open his gates to us. But the news I carried back to my companions was of impious men who had once again rejected our prayers. The pilgrims began to mutter among themselves, saying they could take by force what was refused them out of charity. I pretended to recoil from such proposals, but in preaching resignation I insinuated that the only alternative left us was to die where we stood. Wrathful indignation soon seethed in all their hearts, and I had to cede to the will of that famished horde.

The procession passed through the gates of Rivella without arousing suspicion. When we reached the main square, I suddenly threw off my white robe and galloped toward the governor's palace shouting, "To arms! Long live Carmona!" All the penitents hastily tore off the sheets in which they were wrapped and revealed themselves fully armed. The surprise was so great that no resistance was offered. Drunk with victory, their passions inflamed by the smell of blood, the pious pilgrims were quickly transformed into soldiers. A night of orgy completed the metamorphosis. The Genoese magistrates were massacred, their houses looted, their wives raped. For a whole week wine flowed freely in the taverns and obscene songs echoed through the streets.

I left a small body of soldiers to occupy Rivella; with the rest of my troops I set out to conquer the castles and fortresses which commanded the route leading from Carmona to the sea. The garrisons, decimated by the plague and half-starving, were unable to defend themselves against our assaults. I was not unaware that my perfidy had raised indignation throughout all Italy. But the Genoese, still too weak to undertake a war, were forced to accept my conquests.

Master of Rivella, I immediately ordered high taxes to be paid on all merchandise entering the port. The Florentine traders insisted in vain on being exempted from these taxes; I had no desire to accord them any special privileges. I knew that I was rousing the ire of Florence, but I did not shrink before the prospect of war with the powerful Republic.

I began preparations for the struggle. I was rich enough to enlist the services of most of the captains who had formed bands of marauders all over Italy. I regularly paid them partial wages and in return they agreed to place their men at my command whenever I had need of them. In the meantime, I invited them to wage war on their own, to live and enrich themselves by pillaging the lands bordering on Carmona, thus weakening the cities I proposed to attack while we were still at peace. When I wanted to take a fortified town by surprise, I ostensibly gave leave of absence to one of my captains whom I secretly entrusted with the task of carrying out my project. If he failed, I disavowed him. Without having declared war, I was soon in possession of all the castles and fortresses along my frontiers. By the time the Genoese decided to invade Carmona's plains, I had built up a formidable army, and the best of Italy's condottieri were in my pay.

At first, I let the Genoese and their army of Catalan mercenaries spread out over the countryside. Warned of their approach, the peasants, bringing their crops and livestock with them, took refuge in villages that I had had the foresight to fortify. The enemy soldiers found almost nothing to subsist on in the stripped plains. They attempted to take a few of the villages, but, situated on isolated knolls and ardently defended, our castles defied all assaults. The troops commanded by Angelo de Tagliana split up and exhausted themselves in these traps. It was a simple matter to trick isolated groups of soldiers into ambushes and to make prisoners of the marauders who sought food in abandoned farms. When Tagliana had advanced as far as the river Mincia, I decided to join battle.

It was a fair June morning when our armies stood face to face. A light haze rose from the river and the blue of the sky was tinged with gray. Steel armor sparkled in the radiant light, neighing horses glistened, and the joy I felt in my heart was as fresh as the dew-covered grass. Tagliana, using conventional tactics, divided his army into three corps; I divided mine into small groups. Through the sky's delicate gray, I foresaw a stifling, sun-baked afternoon, and I had pitchers and barrels prepared in advance for watering the horses and refreshing my soldiers after each skirmish. When the combat signal was given, the two armies pounced upon each other with a crashing din. The advantage of my tactics was soon evident. The Genoese troops were unable to shift positions except in large numbers, while my soldiers attacked in small, independent groups, and then fell back to the main line only to spread out and attack again. Nevertheless, grouped around their general, the Catalans stoutly repulsed our assaults. The sun climbed high in the sky, the heat became intense, and we had not yet gained an inch of ground. By the middle of the afternoon our horses were treading over seared, yellow grass, and the air was thick with dust. My men hastily quenched their thirst between attacks, but not a drop of water had wet the lips of our enemies. Through the clanging of steel and the heavy hammering of horses' hoofs could be heard the rippling of water which was flowing less than five hundred paces to the south. Finally, Tagliana's soldiers could no longer resist the temptation; they broke ranks and went down to the river. Then, in a headlong charge, we drove a large number of them into the water where they helplessly drowned in their heavy armor. The rest fled in disorder, leaving some five hundred prisoners in our hands.

I decided to celebrate this victory with festivities worthy of the warrior people we had become. Upon our return to Carmona, I ordered that preparations be made for a huge tournament between the high city and the low. In the morning, children, then adolescents engaged for three hours in various types of combat. During the afternoon, it was the men's turn to face each other. Lightly armored, they threw stones at one another, trying to parry them with their left arms which were wrapped in heavy coats. The men of the high city wore green and those of the low city, red. Next, two groups of more heavily armored men made their appearance in the square. The combatants were clad in coats of iron under which, to soften the blows, they wore cushions stuffed with coarse hemp and cotton. In his right hand each held a lance from which the steel tip had been removed, and in his left hand, a shield. Victory consisted in occupying the center of the square. A great crowd pressed all around the arena; at every window there were smiling women. With gestures and shouts, the spectators urged on their relatives, their friends, their neighbors; they cried out, "Hurrah for the Greens!" or "Hurrah for the Reds!" I had neither friend, nor relative, nor neighbor. Seated under a velvet canopy, I indifferently watched the games while emptying several small pitchers of wine.

"I drink to the prosperity of Rivella and to the ruin of Genoa!" I said, raising my goblet.

They raised their goblets and in docile voices repeated in unison, "To the prosperity of Rivella!" But Palombo, who was head of the weaver's guild, did not join in the toast; he studied his goblet contemplatively.

"Why aren't you drinking?" I asked.

He raised his eyes. "I've heard from an unquestionable source that the Florentine merchants in Rivella have received orders to terminate all trading by the first of November."

"Well?"

"On that date, they'll leave the city and transfer their businesses to Sismone in the Maremma d'Evisa."

The news produced a long silence at the table.

"To hell with the Florentines!" I exclaimed.

"All the other merchants will follow them," Palombo said.

"Misfortune for Evisa and Sismone, then!"

"Florence will stand behind them," he argued.

They all looked at me; in their eyes I read: "The Florentines must be exempted from the tax." But what had I become a conquerer for? To follow the advice of these cautious old men? To prostrate myself before Florence?

"Misfortune for Florence!" I said. I turned toward my captains and raised my goblet. "I drink to our victory over Florence!"

"To our victory over Florence!" they repeated.

The voices of Bentivoglio and Puzzini seemed half-hearted and an ironic smile twisted d'Orsini's lips. I grabbed hold of a wine pitcher and threw it to the ground. "That's how I'll destroy Florence."

They placidly looked at me. The war was over and we were celebrating our victory; they asked for nothing more. As for me, I wanted to hold onto my victory, to keep it alive in my mind. But where was it? In vain I searched their faces for the fervor of that afternoon's battle, for the smell of dust and sweat, for the crushing weight of sun on steel armor. They were full of laughter and petty worries; I no longer cared to listen to their stupid prattle. My shirt was choking me; I stood up and tore it open. The blood rushed to my head, air filled my chest; I felt as though my life were about to burst apart like a blister of fire. The cloth ripped in my fingers and I let my hands, my empty hands, fall back to my sides. In the center of the square, a herald lowered a fence railing, signifying that the Reds had won, and the delirious populace threw flowers and handkerchiefs and shawls at the feet of the combatants. Five of them had been killed, nine others wounded. But these little, puerile beings were capable only of coveting ephemeral, insignificant victories. I could take no pleasure in their games. The sky was the same blue as it was above the banks of the Mincia, but now it seemed faded. Above the walls of Florence, above the banks of the future it flamed red and golden, like that sky burning in my memory.

Palombo was right. In the course of the winter all of Rivella's merchants moved their concerns to Sismone, a port situated in the Maremma d'Evisa. The artisans of Rivella were no longer able to sell their merchandise and soon found themselves without resources. Profiting from the widespread discontent, the Alboni faction aroused the populace and proclaimed Rivella's independence. Any attempt to retake her would have required the possession of a fleet. Therefore, I had to content myself with ravaging the surrounding countryside, with burning crops and farms. But I decided to take my revenge on Evisa in a singular manner.

This city, allied with Florence, was situated at the mouth of the Mincia, the upper part of which flowed through my territory. When the river reached Evisa's ramparts, it split into two branches, each about fifteen hundred feet wide, which served as a natural defense in place of the customary moats. They were too deep to be forded, and, except at one point where it would have been foolhardy to attack, their banks were too muddy to permit the use of boats. I ordered one of my engineers to divert the Mincia. Six months of labor went into constructing a dam of extraordinary strength in order to stop the river from following its natural course. At the same time, to give the river an outlet into Carmona's plains, I had a tunnel dug through a mountain. In their minds' eyes, Evisa's inhabitants saw their lakes transformed into pestilential swamps and their defenses, together with the air's salubrity, gone. They sent emissaries to Carmona to plead with me to give up my plans. My answer to them was that every city had the right to carry out on its own territory whatever works were deemed necessary. But one day, while I was thinking of how Evisa, deprived of her natural defenses, would fall into my hands, a great storm suddenly broke out. The Mincia, swollen by the rains, swept away the dam and in one night destroyed the fruits of six months of labor.

Furious, I sent my captains, Bentivoglio, d'Orsini and Puzzini, to devastate Evisa's outlying lands. Knowing that Florence was raising an army to come to her ally's aid, I formed an alliance with Siena. We put together an army of ten thousand men. My troops and the condottieri's joined forces in Siena, which we used as a base in attempting to break through into Florentine territory. While we skirted the outer edges of her frontier, the Republic's army followed us closely along the inside to prevent our passing through. I made a feint at the state of Arezzo, and when the Florentines sent a large contingent of troops to defend that province, we gained entry by way of Chianti in the valley of the Greva. Following the Arno, we went as far as Florence itself. During the march, an immense amount of booty was taken, for war had not been declared and the peasants, unwarned, did not take the precaution of hiding their belongings and livestock.

For ten days we advanced without encountering any obstacles. The soldiers sang and stuck flowers in their horses' manes; our columns gave the appearance of a peaceful, triumphal procession. And when, from the top of a hill, we caught sight of Florence and her vermilion domes bathed in the sun's brilliant light, a great cry of joy burst forth from every throat. We set up camp and for four days the soldiers lolled about in the fresh grass, passing from one to the other heavy goatskin sacks filled with wine. Steers and cows with full udders wandered among the carts laden with rugs, mirrors and laces.

"And now?" d'Orsini asked. "What are we going to do?"

"What do you want us to do?"

I could not even dream of attacking Florence. She was stretched out at my feet, radiant and calm, a ribbon of green water running through her center. There was no possible way of obliterating that city from the face of the earth.

"We've taken a fairly rich booty," I said. "We'll bring it back to Carmona."

He smiled without answering and I went off, irritated. I was well aware that the campaign had cost a great deal of money and had resulted in nothing. Florence was at my feet and I was powerless to do anything about it. What good then were my victories?

I announced to my troops that we would head back to Carmona that day. All through the camp there were mutterings. We were masters of Tuscany, were we now going to abandon it? Slowly, we packed our belongings. When the time came to set off, I noticed that Paolo d'Orsini was no longer with us. During the night he had passed over into the service of Florence, taking a part of my cavalry with him.

Weakened by this defection, we speedily began our return through the valley of the Arno. The soldiers no longer sang. D'Orsini's men were soon harassing our rear guards, and my troops, bored by their meaningless triumphs, were burning to join in battle. But he knew the country better than I, and I feared his crafty tricks. He followed us all the way to the frontiers of Siena and, within our sight, began attacking the village of Mascola, which was situated on a small hill surrounded by swamps. My men considered themselves insulted and set up a loud clamor for a fight. But a battle seemed to me a dangerous undertaking—the sun-baked crust covering the slimy swamp could support foot-soldiers but would cave in under the weight of a horse.

"I'm afraid of a trap," I said.

"We have more men; we're stronger than they are," said Puzzini with fiery zeal.

I decided in favor of fighting. I, too, was anxious to taste the blood of battle and win a victory over enemies made of flesh and bones. A narrow road which d'Orsini appeared to have left unguarded, crossed through the swamp. I ordered my troops to follow it. Suddenly, after it was too late to retreat, a hail of arrows came flying at them from all directions; d'Orsini had concealed his men behind every bush. Then his light cavalry and his infantry struck at our flanks, and when my soldiers left the road to fight off the enemy, they sank into the muddy swamp and were unable to move. No sooner had our columns been driven into disorder than d'Orsini's foot soldiers ventured onto the road and, thrusting their swords into our horses' bellies, threw over the riders who were so weighted down with heavy armor that they could not get up again. Pietro Bentivoglio discovered an escape by way of a footpath cutting across the swamp; as for myself I galloped straight through the enemy's midst, over the entire length of the road, and left them behind me. But Ludovico Puzzini was taken prisoner along with eight thousand men. Not a single soldier had been slain. All our belongings, as well as all the booty we had taken in Tuscany, fell into the victors' hands.

"Honor demands that we revenge ourselves for this defeat," my lieutenants declared. Their eyes glittered in their humiliated faces.

"What's one defeat?" I said.

D'Orsini's soldiers, who had served under my orders at the beginning of the campaign, considered their prisoners as brothers in arms, less fortunate than themselves, and freed them during the first night of their captivity. In Villana two armorers sold me five thousand sets of armor, and I returned to Carmona with my troops practically intact. I had gained nothing by my victories, and in losing a battle, I lost nothing.

With knitted brows, my lieutenants looked at me uncomprehendingly. I shut myself in my study and remained there for three days and three nights. Tancredo's face, hardened by despair, flashed before my eyes. "What purpose? For whom?" And I heard the voice of the dark-faced monk: "What you have done is nothing."

⚜

I decided to change my methods. Renouncing military parades, pitched battles and useless campaigns, I put all my efforts into weakening the enemy republics by practicing cunning politics.

The cities of Orci, Circio and Montechiaro were broken away from the Florentine alliance by the signing of commercial treaties; agents posing as merchants in cities dominated by Genoa fomented conspiracies, and in Genoa itself, they fed the flames of partisan rivalry. I was careful to respect the institutions of the cities which were brought under my law. Thus, many small republics, tired of a liberty too difficult to defend, preferring security to independence, accepted my protection.

Life was harsh in Carmona. The men slept less than five hours a day, working from dawn well into the night, constantly weaving wool in their somber workshops and compelled to take part in difficult military exercises even in the most torrid heat. The women spent their youths in bearing and nursing children who were trained in all physical activities from their most tender age. But at the end of thirty years, our territory had become as vast as Florence's. As a result of my scheming, Genoa, on the other hand, had fallen into complete decadence. My captains had devastated her countryside and razed her fortresses; her commerce was perishing, her navigation abandoned, and the city was prey to all the disruptions of anarchy. She was dealt a final blow when the duke of Milan attacked her by surprise. Encountering no opposition from the Genoese, General Carmagnola easily made his way through the mountains with his three thousand horses and eight thousand foot soldiers, ravaging the valleys along the march. I immediately set out for the port of Livorno which commanded the mouth of the Arno. I did not even have to lay siege, for the Genoese, unable to defend the city, ceded her to me for the sum of one hundred thousand florins. Proudly, I raised Carmona's banner above Livorno's castle, while my army loudly cheered the most important triumph of my patient maneuvers. With Genoa ruined, Livorno became the principal port of all Italy.

The realization of our wildest hopes seemed imminent when a messenger arrived announcing that the king of Aragon, joining forces with the duke of Milan, was about to attack Genoa from the sea. But suddenly the duke's ulterior aim occurred to me. Genoa was incapable of protecting herself against both of these powerful adversaries. Once he had become master of Liguria, the duke would invade Tuscany, reduce Carmona and then Florence to slavery. In Genoa, I had seen only a strong rival and I had done everything in my power to weaken her, without realizing that her ruin could one day lead to my own.

I was forced to offer my aid to Genoa. Torn apart by the quarrels I had complaisantly stirred up, the Genoese were incapable of boldly deciding to offer resistance, yet had qualms about surrendering to the duke. I tried to rouse their spirits, but they had long neglected to maintain an army and their mercenaries were always liable to quit them at any moment. Following the valley of the Arno, so often ravaged by my captains' incursions, I set out after Carmagnola to halt his advance. Everywhere, fortresses had been dismantled and abandoned, castles destroyed. Unable to entrench ourselves behind solid walls, we were forced to fight in the open fields. But finding enough food to live on in this too-frequently devastated land presented a serious problem. All our past successes now turned against us. After six months of campaigning, my army, hungry, worn out and weakened by fever, was now only a shadow of its former self. It was then that Carmagnola decided to attack.

Carmagnola's forces had grown to ten thousand cavalrymen and eighteen thousand foot soldiers. Compared to his, my cavalry was so inferior in numbers that I decided to risk a new tactic. Against Carmagnola's mounted soldiers, I sent my infantry, which firmly withstood the first assault. Armed with halberds, they hacked at the legs of the charging horses or, grabbing hold of them by the feet, spilled both horses and riders. Four hundred horses had already been slain when Carmagnola gave orders to his cavalrymen to dismount. The battle continued furiously, with a great number of soldiers on both sides meeting death. In the evening, the youngest and most adventurous of my lieutenants secretly led six hundred horsemen through the mountains to the Miossena Valley and, letting out horrifying cries, they pounced upon Carmagnola's rear guard. The Milanese, terrified by this surprise attack, fled in disorder. We had lost three hundred and ninety-six men, but the number of soldiers dead on Carmagnola's side was three times as great.

"Now," I said to the Doge Fregoso, "you mustn't lose a minute. Arm all the men of Liguria, put your fortresses in order, send emissaries to Florence and Venice to ask their help."

He seemed not to hear me. Beneath his long white hair, his face was noble and serene; his clear eyes gazed emptily into the distance.

"What a lovely day," he remarked.

From the terrace, shaded by pink bay and orange trees, I looked down upon Genoa's main street. Women dressed in velvets and silks walked languorously in the shadow of the palace; cavaliers wearing embroidered doublets proudly sauntered through the crowds. Under a porch sat four of Carmona's soldiers, emaciated, dirty and tired; they were watching a group of girls who were chatting with several young men near a fountain.

"If you don't try to defend yourself," I said angrily, "Carmagnola will be outside of Genoa's gates before spring."

"I know," Fregoso replied. "But we're unable to defend ourselves," he added indifferently.

"You *can* defend yourselves," I urged. "Carmagnola isn't invincible, because we've beaten him. My soldiers are tired; now it's your turn."

"There is no dishonor in admitting one's weakness," he said gently with a faint smile on his face. "We here are too civilized not to love peace."

"Peace? What are you talking about?"

"The duke of Milan has promised to guarantee us our constitution and our internal liberty," he answered. "It was not without great anguish that I have decided to renounce the dignities of office my city has bestowed upon me. But I will not shrink before that sacrifice."

"What are you going to do?"

"I shall abdicate," he said with dignity.

I stood up and clenched my fists. "You've betrayed me!"

"I must first consider the interests of my country."

I leaned over the balustrade. Three young girls with flowers in their hair were passing by; their laughter filled the air. My soldiers mournfully watched them, and I knew the images that were flashing through their minds: the parched pink streets of Carmona where even the noblemen went by foot; unsmiling women dressed in black who nursed their children while going about their chores; little girls who climbed the hill carrying buckets of water too heavy for them; men with harried faces eating watery soup in their doorways. The center of the city, where the old hovels had once stood, was now a weed-infested wasteland. We had no time to build palaces, or plant lemon trees, or sing, or laugh.

I turned around. "It's not fair!"

"The duke of Milan would like to come to terms with you, too," Fregoso said.

"I refuse to bargain with him."

That very evening, I set out with my men on the road back to Carmona. More than one was missing. Looking at their dejected faces,

I could almost hear them thinking: "Who are the victors?" And I was unable to answer.

We were approaching Pergola, a city I had always coveted, but which fiercely refused to accept my domination. To take my soldiers' minds off their disillusionment, I decided to make them a present of a tangible victory. I led them to the walls of the proud city and promised them that all the spoils they carried off would be shared only among themselves. Pergola was rich and they grew excited at the prospect of looting her. The north, south and west sides of the city were solidly fortified, and on the east, she was bordered by the Mincia. We had tried several times to capture her, but she withstood all our assaults. Now, however, I had new weapons—heavy mortars which were powerless against moving objects, but extremely effective when used against stone walls. These marvelous contraptions, perfected by my engineers, could each fire sixty shots in a single night. I began by calling upon Pergola to surrender. My soldiers shot arrows over the ramparts which carried messages saying we would destroy the city if they refused to open her gates to us. But the populace, massed behind the battlements, answered only with cries of hate and defiance. I then placed a regiment at each of the city's four gates and had the ground leveled between them to facilitate communication. Next, I ordered the mortars brought up; my soldiers looked incredulously at these engines of war. The first balls that were fired crashed against the walls without visibly shaking them. From the tops of the city's towers, the people of Pergola sang and hurled insults at us. But I was not discouraged. For thirty days we battered the walls and little by little the towers and ramparts fell to pieces. The debris began to pile up in the moat surrounding the city and it was not long before there were penetrable breaches. The besieged inhabitants withdrew from the ramparts; their songs and insults were no longer heard. The final night of the bombardment, while the balls struck against the tottering stones, a leaden silence hung over the city. When dawn came, I saw that we had created a wide breach in the wall and I sent my men to the assault. They raced off shouting joyously; Genoa had been forgotten along with all the enticements of peace. We had carried out a unique exploit: for the first time in history, mortars had battered down powerful ramparts; for the first time, an army had entered a large, fortified city by force.

I was the first to pass through the breach. To our astonishment, we discovered that there was no one lying in wait for us behind the walls, and the streets were deserted. I stopped, afraid of a trap, and my soldiers, intimidated by the silence, held their tongues. We looked up at the roofs and towers. We saw no one. The windows of the houses were closed, the doors open. We cautiously advanced. Not a sound. At every street corner my men aimed their crossbows at the roofs, looking nervously to the right and left, but no stones or arrows flew down upon us. We reached the main square. It was empty.

"Search the houses," I ordered.

The soldiers went off in small groups. Followed by several guards, I entered the governor's palace. The marble floor of the hall was bare, the walls were bare. In the drawing rooms, all the furniture was still in its place, but there were neither rugs, nor tapestries, nor paintings anywhere in the palace. The linen and silver coffers and the jewel boxes were all empty. When I left the palace I learned that mattresses and copper pots had been found on the banks of the Mincia. Under cover of night, the entire populace had fled by way of the river, making off with all their treasures, while we were deluding ourselves in the belief that they were lying in wait for us behind the ramparts.

Surrounded by my silent, motionless soldiers, I stood stock-still in the middle of the square. They had found nothing to pillage in the abandoned houses but some old wrought-iron ornaments. The tavern floors were wet with wine; all the casks had been emptied. In great fireplaces sacks of flour, bread, sides of meat, had been burned to cinders. We had believed that we were conquering a city and we held only a stone skeleton in our hands.

Towards noon, one of my lieutenants brought a woman to me whom the soldiers had discovered in a house on the outskirts of the city. She was small; heavy braids of hair were wound about her head. There was neither fear nor defiance in her eyes.

"Why didn't you leave with the others?" I asked her.

"My husband is sick. They couldn't take him."

"And why did the others leave?" I said angrily. "Do you think that when I conquer a city I have the eyes of babies gouged out?"

"No," she replied. "We don't believe that."

"Then *why?*"

She did not answer.

"More than twenty cities are prospering under my domination. Never have the people of Montechiaro, Orci and Paleva been more happy."

"The people of Pergola are different," she said simply.

I looked at her fixedly; she did not flinch. The people of Pergola. The people of Carmona. Once, long before, I too had uttered these words. I had driven the women and children from the city. Why? . . . I turned my eyes away.

"Let her go," I said to the guards.

She went off unhurriedly.

"Let's get out of here."

My captains mustered their soldiers; they obeyed without reluctance. No one would have wanted to spend the night in that accursed city. I was the last to leave the deserted square; the silence of the stone walls troubled my heart. At my feet lay a corpse. It was I who had killed him, and I no longer knew why.

Eight days later, I signed a treaty with the duke of Milan.

Peace reigned. I disbanded my army, lowered the tax rates, abolished the antiluxury laws. I loaned money to Carmona's traders and became their banker. With my encouragement, industry and agriculture displayed a new vigor. My fortune, which I consecrated to the city, became as legendary as my eternal youth. On the ground where the old hovels once stood, I erected palaces more beautiful than Genoa's. Architects, sculptors and painters from all over Italy were summoned to my court. I had an aqueduct built and fountains spouted in every square. The hill became dotted with new houses and vast suburbs spread out over the plains. Drawn by our prosperity, many foreigners came to settle down inside our walls. I called upon doctors from Bologna to emigrate to Carmona, and I built hospitals. The number of births increased; the population grew rapidly. Soon Carmona had two hundred thousand inhabitants. Proudly, I thought, *They owe their lives to me. They owe everything to me.* It lasted thirty years.

The people, however, were no happier than before. They had better lodgings and were somewhat better dressed, but they worked without respite, and never before had the noblemen and the rich displayed their wealth with such insolence. The ambitions of both the poor and the rich grew ever greater, and from year to year the workers found their conditions less and less tolerable. I wanted to improve their lot, but the master weavers explained to me that if the work hours were reduced, or if wages were raised, the price of goods would have to go up. Then, unable to compete with foreign producers, we would all be ruined, workers and merchants alike. They were right. Unless I could rule the whole world, no drastic reforms were possible. In the summer of 1449 the harvest was bad. Throughout Italy the price of wheat climbed higher and higher and our greedy peasants sold most of their crops to Pisa and Florence. When winter came, bread was so expensive in Carmona that many workers, unable to provide food for their families, had to ask for public charity. I bought up wheat wherever I could and distributed it to the people. But it was not only bread they wanted. They also wanted not to have to beg. One morning, the members of the various guilds, their plans having been kept a closely guarded secret, gathered in arms around their banners. They spread out over the city and pillaged several palaces. The noblemen and the wealthy, caught unaware, could do nothing but barricade themselves in their houses. The weavers, fullers and dyers, effectively in control of Carmona, appointed a council of sixty-four cavaliers who were anxious to take advantage of the revolt to throw me from power. They promised bread to the people and the abolition of their debts. And proclaiming that I had made a pact with the devil, that I should be burned at the stake like a sorcerer, they began an assault on my palace. "Down with the son of the devil!" they shouted. "Death to the tyrant!" From the palace windows, my guards let loose a hail of arrows. The attackers hastily retreated, leaving the square deserted. But a few moments later, they rushed at the door again, attempting to break it down. In the evening, just as the door was about to give way, the noblemen of the surrounding villages and castles, alerted of the attack by messengers, came galloping through the city.

"The revolt has been subdued, my Lord! We have them on the run!" cried the captain of my guards, bursting into my room. Behind him I could hear a joyous clamor and loud metallic clanking. Albozzi, Ferracci and Vincenzo-the-Black, my defenders, were climbing the stone stairs, laughing. Outside, horses were prancing under my windows, and I knew there was blood on their hoofs.

"Stop the massacre!" I violently shouted. "Put out the fires and leave me alone!"

I shut the door, went over to the window and pressed my forehead against the iron grillwork. Against the sky, lit up like a bright dawn, sprouted an enormous mushroom of black smoke. The weavers' houses were aflame and the weavers' wives and children were burning in their houses.

It was late into the night when I stepped away from the window and left the palace. The sky was dark now and the sounds of galloping horses, the savage shouts of soldiers, no longer echoed through the streets.

At the entrance to the weavers' quarters, soldiers were standing guard. The ruins were still smoldering. Dead bodies were lying all about in the deserted streets—women with their chests staved in, children whose faces had been crushed by horses' hoofs. Among the cinders lay horribly charred bodies. At the corner of the street I heard a long wail. There was an almost full moon in the sky, and in the distance a dog howled into the night. *Serves what purpose? For whom?* From the depths of the past, Tancredo was sneering at me.

The dead were buried, the houses rebuilt. I decreed that the artisans were to be freed of their debts. In the spring the almond trees flowered as they had every spring before and the weavers' looms hummed in peaceful streets. But my heart was still filled with ashes.

"Why are you so sad?" Laura asked me. "Don't you have everything in the world a man could possibly desire?"

I had slept all night long in her arms. The days then seemed too long and I welcomed the night and forgetful sleep. My head was resting on her breast. I would have liked to have melted back into the milky languor of her body, but the light of day filtered through my eyelids and I could hear the sounds of life stirring in the city. I was awake and I was bored. I reluctantly got out of bed.

"What, may I ask, *is* there in this world that's desirable?"

"Lots of things."

I laughed. I could easily have given her everything she wanted, but I did not love her. I loved no one. While I was dressing, I felt my legs grow weak, like on the day Catherina was buried, that day when there seemed nothing left for me to look forward to, anywhere, any more. *Day after day, the same gestures,* I thought. *And it will never end! Will I never wake up in another world, a world where even the air tastes different?*

I left the palace. It was the same world; it was still Carmona with her pink streets and her funnel-shaped chimneys. New statues stood in her squares and I was aware of their beauty. But I was also aware that they would stand immobile for centuries on the sites where they had been erected, and they seemed to me as old and as distant as the Greek

Venuses buried in the earth. The people of Carmona walked past them with hardly a glance; they took notice of neither the monuments nor the fountains. What purpose did they serve, then, those chiseled stones? I went outside the ramparts. What purpose did Carmona serve? High up upon her rock, she stood immutable through war, peace, plague, rebellion. And there were a hundred other cities in Italy standing upon their rocks, equally proud, equally useless. What purpose did the sky serve, and the flowers of the meadows? It was a magnificent morning, but the peasants, bent over the earth, had no time to gaze at the sky. And as for me, I was weary by now of seeing it day in and day out for two hundred years, always the same.

I walked aimlessly for several hours. *Everything a man could possibly desire.* I kept repeating these words to myself, but in my soul I was unable to awaken the least desire. How long ago it seemed when every precious grain of wheat weighed so heavily in the hollow of my hand!

Suddenly I stopped. In a small yard where chickens were busily engaged in pecking at one another, a woman was bent over a tub washing her laundry, and seated under an almond tree was a little girl, laughing. The ground was strewn with white petals and the child, gripping the petals in her tiny hands, avidly brought them to her mouth. She was very brown and had large, dark eyes. This is the first time those eyes have ever seen almond flowers, I thought.

"That pretty little girl over there," I called out, "is she yours?"

The woman lifted her head. "Yes. She's thin, isn't she?"

"You ought to feed her better," I said, throwing my purse in the child's lap.

The woman looked at me suspiciously and I went off without so much as a smile from her in return for my gift. Only the little girl was smiling, but not at me. She had no need of me to smile. I raised my head. The sky was a pale, fresh blue, and the blossoming trees sparkled as on the day I carried Sigismondo upon my shoulders. In the eyes of that little girl, the whole world was being born anew. "I shall have a child, a child of my own," I abruptly said to myself.

Ten months later, Laura brought a handsome, robust boy into the world. I immediately sent him off to a castle on the outskirts of Villana. I did not intend to share my son with anyone.

While he was being cared for by his nursemaids, I eagerly made preparation for Antonio's future. First, I consolidated the peace. I did not want him ever to know the bloody vanity of war. Florence had long demanded that I give up the port of Livorno and I agreed to return it to them. A revolution had broken out in Rivella and the prince pleaded for my help, offering to place the city under my protection. I refused.

Atop a hill facing Carmona, I had a marble villa constructed and formal gardens laid out. I drew scientists and artists to my court; I collected paintings and statues and assembled an enormous library. The most distinguished men of the century were placed in charge of Antonio's education. I attended their lessons with him and I, myself, trained my son in all physical activities. He was a handsome child, a bit thin for my taste, but strong. At seven he knew how to read and write Italian, Latin and French. He swam, and could shoot a bow and arrow, and was able to master a small horse.

When he was not at work, he needed companions of his own age to play with. I gathered around him the most handsome and most gifted children of Carmona. Among others, I brought the little girl of the almond flowers to the palace and raised her there. Her name was Beatrice. In growing up, she retained her thin, dark face, her enchanting smile. She played with Antonio like a boy, and of all his comrades, it was she he preferred.

One night while I was lying in bed, bored (at that time I became bored even in my dreams), I decided to take a walk in the garden. It was a hot, smelly, moonless night, streaked with shooting stars. I had taken only a few steps along the sandy paths when I noticed the two of them, strolling on the lawn, holding hands. Over their long nightdresses they had hung garlands of flowers. Beatrice had put some daffodils in her hair and against her heart she pressed a heavy magnolia. They caught sight of me and stood frozen to the spot.

"What are you doing out here?" I asked.

"We're taking a walk," Beatrice answered in a small, clear voice.

"Do you often go for walks at this hour of the night?"

"For him, it's the first time."

"And you?"

"Me?" She looked at me boldly. "I climb out of my window almost every night."

They both stood there before me, guilty and tiny in flower-bedecked robes which hid their bare feet. I felt a sudden sting in my heart. I had given them days of sunshine, of festivities, of laughter, and toys, candies, and picture-books. And yet they conspired together to secretly taste the sweetness of nights I had not given them.

"What would you think of taking a ride with me on my horse?"

Their eyes lit up. I saddled my horse and tossed Antonio in front and Beatrice behind. Her two little arms circled my waist. We galloped down the hill and across the plains while shooting stars fell noiselessly in the heavens above us. The children let out shrieks of joy. I held Antonio tightly against me.

"You mustn't go out secretly any more," I said. "You mustn't do anything secretly. If there's anything at all you want, just ask me. You'll get it."

"Yes, father," he said docilely.

The next day I made them each a present of a horse, and often, when the nights were mild, I took them galloping with me. I had a boat built and fitted out with orange sails to take them sailing on the Lake of Villamosa, on the shore of which we spent the oppressive summer months. When they were tired of playing, swimming, galloping, and running, I would sit down next to them in the pleasant shade of a pine tree and tell them stories. Antonio never tired of asking me questions about Carmona's history. He looked at me in wonder.

"And me, when I grow up what will I do?" he asked sometimes.

I would laugh. "You'll do anything you want."

Beatrice said nothing. With a closed face, she would only listen. She was a wild little girl with long, ponylike legs. She took pleasure in only doing things that were forbidden. She would disappear for hours and then be found clambering on a roof, or swimming too far out in a lake that was too deep, or treading in the dung on a nearby farm, or sprawled out across a path because she had chosen a too-spirited horse.

"Funny little creature!" I would often say, smoothing her hair. She would shake her head rebelliously; she did not like me to f⌐ le her. Whenever I leaned over to give her a kiss, she would draw back and, with dignity, extend her hand.

"Don't you like it here? Aren't you happy?"

"Yes, of course."

She had no idea that, except for the merest chance, she would have been living elsewhere, washing laundry and weeding the earth. But whenever I saw her sedulously poring over a heavy tome or climbing a tree, I would proudly say to myself, "I . . . I alone have shaped her life." And my heart leapt even more joyously when I would hear Antonio laugh; I would think, "He owes his life to me, he owes the world to me."

Antonio loved both nature and the works of man. He loved the gardens, the lakes, spring mornings and summer evenings, and also paintings, books, music. At sixteen he was almost as learned as his teachers. He wrote poems which he sang while accompanying himself on the viol. And he took no less pleasure in hardy activities—hunting, jousting, tournaments. I did not dare forbid him to engage in them, but my mouth grew dry whenever I saw him diving into the lake from atop a rock or jumping on the back of an untamed horse.

One evening, while I was sitting in the library at Villamosa reading a book, Beatrice burst in and approached me hurriedly. I was surprised, for she never came to speak to me unless I called her. She was very pale.

"What happened?"

Her hands were fidgeting with her linen dress. She looked as though she were struggling against something that was suffocating her. Finally she said, "Antonio is drowning."

I ran to the door.

"He wanted to swim across the lake, but he can't make it and I can't save him," she murmured.

I was at the edge of the lake in less than a minute. I tore off my clothes and dove into the water. It was still light and soon I caught sight of a black spot in the middle of the lake. Antonio was floating on his back. When he saw me he moaned and closed his eyes.

He was unconscious when I brought him back to the shore. I stretched him out on my coat and rubbed him vigorously. I felt the heat of my hands penetrating his body. Under my palms, I could feel his young muscles, his tender skin, his fragile bones, and it seemed as if I were molding a completely new body for him. *I'll always be here to save you from all misfortune*, I fervently thought. Gently, I carried my son in my arms, my son to whom I had twice given life.

Beatrice was standing motionless at the door of the house. She held herself erect; tears were streaming down her cheeks.

"He's all right," I said. "Don't cry, now."

"I can see for myself he's all right." She looked at me and in her eyes there was hate.

I put Antonio into his bed. Beatrice had followed me, and when he opened his eyes, it was upon her that they fell.

"I didn't make it across the lake."

She bent over him. "You'll make it tomorrow," she ardently said.

"No! Are you crazy?" I looked steadily at Antonio. "Swear to me you'll never try it again."

"Oh, father!"

"Swear to it. For the sake of all I've done for you, for the sake of your love for me, swear to it."

"All right. I swear."

He closed his eyes again. Beatrice turned around and slowly left the room. I stayed beside him and for a long while I studied his smooth cheeks, his fresh eyelids, the face of my beloved son. I had saved him, but I had not been able to give him the strength to cross the lake. Perhaps Beatrice was right to cry. With a sudden feeling of anguish I thought, *How much longer will he obey me?*

Around the trunks of the cypresses and yews, hanging low above the pink terraces, summer quivered tensely. It glistened in the hollows of marble fountains, rustled in the folds of silken dresses, and its smell rose up from Eliana's golden breasts. Suddenly, the sound of a viol hidden among the bowers, pierced through the silence; at the same instant, a spray of sparkling water gushed from the middle of every basin.

Oh's and ah's sounded along the length of the balustrade, and the women clapped their hands. From the heart of the burning earth, thin crystal shafts shot up toward the sky. Sleeping sheets of clear, fresh water became ruffled, alive.

"Oh!" Eliana exclaimed. The perfumed scent of her breath drifted across my face. "What a magician you are!"

"What's so magical about it?" I said. "Just a lot of gushing water."

The water cascaded down over rock formations, gurgling and laughing. But in my heart, its laughter was transformed into little taps, hard and sharp. *Fountains!* I contemptuously thought.

"The cascade, Bianca! Look at the cascade!" Antonio placed his hand on the young woman's graceful shoulder. I looked at his beaming, happy face and my scornful smile disappeared. Those ridiculous fountains counted for nothing. What really mattered was that I had created this life, this happiness.

Antonio had grown into a handsome young man. He had his mother's glittering eyes and the noble profile of the Foscas. While he was less robust than the men of former centuries, he had a strong, wiry body. Holding a willing shoulder, he smiled at the joyous sound of the water. It was a beautiful day.

"Father," he said, "do I have enough time to play a game of racquet?"

"Who keeps count of your time?"

"But aren't those exiles from Rivella waiting to see us?"

I looked off at the horizon; the deep blue of the sky was beginning to fade. Soon it would melt into the night along with the pink of the earth. *He has so few summers to live. Should I let him lose this beautiful evening?*

"Do you really want to see them with me?"

"Of course!" His young face hardened. "May I ask a favor of you?"

"Go right ahead."

"Let me see them alone."

I picked up a cypress twig and broke it with my fingers. "Alone? Why?"

Antonio reddened. "You always say you'll let me share your power, but you never let me make any decisions of my own. Is it all just a game?"

I pressed my lips together. Suddenly the cloudless sky seemed as heavy as if a thunderstorm were about to strike.

"You haven't enough experience yet," I explained.

"Do I have to wait until I've lived two centuries?"

In his eyes I saw the same fire as I had seen long before burning in the eyes of Tancredo. I put my hand on his shoulder.

"I'd gladly turn over my power to you; it weighs heavily upon me. But believe me, it will bring you only worries."

"That's exactly what I want," Antonio answered sharply.

"And as for me, all I want is for you to be happy. Don't you have everything a man could possibly desire?"

"What's the good of giving me everything if you forbid me to do anything with it?" In a pressing tone of voice, he went on, "You, yourself, would never have been satisfied with this kind of life. I was taught to reason, to think. But what for, if I have to go on blindly following your advice. Did I spend all those years studying and building up my strength just to ride in the hunts like everyone else?"

"I know. You want it all to serve a purpose."

"Yes."

How could I have explained to him that nothing ever serves any purpose, that the palaces, the aqueducts, the new houses, the castles, the conquered cities, were all nothing. His sparkling eyes would have opened wide and he would have said, "But I see things, real things." Perhaps for him they were real. I threw the broken twig to the ground. All my love for him served no purpose.

"It will be as you wish."

His face brightened. "Thank you, father."

He went off running. His white doublet stood out sharply against the dark leaves of the yews. He wanted to mold his life with his own hands, his untried, awkward hands. Was it possible, after all, to shut that life away in a hothouse and cultivate it free from all dangers? Stifled, bound, it would soon lose its brightness, its fragrance. He reached the top of the stairs in three bounds and disappeared inside the house, walking hastily through the marble halls. I could no longer see him. *Someday, everything on earth will be exactly the same as it is now, except that he'll no longer be here. There will be the same dark trees under the same sky, the same vain murmur of laughter and water. And neither on earth, nor in the sky, nor on the seas, will Antonio have left the slightest trace of himself.*

Eliana drew near to me and took me by the arm. "Let's go down by the cascade."

"No."

I turned my back to her and walked toward the villa. I had to see Beatrice. Only with her could I speak and smile without the thought crossing my mind that one day she would die.

I pushed open the door of the library. She was seated at the far end of the oaken table, reading. Silently, I watched her attentive face. With her smooth skin, her black hair and her plain dress she seemed as hard and cold as a suit of armor. Absorbed in her reading, she was unaware of my presence. I went over to her.

"Haven't you done enough reading for today?"

She raised her eyes without showing any sign of surprise; it was difficult to startle her.

"But there are so many books to read," she replied.

"Too many and too few."

The best manuscripts in the world were crammed on the shelves. They raised questions, problems, and it would be centuries before the answers could be known. Why did she persist in this hopeless quest?

"Your eyes look tired. You should have gone to see the water display instead of sitting in here all day."

"I'll go tonight when there's no one in the garden."

With the palm of her hand, she smoothed the page of the manuscript. I could find nothing further to say to her; she was waiting for me to leave. She needed help, and I could have helped her more than any of those unfinished books. But how could I give her what she persisted in not asking for.

"Won't you leave your books for a while? I have something to show you." In the end, it was always I who asked.

Without answering she stood up and smiled faintly, but there was no light in her eyes. Her features were so hard, her face so thin, that everyone found her ugly. Antonio found her ugly. We silently walked through the long corridors and finally I opened a door.

"Look!"

The room smelled of dust and ginger—an odor out of the past, strange in this new villa. The blinds were lowered, and bathed in the yellowish half-light were studded chests, rugs rolled into cylinders, heaps of silks and brocades.

"It's a cargo that just came from Cyprus this morning." I opened one of the chests and there was a sudden sparkling of precious metals and stones. "Choose."

"What?" she asked.

"Anything you like. Look there, at these belts, those necklaces. Wouldn't you like a dress made of that red silk?"

She dipped her hand in the chest and the stones clicked against the jewel-encrusted daggers and swords.

"No, I don't want anything at all."

"You'd be lovely wearing those jewels."

She disdainfully threw back the necklace she was holding in her hand.

"Don't you want people to admire you?" I asked.

"I want them to admire me the way I am." Her eyes glittered, cold and hard.

I closed the chest. She was right. What difference would jewels have made? Just as she was then, with her simple dress, her unpainted face, her hair squeezed into a net—just that way was precisely how I loved her.

"At least choose one of those rugs for your room, then."

"I don't need one."

"What *do* you need?" I said impatiently.

"I don't care for luxury."

I grabbed her arm. I felt like digging my nails into her flesh. Twenty-two years old! And she had opinions, made decisions, felt at home in the world, as if she had lived in it for centuries. She was passing judgment on me.

"Come," I said. I led her to the terrace. The intense heat of the afternoon had given way to a pleasantly warm evening. The water was bubbling and trickling in the fountains.

"You know, I don't care for luxury either. I had this villa built for Antonio."

Beatrice leaned her hands against the warm stone of the balustrade. "It's too big."

"Why too big? I set no limits where he's concerned."

"It's wasted money."

"And why not waste money? What else do you think there is to do with it?"

"You didn't always think like that," she said.

"Yes, that's true."

I had loaned money to the weavers, and Carmona's merchants had amassed fortunes. Some worked as hard as ever hoping to grow even richer, and others squandered away their lives in stupid debaucheries. At one time, Carmona's life was pure and austere, but now brawls broke out every night—husbands with daggers avenging their raped wives, fathers their ravished daughters. And they brought so many children into the world that most of these unfortunate offspring grew up only to have to face poverty. I had had hospitals built and people lived longer than ever before, but in the end, they always died. There were now two hundred thousand inhabitants in Carmona and they were neither happier nor better than in other times. There were more of them, but each still lived alone with his joys and his sorrows. Carmona had been no less full when her ancient ramparts had enclosed only twenty thousand people.

"Tell me," I abruptly said, "two hundred thousand men, is that any better than twenty thousand? Who profits by it?"

She reflected a moment. "What a peculiar question."

"To me, the question seems perfectly natural."

"Ah! to *you* perhaps."

She looked absently at the horizon. She was very distant from me, but in my mouth was a bitter taste, a taste I felt only when I was close to her. A crowd of golden dots was dancing in the air. I wanted to believe that she was no different than those ephemeral insects, but she was just as alive, just as real as I. Her fleeting existence weighed more heavily upon her than my own destiny upon me. For a long while we silently watched the cascade, that moving and yet strangely fixed curtain which tumbled over the rocks, producing bits of bounding white foam. Always the same foam and always different.

Suddenly Antonio appeared at the top of the stairs. A flame lit up in Beatrice's eyes. Why was it he she looked at with so much ardor? *He* wasn't in love with her.

"What did those refugees want?" I asked.

Antonio looked at me gravely. Something quivered in his throat. "They want us to help them capture Rivella."

"What did you tell them?" I anxiously asked.

"I swore that Rivella would be ours within a month."

There was a long silence.

"No!" I finally exclaimed. "We will not begin those bloody wars again."

"Then you're making the decision after all," Antonio violently said. "Tell me the truth. I'll never rule Carmona, will I?"

I looked at the motionless sky. Time stood still. He had drawn his sword and I had killed him. And now Antonio, too, was hoping for my death.

"Do you want the first act of your reign to be a declaration of war?" I asked.

"How much longer do you want us to wallow in your peace?" he retorted.

"It took me a long time and great pains to win this peace."

"And what good is it?"

The spouting water sang its stupid song. If it no longer cheered Antonio's heart, then what good, indeed, was it?

"We're living in peace," Antonio continued. "Our whole history is summed up in that word. The revolution in Milan, the wars of Naples, the rebellions of the Tuscan cities, and we took no part in any of it. Everything happens in Italy as if Carmona doesn't exist. What good is all our wealth, our culture, our wisdom, if we stay here planted on our rock like a giant mushroom?"

"I know," I replied sadly. "But what can be gained by war?"

"How can you even ask? We would have a port, an outlet to the sea. Carmona would be the equal of Florence."

"Rivella belonged to us once, you know."

"But this time we'll keep her."

"The Manzonis are powerful," I warned. "The refugees won't get any help from within Rivella."

"They're counting on the duke of Anjou to help them."

The blood rushed to my head. "We're not going to bring the French here!" I half shouted.

"Why not? Others have called upon them before and they'll be called upon again—perhaps against us."

"And that's precisely why there will soon be no more Italy." I put my hand on Antonio's shoulder. "We're not as strong as we were years ago. Those countries we used to call barbarian are growing and becoming powerful. France and Germany covet our riches. Believe me, our only salvation is in union, in peace. If we want Italy to be able to ward off the invasions that are menacing her, we must consolidate our alliance with Florence, league ourselves with Venice and Milan, obtain the help of Swiss mercenaries. If each city clings to its selfish ambitions Italy is lost."

"You've already explained that a hundred times," Antonio said stubbornly. Angrily, he added, "But we can't be Florence's ally except if we agree to vegetate in her shadow."

"What difference does it make?"

"You'd resign yourself to that! You who have done so much for the glory of Carmona!"

"The glory of Carmona counts little in comparison to the salvation of Italy."

"What do I care about Italy?" Antonio said vehemently. "Carmona is my country."

"Carmona is a city among others, and there are so many cities."

"Do you really mean what you're saying?"

"Yes, I mean it."

"How dare you continue to rule here then!" There was fire in his eyes. "What do you have in common with us? You're a foreigner in your own city."

I silently looked at him. A foreigner. He spoke the truth. I no longer belonged there. For him, Carmona was everything; he loved her with all his mortal heart. I had no right to stop him from fulfilling his destiny as a man, that destiny over which I had no control.

"You're right," I said sadly. "From this day on, it is you who shall rule Carmona."

I took Beatrice's arm and led her to the cascade. Behind me Antonio called in an uncertain voice: "Father!" But I did not turn. I sat down next to Beatrice on a stone bench.

"I suppose it had to happen sooner or later," I said.

"I can understand Antonio," she remarked defiantly.

"Do you love him?" I abruptly asked.

Her eyelashes fluttered. "You know I do."

"Beatrice . . . He doesn't love you."

"I know. But I love him nevertheless."

"Forget him. You weren't made to suffer."

"I'm not afraid of suffering."

"What idiotic pride!" I angrily exclaimed.

He asked for worries; she took pleasure in suffering. What demons possessed them?

"Will you always be the little girl who enjoys playing only forbidden games? Why do you have to ask for the only thing in the world I can't give you?"

"I ask for nothing."

"You can have everything," I said. "The world is big, but it will be yours if only you say so."

"There's nothing I need."

She sat erect on the bench, holding herself rather stiffly; her hands were resting on her knees. Looking at her, it struck me that she really did not need anything. Gratified or deceived, she would always remain the same.

"You were made to be happy and all I want is to *make* you happy." I grabbed hold of her wrist; she looked at me in astonishment. "Forget Antonio. Become my wife. Don't you realize I love you?"

"You?"

"Do you think I'm incapable of loving?"

She withdrew her hand. "I don't know."

"I frighten you. You think I'm the devil."

"No, you're not the devil. I don't believe in the devil, but . . ." She abruptly cut herself off.

"What is it?" I asked.

"You're not a man," she replied with sudden violence. She looked at me steadily. "You're a corpse."

I seized her by the shoulders. I felt like crushing her in my hands. And suddenly, I saw myself in the depths of her eyes—dead. Dead as the cypresses, the unblooming cypresses which know neither winter nor summer, nor spring nor autumn. I let her loose and went off in silence. She remained motionless on the stone bench. She was dreaming of Antonio who was dreaming of his war. And I was alone again.

A few weeks later, Antonio, with the help of the armies of the duke of Anjou, captured Rivella. He was gravely wounded as he led the assault. While festivities were being organized in Carmona to celebrate the victory, I set out for Villana where he had been transported. I found him lying in his bed, ghostly white, his skin stretched taut over his bones. He had a hole in his belly.

"Father," he said with a smile, "are you proud of me?"

"Yes," I answered.

I returned his smile, but inside my breast a volcano was spewing burning lava. Just a hole in the belly, and twenty years of care, twenty years of hope and love were destroyed in one blow.

"Are they proud of me in Carmona?"

"In all Italy there has never been a festival more magnificent than the one that will celebrate your victory."

"If I die, please don't tell anyone until the festival is over. Festivals are so wonderful!"

"I promise."

When he closed his eyes for the last time, there was a look of happiness upon his face. He died, glorious and gratified, as if his victory had been a real victory, as if the word "victory" meant something. For him the future held no dangers; there was no longer any future. He died, having done what he wanted to do. He would forever be a triumphant hero. *But I . . . I shall never see the end of it,* I thought, looking up at the incandescent sky.

I had kept my promise. Beatrice alone knew that Antonio was dead. Joyous and unaware, the people cried out, "Long live Antonio Fosca! Long live Carmona!" For three days the streets of the city echoed with the sounds of parades; tournaments took place in the main square and mystery plays were performed in three of the churches. In the church of San Felice, while the mystery of Pentecost was being acted, sparks symbolizing the fiery tongues of the Holy Ghost fell upon the tapestry and set the church ablaze. But the joyous populace looked indifferently at the mounting flames. They were too busy singing and dancing. Bright torches lit up the square; the façades of the houses were draped with golden banners; burning flares cast a blood-red glow on the marble statues.

"Aren't they going to put out the fire?" Eliana asked. She was standing next to me on the balcony. The necklace of gold and rubies I had given her sparkled against her amber throat.

"It's a holiday. And besides, there are more than enough churches in Carmona." It had taken more than thirty years to build it and now, in a single night, it was being destroyed. Who cared?

I went back into the huge, brightly lit salon. Men and women, dressed in brocade and glittering with jewels, were gayly dancing. Emissaries from Rivella and other cities under my domination were seated under a canopy around the duke of Anjou's ambassadors. The Frenchmen spoke with gruff, loud voices, and the others laughed slavishly at everything they said. Among the dancing couples, I caught sight of Beatrice in a red silk dress. She was dancing with a French nobleman. When the music stopped, I went over to her.

"Beatrice!" She turned and smiled at me defiantly. "I thought you were in your room."

"As you see, I came down."

"You were dancing!"

"Shouldn't I celebrate Antonio's triumph too?"

"What a triumph!" I exclaimed. "Worms are devouring his body."

"Be quiet," she said in a low voice. Her face glowed like a burning ember.

"You're feverish. I can see it in your eyes. Why do you torture yourself? Why don't you break down and cry it out, once and for all?"

"He died victorious."

"You're as blind as he was. Look at them!" I pointed toward the Frenchmen with their insolent faces and their coarse hands, filling the room with raucous laughter. "There are the real victors."

"Well, what of it? They're our allies."

"Much too powerful allies. They'll use the port of Rivella as a base for an expedition against Naples. And once they've taken Naples . . ."

"We can defeat the French, too," Beatrice said.

"No, you're wrong."

After a long silence she finally said, "I'd like to ask a favor of you."

I looked at her small, thin face. "That's the first time . . ."

"Let me leave here."

"Where will you go?"

"I'll go back to live with my mother."

"To wash laundry everyday and take care of the cows?"

"Why not? I just don't want to stay here any more."

"My presence is that insufferable?"

"I loved Antonio."

"And he died without even a thought for you," I harshly said. "Forget him."

"No."

"Do you remember when you were a child, how you loved life?"

"I remember all too well, and that's precisely why I want to leave."

"Stay here. I'll give you anything you want."

"I want to leave. That's all."

"Ah, stubborn mule!" I said. "What kind of a life will you have back there?"

"A life," she answered. "Don't you know that no one can breathe near you? You kill all desires. You give and give, but you never give anything but playthings. Maybe that's the reason Antonio chose to die—because he couldn't really live."

"Go back to your mother!" I said angrily. "And die a living death there."

I spun around and walked rapidly toward the ambassadors. The duke of Anjou's emissary came to meet me.

"What a magnificent festival!"

"A festival like any other," I said.

I recalled the palace's old walls when they were covered from end to end with dried and faded tapestries. Catherina, wearing a woolen dress, was embroidering. Now the stones were hidden under mirrors and silk drapes. The men and women were dressed in silks and gold, but their hearts remained unsatiated. Eliana looked at Beatrice with hate in her eyes, and the other women envied Eliana for her necklace. Husbands were jealously watching their wives dancing in the arms of strangers. All of them were eaten up by ambition, disgust, rancor, indifferent to the pomp and gaiety of the festival.

"I don't see the ambassador from Florence," I remarked.

"A messenger came and gave him a note," Jacques d'Attigny said. "He read it and immediately left the room."

"Ah!" I sighed. "That means war."

I went out on the balcony. Rockets were bursting in the sky, San Felice was still burning, and the people of Carmona were still dancing. They were dancing because their city had won a great victory, because the war was over. But the war was just about to begin.

The Florentines demanded that I return Rivella to the Manzonis, but the French forbade me to do so. To conquer Florence with the help of the French would have meant giving them the whole of Tuscany. And to fight the French would have meant ruining Carmona and making her an easy prey for Florence. Which of the two evils was I to choose? Antonio had died for nothing.

Faces were lifted toward me. The discordant clamor of the crowd became one voice: "Long live Count Fosca!" They were acclaiming me and Carmona was lost.

My hands tightened around the iron railing. How many times had I stood on that balcony, proud, joyous, horrified? What good had come of all my hopes, all my fears, all my passions? Suddenly nothing seemed important; neither peace nor war seemed important. Peace: Carmona would continue to vegetate under the sky like a giant mushroom. War: all that had been built would be destroyed only to be rebuilt the next day. In any event, those people who were dancing in the square would soon die, and their deaths would be as purposeless as their lives. San Felice was still blazing.

I had brought Antonio into the world and he had left the world. If I had never existed, everything that happened on earth would still have happened, nothing would have been any different. *Was the monk right?* I thought. *Can't a man ever do anything worth-while?* My hands choked the railing. And yet I existed. I had a head, two arms and eternity before me. "Oh, God!" I exclaimed aloud.

I struck my forehead with my fist. *There must be a way. There must be something I can do. But where? What?* I now understood those tyrants who burn entire cities to the ground or decapitate a whole populace. They were proving their power to themselves. But the only men they ever killed were those who were already condemned to death, and they destroyed only future ruins.

I turned around. Beatrice was standing against the wall, staring emptily into space. I walked over to her.

"Beatrice, I've just sworn to myself that you'll be my wife."

"No," she said, "I'll never marry you."

"Then I'll throw you into a dungeon and you'll rot there until you consent!"

"You wouldn't do that."

"You don't know me very well."

She stepped back and said in a trembling voice, "You told me that all you wished for was my happiness."

"I want you to be happy and I'm determined to *make* you happy in spite of yourself. I let Antonio lead his own life and he lost it. He died for nothing. I don't intend to make another mistake like that again."

‎🍃

War broke out again. Too weak to take up arms against my powerful ally, I had to refuse to give up Rivella. The Florentines immediately laid siege to several castles situated on the frontiers of my territory. They took a few fortresses by surprise and we tricked their captains into a few ambushes. There were French soldiers serving in my army, and Florence had hired eight hundred Albanian Stradiotes. The battles were bloodier than ever before; these foreign soldiers neither asked for nor gave quarter. But the results were just as uncertain. At the end of five years of fighting, it seemed as if Florence had no chance of ever subduing us, nor Carmona of ever defeating Florence.

"It can last another twenty years," I said. "And there will be neither victor nor vanquished."

"Twenty years!" Beatrice repeated.

She was seated next to me in my study, looking through the window at the quiet evening. The palms of her hands were resting on her knees. There was a wedding ring on her finger, but our lips had never touched. Twenty years . . . She wasn't thinking of the war. She was thinking that twenty years from now she would be almost fifty. I stood up and turned away from the window. I could no longer bear looking at the dull sadness of the dusk.

"Do you hear?" she asked.

"Yes." I heard the woman singing in the street and I also heard the dull rhythmic beating of Beatrice's heart, the same monotonous beating as my own.

"Beatrice!" I abruptly said. "Is it really impossible for you to love me?"

"Let's not speak about that."

"Everything would be different if only you loved me."

"Well, at least I haven't hated you for a long time now."

"But you don't love me."

I stood myself in front of the big, tarnished mirror. A man in the prime of life, with a hard, unwrinkled face. Never did that muscular body know fatigue. I was taller and more robust than the men of that era.

"Am I such a monster?"

She did not answer.

I sat down at her feet. "Anyhow, we seem to have reached a certain understanding. I understand you and I think you understand me."

"Yes, I think so." She lightly touched my hair with the tips of her fingers.

"Well, what do I lack then? Whatever it was that made you love Antonio, don't you find any of it in me?"

She withdrew her hand. "No."

"He was handsome, generous, courageous and proud. Don't I have any of those virtues?"

"You *seem* to have them . . ."

"Seem? Am I an impostor?"

"It's not your fault," she said. "Now I understand that it's not your fault and I don't hate you any more."

"Would you mind explaining that?"

"What's the use?"

"I want to know," I insisted.

"When Antonio dove into a lake, when he led an attack, I admired him because he was risking his life. But you, can you ever do anything courageous? I loved his generosity, and it's true that you give freely of yourself and your possessions with no thought of your wealth, your time, your pains. But you have so many millions of lives to live that you never really sacrifice anything. And I loved his pride. He was a man like any other man, but contrary to most of them, he chose to be himself. I think there's something beautiful about that. You . . . you're an exceptional being, and you know it. That doesn't move me."

She spoke in a clear voice, without hate and without pity, and through her words I suddenly heard a voice from the past, a voice long forgotten, which was saying in anguish, "Don't drink!"

"Then no matter what I do, no matter what I am, I'm worth nothing in your eyes because I'm immortal?"

"Yes, I suppose that about sums it up." She put her hand on my arm. "Listen to that woman singing. Would her song be so moving if she didn't have to die?"

I suddenly got up and took Beatrice in my arms. "But I'm here, I'm alive! I love you and I'm suffering. For the rest of eternity, I'll never meet you again; I'll meet others, thousands, millions of others, but none of them will be you."

"Raimondo." There was pity now in her voice and a trace of tenderness.

"Try to love me," I pleaded. "Try."

I held her tightly against me and felt her body grow limp in my arms. I crushed my mouth against her lips, her breasts quivered against my chest, her hands fell loosely to her sides.

"No," she muttered. "No."

"I love you. I love you as a mortal man loves a woman."

"No!" She was trembling. She broke away and murmured, "Please, forgive me."

"Forgive you? Why?" I asked, astonished.

"Your body frightens me. It's of another kind."

"It's made of flesh like your own."

"That's not what I mean." Tears came to her eyes. "Don't you understand? I can't bear being caressed by hands that will never rot. It makes me ashamed."

"Say rather it horrifies you."

"It's the same thing," she said.

I looked at my hands, my accursed hands. And I understood.

"It's you who must forgive me. I've lived two hundred years and I never really understood until now." I was silent for a moment and then said, "Beatrice, you're free. If you want to leave here, leave. And if ever you love someone again, love him without regrets."

There was a long silence. "You're free," I repeated.

"Free?" she said.

♨

For ten more years our frontiers were ravaged by fires, lootings and massacres. At about this time, Charles VIII, king of France, marched into Italy to claim the throne of the Kingdom of Naples. Since Florence had agreed to ally herself with France, he decided to act as a mediator between us: Rivella would remain in our possession on condition that we pay a heavy tribute to our enemy in exchange.

For years I had been strongly against submitting to the protection of the French. But powerless to do anything about it, I watched in despair as Italy was subjugated to their tyranny and plagued by all the disruptions of civil war and anarchy. "It's all my fault," I said bitterly to myself. If long before I had surrendered Carmona to the Genoese, Genoa would no doubt have succeeded in dominating all of Tuscany, and any foreign invasion would have been smashed against that solid barrier. It was my own stubborn ambition and the ambitions of every separate little city that had prevented Italy from forming a single nation as France and England had done, as Spain had just recently done.

"There is still time," Varenzi would ardently say to me. He was a celebrated scholar, author of a *History of Italian Cities*, who had come to Carmona to plead with me to save our unhappy country. He implored me to work for the unification of the Italian states, and once this great confederation had been formed, I would head its government. At first he had put his hopes in Florence, but the powerful Penitents party, filled with Savonarola's fanaticism, counted on no other forces but those of prayer, and they prayed only for the glory of their own city. Varenzi then turned to me. As weak as Carmona was, impoverished by fifteen years of war, his plans, nevertheless, did not seem fantastic. In the state of anarchy and instability into which Italy was plunged, one resolute man would have sufficed to change her destiny. When Charles VIII reluctantly decided to abandon Naples and recross the Alps, I made up my mind to act. Having secured my alliance with Florence by the scrupulousness with which I paid her the promised subsidies, I began negotiations with Venice. But the duke of Milan heard of my projects and, fearing the power of a league he would not head, he sent emissaries to his nephew, Maximilian, king of Germany, inviting him to accept the crown of Lombardy in Milan and that of the Holy Empire in Rome. He thus hoped to re-establish the ancient authority of the Emperors throughout Italy. He applied pressure to Venice, threatening to leave her at the mercy of the king of France who, it was rumored, was again ready to cross the Alps into Italy. And the Venetians, for their part, ended by sending ambassadors to Maximilian promising him a subsidy.

Maximilian entered Italy and all the little peoples of Tuscany declared themselves his allies, hoping he would put an end to the hegemony of Florence and Carmona. He immediately laid siege to Livorno, which he attacked by both land and sea. Upon hearing of this, Carmona was plunged in deep despair. The hate of our envious neighbors and the duke of Milan's distrust, left us no hope of maintaining our independence in the event that Maximilian succeeded in becoming master of Italy. And if Livorno were taken, all of Tuscany would be in his power. The Florentines had sent a great number of cannon to the port and had established a large garrison there. They had only recently strengthened the city with new fortifications. But Maximilian was backed by the Venetian flotilla and the Milanese army. When we learned that four hundred German horsemen and as many foot soldiers had advanced beyond Cicina in Maremma and had captured the large market town of Balghein, his victory seemed assured. Our only hope was that the six thousand barrels of wheat and the army Charles VIII had promised the Florentine rulers would arrive without delay. But we had long ago learned not to place much trust in a Frenchman's word.

"To think that our whole future is at stake and there's nothing we can do about it!" I said. With my head glued to the window, I anxiously watched the bend in the road for the arrival of a messenger.

"Don't think about it," Beatrice advised. "Thinking won't help any."

"I know. But it's impossible to stop oneself from thinking."

"Oh, yes it is! If you really want to, you can. Thank God, it *is* possible!"

I looked at her bent neck, her fleshy neck. She was sitting at a table covered with paint brushes, powders and sheets of parchment. She still had the same beautiful black hair, but her features had thickened and her body had grown heavy. The fire that used to burn in her eyes was dead. Everything a man could give a woman, I had given her, and yet she preferred to spend her days painting detailed designs on manuscripts.

"Put away those brushes," I abruptly said. She raised her head and looked at me in surprise. "Ride out with me to meet the messengers. It will do you good to get some air."

"But I haven't been on a horse for so long . . ."

"That's the trouble. You never go out any more."

"I'm perfectly satisfied staying in."

I took a few steps across the room. "Why have you chosen to live like this?"

"Did I make the choice?" she slowly said.

"I gave you your complete freedom," I retorted angrily.

"But I'm not blaming you for anything." She turned her head away and bent over her manuscripts again.

"Beatrice, since Antonio died, haven't you ever fallen in love again?"

"No."

"Because of Antonio?"

She hesitated a moment. "I don't think so."

"Why not, then?"

"I guess I'm just not capable of loving."

"Is it my fault?"

"Why do you torment yourself? You think too much. You think much too much." She suddenly smiled at me. "I'm not unhappy, you know," she said lightheartedly.

I went back to the window and pressed my head against the pane, trying not to think—Beatrice's fate had been decided without her, and mine was now being decided without me. But I could not stop myself from thinking. Had Maximilian already taken Livorno? I abruptly left the palace, mounted my horse and galloped to the crossroads. A large crowd had gathered there; some had come by foot, others on horseback. Sitting about on the ground, they anxiously watched the road which led to the sea. Without stopping, I dug my spurs into the horse and sped off along the road. When at last I met the messenger, he informed me that the town of Castagneto had surrendered and that Billona was about to surrender.

No one ate that evening. Beatrice, Varenzi and I shut ourselves in my study, waiting to hear the galloping of another messenger's horse. It seemed as though there was nothing on earth left for me to do but to stand there motionless with my forehead glued to a windowpane, watching an empty road.

"Livorno will be taken tonight," I said.

"What a wind," Varenzi remarked in a somber voice.

The tops of the trees were swaying crazily. On the road, the wind whipped up clouds of dust. The sky was a leaden gray.

"The sea must be rough," Varenzi said.

"Yes. We can't expect any help to arrive tonight."

The road was empty. But further off there were roads swarming with German soldiers, the feathers in their helmets blowing in the wind. They were advancing toward Livorno, massacring the entire population of villages through which they passed. German cannon were bombarding the port. And the swollen sea was as empty as the road.

"He'll give Carmona to the duke of Milan," I said.

"A city like this can never die," Beatrice fervently said.

"It's already dead."

I was the ruler of Carmona and yet my hands hung helplessly at my sides. Out there, foreign cannon were bombarding a foreign city, but every ball struck at Carmona's heart just as surely as if she herself were under attack. And we could do nothing to defend her.

Night fell. We could no longer see the road or hear anything from outside above the howling wind. I went away from the window and began to watch the door through which the messenger would enter. I listened attentively for the sound of his step. But the night passed and the door did not open. Beatrice had crossed her arms on her breast and, her head held straight, she fell asleep in her chair. There was a look of nobility about her. Varenzi was meditating. It was a long night. Time stood still in the bottom of the blue hourglass. No one bothered to turn it.

I remembered all those years, those two long centuries, during which I had struggled for Carmona. I used to believe I held her destiny in my hands: I defended her against Florence, against Genoa, and I worried constantly about the schemes of their rulers; I was kept informed of every move made by Siena and Pisa; I sent spies to Milan. But I wasn't concerned with the wars that took place between France and England, nor what went on in the court of Burgundy, nor the struggles for power between the German electors. I had no idea that those distant battles, those disputes, those treaties, would culminate in this night of impotence and ignorance, that Carmona's fate would be decided not only in Italy, but throughout the whole world. At this very hour it was being decided on the turbulent sea, in the German camp, in the Florentine garrison and, on the other side of the Alps, in the shallow, traitorous heart of the king of France. And no matter what happened now in Carmona, it could no longer have any effect upon Carmona. When dawn finally broke, all hope and all fear were dead in me. No miracle could now bring us victory. Carmona had stopped belonging to me. And in the shame of that useless night watch, I had stopped belonging to myself.

It was not until noon that a rider appeared at the turn in the road.

Livorno had been saved. In spite of the tempestuous weather, a French flotilla consisting of six ships and two large galleons, laden with wheat and crowded with soldiers, had made their way into the port. The Genoese and Venetian fleets had sought protection from the strong winds in the port of Melina, and the French, not having to fight their way through, had safely entered Livorno.

A few days later we learned that a storm had wreaked havoc on the emperor's flotilla and that he had withdrawn his army to Pisa, declaring that he could not wage war with both God and man at the same time. I listened indifferently to this news—it seemed as if it no longer concerned me.

"We must renew our negotiations with Venice," Varenzi said. "Maximilian is short of money and if Venice refuses him further subsidies, he'll have to leave Italy."

The other counselors approved of this suggestion. Years ago they used to say, "The good of Carmona. The salvation of Carmona." But now all I heard was "The good of Italy. The salvation of Italy." How long had they been speaking? for hours or for years? Through the years, their faces and their manner of dress had changed, but there were always the same measured voices, the same grave eyes riveted to a narrow future, almost, in fact, the same words. The autumn sun cast its golden light on the table and played on the chain I was tossing in my hands. It seemed as if I had already lived that precise moment some time in the past. A hundred years before? An hour before? Or perhaps in a dream? Will my life's taste ever change? I thought.

"We'll continue with this discussion tomorrow," I abruptly said. "The meeting's adjourned."

I closed the door of the council room behind me and went to the stables to have my horse saddled. It was suffocating in the palace. I rode along a new street bordered by high white walls which already were turning yellow. *Will I see them again a hundred years from now?* I spurred my horse with both heels. It was suffocating in Carmona.

For a long while, I galloped across the plains. The sky fled by above my head, and under me the earth seemed to bound. I wished that ride could last forever, with the wind blowing in my face and silence in my heart. But my horse's flanks began dripping sweat and the wetness brought me back to reality; words began to form on my lips: "Carmona has been saved again. And now what will I do?"

I followed the road which led up the hill. It twisted and turned and, little by little, I could make out ever greater expanses of the sweeping plains. On the right was the sea and there Italy stopped. She stretched out all around me as far as the eye could reach, but at the foot of the Alps, on the shores of the sea, she stopped. With pains, with patience, I could have had her completely under my domination in ten or twenty years. And then one night my hands would hang helplessly at my sides and, my eyes fixed on the distant horizon, I would wait anxiously for the echo of events taking place on the other side of the mountains and across the seas.

"Italy is too small," I thought aloud.

I drew my horse to a halt and dismounted. I had often stood atop this summit, contemplating the immutable countryside. Suddenly it seemed that the thing I had dreaded a few hours earlier—that Maximilian had conquered Livorno, that Carmona was lost—had actually happened. There was a strange taste in my mouth. The air trembled and all around me everything seemed new. Perched on her rock, flanked by her eight towers gleaming in the sun, Carmona was nothing but a huge mushroom, and Italy herself, a prison the walls of which had collapsed.

Out there was the sea, but the world did not end at our shores. Ships with white sails were making their way toward Spain, and further than Spain, toward new continents. On those unexplored lands, redskinned men worshipped the sun and fought with hatchets. And beyond those lands, were other oceans and other lands. The world ended nowhere and nothing existed outside of it; it bore its destiny in its own heart. And I was no longer on a hill facing Carmona, no longer in Italy; I was in the middle of a vast world, unique and limitless.

I galloped down the hill.

Beatrice was in her room, drawing red and gold designs on a piece of parchment. Next to her was a vase filled with roses.

"Well," she asked, "what did your counselors have to say?"

"Stupidities!" I answered sharply. She looked at me in surprise. "I've come to say goodbye, Beatrice."

"Where are you going?"

"To Pisa. I'm going to see Maximilian."

"What do you expect from him?"

I took a rose from the vase and crushed it in my hand. "I'll tell him that Carmona is too small for me, Italy is too small, that nothing can really be accomplished unless the whole world is ruled by a single man, that if he took me in his service, I could *give* him the world."

Beatrice abruptly stood up. She had grown very pale. "I don't understand," she said, bewildered.

"What do I care if I govern under my name or someone else's. Since that's the only chance open to me, that's the one I'll take. With the Hapsburg fortune at my disposal, perhaps I'll finally be able to do something."

"Are you going to give up Carmona?" A flame was suddenly rekindled in her eyes. "Is that what you mean?"

"Do you think I'm going to stagnate here in Carmona forever? What does Carmona mean to me, after all? I've felt myself a stranger in this city for a long time now."

"You can't do it!" she protested.

"I know, I know. It's the city Antonio died for."

"It's *your* city. The city you saved so many times, the city you've ruled over for two centuries. Are you going to be a traitor to your own people?"

"My people! They've died over and over again! How can I ever feel close to them? They're never the same." I drew near to her and took her hands. "Goodbye, Beatrice. When I'm gone, maybe you'll be able to live again."

The fire that had burned briefly in her eyes, suddenly died out. "It's too late," she murmured.

Filled with remorse, I looked at her thickened features. Had I been less imperious in trying to bring her happiness, she might have loved, suffered, lived. I had lost her more surely than I had lost Antonio.

"Will you ever be able to forgive me?" I asked.

My lips brushed her brow, but she was already just another woman among millions, and my tenderness and remorse had the savor of things long past.

᭛

Evening had fallen. A chilly breeze was blowing in from the river. From the adjacent dining room came the mingled sounds of dishes and voices, and Regina recalled that a moment earlier seven o'clock had sounded. She looked at Fosca.

"And you had the strength to begin all over again?"

"Can you stop life from beginning again every morning?" Fosca replied. "You remember what we were saying one evening—whether you want it or not, your heart beats, your hand stretches out . . ."

"And you suddenly discover yourself combing your hair." She looked around her. "Do you think I'll be combing my hair tomorrow?"

"I suppose so."

She stood up. "Let's get out of here."

They left the inn and Fosca asked, "Where shall we go?"

"Anywhere." She pointed to a road. "There's nothing to stop us from following that road, is there?" She laughed. "Your heart beats and one foot moves forward following the other. The roads have no end."

They began walking slowly down the road. "I'm curious to know what happened to Beatrice," Regina said.

"What do you suppose happened to her? One day she died. That's all."

"That's all?"

"Yes. That's all I know. She had already left Carmona when I returned and I didn't try to find out what happened to her. Anyhow, there was nothing to find out. She's dead."

Regina smiled sardonically. "When you get right down to it, all stories have a happy ending, don't they?"

BOOK II

Along the dusty streets bordering the Arno, heavy-footed German soldiers were tramping aimlessly about among the Pisans whom they dwarfed by a good head. The ancient Medici palace was filled with the sounds of their boots and spurs. I was kept waiting for quite a while. I was unaccustomed to waiting. Finally a guard showed me to a study where I found the emperor seated at a desk. He had straight, blond hair which fell stiffly over his ears and a large, flat nose. He looked about forty. With a courteous gesture, he motioned to me to sit down. He had dismissed his guards and we were alone in the room.

"Count Fosca," he began, "I've long wanted to meet you." He studied me with curiosity. "What they say about you . . . is it true?"

"If you mean that God, until now, has permitted me to conquer old age and death, then it's true."

"The Hapsburgs are immortal, too," he proudly proclaimed.

"Yes," I said. "And that's precisely why they should rule the world. The world alone befits eternity."

"The world is vast," he smiled.

"Eternity is long."

With a sly distrustful look, he silently examined me. "Why have you come to me?" he asked.

"To give you Carmona."

He laughed, revealing his white, even teeth. "I'm afraid that such a gift would cost me very dearly."

"It will cost you exactly nothing. I've reigned over the city for two long centuries now and I'm tired of it. I ask only that you permit me to join you in your ventures."

"And you demand nothing in return?"

"What can any mere man give me, even though he be an emperor?" I said. He seemed so perplexed that I took pity on him. "Soon Italy is destined to become the prey of the king of France—or of you. I'm not concerned with Italy any more; it's the whole world that interests me now. What I would like is to see it brought together in the hands of a single man, for only then will it be possible to mold it to one's desires."

"But why on earth do you want to help *me* bring it together in *my* hands?"

"What difference does it make?" I said. "You, yourself, aren't you struggling for your son? For your grandson who hasn't yet been born, and for *his* children whom you'll never see?"

"But they're my descendants."

"That doesn't make much difference."

With a pained, childish expression, Maximilian reflected a moment and said nothing.

"After I've turned over my castles and fortresses to you," I continued, "nothing in the world could stop you from conquering Florence. And once Florence is conquered, all Italy will be yours."

"Italy will be mine," he said dreamily. His brow, pleated by this effort of the imagination, suddenly relaxed. He smiled silently for a moment and then said, "I haven't paid my men in more than a month."

"How much do you need?"

"Twenty thousand florins."

"Carmona is rich."

"Twenty thousand florins a month."

"Carmona is very rich," I said, smiling.

Three days later, Maximilian entered Carmona. The marble escutcheon, heavily decorated with gilded fleur-de-lis, which had been erected in the center of the city in honor of Charles VIII, was torn down to make room for the emperor's coat of arms. And the people, the very same people who had loudly cheered the king of France four years earlier, now cheered the emperor and his retinue with equal fervor. The women threw them flowers.

An entire week was given over to tournaments and feasts during which Maximilian stuffed himself with enormous quantities of highly spiced meats and large pitchers of wine. One evening, as we were leaving the table after a meal that had lasted three hours, I asked, "And when are we going to march against Florence?"

"Ah! Florence," he said. His eyes were pink and cloudy. Seeing that I was watching him expectantly, he majestically declared, "Matters of state force me to return to Germany."

I leaned forward, "When are you leaving?"

"Tomorrow morning," he said without hesitation.

"I'm going with you."

I watched him as he strode off; his walk was dignified and yet uncertain. Very little could be expected from such an emperor; in one short week I had learned all there was to know about him—ignorant, whimsical, greedy, lacking both ambition and perseverance. Nevertheless, there was a good possibility of bringing him under my influence and steering him in the right direction. And he had a son whose temperament would perhaps better serve my purposes. I was determined to follow him.

I left the palace. It was a clear, moonlit night; the raucous sound of singing voices drifted up from the plains where Maximilian's hordes were encamped. Two hundred years before, I had looked down upon the Genoese tents, red tents among the gray olive trees, and I had kept our gates closed. I passed through the cemetery where Catherina and Antonio were asleep, sat down for a while on the steps of the cathedral, and then made the rounds of the ramparts. The miracle had now been consummated—my life's taste had changed and I saw Carmona through new eyes. It was a foreign city.

In the morning, after I had passed through the postern, I looked back upon the rock bristling with its high towers, the rock that had for so long been the heart of the earth for me. Now, it was only a minuscule particle in that vast conglomeration, the Holy Roman Empire. The earth had no other heart but my own. I was cast naked into the world —a man from nowhere. The sky above me was now no longer a roof; it was an endless road.

For many days and nights we continued riding north. The sky gradually paled, the air grew cooler, the trees less dark, the earth less red. Mountains appeared on the horizon and the wooden-roofed houses in the villages through which we passed were covered with paintings of flowers and birds. Strange odors drifted through the air.

Maximilian chatted constantly with me. He told me that the Catholic kings had proposed a double marriage—his son Philippe with their daughter Jeanne and his daughter Marguerite with the child Don Juan. He was reluctant to agree to this proposal, but I pressed him to accept. It was Spain with her powerful fleet of swift ships that held the key to the world.

"But Philippe will never reign over Spain," Maximilian said to me regretfully. "Don Juan is too young and strong."

"Strong, young men have been known to die."

We were slowly making our way down a precipitous road which smelled of fresh grass and pine trees.

"But the Queen of Portugal is Jeanne's older sister," Maximilian said. "And she has a son."

"He can die, too . . . if God continues to favor the Hapsburgs."

Maximilian's eyes lit up. "May God favor the Hapsburgs!"

Don Juan died six months after his youthful marriage, and a mysterious sickness caused the Queen of Portugal and her son Don Miguel to pass away soon after. When Princess Jeanne gave birth to a son, there was no obstacle standing between him and the throne of Spain. I leaned over the cradle in which the sickly infant was bawling, this child who one day would rule over Spain, Holland, Austria, Burgundy and several of the rich Italian provinces. In his lace dress, he smelled of sour milk, like any other infant. The pressure of my hands would have been enough to shatter his tiny skull.

"We'll make an emperor of this child," I said.

A cloud passed over Maximilian's insouciant face. "How?" he asked. "I don't have any money."

"When the time comes, there'll be money enough."

"Can't we get hold of any now?"

"It's too soon."

He examined me with a perplexed, disappointed look. "Are you coming to Italy with me?"

"No."

"Why not? Don't you believe in my star any more?"

"The glory of your house is even more dear to me than to yourself," I answered. "With your permission, I prefer to stay here and watch over the child."

"Stay here, then." He looked at the infant and smiled. "Teach him not to take after his grandfather."

I remained in the palace of Malines in Belgium while Maximilian campaigned unsuccessfully in Italy, losing battle after battle against the Swiss. I had gained his confidence and he attached great value to my advice. But it was to no avail, since he seldom followed it. I had abandoned all hope in him. His son Philippe had no liking for me, and besides, he was of delicate health. There was little chance that he would ever reign. As for Princess Jeanne, she had become eccentric to the point that those around her grew deeply concerned. All my hopes rested in this child whose first steps, first words, I was still anxiously awaiting. He, too, was fragile and often he threw himself to the ground in nervous fits. I alone succeeded in calming him. I was with him constantly and he knew no other law than the knitting of my brow. But I anxiously asked myself: "Will he live long enough? What manner of man will he be?" If he were to die, if he grew to hate me, I would have had to renounce my great dreams, perhaps for centuries.

The years went by. Philippe died. Jeanne, who apparently was completely insane, was confined to the castle of Tordesillas. And Charles lived, grew steadily to manhood. From day to day my plans became less chimerical; from day to day, strolling through the foggy streets of Malines, I envisioned the future with ever greater hope.

I was quite fond of that sad, calm city. Whenever I walked through her streets, the lace-makers, bent over their spindles behind windows with small glass panes, followed me for a moment with their eyes. But no one knew me, no one knew my secret. I had let my beard grow and even I was sometimes slow to recognize myself when I looked into a mirror. Often I went outside the ramparts, sat down at the edge of the canal and, dreaming, watched the reflections frozen in the moving water. The sages of the century were saying that the time was close at hand when man would completely unravel the secrets of nature and by so doing dominate her. Then, and only then, would he begin to conquer happiness. *That task belongs to me*, I thought. *But first I'll have to hold the whole universe in my hands. Then, no energy will be dissipated, no wealth wasted. I'll put an end to the quarrels which set nations, races and religions against each other. I'll put an end to all injustice. I'll regulate the world as carefully as I did Carmona's granaries. Nothing will be left to the capriciousness of men or the hazards of fate. Reason will govern the earth. My reason.* As evening began to fall, I slowly made my way back to the palace. At the corners of the streets, the first lampposts were already lit. Voices, laughter and the clinking of steins drifted into the air from warm-smelling taverns. Alone and unknown under the gray sky, among men who spoke a language foreign to me, already forgotten even by Maximilian, it sometimes seemed to me that I had just been born.

I leaned over the couch where Charles was resting. His paternal grandfather, Ferdinand, had recently died and Charles was crowned king of Spain. But his subjects made no effort to hide their preference for his younger brother who had been born and had lived among them.

"My Lord, you can't delay the trip any longer," I said. "It would mean losing the crown."

He did not answer. He was suffering from a grave illness and the doctors claimed his life was in danger.

"Your brother's followers are powerful. We have to act fast." I looked impatiently at this tall, pallid adolescent who listened to me with his mouth agape, a vacant expression on his face. Under his drooping eyelids, his eyes seemed lifeless, and his lower lip sagged loosely. "Are you afraid?" I asked.

His lips finally moved. "Yes," he admitted. "I'm afraid." His voice was grave and sincere; it disconcerted me. "My father died in Spain," he went on, "and the doctors said the climate there would be dangerous for me."

"A king must never shrink before danger."

In his slow, slightly stuttering voice, he said, "My brother will make a very good king."

I silently reflected for a moment. If Charles died, nothing was lost —his brother was young enough to become a willing instrument in my hands. But if Charles, who was now Archduke, lost Spain and still continued to live, then the world would be split in two and all my plans would fail.

"But it's you whom God has designated," I said forcefully. "I've often told you what He expected of you—to take this world, this world that's split up into little bits, and make it a single, unified world again, like the day it left His hands. If you give up Spain to Ferdinand, you'll only perpetuate the endless divisions that are ripping the earth apart."

He pressed his lips together. Beads of sweat gathered on his brow. "I could give him everything," he ventured.

I looked at him. He was slow-minded and irresolute, but his very timidity served my purposes. And I did not know Ferdinand.

"No," I said. "Your brother is Spanish. He'll be concerned only with the interests of Spain. You alone can fulfill the mission with which God has entrusted you. It's upon you that the task of insuring the world's salvation has fallen. Your health, your happiness are as nothing compared to that."

I had touched a soft spot. He grew even paler.

"The world's salvation," he said. "It's too much. I'd never be able . . ."

"*You will*, with the help of God."

He sunk his head in his hands and I let him pray in silence. He was still a child who took pleasure in tournaments, music and walks through the countryside; he had a natural foreboding of the monstrous burden I was urging him to bear upon his youthful shoulders. He continued to pray for a long while and then, finally, he looked up and said, "May God's will be done."

A few days later Charles and his court set up quarters amid the sand dunes on the beach at Flessingues. For several weeks, a flotilla of forty vessels lay at anchor off the port awaiting a favorable wind. When it finally came, we set sail for Spain. Leaning against the bulwarks, I watched the sun rise and set day after day. It was not only towards Spain that I was sailing; out there, beyond the horizon, were forests teeming with multicolored parrots and doves that filled their stomachs wtih exotic flowers. There were volcanos which spewed forth streams of molten, bubbling gold, and in the flatlands, men covered with feathers galloped freely about. The king of Spain was the ruler of these savage paradises. *One day I'll sail to those distant shores and see it all with my own eyes. And I'll mold those virgin lands exactly the way I want.*

On the 19th of September, the flotilla arrived within sight of the coast of Asturias in northern Spain. The beach was deserted, but on the side of a mountain I could see a long procession—women, children and old men walking behind mules weighed down with heavy packs. They seemed to be fleeing. Then suddenly from behind a thicket, a salvo of gunfire was let loose. The women of the court shrieked wildly and the sailors grabbed their muskets. Charles' face remained unmoved. Silently he looked upon the land that was his kingdom, unastonished by this rude welcome. He had not come here to seek happiness. After a second discharge of the Spaniards' guns, I cried out with all my might, "Spain! It's your king!"

The whole crew took up the cry, and a moment later I noticed a stirring among the thickets which extended down to the sea. A man, crawling on all fours, appeared out in the open. He must have recognized the arms of Castile in the king's large standards, for he stood erect and waved his musket, shouting, "Spain! Long live the king!" Soon after, from behind the bushes and rocks, mountaineers burst forth with shouts of "Long live Don Carlos!" Later they told us that upon seeing such a great number of ships, they had feared a barbarian attack.

We arrived at Villaviciosa. No preparations had been made to receive us and most of the lords and even the ladies had to sleep on beds of straw. At the break of day, we set off again on our journey to Valladolid. The king was astride a small horse that the English ambassador had obtained for him. Eleonore, his sister, rode at his side. The ladies of the retinue traveled in ox carts and many of the lords straggled along on foot. The road was rocky and we had great difficulty in making our way along it under the blue, obdurate sky.

We met no one at the crossroads and no one was in the fields or on the highway. An epidemic was ravaging the province and the inhabitants were forbidden to leave their homes. Charles, for his part, seemed insensitive to the sun's cruelty, to the ruggedness of this land. Never, during the whole journey, did he show any sign of impatience or melancholy. It seemed that, contrary to the doctors' predictions, the climate of Spain had actually fortified his health. Perhaps it was astonishment at still being alive that caused a timid light to be born in the depths of his eyes, a light I had never before seen. On the day he made his solemn entry into Valladolid, he smiled and said happily, "I feel I'm going to like this country."

Week by week, he seemed to grow more and more alive. He gayly took part in festivals and tournaments, and often he was seen laughing with young people of his own age. Joyously, I thought, *He's alive, he's king! The first battle is won!* As soon as I learned of Maximilian's death, I hastened back to Germany. The moment had come to think of the Empire.

During the last years of his reign, Maximilian had lavished money and promises upon the imperial electors, and he believed that the votes of five out of seven of them had thereby been assured for Charles. But the day after his death, despite the six hundred thousand florins he had paid them, the electors considered the auction opened again. François I, king of France, immediately entered the lists, swearing that if it were necessary, he would spend three million to obtain the Empire. Charles was poor. But across the seas, he owned gold mines, silver lodes and fertile lands. I sought out bankers in Antwerp and convinced them to sign bills of exchange with our colonial riches as guarantee. Then I went to Augsburg where I obtained still more bills of exchange from the Fugger family payable after the election. I immediately sent messengers to convey my offers to the electors, and I personally made the rounds, paying each in turn a visit. From Cologne I went to Trier and thence to Mainz. At every city, a steady stream of messengers sent by François and Henry of England arrived with new offers which the electors impassibly inscribed in their notebooks. François made his payments in hard, ringing crowns, and the margrave of Brandenburg as well as the archbishops of Trier and Cologne began to snap at the bait. One day I learned that François had offered the archbishop of Mainz one hundred and twenty thousand florins and the legateship for all of Germany. That same evening I set out to seek the aid of Franz von Sickingen who commanded the army of the powerful Swabian League. I galloped through the night without stopping, and time, which not long ago stood motionless in the bottom of a blue hourglass, now ran rapidly out under the hoofs of my horse.

Franz von Sickingen hated France. At the head of an army of twenty thousand foot soldiers and four thousand horsemen, we marched on Hochst, a few miles from Frankfurt, while other troops menaced the Palatinate. The electors, frightened, preached the customary sermons, declared that their votes were pure, their hands clean, and elected Charles emperor for the total sum of eight hundred and fifty-two thousand florins.

It was a beautiful autumn day when Charles made his entry into Aix-la-Chapelle. The electors had come to meet him and with bared head, he silently accepted their homage. The procession then passed through the gates of the ancient city. First came the standard bearers, the counts, the lords, the councilors of Aix carrying white batons, the court with its pages and heralds, all of them throwing money to the crowd. Next, flanked by halberdiers, were the high dignitaries, the Spanish grandees, the cavaliers of the Golden Fleece, the princes and the prince-electors. Marshal von Pappenheim, bearing the sword of the Empire, preceded the king who was clad in armor and brocade.

On October 23, 1519, the ceremony took place in Charlemagne's ancient cathedral. The archbishop of Cologne solemnly asked all present: "Do you wish, in the words of the Apostle, to submit yourselves to the rule of this prince and lord?" And the people cried out joyously: "Fiat! Fiat!" The Archbishop then placed the crown upon Charles' head, and as the Emperor climbed to Charlemagne's throne to receive the chevaliers' aubade, a *Te Deum* echoed under the vaulted arches.

When we were finally alone in his study, Charles said to me in a deeply moved voice, "I owe the Empire to you."

"You owe it to God," I corrected. "He created me only to serve you."

I had revealed my secret to him and he seemed hardly surprised—he was too good a Christian for any miracle to astonish him. While he no longer looked upon me with the timid docility of his childhood, he now respected me as a being marked by God.

"God bestowed a great blessing upon me when he placed you near me," he said. "You'll help me to prove myself worthy of it, won't you?"

"Yes, I'll help you."

His eyes gleamed. From the moment the archbishop placed the sacred crown on his head, his face grew firmer, his expression more alive. "I have great things to accomplish," he said fervently.

"And you'll accomplish them."

I knew that he dreamt of revivifying the Holy Empire, but more than that, it was the entire universe I wanted to bring together in his hands. Cortez was conquering the Americas for us and soon gold would begin flowing into Spain. Then we would be able to form powerful armies, and once a federation of the German states was realized, Italy and France could easily be brought under our domination.

"One day the whole universe will belong to you," I said.

He looked at me with an expression of awe. "No man has ever possessed the universe."

"Until now, the time hasn't been ripe."

He remained silent for a moment and then suddenly he smiled. Through the walls of the study, the sound of a viol could be heard. "Aren't you coming to hear the music?" he asked.

"In a moment," I replied.

He rose. "It's going to be a beautiful concert. You really ought to come."

He opened the door. He was young, he was emperor. God had cast His protective shadow over him and the happiness of the world was inseparably mingled in his heart with his own happiness; he could calmly abandon himself to the tender song of the viols. But as for me, my breast was straining against a too-powerful swell. A triumphant voice deafened me to all other sounds, a voice that would never echo in the ears of mortal men, *my* voice, saying: "Now the universe is mine forever, mine alone. The whole universe is my domain and no one, no one, can ever share it with me. Charles will govern for a few years and I . . . I have an eternity before me." I went over to the window and looked up at the starry sky crossed by a belt of milk —millions upon millions of stars. And under my feet, only one earth. *My* earth. Like a gigantic balloon, it was floating peacefully in the ether, marbled with blue, yellow, and green. I saw it all: ships sailing upon the open seas, roads streaking across continents, and I, Raimondo Fosca, with a single sweep of my hand, ripping up deep-rooted forests, draining swamps, changing the courses of rivers. Farms, orchards, and pastures covered the earth, cities sprouted at crossroads, the most humble weavers lived in large, sun-brightened houses, granaries were filled with pure wheat. Everyone was rich, strong and handsome; everyone was happy. "I'll create a paradise on earth," I said half aloud.

Charles was gently caressing the rainbow-colored feather coat. He had a special liking for rich goods and precious metals. When the sailors opened the chests and set down before him large alabaster vases full of turquoise and amethysts, his beaming eyes opened wide.

"What riches!" he ardently exclaimed.

He looked at the gold coins and ingots heaped high in one of the chests, but I knew it was not of these riches that he spoke. Beyond the gray walls of the Brussels palace, he saw a fiery jet of gold spouting upward toward the blue sky, he saw rivers of vermilion lava bubbling down the sides of a volcano, he saw great avenues paved with glittering metals, and gardens in which solid gold trees were growing. I smiled. Through the sparkle of these thousands of little suns, I too saw ingot-bearing galleons entering the port of Sanlucar, and I imagined myself scattering a rain of brilliant confetti over the old continent with reckless abandon.

"How can you even hesitate?" I said.

Charles' hand let go of the soft, smooth coat. "Those men have souls, too," he said.

With slow, measured steps, he began to pace up and down the long gallery. He had slipped the letter from Cortez inside his doublet, the letter that the captain with the cracked lips had given him. On Good Friday of the preceding year, Cortez had landed on a desolate shore and there founded a city to which he gave the name of Vera Cruz. In order to prevent his men from returning to Spain, he had all of his ships scuttled with the exception of one, which he sent back to Charles laden with the treasures of the Aztec emperor, Montezuma. He was asking for help to put an end to the intrigues of the governor, Velasquez, who wanted at all costs to stop him from continuing his expedition. And Charles hesitated.

I looked at him impatiently. The letters from the Dominicans of Hispania and Father Las Casas' report had deeply disturbed his soul. We learned that, despite laws to the contrary, the Indians were still being branded like slaves, beaten, and even massacred. Too weak for the work forced upon them, they died by the thousands. But as for me, I refused to concern myself with those ignorant savages who were filled with all manner of absurd superstitions.

"Send over some reliable men who'll see to it that the laws are properly upheld," I suggested.

"At such great distances, what man is reliable?" He began to pace back and forth again alongside a table covered with crystal bowls, jade necklaces, and figurines of hammered gold.

"The good fathers exaggerate," I said. "They always exaggerate."

"If just one of the things they reported were true, it would be enough . . ."

"The black people of Africa don't have souls. You know that. And neither do those savages in America."

"But the cure seems to me no less horrible than the sickness," the emperor said thoughtfully. He no longer looked at the tempting ingots. He looked at nothing. His face took on that vacant, sleepy expression of his adolescence.

"Well, what do you propose doing?" I asked.

"I don't know."

"Are you going to turn down an empire paved with gold?" I plunged my hand into the chest and let the coins slip through my fingers.

"I don't know," he repeated dully. He looked very young and very unhappy.

"You haven't the right to throw it all away. God created all these riches to serve mankind. There's fertile land over there that will never be cultivated if we don't force it from the Indians. Think of the misery of your subjects. They'll all grow prosperous when the gold from the Americas flows through your ports. Out of pity for those savages, are you going to condemn the German peasants to death by starvation?"

He did not answer. Never before had he been forced to make so grave a decision. He could not know how brief and unimportant a thing a human life was. In any case, in less than a hundred years, none of those wretched creatures who were causing Charles so much anguish would be alive to remember their sufferings. And in my eyes, they were all dead even now. Charles, however, was unable to consent so easily to depriving them of their lives—he measured their joys and their sorrows as he measured his own. I abruptly walked over to him.

"Do you imagine that you can ever do good in this world without doing evil? It's impossible to be just to everyone, to make everyone happy. If your heart is too tender to consent to necessary sacrifices, you ought to shut yourself away in a monastery."

He pressed his lips together. Something hard and cold gleamed under his half-closed eyelids. He loved the century in which he was living; he loved luxury and power.

"I want to govern without causing anyone an injustice."

"Can you govern without wars, without gallows? Once and for all, you have to look things in the face!" I said sharply. "If you learn to do that, you'll stop wasting precious time. The best of princes always have hundreds of deaths on their consciences."

"There are just wars and necessary repressions," he countered.

"You have to justify the suffering you cause to some men by the good works you accomplish for the benefit of all."

I remained silent for a moment; I could not tell him what I was really thinking: that a life, even the best of lives, weighs no more than the flight of a gnat, but that the roads, the cities, the canals we could build, would remain on the surface of the earth throughout eternity; that for eternity, we could rip a whole continent from the dark shadows of virgin forests and idiotic superstitions. I could not tell him these things because Charles was unconcerned with an earthly future he would never see with his own eyes. But I did know the words that were capable of awakening a response in his heart.

"Bear this in mind: it will be only worldly misery that we inflict upon those poor savages. And ultimately we'll bring eternal truth and happiness to them and to their children and to their children's children. When all those ignorant people are finally led into the Church's fold where they and their descendants will remain for centuries and centuries to come, won't you be justified in having aided Cortez?"

"But men who are now in mortal sin will die by our hands," he said hesitantly.

"In any case, they would have died in idolatry and crime."

Charles fell into a chair.

"Never commit an evil act when it serves no purpose," I said. "God can demand no more than that from any emperor. He must know that evil is sometimes necessary—after all, He, Himself, created it."

"Yes." He looked at me distressfully. "But I'd like to be sure," he said.

I shrugged my shoulders. "You'll never be sure."

He sighed, and for a moment he silently tugged at his collar. "All right," he said. "All right."

Charles rose abruptly and went to his private chapel. It was well into the night when he finally emerged.

♨

"The whole city has gone completely mad," I said, leaning against the window sill.

It had begun the evening before, when the carriage with the wreathed columns and heavy leather curtains first entered the city. By the thousands, they came to meet it: peasants, artisans, merchants, some astride horses, others on donkeys. To the sound of fifes and drums, to the sound of the church bells, they marched triumphantly through the north gate of the city. The inn of the Cavaliers of Saint Jean was overflowing with men, women, priests and notables who crowded the corridors and stairways. Posted atop the surrounding roofs were youths, children, and even a few old men. When the monk alit from his coach, the mob surged toward him, shouting wildly; women threw themselves to their knees and kissed the edges of his mud-spattered frock. All day long, through the walls of the archbishop's palace, we could hear their chants and their cries. And that night, the tumult again broke out. Standing upon tables, barrels and the rims of fountains, orators proclaimed the miracles Luther had accomplished, brass bands paraded through the streets, and from the taverns could be heard both exalted canticles and the noise of brawls. I had seen cities celebrating before; the people of Carmona used to sing out joyously on days of victory, and I knew why they were singing. But what was the meaning of all this senseless clamor? I slammed the window shut.

"What a carnival!"

I turned around and saw Balthus and Morel silently watching me, and despite the friendly feelings I had for them, it was irritating to feel their eyes constantly upon me.

"That man is fast becoming a martyr, a saint," Balthus said.

"The natural result of persecution," Pierre Morel remarked.

"You know, of course, that I've had no hand in this whatsoever," I said.

When Charles convoked the Diet of Worms, it was my understanding that we were going to settle the question of the Constitution of the Empire and establish a basis for a federation presided over by the emperor. I was therefore greatly annoyed when he stubbornly pressed for Luther's condemnation, and I was even more annoyed when the Diet, refusing to make a pronouncement without hearing the accused, obliged us to convoke him. We were losing precious time.

"How did Luther impress the emperor?" Balthus asked.

"He considered him inoffensive," I replied.

"And if we don't condemn him, he'll stay inoffensive."

"I know."

At that very moment everyone throughout the palace, throughout the city, was feverishly arguing the case. Charles' councilors were divided into two opposing groups; some wanted to banish the heretic from the Empire and ruthlessly persecute his partisans, while the others pleaded for tolerance. The latter, like myself, held that these spiritual quarrels among monks were insipid at best, and that the temporal powers ought not to take part in arguments concerning faith, indulgences and sacraments. They also felt that Luther was less dangerous to the Empire than a Pope engaged in negotiating an alliance with France. I agreed with them, but that evening their insistence suddenly troubled me. Were these really reasonable, disinterested men, freed from all superstitions, who were so anxiously awaiting the emperor's decision?

I abruptly asked, "Why do you defend him with such zeal? Has he won you over to his ideas?"

For a moment they seemed disconcerted. "If Luther is condemned," said Pierre Morel, "they'll start burning people at the stake again in Holland and Austria and Spain."

"You can't force a man to deny what he believes to be the truth," Balthus remarked.

"But suppose he's wrong?"

"Who has the right to decide?"

Perplexed, I looked at them steadily. They were not saying everything that was on their minds. I was certain now that there was something in Luther that attracted them. But what? They did not trust me enough to tell me, and I wanted to know. All night long, while the celebration continued unabated under my windows, I reread Jean Eck's reports and Luther's pamphlets. At one time I had been curious enough to go through all of his writings and I found absolutely nothing reasonable in them. I considered the fervor which he brought to bear in combatting the Roman superstitions no less stupid than the superstitions themselves. As for Luther himself, I saw him for the first time that afternoon; Jean Eck was interrogating him before the Diet. In a stammering voice he declared that he needed a little more time to prepare his defense, and Charles, seeing and hearing him, gayly said to me, "It will take more than that little monk to make a heretic of *me*."

Why then the frenzied voices echoing through the night? Why were learned, reasonable men waiting so anxiously for dawn?

The next day, when the session began, I impatiently watched the door through which the monk would enter. Charles, wearing his black and gold Spanish clothes, was seated on his throne, impassive. A small velvet beret covered his short hair. Surrounding him, looking like statues, the dignitaries in their ermines and the princes in their golden attire stood stiff and motionless. In the corridors, cries of "Hurrah! Hurrah!" rang out. It was Luther's followers who were shouting. He entered the room, pushed his hat to the back of his head, uncovering his badly cut hair, and walking up to the emperor, greeted him with assurance. No longer did he appear intimidated. He settled down at a table on which his books and pamphlets had been stacked, and he began to speak. I studied his thin, sallow face with its prominent cheekbones and dark, glittering eyes. Where did those persuasive powers he possessed come from? There seemed to be a great driving force in him, but again he spoke only of sacraments and indulgences. I was bored by all that nonsense and I thought, *We're wasting time. All these monks should be exterminated, the Dominicans along with the Augustinians. Churches should be replaced by schools, sermons by lessons in mathematics, astronomy, physics. We should be discussing Germany's constitution right now instead of listening to these puerile speeches.* Charles, however, listened attentively to Luther's words while fingering the medallion of the Golden Fleece which rested on his pleated shirt. The monk's voice grew excited. He began speaking with fire, and in the too-narrow room, stifling from the summer's heat, everyone fell silent. In a frenzied outburst, he said, "I cannot, will not, retract a single word of what I have said or written, for to act against one's conscience is neither safe nor honest."

I winced. His words struck at me like a challenge. But it was not only the words; it was the tone in which he spoke them. This man had the audacity to maintain that *his* conscience was more important than the interests of the Empire, indeed, than the interests of the world. *I* wanted to gather the universe in my hands and *he* declared that he was a universe in himself. His arrogance populated the world with thousands of stubborn wills. And this, surely, was why the people and even the sages listened intently to him. He stirred up that rage of pride in their hearts which had devoured Antonio and Beatrice. And if he were permitted to continue his preachings, in time he would have everyone believing that each man was sole judge of his relations with God and judge also of his own acts. How then would I ever be able to make them obey?

He continued to speak, attacking the Church's established dogma. But I began to see that it was not only dogma, grace, faith that was in question; something else was at stake: the very works of which I had so long dreamed. They could be realized only if men were brought to renounce their self-love, their whims, their follies. And it was precisely this that the Church taught. She enjoined people to obey one set of laws, to bow before one faith; and if I were powerful enough, those laws would be mine. Through the mouths of priests, I could make God speak in whatever manner I wanted. But if each individual sought God in his own conscience, I knew it would not be I whom he would encounter. "Who has the right to decide?" Balthus had said to me. That was why they defended Luther—they wanted to decide, each man for himself. But then the world would be even more divided than it had ever been before, and it had to be governed by a single will— *mine.*

Suddenly there was a stir in the assembly. Luther declared that the council of Constance had made decisions which went against the most explicit passages in the Scriptures. At these words, Charles V slammed his gloves against his knee and abruptly stood up. A deathly silence hung over the assemblage. The emperor walked over to a window and for a moment looked up at the sky. Then he turned around and ordered the room to be cleared.

"You're right, my Lord," I said. "Luther is even more dangerous than the king of France. If you let him do as he pleases, that little monk will destroy your empire."

His eyes anxiously questioned me. Despite his abhorrence of heresy, he would have believed he were disobeying God himself if he condemned Luther against my advice.

"Do you really think so?" he said, surprised.

"Yes. My eyes have been opened."

A hundred arms were raised up to carry Luther aloft triumphantly. Outside they were acclaiming him, acclaiming pride and folly. Their stupid shouts ripped through my ears, and again I felt the monk's feverish eyes on my face, those eyes that had challenged me. He wanted to turn people away from their true good, their true happiness, and they were so lacking in sense that they were ready to follow him. If they were left to their own devices, they would never discover the road to an earthly paradise. But I was there; I knew where they had to be led and by what path. I had fought for them against famine, against plague, and I was prepared, if necessary, to fight for them against themselves.

The next morning the emperor stood before the Diet and declared: "One monk, relying solely upon his own judgment, has placed himself in opposition to a faith upheld by Christianity for more than a thousand years. I have vowed to defend that holy cause, be it at the price of my domains, my body, my blood, my life, my soul."

A few days later, Luther was banished from the Empire. An edict was published in Holland forbidding, under pain of severe punishment, the printing of any work treating of questions of faith without authorization from the proper church officials. The magistrates were ordered to prosecute Luther's partisans.

Just at the time the question of the constitution was to be taken up, we were forced, to our great disappointment, to dissolve the Diet. François I, infuriated by the defeat he had suffered at the hands of Charles in their contest to win the imperial crown, was preparing to declare war against us, and in addition, disturbances were breaking out all over Spain. Charles had to leave for Madrid. He confided the government of Germany to his brother Ferdinand and requested that I remain behind to watch over him. Luther's condemnation did nothing to mollify the unrest that prevailed throughout the Empire. Monks abandoned their monasteries and wandered through the countryside preaching heretical doctrines; armed bands of students, workers, adventurers, set fire to libraries, churches and rectories. Every city gave birth to new sects even more fanatical than Luther's, and riots were constantly breaking out. In every village prophets arose who harangued the peasants to throw off the yokes of their princes. The ancient revolutionary banner appeared in all the corners of the land—a white flag which pictured a golden shoe surrounded by luminous rays and inscribed with the motto, *Let Those Who Want Freedom March Towards This Sun.*

"There's nothing to worry about," Ferdinand said. "All we need is handful of soldiers to restore order."

"To restore *dis*order, you mean. Those poor people are right; reforms *are* needed."

"What reforms?"

"That's precisely what has to be studied."

I had not forgotten the massacre of Carmona's weavers, and when, two centuries before, I first wanted to hold the world in my hands, my chief aim had been to modify the economy. Yet never before was the distribution of wealth more unreasonable than at this very moment. Merchandise flowed into our ports, the whole world had been opened to commerce, and our ships brought us valuable cargoes from every corner of the earth. But the masses of peasants and the small merchants were poorer than at any other time I could remember. A pound of saffron which was worth two and a half florins and six kreutzers in 1515, now cost four and a half florins and fifteen kreutzers. Bread cost fifteen kreutzers more per pound; a quintal of sugar sold for twenty florins instead of ten; Corinthian grapes cost nine florins instead of five. The price of every commodity had augmented while at the same time wages were constantly lowered.

"It's an intolerable situation," I angrily said to the financiers I had gathered together. They all looked at me with an indulgent smile; it was no doubt my naivety that made them smile. "Speak," I said to Muller, a banker. "What's the reason for this insane spiraling of prices?"

They spoke and I learned that the misery of this era resulted precisely from the rapid development of commerce. The gold which the conquistadors obtained by the blood and sweat of the Indians, flooded the old continent and caused rises in the prices of every commodity. Powerful companies were formed which chartered vessels and soon monopolized almost all commerce. Having crushed the smaller traders, they were able, within a few years, to sell their merchandise for double its cost and even more. This one-sided enrichment led eventually to the depreciation of agricultural products; the value of money declined; wages went down at the same time that prices soared. A handful of men accumulated monstrous fortunes and dissipated them on absurd luxuries, while the masses of people wasted away from hunger.

"You will have to pass and enforce laws putting an end to monopolies, usury and speculation," Muller advised me.

I remained silent. All of Germany's princes, including the emperor himself, were in debt to these powerful companies from which they continually borrowed money at usurious rates. My hands were tied. François I had attacked the kingodm of Navarre, Luxemburg and Italy, and Charles, who was forced to take up arms against him, pleaded with me to find money to pay his troops. Our fate was in the hands of bankers and powerful merchants.

A few weeks later a revolt broke out in Forscheim in Franconia, and it spread across the whole of Germany. The peasants demanded equality, fraternity and the redistribution of land. They burned down castles, abbeys, churches; they massacred priests and lords and divided the domains of their princes among themselves. By the end of the year, they were the masters everywhere.

"There's only one solution," Ferdinand said. "We'll have to call upon the Swabian League."

He rapidly paced back and forth in the large, bright salon, and the princes who had come to ask his help followed him about with respectful, anxious looks upon their faces. There was so much fear and hate in their hearts that the air in the room seemed venomous. Out there, in the country, the peasants were singing and dancing around joyful fires. They had drunk and eaten their fill, and in their breasts, a new flame was burning. I thought of the weavers' charred houses, of the women and children trampled by horses, and I murmured, "Those poor people!"

"What did you say?" Ferdinand asked.

"I said there's only one solution."

The princes nodded their heads approvingly. Thinking only of their own selfish interests, they crushed their peasants with drudging work and unreasonable taxes. I, on the other hand, wanted to create a world in which justice and reason would prevail, a world in which men would find peace and happiness. And yet I said the same thing as they—only one solution. My thoughts, my desires, all the experience accumulated during the centuries through which I had lived, counted for nothing, were worthless. I was bound hand and foot. A monstrous mechanism had been wound up, set in motion, and each wheel inexorably turned another. In spite of myself, I was forced to the same decision as Ferdinand, the same decision as anyone else in our places would have had to make. *Only one solution . . .*

The peasants owed their fragile victory only to the surprise and isloation of their lords. As soon as the noblemen regained possession of themselves and united their forces, they rapidly and ruthlessly quashed the rebellious hordes. Desirous of rejoining the emperor, I then set out for Holland to obtain passage to Spain. On horseback, I crossed the same pine-tree forests, the same meadows and moors through which I had galloped five years earlier when I had carried Charles' offers to the electors. At that time my heart was bursting with hope and I had thought, *I shall hold an empire in my hands!* I had succeeded; I was at the summit of power. And what was I able to do? I wanted to build the world anew and I spent my time and energy in defending myself against anarchy, heresy, against the ambitions and obstinacy of selfish men. I defended myself by destroying. I passed through ravaged lands where villages were in cinders, fields left uncultivated and cattle, half-dead, wandering aimlessly around abandoned farmhouses. Not a single man could be seen on the roads or in the fields, only women and children with hungry, emaciated faces. All the rebellious cities, villages and hamlets had been set aflame, and the peasants tied to trees and burned alive. At Konigshoff they were tracked down like a pack of wild boar. In a last, futile effort to save themselves they climbed up trees, but were slaughtered nevertheless with pikes and musket shots. Those who fell to the ground were trampled under horses' hoofs. In the village of Ingolstadt, four thousand peasants were massacred. Some sought refuge in the church; they were burned alive. Others gathered in the castle, huddling together, half-burying themselves in the earth in a vain attempt to escape detection, pleading for God's mercy; none were spared. Even now the noblemen's wrath continued unabated. Torturing and executions took place every day; the luckless peasants were burned to death, their tongues ripped from their mouths, their fingers cut off, their eyes gouged out.

"Is that how it is to reign?" Charles said.

The blood had drained from his face and a corner of his mouth was quivering. For two hours he had listened to me without uttering a word and now he looked at me in anguish. *Is that how it is to reign?*

In Spain, too, much blood had to be spilled to put down the revolts, and the repression was still continuing in Valencia, Toledo and Valladolid, where every day heads fell by the hundreds under the executioners' axes.

"Have patience," I said. "A day will come when we'll have rid the earth of evil. Then we shall start to build."

"But this evil is our own doing," he protested.

"Evil brings forth evil," I said. "Heresy calls for the stake and revolts for repression. It will all come to an end . . ."

"But *will* it ever come to an end?"

All day long he wandered silently through the palace. Toward evening, during a session of the council, he fell to the floor; overcome by nervousness, and burning with fever, he was carried to his bed. As I often did when he was a child, I stayed at his bedside day and night, but I found no words of hope to speak to him. The situation was indeed black. But by a stroke of good luck, we were able to enlist the services of a brilliant general, the High Constable Charles de Bourbon, who had quarreled with the king of France and, as a result, offered us his assistance. But we had to pay very dearly for his treason, and we lacked money. We feared that our worn-out troops would mutiny and we were badly in need of artillery. The possibility that we would be driven from Italy caused us great concern.

Charles lay prostrate in bed for a whole week. He had just gotten up and was taking a few exploratory steps about the palace when a courier arrived on the run, panting heavily. The French army had been shattered, half of France's highest nobility had perished and the king himself was taken prisoner. Charles did not say a word. He went into his private chapel and prayed. Then he gathered all his councilors together and gave the order to cease hostilities on all fronts.

Less than a year later, on January 14, 1526, to be exact, the treaty of Madrid was signed. François gave up all rights in Italy, recognized Charles' claims on Burgundy, withdrew from the league against the emperor and promised to lend his aid in fighting the Turks. To guarantee his commitments, he left his son with us as a hostage. Charles personally accompanied him on the road leading to Torrejon de Villano, a few miles from Madrid. Having embraced him for the last time, he took him aside and said to him, "Brother, you're well aware of everything we have agreed to. Now tell me quite frankly if you intend to live up to those agreements."

"I intend to live up to them completely," said François. "If you find me conducting myself otherwise, you may consider me evil or a traitor."

I had not heard him speak those words (Charles repeated them to me as we were returning), but I saw the charming way the king of France smiled at the emperor, I saw him lift his feathered hat and bid him goodbye with a sweeping gesture. Then he galloped off at full speed on the road to Bayonne.

✷

Charles' finger crossed the Atlantic and came to rest upon a little black circle—Vera Cruz.

Geographers, for the first time, had plotted the farthest reaches of the New World—Tierra del Fuego, the shores of which Magellan had sailed past in rounding the Horn and which was inhabited by large-footed Indians. On the yellow and green continents which emerged from the sea, they had inscribed magical names, America, Tierra Florida, Tierra de Brazil. I, too, placed my finger on the large, new map. Mexico City.

It was only a black spot on a sheet of parchment, but among the lakes which reflected its splendor, in the region of the world where the air was most transparent, it was also the capital of Cortez. Upon the ruins of the ancient quarters, Mazeltan, Tecopan, Artacalaco and Culpupan, stood the four districts of San Juan, San Pablo, San Sebastian, and Santa Maria. Churches, hospitals, monasteries and schools rose up along the city's wide avenues. And even now new cities were being founded in the wild terrain surrounding the capital. I drew my finger along a black line which represented the Cordillera de los Andes with its snow-covered peaks, and I pointed to a virgin region to the west of the chain on which *Tierra Incognita* was written.

"The Eldorado," I said. "Pizarro is probably crossing those mountains at this very moment." I touched a meridian line located three hundred fifty miles above the Cape Verde Islands which, since the treaty of Tordesillas, separated the Portuguese possessions from the Spanish domains. "One day," I murmured, "we'll wipe out that frontier."

Charles lifted his eyes to the portrait of Isabella. Beneath her light auburn hair there was a faint smile upon her beautiful, regal face. "Isabella will never have any claim to the Portuguese crown," Charles said.

"Who knows?"

My eyes wandered over the Indian Ocean, across the countries of spices, from the Molucca Islands to Malacca and then to Ceylon. Isabella's nephews could die, or soon we would be strong enough, perhaps, to set off a war which would make Charles master of the whole peninsula as well as Portugal's vast colonial empire. With the king of France defeated, we now had our hands free to strike elsewhere.

"You're insatiable," Charles gayly remarked. He was stroking his silky beard and his blue eyes were laughing in his florid face. He had grown into a robust man; he appeared almost as old as myself.

"And why not?" I asked.

He shook his head. "You have to learn how to set a limit to your desires."

I raised my eyes from the yellow and green chart and looked up at the plaster ceiling, the tapestries, the paintings. The palace of Granada had been draped with precious silks to receive Isabella. Spouting fountains were singing in the garden, and brooks were rippling among the pink laurel bushes and orange trees. I walked over to the window. The queen, surrounded by her ladies-in-waiting, was strolling slowly along the paths. She was wearing a long, silk, russet-colored gown. Charles loved her. He loved this palace, the fountains, the flowers, the rich clothes, the tapestries, the hearty meals, the spicy sauces. He loved to laugh and for over a year now, he had known happiness.

"Don't you want to rule over an empire of the world?" I asked.

"No. Let's accomplish what we've set out to do. That will be quite enough."

"We'll accomplish it," I assured him.

I smiled. I was unable to set a limit to my desires. I could not stop at furnishing a palace, loving a woman, listening to a concert, being happy. But I was pleased at least that Charles was able to enjoy all these things. I thought of the sickly child, the sleepy adolescent, the hesitant youth of whom I had vowed to make an emperor and I admired the calm, handsome man he had grown into. I thought, *His power, his happiness, is my achievement. I've built a world and I gave that man his life.*

"You once said to me: 'I'll do great things.' Do you remember?" I asked.

"Yes, I remember."

"And you've already created a world," I said, placing my hand on the map with the fabulous names.

"I owe it all to you. You showed me what my duty was."

Cortez's success, the victory at Pavia, the alliance with Isabella, all seemed obvious signs to him that he had obeyed God's will. How could he now regret the massacring of a few red or black tribes? A week earlier, in the port of Sanlucar, I had personally supervised the loading of plants and animals which we were sending to Cortez to live and thrive under the skies of the Americas. An armada was being readied to set sail for the new continent. On the docks, enormous quantities of merchandise, destined to be loaded on the galleons and even the warships, were piled high. No longer was it soldiers who were embarking, but rather farmers and colonists. Charles was sending Dominican and Franciscan monks to Vera Cruz to establish and staff hospitals and schools, and for my part, I put a large sum of money at the disposal of Nicolas Fernandez, a doctor from Toledo, to organize a scientific expedition. He took naturalists with him who were to catalogue the American flora and fauna, and geographers to map uncharted areas. To the colonies of New Spain, the ships were bringing cane sugar, vine roots, mulberry trees, the larva of silk worms, hens and cocks, rams and ewes. Donkeys, mules and pigs were already being raised there, and orange and lemon trees were being widely cultivated.

Charles touched the little black circle which represented Mexico

City. "God willing," he said, "one day I'll go see with my own eyes this realm He has bestowed upon me."

"With your permission, I'd like to accompany you."

For a moment, we silently dreamed side by side. Vera Cruz, Mexico. For Charles it was *only* a dream. The Americas were far off, his life short. But as for me, I would see them, come what may. I abruptly stood up and Charles, slightly startled, looked at me questioningly.

"I'm going back to Germany," I announced.

"Are you bored already?"

"You decided to convoke a new Diet. Why wait any longer?"

"God Himself rested on the seventh day," Charles said.

"That was God."

Charles smiled. He was unable to understand my impatience. In a moment, he would begin dressing himself immaculately for the evening festivities. He would dine on a large roast of one sort or another and, smiling at Isabella, he would listen to music. But I could no longer wait; I had waited too long already. I had to hasten the arrival of the day when, looking about me, I could say to all the world: "I *was* able to accomplish something. *There* is what I have done!" Not before my eyes came to rest on those cities torn by my desires from the bowels of the earth, on those plains peopled by my dreams, not before that moment would I be able, like Charles, to let myself fall into a chair, smiling and relaxed. Only then would my life beat evenly and peacefully inside me without hurling me toward a future full of uncertainty and disappointments. All around me, time would be a great, calm lake in which I would restfully wallow, like God in His clouds.

A few weeks later, I again rode through Germany. It now seemed to me that I would finally reach my goal. The peasants' revolt had put a fright into the princes, the Lutheran question seemed capable of solution, and there was an excellent possibility of uniting all of Germany's separate states into a single confederation. Then I would turn toward the New World, the prosperity of which would once again flood the old continent. I looked about me at the devastated countryside. New houses were already being erected in razed villages; men were laboring in the fallow fields, and women, seated on doorsteps, were gently cradling new-born infants in their arms. I looked indifferently at the evidence of fires and massacres that were still present. *After all, what does it matter?* I thought. The dead were no longer, the living were alive—the world was just as full as ever, the same sun was shining in the same sky. There was no one to feel sorry for, nothing to regret.

✺

"There'll never be an end to it!" I said angrily. "Our hands will never be free!"

No sooner had I arrived at Augsburg than I learned that François I, his promises cast to the winds, had leagued himself with Pope Clement VII as well as the rulers of Venice, Milan and Florence for the purpose of resuming his wars against the emperor. He had also formed an alliance with the Turks who had just demolished an army of twenty thousand men commanded by Louis of Hungary and who were now dangerously menacing the whole of Christianity. Once again I was forced to put aside my projects and tend instead to a thousand urgent problems.

"Where are you counting on getting money from?" I asked Ferdinand.

We were sorely in need of money. In Italy the imperial troops, under the command of the Duke of Bourbon, were demanding adequate provisions and all of their back pay. They were on the verge of open mutiny.

"I was thinking of borrowing from the Fuggers again," he replied.

I knew that that would be his answer, and I also knew the dangers of resorting to this over-used expedient. The bankers of Augsburg insisted upon guarantees, and little by little Austria's silver mines, the most fertile lands of Aragon and Andalousia, all our most important sources of revenue, were falling into their hands. The gold from the Americas belonged to them long before it entered our ports. Thus, the treasury always remained empty and we were continually forced to ask for new loans.

"And what about men?" I asked. "Where will we get men?"

He was silent for a moment and then, avoiding my eyes, he murmured, "The Prince of Mindelheim has offered us his assistance."

I jumped up. "Are we going to lean on a Lutheran prince?"

"What else can we do?"

I remained silent. *Only one solution . . . What else can we do? . . .* The mechanism has been wound, the wheels were meshing, inexorably turning, and all for nothing. Charles had dreamed of reviving the Holy Empire; he had vowed to defend the Church at the cost of his domains, his blood, his life. And now we were about to accept the aid of his enemies to fight a Pope in whose name we had burned hundreds of people at the stake in Spain and Holland.

"We have no choice," Ferdinand insisted.

"No," I said. "There's never any choice."

At the beginning of February we marched into Italy—eight thousand Bavarian, Swabian and Tyrolian mercenaries, all Lutherans, led by the Prince of Mindelheim. We went first to join forces with Bourbon who was waiting for us in the valley of the Arno. A heavy rain poured down on us day and night, and the roads everywhere were transformed into bogs.

Just as we arrived in the camp, mutinous troops were marching toward the general's tent, shouting, "Money or blood!" In their hands, ready to fire, they were carrying loaded muskets. Their trousers were in tatters and the faces of many of them bore long scars. They looked more like brigands than soldiers.

I brought one hundred thousand ducats with me which were immediately distributed, but as the soldiers took the gold, they made sarcastic remarks about the smallness of their shares. They demanded twice as much. To restore order, the Prince of Mindelheim shouted to them: "We'll find gold enough in Rome!" Wasting no time, the combined armies set out on the road to Rome, vowing to make up for their privations by looting the Church's treasures. We tried in vain to dissuade them, but by now they were so inflamed that a messenger who brought us news that the Pope had made peace with Charles had to flee to save his skin. On the way we were joined by bands of Italian outlaws who smelled the scent of pillage in the air. There was no possible way of stopping that unruly horde which swept us along with it. We were prisoners of our own troops. *Is that how it is to reign?*

Under the beating rain, we silently rode along amid their raucous yelling. It was I who had brought these men together, provided them with money and food, and now they were dragging me with them toward the most absurd catastrophe imaginable.

At the beginning of May, fourteen thousand bandits arrived at the walls of Rome, lustily shouting for booty. Bourbon, to save his throat from being slit, was forced to lead them in an assault. He was killed at my side on the first wave. After having been twice repulsed by the Pope's troops, the Lutherans, the Spanish mercenaries, and the Italian brigands invaded the city on their third attempt. For seven full days they massacred priests and laymen, rich and poor, cardinals and kitchen helpers. The Pope fled, saved by his Swiss guards who fought savagely to the last man; later, he surrendered himself to the Prince of Orange who had taken Bourbon's place.

Bodies dangled over the balustrades of balconies, swarms of blue flies buzzed around human flesh rotting in the squares, bloated corpses drifted in the Tiber's oily waters. There were red puddles in the streets and bloody rags among the filth in the gutters. I saw dogs greedily tearing at nauseating pink and gray entrails. The air smelled of death. Women wept in their homes while soldiers went about the streets, singing.

I did not weep; nor did I sing. "Rome," I said to myself. "This is Rome." But the word no longer moved me. Rome had always been a more beautiful and more powerful city than Carmona, and if years ago someone had said to me: "One day you will conquer her; your soldiers will drive out the Pope and hang her cardinals," I would have shouted for joy. Later I revered Rome as the noblest city of Italy, and if someone had said to me: "Spanish and German soldiers will massacre her citizens and sack her churches," I would have shed tears. But that day, Rome meant nothing to me. I saw in her ruins neither a victory nor a defeat, only a meaningless fact. "What difference does it make?" I had spoken those words all too often. But if burned villages, torturings and massacres had no importance, what mattered new houses, bountiful harvests and children's smiles? What hope was left to me? I no longer knew what it was to suffer or rejoice. A dead man. Gravediggers removed the corpses from the streets and squares, the splotches of blood were washed clean, the debris cleared away and women timidly left their houses to fetch water from the fountains. Rome was being reborn, and I . . . I was dead.

For days, I wandered deathlike through the city. And then, suddenly, one morning as I stood on the banks of the Tiber looking at the massive silhouette of the castle of Sant' Angelo, something beyond that lifeless scene, beyond the emptiness in my heart, began to live again. It lived at once outside of me in the deepest part of me—the smell of dark yew trees, a section of a white wall under a blue sky, my whole past. I closed my eyes and I saw Carmona's gardens. In those gardens there used to walk a man who burned with desire, anger, and joy. I was that man; he was I. Out there, far off on the horizon,

I existed with a full heart, a living heart. That very day I took leave of
the Prince of Orange and galloped out of Rome onto the open roads.

Wars were raging throughout all of Italy. I, too, had fought in those
valleys, on those plains; we would burn a few crops, lay waste to a
few orchards, but with the passing of a single season, all traces of our
destructiveness would disappear. The French and Germans, however,
ruthlessly ravaged these lands which were foreign to them and took
no pity on their inhabitants. Entire hamlets were burned to the ground,
granaries destroyed, livestock massacred, dams smashed, and fields
flooded. More than once I saw bands of children searching for edible
herbs and wild roots along the roadside. The world was growing
bigger, populations were increasing, cities spreading out. Forests and
swamps were being turned into fertile land, new tools had been
invented. But the fighting grew more and more savage; by the thousands men died in battle, were massacred. They learned to destroy as
fast as they learned to build. It almost seemed as if there were a stubborn God in heaven who was determined to maintain an immutable
and absurd equilibrium between life and death, prosperity and misery.

The countryside grew familiar; I recognized the color of the earth,
the smell of the air, the songs of the birds. I spurred my horse. A few
miles further on, there used to live a man who passionately loved
his city, a man who smiled at the flowering almond trees, who clenched
his fists, who felt the blood coursing through his veins. I was anxious
to rejoin that man, to dissolve into him. My throat dry, I rode rapidly
across the plains planted with olive and almond trees. And then
Carmona loomed up before me, perched on her rock, surrounded by
her eight gilded towers, the same as always. I looked at her for a long
while. I had drawn my horse to a halt and I waited; I waited and
nothing happened. I saw only a familiar scene, a place I felt I had just
left the day before. In one glance, Carmona had entered into my
present. She stood there before me, ordinary and indifferent, and my
past remained out of reach.

I rode up the hill, thinking, *He's waiting for me behind the ramparts.* I passed through the gate and I recognized the palace, the shops,
the taverns, the churches, the funnel-shaped chimneys, the pink
streets and the delphiniums growing against the walls. Everything was
in its place, but my past was nowhere to be found. For a long while
I stood motionless in the main square, I sat down on the steps of the
cathedral. I wandered through the cemetery. Nothing happened.

The looms were humming, the coppersmiths were hammering on cauldrons, children were playing on the hilly streets. Nothing had changed; there was no emptiness in Carmona; no one needed me. No one had ever needed me.

I went into the cathedral and looked at the flagstones under which lay Carmona's princes. Under the vaulted arches, the priest had murmured, "May they rest in peace." They were resting in peace. And I, too, was dead, but I was still here, a witness to my absence. *Never will there be any rest for me,* I thought.

><

"Germany will never be united as long as Luther has a single follower," Charles said fiercely.

"The more ground Luther loses, the more the new sects gain. And they're even more fanatical than the Lutherans," I said.

"All of them have to be wiped out," Charles exclaimed, bringing his powerful hand down sharply against the table. "It's time we did something!"

It *was* time we did something. He was right. For ten years it had been going on, gaining momentum. Ten years of pompous ceremonies, of petty worries, of useless wars, of massacres. Except in the New World, we had still built nothing. For a single year, however, there had been a rebirth of hope; François I had given up his rights in Italy, Austria and Flanders; Germany, massed behind Ferdinand, had driven back the Turks before Vienna; Isabella had borne Charles a robust son, and the succession to the thrones of Spain and the Empire was thus assured; Pizarro had set out to conquer a new empire which promised to be even richer than Cortez's; and Charles, at the end of February 1530, was crowned Holy Roman Emperor by the Pope in the cathedral of Bologna. But trouble soon began to break out in Italy and Holland. The Lutheran princes joined forces and François plotted with them. Suleiman the Magnificent again threatened Christianity, and Charles, having gathered the Catholic princes around him, began preparations for a campaign against the Turk.

"I'm beginning to wonder if burning heretics is really the way to stamp out heresy," I said.

"They don't listen to our preachers," Charles retorted.

"I'd like to try to understand them. I don't understand them," I murmured.

He knitted his brows. "The devil is in their hearts."

He who had displayed so much scrupulousness about permitting the Indians to be maltreated, had nevertheless encouraged the zealousness of the Inquisition in Spain and Holland. He considered it his Christian duty to fight demons.

"I'll do my best to drive out the devils," I promised.

I knew what was irritating Charles. To lean now on the Lutherans against the Pope, now on the Catholics against the Lutheran league, was like riding a seesaw; it could lead us nowhere. We would never succeed in realizing our dream of political unity until we had put down all eruptions of spiritual discord. I was certain that we could do it; we had only to find the right method. Persecutions tended to make the heretics' obstinacy even more unbendable, and our preachers spoke a false and fanatical language to them. But was it not possible to make them listen to the voice of reason and show them where their true interests lay?

"What do you mean by their true interests?" asked Balthus, with whom I was discussing my ideas. He looked at me quizzically. It was men of his kind whose assistance I needed, but ever since Luther's condemnation, he never spoke to me without a certain reticence.

"You're right," I said. "We have to find out what's at the bottom of it all." I looked at him steadily. "Do you know?"

"I don't associate with heretics," he said with a prudent smile.

"Well, *I'm* going to associate with them. I've got to learn exactly how they think."

When Charles left at the head of his army, I set out for Holland; upon arriving I questioned the nuncio Aleander. Having learned that the sect with the largest number of adherents was the Anabaptists, thus named because they performed second baptisms on each other, I asked about getting into contact with them. I was told that it would not be difficult to introduce myself among them, for they took little pains to conceal their doings; they seemed to be seeking martyrdom. I did in fact succeed quite easily in gaining admittance to several of their meetings. Squeezed into the back room of a shop illuminated by two oil lamps, workers, artisans and small merchants listened with feverish eyes to the inspired orator who was dispensing sacred words to them. Most often the speaker was a small man with soft, blue eyes who claimed to be the incarnation of the prophet Enoch. His sermons were usually insignificant; he preached the coming of a new Jerusalem where justice and brotherhood would reign. But he declaimed these dreams of his in an exalted, moving voice. There were always a good many women in the assemblage and several very young people. They listened passionately to him, their breathing became heavy, soon they began to cry out, fall to their knees and, weeping hysterically, clasp each other in their arms. Often they even ripped their clothes apart and dug their fingernails into their faces. Women threw themselves to the floor, their arms stretched out in the form of a cross, and men trampled over their prostrate bodies. Afterwards, they went calmly back to their homes. The president of the Inquisition, who from time to time ordered a handful of them to be burned at the stake, told me how struck he was by their gentleness and obedience; the women sang as they went to be tortured. On several occasions I tried to talk to the prophet, but he always smiled without answering.

I stayed away from the shop for several weeks. When I again found myself there one evening, the prophet seemed to have changed his text and tone. He spoke much more violently than before and at the end of his sermon he cried out passionately, "It's not enough to tear the rings off the fingers of the rich and the golden chains from their necks. Everything that is must be destroyed!"

The assemblage feverishly repeated after him, "We must destroy! We must destroy!" They shouted with such intense passion that a feeling of anxiety overtook me. When the meeting broke up I grabbed the prophet's arm.

"Why do you preach destruction?" I asked. "Tell me."

He looked at me gently. "We must destroy."

"No," I protested. "We must build."

He shook his head. "We must destroy. Nothing else is left to man."

"Yet you preach the coming of a new Jerusalem."

He smiled. "I preach it because it doesn't exist."

"You mean you don't really hope that it will ever come about?"

"If it came about, if all men were happy, what would there be left for them to do on earth?" He seemed to be looking into the very depths of my heart; in his eyes there was anguish. "The world weighs so heavily upon our shoulders . . . There is only one way to salvation —undo all that has been done."

"What a strange way to salvation!" I remarked.

He laughed maliciously. "They want to turn us into stones but we won't let ourselves be turned into stones!" His great, prophetical voice suddenly boomed out into the night. "We shall destroy, we shall devastate, we shall live!"

Not long after that, the Anabaptists spread out through all the cities of Germany, burning churches, the houses of the rich, convents, books, furniture, anything and everything they laid their hands on. They set fire to crops, raped women and engaged in bloody orgies. They massacred all those who attempted to interfere with their wild fury. I learned that the prophet Enoch had become the ruler of Münster, and from time to time I heard reports of horrible bacchanales which took place under his law. When the bishop finally regained possession of the city, the prophet was locked in an iron-barred cage which was suspended from one of the cathedral's towers. I decided not to waste any effort puzzling over this man's extravagant destiny, but with no little anxiety I could not help thinking: "Famine can be conquered, plague can be conquered, but can man ever be conquered?"

I knew that the Lutherans, too, looked with horror upon the havoc the Anabaptists had wreaked. Anxious to exploit this sentiment, I asked to speak to two Augustinian monks whom the ecclesiastical tribunal of Brussels had just condemned to the stake.

"Why do you refuse to sign this paper?" I asked, showing them a certificate of retraction. They smiled but did not answer. Both of them were thick-featured, middle-aged men. "I know," I resumed. "You scorn death; you're eager to reach Heaven. All you think of is your own salvation. Do you believe that God approves of such selfishness?" They looked at me with a slight expression of astonishment; the words I spoke were not those they were accustomed to hearing from the Inquisitors. "Surely you've heard of the horrors the Anabaptists have perpetrated in Münster and all over Germany?"

"Yes."

"Well! You're the ones who are responsible for those crimes, just as responsible as you were ten years ago for the revolt."

"You know full well the words you speak are false," one of the monks said. "Luther long ago repudiated those wretched creatures."

"Yes, and vehemently. But only because he felt guilty. Reflect a moment," I said. "You insist upon the right to search your hearts for the truth and to preach what you find there to all the world. Isn't that right? Well, what's to stop lunatics and fanatics from also crying out *their* truths? You've seen how many new sects have been born, how much destruction they have wrought."

"Their preachings are in error," the monk protested.

"But how can you prove that, since you reject all authority?" In a pressing voice I added, "It may be true that the Church has often failed us in her obligations. I even admit that her teachings are sometimes in error and I don't forbid you to condemn her in the secret of your hearts. But why, why must you attack her openly?"

With their heads bent toward the ground and their hands hidden in the sleeves of their robes, they listened to me attentively. I felt so certain of being right that I thought for a moment I was going to convince them.

"All men must become united," I continued. "They've got to fight poverty, injustice, war, nature's hostility. They mustn't waste their energies in vain disputes or sow seeds of dissension among themselves. Can't you sacrifice your own beliefs for the good of your brothers?"

They raised their heads and the monk who had until now remained silent said, "There is only one good—to act according to the dictates of one's conscience."

The next day, flames crackled in the center of Brussels' main square. A horrible smell of burned flesh drifted up to the sky. With bowed heads, the crowd that had gathered around the stakes silently prayed for the souls of the martyrs. From a window, I watched the black cinders whirling about in the air. *The fools!* The flames were devouring them alive, and they had chosen it. Like a fool, Antonio had chosen to die; like a fool, Beatrice had refused to live. The prophet Enoch starved to death in a cage suspended from the top of a tower. I stared at the stakes and asked myself if they were really fools or if there existed in the hearts of mortal men a secret I was unable to fathom. The flames died out. All that remained in the center of the square was a heap of formless ashes. I wished I could have questioned those ashes which the wind had begun to scatter through the city.

In the meantime Charles had triumphed over Suleiman, had carried the war against the Infidels into Africa, had driven the pirate Barbarossa from Tunis and had put Moulay Hassan, who agreed to recognize Spain's dominance, on the throne. He then left for Rome to celebrate Easter. In Saint Peter's Church he sat on a throne next to the Pope. Together they performed their acts of devotion and together they left the basilica. For the first time in centuries the Empire displayed a power equal to the Papacy's. But at the very moment when this triumph burst over the face of the earth, we learned that François I had suddenly laid claim to the Duchy of Milan for his second son and that he had just sent an army to Turin.

"No!" Charles exclaimed. "I don't want any more wars. Always wars! What good are they? They only wear us down." He, who was always the supreme master of his emotions, now rapidly paced back and forth, nervously stroking his beard. "This is what I'll do," he continued. "I'll engage François in personal combat. The stakes? Milan against Burgundy. And the one who loses has to serve the victor in a war against the Infidels."

"François won't take up the challenge," I said.

It was now perfectly apparent; never would there be an end to it, never would our hands be free. Once delivered from the French, we would have to march against the Turks, and once the Turks were defeated, we would again have to take up arms against the French. No sooner than a revolt was put down in Spain, another would break out in Germany; weaken the power of the Luthern princes and we would be forced to fight the arrogance of the Catholics. We consumed ourselves in useless struggles and we no longer even knew what the stakes were. German federation, developing the New World—we were never free to devote ourselves to those great projects.

Charles decided to attack Provence. We marched to Marseille but failed to take the city and were forced to retreat to Genoa and embark for Spain. The Treaty of Nice which followed cost us Savoy and two-thirds of Piedmont.

Charles spent the winter in Spain with Queen Isabella, whose health was a matter of grave concern. The first of May, after a miscarriage, she came down with a violent fever which ended her life a few hours later. The emperor shut himself away for several weeks in a convent near Toledo. When at last he emerged from his seclusion, he had aged ten years. His back was bent, his complexion sallow and his eyes faded.

"I thought you'd never come out of that convent," I said.

"I would rather have not come out." Sitting motionless in his chair, Charles stared through the window at the steely blue sky.

"Well, then, why didn't you stay there? You're the ruler, aren't you?"

He turned his head and looked at me. "It was you who once told me that my health, my happiness counted for nothing."

"Ah, you still remember that."

"Now, if ever, is the time to remember it." He passed his hand across his brow; it was a new gesture he had acquired, the gesture of an old man. "I want to leave Philippe an empire that's still intact," he said.

I bowed my head and remained silent. The Castilian summer's burning heat noiselessly closed in on us. How did I ever have the audacity to dictate his duty to him? How did I dare say to myself one day while listening to the fountains of Granada, "I gave that man his life, his happiness"? Now I would have to say, "It was I who gave him those lifeless eyes, that sad mouth, his shuddering heart. His unhappiness is all my doing." It was cold in his soul and I felt that coldness as keenly as if I had touched my hand to a corpse.

For several weeks we were plunged in a sort of torpor. A message from Charles' sister Marie, who governed Holland in his name, pulled us out of it. Trouble had broken out in Gand. For the past several years the ancient city had been cast under the shadow of prospering Antwerp. Her merchants saw their orders constantly diminishing, and her idle workers were living in poverty. When the regent proposed that every city contribute to a national tax, Gand refused to pay. Rebels tore up the municipal constitution, which had been accorded the people of Gand in 1515, and they proudly wore small bits of parchment attached to their clothes as a rallying sign. They had killed a magistrate and began pillaging the city. We asked the king of France to allow us safe passage through his territories—which he accorded us—and on the 14th of February Charles V entered Gand with Marie, the Pope's legate, ambassadors, princes, German noblemen and Spanish grandees. Behind them followed the Imperial Cavalry and twenty thousand foot soldiers; the procession with all its baggage took five hours to pass through the gates of the city. Charles settled down in the castle where he had been born forty years earlier; his troops were dispersed throughout the city. They immediately began a reign of terror, and before three days had gone by the leaders of the revolt were forced to cede. On the 3rd of March the trial began. The attorney-general of Malines set forth the city's crimes before the sovereigns, and a delegation of Gandians came to plead with Marie for mercy. But she turned a deaf ear to the latter and insisted upon pitiless reprisals.

"Aren't you tired of punishing?" I asked Charles.

He looked at me in astonishment. "What do my feelings have to do with it?" From all outward appearances he seemed to have found a certain serenity. He ate and drank heartily and still continued to give as much care as ever to his toilette. Nothing in his conduct drew any suspicion to the emptiness in his heart.

"Do you really believe that these men are criminals?"

He raised his eyebrows. "Were the Indians in America criminals? You were the one who taught me that no one can govern without committing evil."

"With the condition that the evil committed serve some ultimate purpose," I added.

"We have to set an example," he explained.

I studied him for a moment and then said, "I admire you."

He turned his head away. "I have no right to endanger Philippe's heritage."

The next day the executions began. Sixteen of the leaders were beheaded while the Spanish mercenaries looted the houses of the rich and raped their wives and daughters. The emperor ordered one of the city's quarters demolished and a citadel erected upon its ruins. All of Gand's public wealth was confiscated; her arms, cannon, munitions and her great bell, known to the populace as Roland, were taken away from her. All her privileges were abolished and her citizens were required to make public apologies.

"Why?" I murmured. "Why?"

Marie, seated beside her brother, was smiling. Thirty of the city's notables, dressed in black, their heads and feet bare, were kneeling at the sovereign's feet. Behind them, in shirtsleeves and with ropes around their necks, were six delegates from each guild, fifty weavers and fifty members of the popular party. All bowed their heads and clenched their teeth. They had wanted freedom, and to punish them for this crime we forced them to crawl before us on their knees. Throughout Germany, thousands of men had been beaten, quartered, burned; thousands of noblemen and merchants had been beheaded in Spain; in the cities of Holland, heretics, lashed to stakes, writhed in searing flames. Why?

That evening I said to Charles, "I'd like to leave for America."

"Right now?" he asked.

"Now."

It was my last hope, my only desire. The year before, we had learned that Pizarro and his army had captured the gold-bedecked Peruvian emperor and had taken possession of his domains. The first galleon arriving from this new realm entered the port of Seville bearing forty-two thousand four hundred eighty-six gold pesos and one thousand seven hundred fifty silver marks. There, no energy was being wasted in propagating a vacillating past by means of useless wars and cruel repressions. There, men were planning a new future, constructing, creating.

Charles went over to the window and looked down at the gray waters squeezed in between the canal's stone walls. In the distance, the dark mass of the belfry, its proud bells gone, could be seen.

"I'll never see the Americas!" he said.

"You'll see them through my eyes. You know you can trust me."

"Later," he said. It was not an order; it was a plea. He must have been in great distress to speak to me in that supplicating tone. With firmness now, he said, "I need you here."

I lowered my head. I wanted to see the Americas *then* and I wondered if I would still want to later. It was then that I should have left.

"I'll wait," I said.

I waited ten years. Everything constantly changed and yet everything remained the same. In Germany Lutheranism was gaining steadily, the Turks were once more threatening Christianity, and the Mediterranean again became infested with pirates from whom we unsuccessfully attempted to take Algiers. There had been another war with France which resulted in the treaty of Crépy-en-Valois, whereby the emperor gave up all claims to Burgundy, and François I renounced his rights to Naples, Artois and Flanders. After twenty-seven years of fighting, which had drained the strength of both France and the Empire, the two adversaries found themselves face to face with not the slightest change in their respective positions. Charles was happy to hear that Pope Paul II had convoked a Holy Council at Trent, but the Lutheran princes, immediately upon learning of the Pope's plans, set off a civil war. Despite the torturous pains the gout was inflicting upon him, Charles personally took command and acquitted himself heroically, wreaking havoc upon the enemies' forces. But the emperor's governor in Milan committed the blunder of occupying Piacenza, and the Pope, furious, began negotiations with Henri II, the new king of France. As a result, the Council was moved from Trent to Bologna. At Augsburg, Charles was forced to accept a compromise which satisfied neither Catholics nor Protestants. Both sides obstinately rejected the project for which we had cease-lessly struggled ever since Charles became emperor, that of a German constitution.

"I should never have signed that compromise," Charles said. He was slumped in a large, deep armchair, his gouty leg resting upon a footstool. It was thus that he passed his days when events did not compel him to mount a horse.

"There was nothing else you could do," I said.

He shrugged his shoulders. "I've heard that too often."

"You've heard it because it happens to be true."

The only solution . . . we have no choice . . . nothing else you could do . . . Through the years, the centuries, the mechanism slowly un-wound itself. Only a fool could believe that the will of a single human being was able to change its movement. What did our great plans matter?

"I should have refused," he said. "No matter at what price."

"It would have meant war and you would have been defeated."

"I know."

He passed his hand across his brow; the gesture had become habitual. He seemed to be asking himself, "Why not be defeated?" And per-haps he was right. In spite of everything, there *were* men whose desires had left their marks on earth—Luther, Cortez . . . Was it because they had accepted the idea of being defeated? As for us, we had chosen victory. And now we were asking ourselves, "What victory?"

"Philippe will never be emperor," Charles said after a brief silence.

He had known it for a long time. Ferdinand's ambition to bequeath an empire to his own son was too fresh, too strong. But never before had Charles openly admitted this defeat even to me.

"What's the difference?" I said.

I looked at the faded tapestries, at the oaken furniture and, through the window, at the wind-driven autumn leaves. Here in Europe everything had become fixed and covered with dust—the dynasties, the frontiers, the routines, the injustices. What use was there in trying to hold together the debris of this old, worm-eaten world?

"Make Philippe a Spanish prince and emperor of the Americas. America is the only place left in the world where men can build and create . . ."

"Can they?" Charles asked skeptically.

"How can there be any doubt in your mind? You've conquered a virgin world over there, you've erected churches, built cities, you've sown seeds and reaped harvests . . ."

He shook his head. "Who knows what's going on in America?"

The situation was in fact confused. A war had broken out between Pizarro and one of his lieutenants. The latter had been defeated and was condemned to death, but soon after, his partisans succeeded in killing Pizarro. The viceroy, whom the emperor had sent to settle these disputes, was assassinated by Pizarro's soldiers, and they in turn were defeated and beheaded by the emperor's troops. All that could be said with certainty was that the new laws were not being observed and that the Indians were still being maltreated.

"There was a time when you wanted to see America for yourself," Charles said.

"Yes."

"Do you still want to?"

I hesitated a moment before answering. Something—perhaps it was a desire—still beat weakly in my heart. "My only wish is to serve you always."

"Well, then," he said, slowly rubbing his gouty leg, "go see what we've done there. I have to know. I have to know what I'm leaving to Philippe." He lowered his voice to a whisper. "I have to know what I've done in thirty years of ruling."

Six months later, in the spring of 1550, I boarded a caravel in the port of Sanlucar de Barrameda and, together with three cargo vessels and two warships, we set sail for the new world. Day after day, leaning against the bulwarks, I watched the foamy path the ship left behind on the water's surface, the same path that the caravels of Columbus, Cortez, and Pizarro had left. Often I had traced it with my finger on parchment maps, but now the sea was no longer a shaded area on a scrap of paper that I could cover with my hand; it undulated and sparkled, it stretched out into the distance farther than any man could see. "How can anyone ever possess the sea?" I thought. In my studies in Brussels, Augsburg and Madrid, I had dreamed of holding the world in my hands—the world, a smooth, round sphere. But now, as we sailed day after day over the blue waters, I often asked myself, "What, after all, *is* the world? *Where* is it?"

One morning while I was lying on the bridge with my eyes closed, a sudden gust of wind carried to my nose an odor that I had not smelled for five months, a warm, spicy odor, the odor of land. I opened my eyes. Before me, stretching out as far as the eye could see, was a level coast shaded by a forest of giant-leaved trees. We were nearing the Bahama Islands. I gazed in awe at the immense green platform which seemed to be floating upon the sea. Half a century ago a look-out had shouted "Land!" and Columbus' sailors had fallen to their knees. We heard the chirping of birds, the same as they chirped then, the same as they will always chirp.

"Are we going to put into port here?" I asked the captain.

"No," he answered. "The islands are deserted."

"Deserted? . . . Then it's true!"

"Didn't you know?"

"Yes, that's what I was told, but I didn't believe it."

In 1509 King Ferdinand had authorized selling the natives of the Bahamas as slaves. Father Las Casas declared that they had been tracked down like wild game with the help of bulldogs and that fifty thousand Indians had either been wiped out or dispersed.

"Fifteen years ago there were still a few colonists left on the islands," the captain said. "They lived off pearl trading. A good diver brought as much as a hundred and fifty ducats even then. But it wasn't long before the race died out and the last of the Spaniards had to leave."

"How many islands are there in this group?" I asked.

"About thirty."

"And they're all deserted?"

"Every last one of them."

On the map which the geographers had drawn up, the island group was nothing but a semicircle of insignificant spots. But now, as we slowly sailed past them, I saw each separate island glowing as radiantly as the gardens of the Alhambra. They were filled with brilliant flowers, colorful birds and sweet-smelling odors; the sea, held prisoner between coral reefs, settled into placid basins which the sailors called "gardens of water"; polyps, medusas, algae and coral sparkled in the transparent waters where red and blue fish swam lazily about. From time to time I saw a solitary dune, like a stranded ship, emerge from the water's surface; occasionally one of these sand hills would be covered with a web of creeping lianas and encircled by a ring of palm trees. No longer did boats glide over the warm lakes in which an occasional fresh-water spring bubbled; no hand was present to part the thick curtain of lianas. Those delightful lands, where a nude, languorous people lived in carefree indolence, were lost to man.

"Are there any Indians left in Cuba?" I asked as we entered the narrow channel which led to the Bay of Santiago.

"About sixty families. They used to live in the mountains and were resettled in a village at Guandora, near Havana," the captain answered. "In this region here, there still ought to be a few tribes, but they keep themselves pretty well hidden."

"I see."

The Bay of Santiago of Cuba was large enough to hold with ease the entire armada of the kingdom of Spain. I looked at the pink, green and yellow cubicles which rose story upon story along the sides of the mountain and I smiled. I liked cities. The moment I set foot on the cobblestone streets, I happily breathed in the smells of tar and oil, the smells of Antwerp and Sanlucar. I made my way through the milling crowd in the port district. Ragged children clung to my clothes, shouting, "Santa Lucia!" I threw a handful of change to the ground and asked the brightest looking lad in the band to guide me through the city.

A wide, reddish-brown, palm-shaded avenue led to a church of dazzling whiteness.

"Santa Lucia," said the child. His feet were bare and his head was a black ball, completely shaven.

"I'm not interested in churches," I said. "Take me to where the shops are, and the market place."

We turned the corner; all the streets were straight and laid out like a checkerboard, and the houses, covered with bright stucco, were modeled after those of Cadiz. But Santiago bore no resemblance to any Spanish city I knew; it was hardly a city at all. The yellow dust of still-unpaved streets soiled my boots, and the big, open squares were still-vacant lots in which century plants and cactuses grew uninhibited.

"Did you just come from Spain?" the child asked, looking up at me with beaming eyes.

"Yes," I answered.

"When I grow up, I'm going to work in the mines," said the child. "I'll make a lot of money and then I'll go to Spain."

"Don't you like it here?"

He spat contemptuously on the ground. "Everyone here is poor."

We arrived at the market place. Women squatting on the ground were selling cactus fruits, split open and spread out on palm leaves. Others were standing behind counters covered with round loaves of bread and baskets filled with grain, beans, and chick-peas. There were also merchants selling ironware and material. The men, all of them barefooted, wore faded cotton clothing, and the women, also bare-footed, were dressed in tatters.

"How much is a bushel of wheat?" I asked. I was wearing the clothes of a nobleman and the merchant looked at me with surprise.

"Twenty-four ducats."

"Twenty-four ducats! That's twice as much as in Seville."

"That's the price," the man said sullenly.

I slowly walked around the square. A ragged little girl darted in front of me. She stopped at every stand where bread was sold, finger-ing and reflectively weighing the round loaves in her hands, unable to decide which one to choose. The merchants smiled at her. In this country of reversed values, iron cost more than silver, bread was more precious than gold. A bushel of beans which cost two hundred seventy-two maravedis in Spain, cost five hundred seventy-eight here; a horseshoe cost six ducats, and two nails forty-six maravedis; a ream of paper sold for four ducats, and a bolt of fine Valencian scarlet cost forty ducats; a pair of laced boots were worth thirty-six ducats. The rise in prices, which was just now beginning to be felt in Spain, fol-lowing the discovery of the silver mines in the Potosi Mountain, had already reduced the people here to abject poverty. I looked at the tawny faces hollowed by famine and I thought, *In five years, ten years, this is how it will be throughout the kingdom.*

After wandering all day long through the city, plagued by the wailing of women and old men begging for alms, by the shrill plead-ing of children, I dined at the governor's palace, where I was sur-rounded on all sides by luxurious splendor. From their heads to their toes, the lords and their ladies were covered with silk; even the walls of the palace were draped with silk. The table was even more sumptuous than Charles's. I questioned my host regarding the natives' lot, and he confirmed what the captain of my boat had told me. Behind Santiago and near Havana there were still a few plantations cultivated by Negro slaves. But on the whole, the island of Cuba, which was as long as the distance which separated Valladolid from Rome and populated until only recently by twenty thousand Indians, was deserted.

"Can't these savages be subdued without massacring them all?" I asked, making no effort to conceal my displeasure.

"There were no massacres," replied one of the planters. "You don't know the Indians. They're so lazy they'd rather die than do anything the least bit tiring. They would kill themselves just to get out of working. They hung themselves or refused to eat. Whole villages committed suicide."

A few days later, on a boat sailing to Jamaica, I questioned one of the monks who had come on board at Cuba.

"Tell me, is there any truth in what they say, that the Indians committed suicide out of sheer laziness?"

"The truth, my son, is that their masters literally worked them to death," said the monk. "The others, seeing what was in store for them, chose to end their lives as quickly as possible. They ate dirt and stones to hasten their deaths. And they refused to let themselves be baptized—they weren't taking any chances on meeting the good Spaniards in Heaven."

Father Mendonez's voice trembled with indignation and pity. He spoke to me of the Indians for a long while. Instead of the cruel, dull-witted savages that Cortez's lieutenants had described, he painted me a picture of men so gentle that, unused to wielding arms, they frequently wounded themselves with the sharp edges of the Spaniards' swords, a few of which had fallen into their hands. They lived in huge huts built of branches and reeds where they took shelter by the hundreds. For food, they hunted, fished and cultivated corn, and they spent their leisure in wreathing hummingbirds' feathers. They did not covet worldly possessions and they were devoid of hate, envy, and cupidity. Poor, carefree, and happy, they were content to peacefully live out their lives. I looked at the herd of wretched emigrants lying on the deck, crushed by the sun and by fatigue. Carrying small bundles in their hands, they had left the unyielding soil of Cuba to seek their fortunes in the mines. And I thought, "For whom are we laboring?"

Soon, a group of jagged mountains appeared on the horizon. Below their azure crests, I could see deep valleys and glades of varied shades of green, from near black to very pale. Jamaica. Of sixty thousand Indians who had lived on this island, Father Mendonez told me that there were barely two hundred left.

"Then bringing in the Africans didn't save a single Indian's life?" I asked.

"When you have wolves caring for lambs, there's no way of saving them," said the monk. "And how, may I ask, does one wipe out one crime by another, equally outrageous?"

"But Father Las Casas himself was in favor of that measure."

"When Father Las Casas died, he was tormented by remorse."

"He's not to blame," I said sharply. "What man can foresee the consequences of his acts?"

The monk looked at me and I turned my eyes away. "Prayer, much prayer is needed, my son," he said.

I was aware that the planters were accorded by law the right to burn their black slaves in slow, torturous degrees, or to quarter them at the slightest provocation. In far off Madrid where I had often listened unblinkingly to tales of horror, it was all too easy to believe that the planters rarely, if ever, exercised this right. It was said that certain colonists fed their dogs on the flesh of native children; it was said that Governor Nogarez, through pure capriciousness, had massacred more than five thousand Indians. And stories were also circulated of volcanos which spewed forth molten gold, of Aztec cities built of solid silver. But for me, the Antilles were no longer just a collection of legends, for now I had seen these emerald islands and their azure mountains with my own eyes. Inside the rings of golden sand which covered their shores, real men lashed other human beings with real whips.

We put in at Port Arthur and set sail again soon after. The heat grew more stifling from day to day and the sea was absolutely motionless; not a wrinkle marred the water's surface. Sprawled out in the fore part of the ship, the emigrants, their sallow faces dripping sweat, were trembling with fever.

It was morning when we sighted Porto Belo, nestled between two green promontories at the end of a long bay. The vegetation which covered the surrounding hills was so dense that not an inch of earth was visible; it seemed as if two enormous plants, each four hundred feet high, had sprouted from the sea, their roots plunging deep into the water. The burning air vibrated in the city's streets. I was told the climate was so unhealthy that foreigners who were unable to procure mules to make the journey across the isthmus died of fever within a week. At my request the governor obtained mounts for all my fellow voyagers. We left behind only those who had fallen victim to the dreaded fever.

For days and days we traveled along a mule trail which wound its way through a giant forest. Above our heads, the trees formed a thick arch, completely shutting off the sky from our vision. Enormous roots which had broken through the road hindered our progress, and we also had to make frequent stops to cut away the lianas which had overgrown the ground since the last trip. All around us, the shadowy air was stifling and moist. Four men died on the way, and three others, unable to continue on, lay down along the roadside and were left behind. Father Mendonez told me that these lands, too, were deserted. In three months, seven thousand Indian children had died of starvation on the isthmus.

All traffic to or from Peru and Chile passed through Panama, a big, prosperous city. Walking through the streets, I saw merchants clothed in silks, women covered with jewels, mule teams with splendid harnesses. The spacious houses of the wealthy were sumptuously furnished. But the air here was so unhealthy that the inhabitants, amid all their ephemeral riches, perished each year by the thousands.

We boarded a caravel which skirted along the coast of Peru. Those emigrants who had survived the rigors of the voyage, continued on toward Potosi. As for myself, I left the ship with Father Mendonez at Callao, about nine miles from the City of the King; we reached the capital without difficulty.

The city was laid out like a checkerboard, with wide streets and large squares. It was so vast that its citizens called it "the city of magnificent distances." Its adobe houses, the outside walls of which were bare and windowless, were built around patios, like the houses of Andalusia. Refreshing fountains spouted water at every crossroad and the air was light and warm. Nevertheless, the climate did not agree with the Spaniards, and I found the same wretched crowds in the streets as I had seen in Santiago of Cuba. Here, too, gold and silver did not help the people escape from their plight. A cathedral with solid silver columns and walls of precious marble was being erected. For whom?

After the cathedral, the city's most beautiful building was an immense, bare-walled prison. Through the window of his gold-encrusted carriage, the viceroy proudly pointed it out to me.

"In there, all the rebels of the realm are imprisoned," he said.

"What do you mean by rebels?" I asked. "Those who revolt openly against the authorities, or those who refuse to obey the new laws?"

He shrugged his shoulders. "No one obeys the new laws. We would have to reconquer Peru from her conquerors if we wanted the words 'royal authority' to mean anything."

The laws promulgated by Charles V required that the Indians be liberated, that they be given a salary and that they be compelled to work only in moderation. But everyone I questioned declared that the enforcement of these laws was impossible. Some held that the Indians could not be happy except as slaves; others demonstrated, figures in hand, that the immensity of the work we had accomplished and the Indians' natural laziness made a harsh regime necessary; and still others said simply that the king's lieutenants had no way of making themselves obeyed.

"We decided to refuse absolution to colonists who treated the Indians like slaves," said Father Mendonez. "But our bishops threatened to deprive us of our priestly prerogatives if we persisted with this idea."

He took me to visit a mission where old, sick Indians were cared for and orphans fed. In a court shaded by palm trees, children were squatting around large bowls of rice. They were handsome, brown-skinned children with high, prominent cheek bones and straight, black hair. Their large eyes were dark and glittering. In unison they plunged their little brown hands into the bowls and in unison brought them to their mouths. They were the children of men and not little animals.

"They're quite handsome," I said.

The priest placed his hand on the head of a small girl. "Her mother was beautiful too, and her beauty cost her her life. Pizarro's soldiers hung her and two of her friends to prove to the Indians that they were insensitive to their women."

"And this one?" I asked.

"He's the son of a chief who was burned alive because the tribute offered by his village was deemed insufficient."

Thus, as we slowly circled the courtyard, the history of the conquest unfolded itself before our eyes. As they penetrated ever deeper into the country, Pizarro's men forced each village to surrender up all the wares that had taken the people years to amass. Whatever food the conquerors did not eat, they wasted or burned. They killed off entire herds, destroyed crops; wherever they set foot they left behind them a wasteland so ravaged that the natives died of hunger by the thousands. At the slightest pretext a village would be burned, and if the unfortunate inhabitants tried to flee their blazing homes, they were cut down by arrows. In more than one city the entire populace committed suicide at the approach of the conquistadors.

"If you still want to see this unhappy country for yourself, I'll get you a guide," Father Mendonez offered. He pointed to a tall, brown young man who was leaning against a palm tree; he seemed to be dreaming. "He's the son of a Spaniard and an Inca. His father— this happens often—abandoned his mother to marry a Castilian lady, and the child was left in our care. He's familiar with the history of his ancestors and he knows the region well. I have often taken him along with me on my trips."

A few days later, accompanied by Filipillo, the young Inca, I left the City of the King. The viceroy had placed a number of strong horses and ten Indian porters at my disposal. A thick fog hung over the coast, completely hiding the sun, and the ground was wet with dew. We set out on a road which ran along the side of a hill covered with luxuriant grasslands. It was a wide, flagstone highway, sturdier and smoother than any of the old world's roads.

"The Incas built it," my guide proudly told me. "The whole empire was covered with roads like this. Couriers, fleeter than these horses, ran from Quito to Cuzco, carrying the emperor's orders to all the cities."

I greatly admired this magnificent construction. The Incas had also built stone bridges across rivers, and they spanned the numerous deep ravines along the way with structures made of woven vines held down on either side by wooden stakes.

We rode on for several days. I was astonished by the vigor of our Indian porters. Bearing heavy loads of provisions, blankets, and equipment, they marched almost forty miles a day without flinching.

I soon learned that their strength came from constantly chewing the green leaves of a plant they called *cola*. Whenever I called a halt, they would throw down their packs and sprawl themselves out on the ground, apparently completely exhausted. Then they would start chewing a fresh leaf, rolled into a ball, and almost immediately they would become alive again.

"This is Pachacumac," Filipillo announced.

I drew my horse to a halt and repeated aloud, "Pachacumac!" The word evoked an image in my mind of a city of splendid palaces made of sculptured stone and cedar wood, of gardens filled with fragrant flowers, of great stairways leading down to the sea, of fish preserves and aquatic birds. I envisioned palace terraces planted with trees of solid gold, bearing golden fruits and flowers, and with golden birds perched on their branches. *Pachacumac!* I opened my eyes wide.

"But I don't see anything," I said, perplexed.

"There is nothing left to see," said the Inca.

We rode on a little farther to a terraced hill which served as a pedestal for a monument. All that remained of the monument was a section of wall built of enormous blocks of red-painted stone placed one atop the other without cement. I looked at my guide. Seated erect on his horse, his head held high, he looked at nothing.

The next day we left the coast and began to ride up into the mountains. Little by little we rose above the mist which hung over the seaboard. The air became drier, the vegetation richer. From afar, the hills seemed to be covered with a golden gravel, but as we drew nearer, we saw great fields of sunflowers and yellow-hearted daisies. Tall, slender, grassy plants and blue cactuses also grew abundantly in the meadows. Although the road climbed steeply, the temperature remained even. We passed through several abandoned villages where the adobe houses were intact but invaded by vegetation. My guide told me that at the approach of the Spaniards, the villagers had fled across the Andes, taking all their treasures with them. No one knew what had become of them.

In even the smallest of these villages, the people used to weave brightly dyed cotton, agave fibers, and llama wool. They molded pottery of red clay and painted faces or geometrical designs on them. Now, everything was dead.

I patiently questioned the young Inca, and bit by bit, as we crossed an immense plateau eight thousand feet above the sea, where blue cactuses were still growing, I found out what the empire of his fore-fathers had been like. The Incas had little use for the concept of private property; in each village the land belonged to everyone and was redistributed each year. A certain area, called "Land of the Incas and the Sun," was set apart to provide for the officials and to build up a surplus which was stored away for use in times of scarcity. Each Indian, on appointed days, took his turn cultivating this land; he also helped to work the fields of the sick, of widows, and of orphans. He performed his tasks willingly, indeed, lovingly, and often friends and sometimes even the entire populace of a village would be invited to work a plot of ground. Those who were asked went as eagerly as if they had been invited to a wedding celebration. Every two years a general distribution of wool took place, and in the warmer parts of the realm, cotton grown on the royal lands, was handed out to all. Each man was mason and smith as well as cultivator of his allotted field, and he did everything in his own home that needed to be done. There were no poor people among them. As I listened to Filipillo, I thought, *That, then, was the empire we destroyed, the empire I dreamed of establishing on earth and that I did not know how to build!*

"Cuzco!" the Inca cried out.

We had arrived at the top of a mountain pass and, looking down, saw below us an expanse of green flatlands dotted with villages—the delightful valley of the Vulcanida. In the distance, the white cone of the Azuyata and the snowy peaks of the Andes loomed up. The city was sprawled out at the foot of a hill crowned with ruins. I spurred my horse and galloped toward the ancient capital of the Incas.

We crossed fields of alfalfa, barley and corn, and rode through cola gardens. The plains were streaked with canals the Incas had dug out, and the hills had been terraced to prevent the land from eroding. These builders of roads and cities had also been more adept at farming than any of the old continent's peoples.

Before entering the city, I climbed the hill; the ruins were those of a fortress where the emperor had entrenched himself against the onslaughts of Pizarro's troops. It was composed of three concentric ramparts made of dark limestone blocks, perfectly fitted together. I do not know how long I stood there among those stones.

Once inside the walls of Cuzco, I saw that the city had not been entirely destroyed; several of her towers were still standing, and a few handsome stone houses still lined her streets. But in most cases, all that remained intact of the city's buildings were the foundations, upon which the Spaniards had hastily constructed flimsy brick dwellings. Despite its pleasant surroundings, despite the large number of Indians and colonists who lived there, the city seemed crushed under the weight of some dark malediction. The Spaniards complained of the intolerable climate and of the hate they felt all around them. They told me that every year on the anniversary of the conquistadors' entry into the city, aged Incas put their ears to the ground hoping to hear the roaring waters of a subterranean river which they believed would one day carry off the Spaniards.

We spent only a few days in Cuzco and then continued on our journey. The air of the high plateaus was so dry and cold that frequently we saw dead mules lying in a state of perfect preservation along the roadside; corpses, it seemed, did not decompose in these regions. From time to time, we came across the ruins of palaces, temples, and fortresses—enormous triangular or hexagonal adobe structures built without arches or vaults. All that remained of most of these once magnificent buildings was debris. At one end of a large, dried-up lake, we found the vestiges of the splendid city of Piahocanacao. Granite and porphyry lay shattered on the ground; what had once been a temple was now a mountain of rubble; rows of large, flat stones indicated where the streets had been. A long stretch of the highway leading to the city was bordered by gigantic, roughly carved statues.

All the villages we passed through were deserted. More often than not, they had been burned to the ground. On one occasion we saw an old man standing in the doorway of a newly built hut; he had neither nose nor ears, and his eyes had been gouged out, leaving horrid hollow sockets. When Filipillo spoke to him, he seemed to hear, but he remained silent.

"I suppose they ripped out his tongue, too," said the Inca.

He told me that the Spaniards suspected there were gold veins in this region and had therefore atrociously tortured the natives to make them reveal their location. But the Indians fell into a stubborn, impenetrable silence.

"Why?" I asked.

"You will see the mines of Potosi," the Inca replied, "and you will then understand why they wanted to save themselves and their children from such a fate."

I soon came to understand. A few days later, we passed a column of about four or five hundred Indians who were being led to the mines. They were attached to each other by iron collars locked around their necks and a "G" was branded on their cheeks. They were completely exhausted and staggered pitiably as they marched along. The Spaniards riding on either side of the column drove the Indians on with bullwhips.

"They are coming from Quito," my guide said. "And there may have been more than five thousand when they left there. Once, ten thousand died while marching through the hot lands. Another time, out of six thousand who started, two hundred arrived alive. When they fall to the ground from exhaustion, the Spaniards do not even take the trouble to unlock them. They simply cut off their heads."

That evening for the first time in a long while, we saw smoke rising from the huts of a village. Seated in the doorway of her home a young Indian woman was cradling a child in her arms and singing. Her song had such a melancholy tone that I wanted to learn the words. My guide translated them for me thus:

> *Was it in the puckey-puckey's nest*
> *That my mother gave me birth*
> *To suffer so much sorrow,*
> *To weep at this very hour*
> *Like the puckey-puckey in his nest?*

He told me that since the conquest, the songs with which mothers lulled their babes to sleep were all as sorrowful as the one I had just heard. Only women and children were left in the village, the men having been taken away to work in the Potosi mines. And it was thus in every village and settlement through which we passed all the way to the volcano.

Capped by snow and spitting fire, the Potosi rose up twelve thousand feet above the plateau which formed its base. The mountain was a labyrinth of galleries where veins of silver, some as much as two thousand feet thick, were being mined. At its foot, a city had hastily been erected. I walked about among the wooden shacks in search of my shipboard companions. I found only about ten; the others had died on the way. As for those who had reached Potosi, they had great difficulty in adapting themselves to the climate of this high plateau; the women, especially, suffered from mountain sickness. All of their children were born deaf and blind and died within a few weeks. They told me that a man working on his own was barely able to mine enough silver to pay for his basic needs. They had lost all hope of making their fortunes here or even of saving enough to return to their own country. Only the big, influential contractors, who were able to obtain the forced labor of hordes of Indians, grew rich.

"Look," said my young guide. "Look at what they have done to my people."

For the first time his impassive voice trembled, and by the light of a torch I could see tears in his eyes. In the dark galleries, an entire race slaved, a race no longer of living men but of phantoms. They were fleshless and featureless; their brown skins were stretched taut over bones that were as brittle as dead wood; they stared blankly before them and seemed to hear nothing; with automatonlike movements, they swung their primitive tools against the walls. At times, one of these black skeletons, without uttering a sound, would slump wearily to the ground, only to be beaten with whips or iron bars; if he failed to rise quickly enough to suit the Spaniards, they would kill him outright. For more than fifteen hours every day of the week they excavated earth, and the only food they were given was a few morsels of bread made of pulverized roots. None of them survived more than three years.

From morning till night, trains of mules laden with silver went down toward the coast. Every ounce of metal had been bought with an ounce of blood. And yet the emperor's chests remained empty and his people continued to live in poverty. We had destroyed a world, and we had destroyed it for nothing.

"Then I've failed everywhere," said Charles V.

All night long I had spoken to him of the Americas, and the emperor silently listened to me. The first light of day began to filter into his heavily tapestried room, illuminating his face. I felt a wrench in my heart. In three short years he had become an old man. His eyes were dull, his lips livid, his face drawn; he had difficulty in breathing. He was sunk in his armchair and an ivory-knobbed cane was lying beside the blanket that hid his gout-twisted legs.

"Why?" he asked in bewilderment.

During the three years of my absence, he had suffered a number of heartbreaking defeats. He had been betrayed by Maurice of Saxony who had taken command of the Lutheran forces; he was forced to flee before this turncoat and later to accept a treaty which in one blow destroyed everything he had done during his whole life to establish religious unity; he had failed in Flanders, having been unable to retake the lands left by Henri II; revolts had again broken out in Italy, and the Turks continually harassed the Empire.

"Why?" he repeated. "What was my mistake?"

"Your only mistake was to reign," I answered.

He fingered the medal of the Golden Fleece which was resting on his velvet doublet. "I didn't want to reign, you know."

"Yes, I know."

I looked at his wrinkled face, his gray beard, his lifeless eyes. For the first time, I felt older than he, older than any man had ever been, and I took pity on him, as if he were a child.

"I was wrong," I said. "I wanted to make you ruler of the Universe. But there isn't any Universe."

I arose and began pacing the room. I had not slept all night long; my legs were leaden. Now I finally understood—Carmona was too small, Italy too small, and the Universe did not exist.

" 'Universe'! What a convenient word!" I said. "What do today's sacrifices matter? The Universe is always there, in the far-off future. What does it matter if people are burned at the stake, massacred by the thousands? The Universe is somewhere—always somewhere else, of course, but somewhere. And it's *nowhere!* There are only men, men forever divided."

"It's sin that divides them," said the emperor.

"Sin?"

Was it sin or folly or something else? I thought of Luther, of the Augustinian monks, of the Anabaptist women who sang while writhing in the flames, of Antonio and Beatrice. In all of them, there was a force that undermined my carefully reasoned predictions and steeled them against bending to my will.

"One of the heretical monks whom we condemned to the stake said to me before dying, 'There is only one good: to act according to one's conscience.' If that's true, it's insane to want to dominate the world. Nothing can be done for man; his good depends only upon himself."

"There *is* only one good," said Charles, "to seek salvation."

"But do you believe you can force salvation upon others or can you seek it only for yourself?"

"With God's grace, only for myself." He brought his hand to his brow. "I used to think it was my duty to force others to seek salvation, and that was my mistake. It was a temptation placed before me by the devil."

"As for me, all I ever wanted was to create happiness for them. But they're beyond my reach."

I stopped talking. I heard their festive shouting and their bloody howls; I heard the voice of the prophet Enoch: "Everything that is must be destroyed!" It was I against whom he preached, I who wanted to make of this earth a paradise in which every grain of sand would have had its place, in which every flower would have bloomed in its proper time. But they were neither plants nor stones; they did not want to be transformed into stone.

"I had a son," I resumed, "and he chose to die because it was the only choice he could make for himself; I left him nothing else to live for. I had a wife, too, and because I insisted upon giving her everything, she no more lived than if she were dead. And there are those whom we burned alive and who died thanking us. It's not happiness they want; they want to live."

"To live? But after all, what does that mean? This life is nothing," he said, shaking his head. "What madness to want to dominate a world that's really nothing!"

"There are moments when a fire burns in their hearts; that's what they mean by living."

Suddenly a flood of words came to my lips. Perhaps it was to be the last time for years to come, for centuries, that it would be given to me to speak.

"I understand them," I said. "Now I understand them. It's never what they *receive* that has value in their eyes; it's what they *do*. If they can't create, they must destroy. But in any case, they have to rebel against what is, otherwise they wouldn't be men. And we who aspire to forge a world for them and imprison them in it, they can't help but hate us. The very order, the peace that we dream of for them, would be their worst possible curse."

Charles had sunk his head in his hands. He was no longer listening to the strange ideas I was uttering; he was praying.

"Nothing can be done either for them or against them," I concluded. "Nothing can be done."

"We can pray," said the emperor. He was pale and his mouth sagged at the sides as it often did of late when his leg was racking him with pain. "The test is over. If not, God would have left a little hope in my heart."

A few weeks later, Charles V retired to a small house in Brussels, situated in the middle of an estate near the gate of Louvain. It was a one-story lodge filled with scientific instruments and clocks. The emperor's room was small and bare, like a monk's cell. When the death of Maurice of Saxony delivered him of his most powerful enemy, he refused to take advantage of it. He decided to trouble himself no longer with Germany's problems, and at the same time he gave up the constant intriguing to insure his son's falling heir to the Empire. For two years he busied himself with putting his affairs in order, and during that period all his undertakings were crowned with success. He drove the French from Flanders, signed the treaty of Vaucelles and brought about the marriage of Philippe and Mary Tudor, Queen of England. But his decision to abandon the Empire remained unshaken.

On the 25th of October, 1555, in the great hall of the Brussels palace, a solemn assemblage was awaiting the arrival of the emperor; dressed in mourning clothes, he entered the room leaning on the arm of William of Orange. After the Councilor Philibert of Brussels finished reading an official declaration of the imperial will, Charles arose to speak. He recalled that forty years earlier, in the same hall, he had received title to Aragon, Navarre, Granada, Naples, Sicily, Sardinia, Spanish America and Castile; that three years later, upon the death of his grandfather Maximilian, he inherited all the Hapsburg realms, and that the Imperial Crown was then bestowed upon him. He told how he had found Christianity severed and his domains surrounded by hostile enemies against whom he had to defend himself all his life. His strength had now left him, he explained, and he wanted to give the Netherlands to Philippe and the rest of the Empire to Ferdinand. He told his son to respect the faith of his ancestors, to respect the peace and the law. As for himself, he said he had never knowingly wronged anyone.

"If I ever hurt anyone unjustly, I beg that person's forgiveness," said Charles.

While pronouncing these final words, he had grown very pale; when he took his seat, tears were streaming down his cheeks. No member of the assemblage was able to restrain himself from weeping. Philippe threw himself at the feet of his father, who drew him into his arms and tenderly kissed him. I alone knew why he was weeping.

On the 16th of January, 1556, he signed a paper in his room whereby Castile, Aragon, Sicily, and Spanish America were turned over to Philippe. For the first time in years I saw him laugh and banter. That evening he ate a sardine omelette and a large portion of eel paté. After the meal, he passed a pleasant hour listening to a viol concert.

He had a house built in the heart of Spain, near the monastery of Yuste, and one day asked me, "Will you come there with me?"

"No," I answered.

"What can I do for you?"

"Didn't we agree that no one can do anything for anyone?"

He looked at me gravely. "I shall pray God that one day he grant you rest."

I went with him as far as Flessingue and stood there on the beach, watching the ship that carried him off.

And then the sails disappeared on the horizon.

🖿

"I'm tired," Regina said.

"We can sit down, if you like," Fosca suggested.

They had been walking for quite a long while and had gone deep into the forest. The night was warm under the blanket of trees. Regina felt like stretching out among the ferns and sleeping forever. She sat down.

"Don't go on," she said. "It's not worth the trouble. It will be the same story to the very end. I know it."

"The same story, and every day different," said Fosca. "You have to hear it out."

"A little while ago you didn't want to tell it to me."

Fosca lay down on the ground next to Regina. For a moment he silently contemplated the dark leaves of a chestnut tree. "Can you picture that sail disappearing on the horizon and me standing on the beach, watching it disappear?"

"Yes, I can," she said. And it was true; now, she could.

"When I've finished my story, I shall watch you disappear down the road. I suppose you know that you have to disappear."

She buried her face in her hands. "No, I don't know. I don't know anything any more."

"But I *do* know. And as long as I can go on talking, I'll talk."

"And after?" she asked.

"Let's not think about after. Let it be enough for me to speak and for you to listen. For the time being, we have no questions to ask each other."

"All right, go on," she said.

BOOK III

The marsh extended as far as the eye could reach. I continued straight across it. The spongy ground gave way under my feet and water squirted from the rushes with a feeble sigh; on the horizon, the sun was setting. Far out on the plains and seas and behind the mountains, there was always a horizon, and every evening the sun would set. Many years had passed since that day I threw away my compass and began my solitary wanderings over these monotonous lands, no longer counting the days or the weeks or the months, unaware of the hour. I had forgotten my past, and my future . . . my future was this endless plain which stretched out to the sky. I was exploring the ground with my foot, trying to find a piece of solid earth where I might settle down for the night, when I caught sight of a large pink pond not far off. I walked toward it and discovered that it was actually a bend in a river which was winding its way through the rushes and tall grass.

A hundred years, or even fifty years earlier, my heart would have beat wildly. I would have thought, "I've discovered a great river. I alone know of it!" But now, the river, reflecting the pink sky, was a matter of almost complete indifference to me. My only thought was that crossing it at night would be out of the question. When finally I found a patch of solid ground, hardened by the first frost, I threw down my pack and took out a fur blanket. Then, with my ax, I set to work on a tree stump and gathered up a large bundle of wood which I set afire. Every evening I lit a fire so that in the absence of my own life's flame there would be a crackling, an odor, a red, burning life in the night, mounting from the earth toward the sky. The river was so calm that not even the slightest murmur could be heard from its waters.

"Hello! Hello!"

I was electrified. It was a human voice, the voice of a white man.

"Hello! Hello!" I shouted back.

I threw an armful of wood into the leaping flames. Still shouting, I hastened to the river and saw a faint light on the other bank; he too had lit a fire. He shouted something, but I was unable to make out what he was saying. He seemed to be speaking French. Our voices crossed in the humid air, but the stranger could probably no better understand me than I him. Finally, he stopped trying and I cried out three times at the top of my voice, "Until tomorrow!"

A man! A white man! As I lay rolled up in my blanket, I felt the warmth of the fire on my face and I began to think back. Ever since I had left Mexico, I had not set eyes upon a single white man's face. Four years! (I had already started counting again.) I had seen a flame flicker on the other side of the river, heard the faint sounds of a voice, and now I could not stop myself from repeating over and over, "Four years! Four years that I haven't seen a white man!" Between us, across the night, a silent dialogue had begun. "Who is he? Where has he come from? What is he after?" I asked. And he was asking the same questions, and I answered him. *I answered!* Suddenly, on the bank of that river, I found myself once more with a past, a future, a destiny.

A hundred years earlier, I had boarded a ship at Flessingue and set out on a tour of the world. I had hoped to get along without the companionship of other human beings. I wanted to be nameless, face-less, a shadow that would see all and itself remain unseen, unknown. I crossed oceans and deserts and sailed on Chinese junks. At Canton, I looked upon a massive block of solid gold valued at over two hundred million. I visited Kathung and, garbed in a priest's robe, scaled Tibet's high plateaus. I saw Malacca, Calcutta, and Samarkand. In Cambodia, in the heart of a dense forest, I gazed in awe upon a temple as vast as a city, a temple with almost a hundred towers. I dined at the tables of the Grand Mogul and of Abalana, the shah of Persia. I made my way through the islands of the Pacific by a hitherto unknown route. I fought against Patagonians. Finally, having reached Vera Cruz and from there, Mexico, I set out alone on foot to explore the heart of this unknown continent. For four years I strode over prairies and through forests, going nowhere in particular, without compass, lost under the sky and in eternity. And just a little while ago, I was still lost. But now I was lying at a precise point on the planet, a point the latitude and longitude of which could be determined by an astrolabe. It was certainly to the north of Mexico. But how many thousands of miles? To the east or west? The man who was sleeping on the other bank knew where I was.

As soon as dawn broke, I stripped off my clothes and put them together with the blanket in my pack made of buffalo hide. I strapped it to my back and plunged into the river. The icy water took my breath away, but the current was weak and I soon reached the opposite bank. After drying myself with the blanket, I put my clothes back on. The stranger was sleeping next to a small pile of cinders. He was about thirty, his hair was light brown and the lower part of his face was hidden beneath a short, bushy beard. I sat down next to him and waited.

He soon opened his eyes and looked at me in surprise. "How did you get over here?" he asked.

"I crossed the river."

His face lit up. "You have a canoe?"

"No, I swam across."

He threw off his blanket and jumped to his feet. "Are you alone?"

"Yes."

"Are you lost, too?"

"I can't get lost," I replied. "I'm not going anywhere."

He ran his fingers through his tousled hair. He seemed perplexed. "Well, *I'm* lost," he said bitterly. "My companions either lost me or abandoned me. We had reached the source of a river we had started out on at Lake Erie. An Indian there told me that when we got to the source, we'd find a trail leading to another river, a very big river. I set out with the two other men to look for it. We discovered it and started following it down. But on the third day I woke up and found myself alone. I thought my companions had gone on ahead, but I've come as far as here looking for them and I still haven't found any trace of them." He grimaced. "They were carrying all the provisions."

"You should retrace your steps," I suggested.

"Yes, but will the others be waiting for me? I'm afraid of a plot." He looked at me and smiled. "What a wonderful feeling it was when I saw your fire last night. Do you know this river?"

"This is the first time I've ever seen it."

"Oh," he said disappointedly. He glanced at the slimy water slowly winding its way through the swamp. "It flows from northeast to southwest. There's no doubt that it empties into the Pacific, is there?"

"I have no idea," I answered. I, too, looked at the river, and suddenly it was no longer just so much rippling water. It was a road, it led somewhere. "Where were you going?" I asked.

"I'm trying to discover a route to China. And if this river really leads from the lakes to the ocean, I've found it." Again, he looked at me and smiled. It seemed strange that a man could still smile at me. "And you?" he asked. "Where did you start out from?"

"Mexico."

"On foot? And alone?" he asked, dumbfounded.

"Yes."

He looked at me with a sort of eagerness. "What do you do for food?"

I hesitated a moment. "From time to time I kill a buffalo and the Indians give me a little corn."

"I haven't eaten for three days now," he said with all the cheerfulness he could muster. There was a brief silence. He was waiting.

"I'm sorry," I said, "but I haven't any food. I can sometimes go for one or two weeks without eating. A secret I learned in Tibet."

"Ah!" He pressed his lips together and his face became drawn. But an instant later he forced himself to smile again. "Teach me the secret, fast," he said.

"It takes years," I replied.

He looked all around and then silently began to fold his blanket. "Isn't there any game around here?" I asked.

"None. The prairie begins about a day's walk from here, but it's been burned." He spread a sheet of buffalo hide on the ground and began to cut out a pair of new moccasins. "I'm going to try to find the others," he said.

"And if you don't find them?"

"Then it's all in the hands of God."

He hadn't believed me. He thought I did not want to share my provisions with him. But on the contrary, I would gladly have given him something, anything, in exchange for his smile.

"I know where there's an Indian village about five days from here," I said. "They'll surely give you some corn."

"Five days!"

"It will set you back ten days. But between the two of us, we could carry enough to live on for several weeks."

"You're coming back to Montreal with me?"

"Why not?"

"Well, let's get started then," he said.

We swam across the river—the water was warmer than in the early morning—and we trudged through the swamp the whole day long. My companion seemed very tired. He spoke little. I learned, however, that his name was Pierre Carlier and that he came from Saint-Malo. When he was still only a child, he had sworn to himself he would become a great explorer. He had sold everything he owned to raise enough money to come to Montreal and organize an expedition. He had spent five years exploring the Great Lakes, linked to the Atlantic by the Saint Lawrence River, hoping to find a waterway leading to the Pacific. His money was almost gone and his government refused to help him. They wanted the French colonists to settle down in Canada and not go wandering about in unexplored lands.

We reached the prairie on the second day. The Indians had set fire to it here as well as everywhere else. It was the hunting season. From time to time, we came across the bones of buffalo and saw their tracks in the ground. But we knew that for miles around not a single living animal would be found. Carlier stopped speaking altogether. He was completely exhausted. During the night I discovered him gnawing on the buffalo hide from which he cut a new pair of moccasins every day.

"Can't you really give me anything to eat?" he asked me the next morning.

"You can go through my pack," I said. "I have absolutely nothing."

"Then I'm afraid I can't go on." He stretched himself out on the ground, folded his hands behind his neck and closed his eyes.

"Wait for me," I said. "I'll be back in four days."

I left a gourd filled with water within reach of his hand and set off at a rapid pace. I had no trouble finding the way. My footprints were still visible in the marsh, and the grass I had trod over on the prairie indicated my trail. I continued on without let up until nightfall and set out again the next day at dawn. I reached the village in two days. It was empty. All the Indians had gone off on the hunt. But I found corn and meat stored away in a hiding place.

"Easy, Carlier," I said, "easy." He bit greedily into the chunk of meat. His eyes glittered.

"Aren't you eating?" he asked.

"I'm not hungry."

He smiled. "It's wonderful to eat."

I returned his smile. Suddenly, I had a strong desire to be that man who was hungry and who ate, that man who was so passionately searching for a route to China.

"And now what are you going to do?" I asked.

"I'll go back to Montreal and try to raise enough money to organize a new expedition."

"I have some money." In the bottom of my pack there were jewels and gold ingots.

"Are you the devil by any chance?" he cheerfully asked.

"Suppose I were the devil?"

"I'd gladly sell you my soul in exchange for the route to China. I'm not concerned about the other life. This one is enough for me!"

There was so much ardor in his voice that the desire to be him, Carlier, the explorer, again tore through my heart. *Is there still a chance for me to become a living man again?* I thought.

"Well, I'm not the devil," I said.

"Who are you?"

A word formed on my lips: *nobody*. But he was looking at me, questioning me. I had saved his life. For him, I existed. And I felt a long forgotten burning in my heart. My own life was beginning to take form again.

"I'll tell you who I am," I said.

◆

The oars struck the water with an even rhythm, and the canoes slowly glided down the winding, lazy river. Carlier was sitting next to me. Resting on his knees was an open journal in which he entered the daily events of our exploration and in which he was now busy writing. I was smoking. I had learned the habit from the Indians. From time to time Carlier lifted his head. He looked at the fields of wild rice and the savannas where clumps of trees rose up at scattered intervals. Occasionally a bird would dart up from the river bank with a shrill screech. The air was warm. The sun was beginning to sink in the sky.

"I like this time of day," he said.

"You say that all day long."

He smiled. "Well, I like this season . . . and this country."

He started to write again. He noted down the trees, the birds, the color of the sky, the varieties of fish. All these things were important to him. In his notebook, each day had something special, distinctive about it, and burning with curiosity he looked forward to the adventures which still separated him from the river's estuary. For me the river simply had an estuary like all other rivers, and beyond that estuary stretched the sea, and beyond the sea other lands and other seas, and the world was round. There was a time when I thought it infinite. Upon leaving Flessingue, I still had hope of spending eternity discovering it. Standing on the peak of a mountain, below a blanket of clouds, I had glimpsed a patch of golden plain through a crevice, and I had been thrilled. I had known the feeling of joy in looking down upon an unknown valley from the heights of a pass, in wandering through a gap closed in by gigantic walls, in landing on a virgin island. But now I knew that behind each mountain there was a valley, that every gorge had an issue, every cavern walls. The world was round and monotonous—four seasons, seven colors, a single sky, water, plants, flat or hilly land. Everywhere, the same boredom.

"Northeast to southwest," said Carlier. "It's not changing direction." He closed his notebook. "It's like strolling through a park."

In Montreal we had carefully chosen trustworthy men and we loaded down six canoes with provisions, clothing, and instruments. We were already a month's journey beyond the place where we had first met, and the expedition had still not encountered any serious obstacles. The savannas abundantly provided us with buffalo, deer, moose, wild turkey, and quail.

"After we've reached the estuary, I'm going to return to the source," he said. "There has to be a waterway between the river and the lakes." He looked at me rather anxiously. "Don't you believe there's one?" Every night he repeated the same words, and every night with the same ardor.

"Why not?" I said in reply.

"Then we'll charter a ship, won't we? and sail all the way to China." His face hardened. "I don't want anyone to sail that route before me."

I drew on my pipe and blew a cloud of smoke through my nostrils. I tried to share in his life and make his future mine, but it was useless—I could not be him. His hopes, his perpetual anxieties, were no less foreign to me than the unique tranquility of that hour.

He put his hand on my shoulder. "What are you thinking of?" he asked tenderly.

For all of three centuries no man had ever put his hand on my shoulder, and since Catherina's death, no one had ever asked me, "What are you thinking of?" But Carlier spoke to me as if I were no different than any other man, and it was for that reason, above all, that I cherished his friendship.

"I'd like to be in your place," I said.

"You? In my place?" Smiling, he held out his hand to me. "Let's change!"

"You don't know what your're asking for."

"Ah!" he said fervently. "If only I were immortal!"

"There was a time when I used to say that, too."

"Then I'd be certain of finding the route to China. I'd sail down every river on earth. I'd plot maps of every continent."

"No," I said. "You'd soon lose all interest in China, you'd lose interest in everything, because you'd be alone in the world."

"Are you alone in the world?" he asked me reproachfully. His face and movements were virile, but a feminine softness often appeared in his voice and eyes.

"No," I answered, "not now." Far off in the savanna an animal cried out raucously. "I never had any friends," I said. "People always looked upon me as a stranger—or as a dead man."

"Well, I'm your friend," he reassured me.

For a long moment we silently listened to the soft murmur of the oars plowing the water. The river was so sinuous that we could not have gained very much ground since the morning. Suddenly Carlier stood up.

"A village!" he shouted.

At first I saw only smoke rising in the air, and then, sheltered behind a clump of trees, cone-shaped huts made of matted rushes appeared. Indians were standing on the bank, howling shrilly and waving their bows.

"Quiet," Carlier ordered.

The men continued to row without saying a word. Carlier opened a sack that contained merchandise we brought with us for trading with the natives—bolts of goods, mother-of-pearl necklaces, needles, and scissors. The Indians' dugouts now barred our way. Holding a multi-colored shawl in his hands, Carlier began to speak to them in a soft, controlled voice, and in their tongue. I understood nothing of what they were saying; for many years now, all effort seemed useless to me and I had neglected to learn the savages' language. Soon the Indians stopped their howling and motioned us to come ashore. At the same time they advanced in our direction without any display of hostility. They were dressed in brightly colored deerskin clothes, trimmed with porcupine bristles. While we were landing our boats and making them fast, the Indians talked quietly among themselves. Finally, one of them walked up to Carlier and spoke to him volubly.

"They want to take us to their chief," Carlier said. "Let's go with them. But don't part with your guns under any pretext."

The chief was seated on a mat of rushes in the middle of the village grounds. A dozen perfect pearls were hanging from each of his ears and others dangled from his nose. In front of him were two hollow stones filled with tobacco; he was smoking a pipe decorated with feathers. Removing the pipe from his mouth, he motioned us to sit down. Carlier spread out before the chief the gifts he had brought. The chief thereupon smiled benevolently. They began to talk. In a low voice, one of the members of the crew translated their conversation for me. Carlier explained that he wanted to continue down the river to the sea. The chief appeared very displeased with this project. He told Carlier we would soon come to another river that was completely unnavigable. Not only was it riddled with treacherous rapids and precipitous falls, but tree trunks, he claimed, would be sent crashing against our canoes by the turbulent waters, and savage tribes living along its banks would not hesitate to attack us with hatchets. Carlier resolutely answered that nothing could stop him from continuing on. The chief resumed his lengthy discourse which Carlier opposed with the same firmness. Finally, a faint smile appeared on the chief's lips.

"We will talk about it tomorrow," he said. "The night will bring you counsel."

He clapped his hands. Servants brought forth bowls of rice, boiled meat, and corn which they placed before us on the ground. We ate in silence from glazed earthenware bowls. Gourds filled with a strong alcoholic drink were passed around by the servants. But I noticed that the chief did not offer us his pipe.

Towards the end of the feast, several of the Indians began beating on drums. Others violently shook gourds filled with pebbles. Soon the whole tribe started to dance, brandishing their tomahawks. The chief shouted an order and two men emerged from a hut carrying on their shoulders a live crocodile bound from head to tail with thin twine. The rhythm and the dancing redoubled in violence. Awe-struck, I watched the Indians attach the reptile to a tall, red-painted stake which stood at one end of the grounds. The chief arose, solemnly walked up to the crocodile, took a knife from his belt and cut out its eyes. He then returned to his seat. With terrifying howls, the warriors proceeded to cut long gashes in the hide of the living beast. Then they riddled it with arrows. Carlier and the crew members grew white. The Indian chief, impassive, continued to smoke his pipe.

I took a gourd which a servant held out to me, raised it to my lips and drank heartily. I heard Carlier's voice ordering, "Don't drink!" But the men continued to drink nevertheless. As for himself, he hardly wet his lips. The chief said something to him in an imperious tone of voice and Carlier merely smiled back. When the gourd was again passed to me, I took several long swallows. The beating of the drums, the Indians' hooting, their frenetic dancing, the eeriness of the killing I had just witnessed, and the fiery liquid running down my throat, all combined to make my blood boil up and beat feverishly in my veins. I felt as if I, myself, were becoming an Indian. They were dancing. From time to time one of them would swing his tomahawk at the red stake to which the crocodile was bound and then loudly sing out the praises of all the heroic deeds he had performed during his life. I drank another long swallow. My head was a gourd full of pebbles, my blood was fire. I was a savage Indian, born and raised on the banks of this serpentine river. Horrible tattooed gods reigned in my heavens; the rhythm of the drums and the cries of my brothers gladdened my heart. One day I would go off to a paradise of dances, feasts and bloody victories . . .

When I opened my eyes I found myself rolled in my blanket, up-stream from the place at the village where we had come ashore. My head was throbbing painfully. I looked at the river's yellow waters; the air around me had a flat, familiar taste. *I'll never be like those savages. This stale taste of my life will never change. Always the same past, the same feelings, the same rational thoughts, the same boredom. For thousands of years! Never will I escape from myself!* I looked at the yellow waters and suddenly I jumped to my feet. The boats were no longer there!

I ran over to Carlier. He was still asleep. The whole crew was asleep with their guns lying beside them. The Indians had probably been reluctant to murder them for fear of setting off a war with the white men. But during the night, they had set our canoes adrift. I put my hand on my friend's shoulder. When he opened his eyes, I pointed to the river's empty waters.

Grouped together in a clearing by the river, we spent the entire day discussing the possibilities that lay open to us. The crew members were obviously dismayed. To attack the Indians and take their boats and provisions was out of the question; they greatly outnumbered us. To hollow out tree trunks with our hatchets and continue down the river was too hazardous; the villages would probably be hostile and we no longer had merchandise to exchange for food. Furthermore, if we were to encounter rapids, we would have to have solid canoes.

"There's only one solution," I said. "We'll have to build a fort to protect ourselves against Indian raids. Then we can store up game and smoked fish to see us through the winter. In the meantime, I'll go by foot to Montreal and as soon as the ice melts on the rivers, I'll come back with canoes, food, arms and men."

"But Montreal is two thousand miles away," Carlier said.

"I can cover them in three or four months."

"Winter will overtake you on the way."

"I can walk through snow."

Carlier lowered his head and pondered for a long while. When he raised it again, his face was grave. "I'll go to Montreal myself," he said.

"No."

"Why not? I can walk fast, too, and I can walk through snow."

"You can also die," I said. "What will become of these men?"

He stood up and plunged his hands in his pocket. Something moved in his throat. I recalled the day when another man—I had forgotten who—had stood before me with that same expression on his face, that same lump bobbing in his throat.

"You're right," he said finally.

He turned around and took a few steps, kicking a stone along with his foot. I suddenly remembered; it was Antonio who had looked at me with those eyes.

◆

"Look!" I cried out to my companions. "Fort Carlier!"

Their oars stopped dead in the water. The fort was located a little past the second bend in the river; in a straight line it was only a few hundred feet away. It was a sturdy structure made of large, dark logs enclosed within a triple stockade. No one seemed to be there. I stood up in front of the canoe and shouted, "Hello! Hello!" and I continued shouting until we came alongside the fort. I jumped to the bank, grown over with young, tender grass and spring flowers, and ran toward the stockade. Carlier was leaning on his gun, waiting for me in front of the gate of the first enclosure. I grabbed him by the shoulders and said warmly, "It's good to see you again!"

"You too," he said, without smiling. His face was white and puffed up; he had aged a great deal.

I pointed to the eight big canoes loaded down with food, arms, and merchandise for trading. "Look!"

"Yes, I saw them," he said. "Thanks."

He pushed the gate open and I followed him into the fort. The building consisted of a single large room with a low ceiling and a floor of hard, trampled earth. A man was lying in a corner on a bed of straw and furs.

"Where are the others?"

"The two others are in the attic. They're keeping watch on the savanna."

"The *two* others?"

"Yes," he said.

"What happened?" I asked.

"Scurvy. Thirteen men died. This one here stands a chance of pulling through, now that it's spring. A few weeks ago, I made up an extract from the leaves and branches of those white spruces out there, and I've been forcing him to drink it down. I came close to dying, myself, and that's what cured me." He looked at me and finally seemed to see me. "You got here none too soon!"

"I brought plenty of fresh fruit and corn along with us," I said. "Come take a look."

He went over to the man. "Do you need anything?"

"No," he answered.

"I'm going to bring you some fruit," Carlier said. He turned and followed me to the canoes.

"Did the Indians attack you?"

"Three or four times the first month. But we fought them off. There were a lot of us then."

"And after?"

"After? Well, we hid our losses from them. We buried the dead at night. Or rather, we satisfied ourselves with covering them with snow; the ground was too hard to dig graves." His eyes wandered off. "When spring came, we had to bury them again. There were just five of us left then, and my knee had begun to swell."

My men had secured the canoes to shore and were plodding back and forth between the fort and the river, doubled under the weight of cases and sacks.

"Do you think the Indians will try to stop us from going on?" I asked.

"No," Carlier replied. "The men left the village two weeks ago and they haven't come back yet. I think there's a war going on in the prairie."

"We'll start out again as soon as my crew has had a chance to rest up a little. It won't be more than three or four days." I pointed to the canoes. "They're good, sturdy boats. We won't have any trouble going over rapids with those canoes."

He nodded his head. "That's all right with me."

We spent the following days preparing for our departure. I noticed that Carlier hardly questioned me at all about my journey; he spoke to me mainly of the hard winter they had passed at the fort. To cover up his losses from the Indians, he made every able-bodied man act a part in a perpetual play; he had them leave the fort and he pretended to chase after them as if they had disobeyed his orders. Although he told these stories in a cheerful tone of voice, he never smiled. It seemed as if he no longer knew how to smile.

On a beautiful May morning we set out again on our expedition. The man who had been suffering from scurvy was beginning to feel better and we carefully placed him in the bottom of one of the canoes. There were only women and old men left in the Indian village, and we rowed past without incident. The days began to run out again, slow and monotonous, metered by the sound of the oars.

"The river is still flowing from northeast to southwest," I said to Carlier.

His face brightened. "Yes, I know."

"One day there'll be forts and trading posts all along this river," I said. "And where Fort Carlier now stands, there'll be a city bearing your name."

"One day," he said. "But I won't be here to see it."

"What's the difference? You'll have done what you wanted to do."

He looked at the yellow waters and the flowering savanna, at the branches of the firs from which tender, green needles were growing. "That's what I used to think, too," he said.

"And now?"

"Now I can't stand the thought that you'll see all those things and I won't," he replied bitterly.

I felt a sharp bite in my heart and I thought, *It's happened, then. With him, too, it's happened.*

"Other men will see them, too," I said.

"But they won't have seen things the way they are now. And one day they'll die, each in his turn. I don't envy *them* in the least."

"And you shouldn't envy me, either."

I looked at the muddy river, at the flat savanna. At times it seemed as if the world belonged to me alone, as if none of its transitory visitors would ever contest its ownership with me. But then there were times when, seeing the love with which these ephemeral beings looked upon the world, I had the feeling that only for me was it deaf and mute and faceless. I was riveted to it and yet, at the same time, excluded from it.

The days grew warmer, the river wider. At the end of a week's time, it had reached the proportions of a lake, and soon after we saw that it emptied into another river, the blue waters of which flowed precipitously from our right to left.

"There it is!" I cried out. "The great river!"

"Yes," Carlier said quietly. There was a look of deep anguish on his face. "It flows from north to south."

"It can change course a little farther on."

"Not a chance. We're hardly six hundred feet above sea level."

"Wait awhile," I said. "It's still too soon to tell."

We continued on. For three days the yellow and blue waters flowed side by side without mingling; then the yellow finally vanished in that great limpid serpent which was winding its way through the plains. There was no longer any possible doubt of it—we had found the great river. It had neither rapids nor cataracts, but it *did* flow from north to south.

All one morning, Carlier sat on the river's edge, his eyes fixed on the horizon toward which the current carried its cargo of branches and tree trunks. I put my hand on his shoulder.

"It's not the route to China," I said, "but it's certainly one of the important rivers of the world, and no one before ever knew of its existence. Don't forget that Columbus believed he had landed in India when he actually chanced upon a new world."

"I don't care one whit about this river," Carlier said, clearly enunciating each word. "I wanted to find the route. That's all. We may just as well go back to Montreal, for all I'm concerned."

"What kind of foolishness is that? Let's go on to the estuary. You can look for the route again some other time."

"But there isn't any," Carlier said hopelessly. "The northern part of the lakes was explored time and time again and nothing was found. The great river was the last chance."

"Well then, if it doesn't exist, why torment yourself for not having found it?"

He shrugged his shoulders. "You can't understand. Ever since I was fifteen, I kept promising myself I'd discover it. I even bought a Chinese robe at Saint-Malo; it's with the rest of my things in Montreal. I would have taken it along with me to China."

I remained silent for a moment. I did not, in fact, understand him. Finally, I said, "If, as I believe, you've just discovered the river that will permit boats to cross this continent from north to south, you'll be as famous as if you had found the route to China."

"I don't care about being famous," he said in a sudden burst of rage.

"You'll have rendered just as great a service to mankind. As for China, they can always go by the old route; they'll get along well enough."

"And they'd have gotten along just as well without this river, too."

He sat on the bank of the river all day long without taking a bite of food. I patiently attempted to hearten him and the next morning he agreed to continue the expedition.

The days passed. At one point, a slimy subsidiary hurtled enormous tree trunks into the mainstream. Our rowers had great difficulty in avoiding them, for the waters of the two rivers, in meeting, created whirlpools which our canoes were repeatedly sucked into. We succeeded, however, in pulling away from that dangerous stretch without damage. A few miles farther, we sighted a village; our guns were already in our hands when one of the men in the lead canoe cried out, "Everything is burned!"

We drew alongside the village. Nothing but piles of cinders remained of most of the huts. In the center of the village, headless, mutilated bodies were tied to stakes; still more bodies were heaped high in one of the unburned huts. At the river's edge we found embalmed heads, the size of fists, from which the skulls had been removed. All the villages we encountered during the following days were similarly ravaged.

The river widened. The climate grew warmer and the vegetation was now semitropical. Frequently, the men had to shoot alligators to keep them away from the boats. The marshy banks were covered with reeds, among which clumps of aspen trees rose up here and there. One day we found a crab buried in the mud; I leaned over, cupped my hand and quickly brought a little water to my lips. It was briny.

A short distance further on, the river divided into three branches. After hesitating for a few minutes, we chose the middle channel. For two hours we slowly made our way through a labyrinth of low islands, sand banks and reeds. Then suddenly one of the crew members stood up and let out cries of joy. We had emerged on the sea.

"Aren't you happy now?" I asked Carlier.

The men pitched camp for the night. During the day they had killed several wild turkeys which they put up to roast, and they laughed and sang merrily.

"There's something wrong with my astrolabe," Carlier told me. "I can't get the longitude."

"What's the difference?" I said. "We'll come back. We'll come back by sea, with a real ship. It's a great discovery!"

Carlier's face remained grave. "Your discovery," he said.

"What makes you say that?"

"It was you who saved my life on the prairie. It was you who went to Montreal for help. It was you who persuaded me to continue the expedition. Without you I wouldn't be here right now."

"And neither would I be here without you," I said gently.

I lit my pipe and sat down beside him. I looked out at the sea: always the same sea, the same sounds, the same smells. I glanced over his shoulder and watched him write down a few numbers in his journal.

"Why haven't you written anything in there for so long?" I asked.

Carlier shrugged his shoulders.

"Why?" I repeated.

"You were always scoffing at me!"

"I was *scoffing* at you?"

"Oh, you never said anything, but I saw it on your face." He let himself fall back, put his hands under his head and stared up at the heavens. "It's a terrible thing to have to live under that gaze of yours. You look at people from so far off; you're on the other side of death. For you, I'm already dead, a corpse: age thirty in the year 1651; searched for a route to China; failed; discovered a great river that others would have discovered a little later without him." With no trace of bitterness, he added, "If you had wanted, you wouldn't have needed me to make this discovery."

"But I was incapable of even *wanting* to make it," I said.

"And I, why should I want to? Why should I take an interest in things that don't interest you? Why should I be happy? I'm not a child."

A thick fog crept into my heart. "Would you prefer that we part?" I asked.

He did not answer, and deeply distressed I thought, *If I leave him, where will I go?*

"It's too late," he finally said.

We went back up to Montreal and the next spring chartered a ship which we took to sea, sailing it down the Atlantic coast of the American continent. After circling Florida, we skirted along a coastline that was at the same latitude Carlier had measured at the mouth of the great river. Unfortunately, we did not know the longitude of the estuary and a dense fog hung over the entire littoral, obscuring our view. We sailed slowly and very cautiously, for we had to stay as close to the shore as possible and were afraid of running aground on sandbanks or reefs.

"Look!" cried a sailor. He was one of the men who had taken part in the preceding expedition. Pointing in the direction of the coast, which was barely visible through the white fog, he asked, "Don't you see anything?"

Leaning against the bulwark with both hands, Carlier peered intensely into the mist. "All I see is a sandbank," he said.

As for myself, I, too, saw only reeds and strips of land covered with gravel.

"Water!" Carlier suddenly exclaimed. "I can see water!" He spun around and cried out, "Lower a canoe!"

A few moments later we were rowing toward the shore. Winding its way among a labyrinth of flat islands and strips of land, the great, muddy river emptied itself into the sea through an opening several miles wide. We went back to the ship, certain of having found the estuary for which we were searching.

Our plan was to sail up the river and its subsidiary as far as the trail where I had first met Carlier. There, we would build a fort, store up fruits and vegetables for the winter, leave a few men behind to guard the ship, and the rest of us would return by canoe to Montreal where we would proclaim our discovery. We had no doubt that aid would then be accorded us to establish trading posts, to explore the sources of the great river, to search for a waterway connecting it to the Saint Lawrence by way of the lakes and perhaps even to construct canals. Soon, villages would spring up. The new continent had been opened wide to all of mankind.

The ship put about. Slowly, it sailed toward the widest channel, preceded by a canoe which led the way. As we came nearer, the shock of the turbulent waters issuing from the river caused the ship to pitch heavily from stem to stern. Just as we were about to enter the channel, there was a dull thud. The ship had struck a reef.

"Cut down the masts!" Carlier cried out.

The bewildered crew did not respond to his order. The wounded ship continued to pitch and roll dangerously; its masts, heavy and menacing, creaked and swayed. I grabbed an axe and started to chop away at one of them, while Carlier set to work on the other; the two masts came down with a great crash. But the ship obstinately continued to sink deeper into the water. We lowered the canoes and rowed them to shore. We were able to salvage only a few small bundles of merchandise and a little food before the ship had completely disappeared, two hours later.

"We'll go up the river by canoe," I said cheerfully to Carlier. "What's one boat? Your discovery is worth a fortune! You'll have twenty boats just for the asking."

"I know." He looked out at the sea, separated by a blue line from the torrent of yellow water and the alluvial deposits. "There's no turning back now," he said.

"Why should there be any question of turning back?"

"You're right," he replied.

He took my arm and we started out in search of dry ground where we could pitch camp.

We spent the next morning hunting buffalo and fishing for trout.

Then, having divided the crew members among the four canoes, we began our voyage upstream. On either side of the river, monotonous plains stretched out endlessly into the distance. Carlier seemed preoccupied.

"Does this land look familiar to you?" he asked me.

"I think so," I said hesitantly.

The same tall reeds capped by pale green tufts lined the banks of the river. Farther inland, there were the same flowers, the creeping vines, the clumps of aspens. Alligators were asleep in the warm mud.

We continued rowing for four days; on the afternoon of the fifth, we sighted a village. Its windowless huts were made of mud and had large, square doors. I did not recognize the place. Standing on the river's edge the Indians were waving their arms in what appeared to be a friendly way. They were wearing white loincloths tied around their waists with a rope from which two large tassels hung.

"There were no villages less than two weeks' journey from the estuary," Carlier said.

We beached our canoes. The chief of the tribe, a benevolent-looking man, welcomed us into his hut which was decorated with leather shields. Although it was broad daylight outside, the room was lit up by torches made of dried, twisted reeds. Carlier asked the chief the name of the river and he replied that it was called simply the "red" river. Carlier further asked if he knew of another large river in the region, and the chief said that far to the east there was a river that was wider and longer than any other he knew. We offered him a few gifts, and in exchange for a package of needles, an awl, a pair of scissors and a few yards of goods, he gave us an abundance of corn, dried fruits, salt, turkeys, and chickens.

"Well, what do we do now?" Carlier asked when, after having smoked the peace pipe, we had taken leave of the chief.

"We'll just have to find the great river," I replied.

Carlier lowered his head.

I reflected a moment. "I'll go look for the river," I said. "After I've found it, I'll come back and lead you there. The land here is rich and these Indians received us as friends. You'll be able to wait here for me as long as necessary."

"I'm going with you," Carlier said.

"No. It's a long way to the river and we don't know the country or its peoples. What I can do alone, I can't do with you along."

"I'm going with you, or I'm going without you," he said stubbornly. "One way or the other, I'm going."

I looked at him. A word I had uttered centuries ago came to my lips. "What foolish pride!" I said.

He began to laugh; I did not like that laugh.

"Why are you laughing?"

"Do you think anyone can live with you, or even near you, and keep a single ounce of pride?" he said.

"Let me go alone."

"You don't understand! You don't understand *anything!* I *can't* stay here. If I could stay put, I would have stayed in Montreal, I would have stayed in Saint-Malo. I would have settled down in a quiet, little house with a wife and children." He pressed his lips together. "I've got to feel that I'm alive—even if I have to die trying."

During the following days, I tried in vain to talk him out of it; he refused even to answer me. Carefully, he filled a pack with provisions, adjusted his instruments and one morning he said to me, "Let's go."

Both of us were heavily loaded down. We brought along buffalo hides from which we made moccasins every morning; a single day of walking was enough to wear out a pair. We took guns, cartridges, hatchets, fur blankets, a canoe made of buffalo skins and a two months' supply of food. Heeding the Indians' advice, we set out on a buffalo trail; following the tracks of wild animals was the surest means of not missing any waterway. We walked along in silence. I was happy to be walking toward a goal. Ever since I joined Carlier, there had always been a goal before me, a goal that gave me a future and at the same time masked the future. The more difficult it was to reach this goal, the more confidence I felt in the present. The great river seemed very difficult to reach and every minute was sufficient unto itself.

At the end of a week's time it began to rain. We crossed a prairie where the tall, rough grass scraped our hands and arms as we pushed our way through it. The ground was heavy with water, making it difficult to walk. At night the drenched trees provided us scant shelter. Next, we came upon a forest and had to cut our way laboriously through an old, unused buffalo trail overgrown with vegetation. We crossed several rivers. Under the gray blanket which uniformly covered it, the country seemed deserted. No birds, no animals fled at our approach. And our supply of food was dwindling.

Noiselessly, we approached the first village we sighted since setting out. Ferocious outcries and the beating of drums filled the air. I darted from tree to tree; on the village grounds I saw a circle of Indians dancing wildly around other Indians who were bound hand and foot; the war was still raging on the plains. After that, we took care to avoid villages. On another occasion, we spotted a column of painted Indians heading toward us. They were letting out animal-like roars and were apparently on the warpath. We hid ourselves in the foliage of a tree and luckily escaped detection.

It rained more or less steadily for thirty-five days, and during that period we came upon no less than twenty streams. Finally, a strong wind arose and swept clean the sky. Our journey became easier. But we had only a two weeks' supply of food left.

"We'll have to turn back," I said to Carlier.

"No," he protested. His face had regained its former aspect—tanned and youthful, hardened by a beard and softened by long, supple hair. But he had not regained his precise, carefree eyes, eyes which now gazed absently about him. In a buoyant tone of voice, he said, "Now that the rains have stopped, we'll be able to kill some buffalo."

"But we won't kill a buffalo every day." In this dank climate it was impossible to preserve a piece of meat for more than twenty-four hours.

"Then we'll come across villages where they'll sell us corn."

"The war is still on," I reminded him.

"They're not fighting everywhere."

I gave him an angry look. "Aren't you in somewhat of a hurry to die?"

"To tell you the truth, it's all the same to me whether I live or die," he said.

"If you die, your discoveries will be buried with you. You don't for a moment imagine that any of your men will worry about looking for the great river, do you? They'll take root where we left them and mix with the Indians." After a brief silence, I added, "And I won't look for it either."

"I don't care one way or another any more." Carlier put his hand on my shoulder; many months had gone by since the last time he had made this friendly gesture. "You convinced me that the route to China wasn't so important. Well, the great river isn't so important either."

"Let's go back," I said. "We'll organize a new expedition."

He shook his head. "I've run out of patience."

We continued on. I killed a small deer, a few wild chickens and a few quail, but our provisions shrank from day to day. When we at last came upon the great river, we had only a three days' supply of food left.

"You see! I made it!" Carlier exclaimed. He stared coldly at the river; there was an ugly look on his face.

"Yes, and now let's head back."

"I made it!" he repeated. A sly smile formed on his lips, as if he had played a good trick on someone.

I pressed him to leave and he followed me indifferently. He did not speak, he looked at nothing. The second day, I killed a turkey, four days later, a red deer. But after that, we went a whole week without encountering any game. Our provisions were now completely gone. I killed a buffalo and roasted a huge chunk of loin which we took along with us; two days later it had to be thrown away.

We decided to take our chances in the next village we should come upon. One morning we saw some huts; upon approaching them, we noticed that no smoke was rising from the village and that no sound could be heard. But I recognized the smell—the foul smell of the meat we had thrown away. Hundreds of bodies were sprawled out on the village grounds; the huts were empty, the storage places for corn and meats were empty.

We continued to walk for two more days and on the third morning, as I was about to lift my pack, Carlier said to me, "I'm staying here. Goodbye."

"I'll stay with you."

"No, leave me alone."

"I'm staying," I insisted.

All day long I scoured the prairie. Once, very far off, a small deer darted from the brush; I shot at it and missed.

"Why did you come back," Carlier asked.

"I'm not going to leave you."

"Go away," he pleaded. "I don't want to die with you looking at me." I hesitated. "All right, I'll leave."

He looked at me distrustfully. "Are you telling me the truth?"

"Yes, that's the truth. Goodbye."

I turned around and walked until I was out of his sight. Then I sat down and leaned my back against a tree. *And now? What's going to become of me now?* If I had never met him, I might have continued to wander aimlessly over the continent for a hundred years, a thousand years. But I *had* met him, I had stopped, and now I could no longer take up my solitary journey again. I watched the moon climbing in the sky and suddenly, through the silence, I heard a single gunshot. I did not move. *For him, it's finished. But for me will it never be possible to crawl out of this body of mine and leave behind only a few dry, naked bones?* The moon was shining as it had shone one night when I dragged myself out of a canal, joyful and shivering, as it had shone on another night above burnt-out houses. That night a dog was howling at death, and now, inside me, I heard that long plaint rising toward the circle of frozen light suspended in the heavens. Never would the light of that dead satellite be obliterated, and never would that bitter taste of solitude and eternity be washed from my life.

※

"Yes, I suppose it had to end that way," Regina said. She stood up and brushed off the sprigs clinging to her skirt. "Let's walk a little."

"It could have ended differently," Fosca said. "He made the choice."

"It had to end that way," she repeated.

The road led to a glade, at the far end of which the roofs of a village could be seen. They walked along in silence.

"I won't have the courage," Regina said, breaking the silence.

"Do you need courage? In just a few more years . . ."

"I'm afraid you don't know what you're talking about."

"It must be reassuring to know that you can stop living whenever you want," Fosca said. "Nothing then is irreparable."

"And I wanted so much to live," Regina said.

"I tried. I went back to Carlier, took his gun and shot myself in the chest and then in the mouth. It stunned me for a while. And then I found myself alive again."

"What did you do after that?" She did not really care what he did; she knew only that he was right. As long as he spoke, as long as she listened to him, there were no questions to ask. She wished his story would never end.

"I walked to the sea and came upon a village lying on the coast. The chief let me live there and I built a hut for myself. I wanted to become one of them, one of those men who lived naked under the sun. I wanted to lose myself."

"It didn't work out?"

"A good many years went by, but the day finally came when I had
to face myself again, and there were still just as many years ahead to
live."

They continued to walk until they reached the village. All the doors
were locked, the shutters closed; not a sound, not a light. In front of
the *Soleil d'Or* was a green bench. They sat down. Through the shutters,
they could hear a sleeper snoring evenly.

"And then?" Regina asked.

BOOK IV

I began to run. My heart was pounding wildly. The yellow waters had leapt from the river bed with a thunderous roar and were rushing toward me. If the foam touched me, my body would be covered with black spots and all at once I would be nothing but ashes dissolving in the boiling water. I ran. My feet barely touched the ground. At the top of the mountain a woman was motioning to me. Catherina! She was waiting for me. I had only to touch her hand and I would be saved. But the ground held fast to my feet; I was in a swamp. I could no longer run. Suddenly the ground gave way. I barely had time to raise my hand and cry out *Catherina!* before I was swallowed up by the molten earth. *This time I am not dreaming. This time I am finally dead for good.*

"Sir!"

All at once the dream shattered into a thousand pieces. I opened my eyes. I saw the canopy of the bed, the window, and through the window, the tall chestnut tree with its branches swaying in the wind; the everyday world, with its distinct colors, its precise configurations, its unchanging, humdrum activities.

"The carriage is waiting, sir."

"Very well."

I closed my eyes and put my arm over them, shutting out the light. I wanted to fall asleep again, to flee somewhere else, not to another world —if it were a world, it would have been the same for me—but to the strange realms of my dreams, those dreams of which I was so fond, dreams in which I escaped along a mysterious thread to the other side of the heavens, to the other side of time itself. There, no matter what happened, I would no longer be myself. I pressed my arm against my face; golden spots danced in the greenish shadows. But I could not fall back to sleep. I heard the sound of the wind in the garden, the sound of footsteps in the corridor; each step rang sharply in my ears. I was awake, and once again the world lay soberly under the sky, and I was lying in the middle of the world with that bitter taste of my life on

my lips. Forever. *Why did he wake me up? Why did they wake me up?*
I angrily thought.

It had happened twenty years earlier. I had passed a good many years
in the Indian village. The sun had burned my skin. Like a snake, I
sloughed it off, and a witch doctor tattooed sacred symbols on my new
body. I ate their foods, sang their war chants; several of their women
lived successively under my roof. They were warm and brown and
velvety. Lying on a straw mat one day, I watched the shadow of a
palm tree extend itself along the sand. It was slowly creeping toward a
large rock sparkling in the sun. The shadow would soon touch the rock;
I *knew* that in just a few moments it would touch the rock, and yet I
could not see it move. Day after day I watched it and never was
I able to catch it moving. I watched closely, intently, and although I
noticed it had advanced the merest fraction of an inch, I could not see
it advancing. And I might have spent years, centuries, watching that
shadow huddle first at the foot of the tree and then lengthen itself
insiduously. I might even have been able to lose myself completely;
the rest of the world might have vanished leaving only the sky, the sea,
the shadow of that palm tree in the sun and myself, who had ceased to
exist. But one day, at the precise instant when the rock was beginning
to turn gray, they appeared and said, "Come with us." They took me
by the arm and pushed me toward their boat; they dressed me in their
clothes and then deposited me on the shores of the old continent. And
now, Bompard, standing in the doorway, was saying, "Shall I have
the horses unhitched?"

I raised myself to my elbows. "Can't you let me sleep in peace?"

"You asked for the carriage at seven."

I got out of bed. I knew that it was useless to try to fall back to
sleep. They had awakened me and now a series of questions, one
insistently following the other, raced through my head. What shall we
do? Where shall we go? And whatever I did, wherever I went, there
was no way of escaping from myself.

I straightened my wig and asked, "Where shall we go?"

"You had planned on visiting Madame de Montesson."

"Haven't you anything more amusing to suggest?"

"Count de Marsenac has been complaining about not seeing you
lately at his suppers."

"And he'll never see me at them again," I said.

How could I ever amuse myself at their timid orgies, I who had heard the screams of children being trampled and women being raped in the streets of Rivella, in the streets of Rome and Gand.

"Think of something else."

"But everything bores you," he said.

"Ah! It's suffocating in this city!"

Paris had seemed immense to me when I first arrived there with a sack full of diamonds and gold ingots slung over my shoulder. But it wasn't long before I had made the rounds of all her cabarets, her theaters, her salons, her squares and gardens. I knew that with a little patience it would be possible in time to name all her inhabitants one by one. And nothing ever happened there but the predictable; even the murders, the brawls, the knifings, were all accounted for in the statistical records the police had established.

"There's no reason why you have to stay in Paris," Bompard said.

"It's suffocating on earth. Everywhere."

The earth, too, had seemed immense to me at one time. I remembered that at one time, atop a hill, I had said to myself, "Out there is the sea, and beyond the sea other continents, without end." But now I knew that the world was round; its circumference had even been measured, and its precise curvature at the equator and between the poles was presently being determined. And they were bent upon making it still smaller by relentlessly inventorying the most minute, the most obscure places and things. They had just drawn up a map of France of such infinite detail that not a single village or stream went unmarked. What good was it to leave? Even before starting out, every voyage was already ended. They had catalogued the plants and animals that thrived on the planet. There were, after all, only a very small number of them, and a very small number of landscapes, of colors, of tastes, odors, faces, for they were always the same, vainly repeating themselves in thousands of copies.

"Well, go to the moon then," Bompard said.

"That's my only hope—to split open the sky."

We went down the stairs in front of the house and I said to the coachman, "Madame de Montesson's."

Before entering the salon I stopped a moment in the hall and derisively looked at myself in a mirror. I was wearing a plum-colored, gold-embroidered, velvet suit; after twenty years, I was still not used to these masquerade costumes. Under my white wig my face seemed to belong to a stranger. But the others appeared to feel perfectly at ease in their absurd clothes. They were small and puny and would have cut a sad figure in Carmona or at the court of Charles V. The women, with their white-powdered hair and red splotches flaming on their cheeks, were, for the most part, ugly. The faces of the men annoyed me; they were constantly in motion: they smiled, their eyes crinkled, their noses twitched, they never stopped speaking or laughing. From the hall, I heard them laughing. In my time, it was left to buffoons to divert us; we laughed in great bursts, but not more than four or five times in an evening, not even happy, carefree Malatesta. I went through the door and noticed with satisfaction that their faces froze, their laughter faded. No one except Bompard knew my secret, but I frightened them. I had amused myself by ruining several of these men and humiliating many of the women. At each of my duels, I had killed my opponent and a legend had grown up around me.

I walked over to the chair in which the mistress of the house was sitting; a circle of people surrounded her. She was a gay, malicious old woman whose verbal stabs sometimes succeeded in diverting me. And I knew she liked me, for she said I was the most malevolent man she had ever known. But for the moment, talking to her was out of the question. Old Damien and little Richet were monopolizing the conversation. They were discussing the role of prejudice in human life. Richet took the defense of objective reasoning. I hated old men because they could feel their whole lives behind them, round and full like a huge cake. And I hated young people because they could feel their futures before them. I hated that look of enthusiasm and intelligence that animated all their faces. Madame de Montesson alone listened coldly to the dispute, pushing her needle back and forth through the tapestry she was working on.

"Both of you are wrong," I abruptly said. "Neither reason nor prejudice is beneficial to man. Nothing is beneficial to man because men are incapable of doing anything for themselves."

"It's just like you to say that," said Marianne de Sinclair disdainfully. She was a tall, rather pretty young woman who filled the function of reader to Madame de Montesson.

"Men can create their own happiness and that of others," said Richet.

I shrugged my shoulders. "They'll never be happy."

"You're wrong. They'll be happy the day they become reasonable," he said.

"They don't even *want* to be happy," I retorted. "They're only too happy to kill time while waiting for time to kill them. You—all of you

—you're simply killing time by dazzling yourselves with your own brilliance."

"What do you know about men?" said Marianne de Sinclair. "You hate them."

Madame de Montesson raised her head and held her needle in suspension above her tapestry.

"Oh! Enough of that!" she exclaimed.

"Yes," I agreed, "enough talk."

Talk. That was all they had to offer me—freedom, happiness, progress. It was on such tasteless meat as this that the people of that era were fed. I turned around and walked to the door; it was suffocating in their tiny rooms, crowded with furniture and knicknacks. There were rugs, Ottomans, and tapestries everywhere, and the air, heavy with perfume, gave me a headache. I glanced around the salon; they had begun their prattling again. I was able to freeze their enthusiasm for a brief moment, but it did not take them long to become animated again. Marianne de Sinclair withdrew to a corner with Richet, where, with gleaming eyes, they engaged in earnest conversation. They agreed with each other and both agreed with themselves. I felt like cracking open their heads with a solid blow of my heel. I went through the door. On the adjacent balcony men were seated around gaming tables. Contrary to the others, they did not speak, did not laugh; their lips were pressed tightly together, their faces were stone. Winning or losing money—that, apparently, was the principal diversion they had found in life. In my time, horses galloped across plains, we held lances in our hands. In my time . . . Suddenly I thought, "But this century, this year, this day, isn't this also my time?"

I looked at my shoes with their jewelled buckles, at my lace cuffs. For twenty years it seemed to me that I had been playing a game, and that one day, at the stroke of midnight, I would return to the land of shadows. I glanced up at the clock. Above its gilt face, a porcelain shepherdess was smiling at a shepherd. A little earlier, the hands were pointing to midnight; they would point to midnight tomorrow and the day after tomorrow, and I would still be there. There was no other land for me but this planet, and I felt as if I no longer belonged. An outsider. I had been at home in Carmona and in the court of Charles V, but that was long before. The years that would now stretch out endlessly before me would be years of exile. All my clothes would be costumes and my life a perpetual play.

The Count de Saint-Ange walked past me; he was very pale. I stopped him. "Aren't you playing any more?" I asked.

"I've already played too much," he answered. "I lost everything."

There were beads of sweat on his brow. He was weak and stupid, but he was a man of his times, at home in the world in which he lived, and I envied him. I took some money from my pocket. "Here, see if you can win something back."

He grew even paler. "And if I lose?"

"You'll win. In the end one always wins."

With a brusque gesture he took the stake and sat down at a table. His hands were trembling. I leaned on the back of his chair; that particular game amused me. If he lost, what would he do? Kill himself? Throw himself at my feet? Would he sell me his wife like the Marquis de Vintenon? Sweat gathered on his upper lip. He was losing. He was losing and he felt his life beating in his chest, burning in his temples. He was risking his life. He was living. *And I? Will I never feel what even the most wretched among them feel?* I stood erect and walked to another table. *At least I can lose my fortune.* I sat down and threw a fistful of gold Louis on the felt-covered table.

A stir swept across the balcony. Baron de Sarcelles came over and sat down in front of me. He was one of the richest financiers in Paris.

"Well, now," he said. "This is a game that promises to be interesting."

He too threw a handful of gold Louis on the table and we played out our cards in silence. After half an hour, not a single Louis was left before me and my pockets were empty.

"I'll bet fifty thousand crowns on my word," I said.

"Very well."

A crowd of people was now pressing around our chairs, holding their breath, staring at the bare green felt. When Sarcelles laid down his hand and I threw my cards into the pack, sighs and gasps escaped from their mouths.

"Double or nothing," I said.

"Double or nothing."

He dealt the cards. I looked at their shiny backs and felt my heart beginning to beat a little faster. If I could lose, lose everything, perhaps my life's taste would change . . .

"Pat," said Sarcelles.

"Two cards," I said. I looked at the cards. Four kings. I knew I had Sarcelles beaten.

"Raise you ten thousand," he said.

I hesitated for a second. I could have thrown in my cards and said, "You win." But something—perhaps it was anger—made a knot form in my throat. Was I reduced to *that?* Was I going to cheat myself out of winning? Was it forever forbidden to me now to live without cheating?

"I'll see you," I said, laying down my cards.

"The money will be at your home before noon tomorrow," Sarcelles promised.

I bowed, crossed the room and went back into the salon. The Count de Saint-Ange was leaning against a wall; he looked as if he were about to faint.

"I lost everything you loaned me," he said.

"He who doesn't want to lose, doesn't lose," I admonished him.

"When would you like to be paid?"

"In twenty-four hours. Isn't that the way it's usually done?"

"I can't," he said. "I haven't got that much money."

"Then you shouldn't have borrowed."

I turned my back to him and my eyes met those of Mademoiselle de Sinclair. They were sparking with anger.

"There are crimes the law doesn't punish, yet which are even more infamous than murder," she said.

"I'm not against murder," I said blandly.

We silently stared at each other. That woman, at least, wasn't afraid of me. She abruptly turned away; I took her by the arm.

"You have a great aversion for me, haven't you?"

"What other feeling can you expect to inspire?"

I smiled. "You don't know me well enough. You ought to invite me to your little Saturday gatherings. I promise I'll open my heart to you . . ."

My words seemed to strike a soft spot; her cheeks flushed slightly. Madame de Montesson was unaware that some of the salon's habitués had been visiting her reader's home. And she wasn't the woman to pardon Marianne for that.

"I only invite my friends," she said.

"It's better to have me for a friend than an enemy."

"Are you trying to bargain with me?"

"Take it as you like."

"My friendship cannot be bought," she said, rather heatedly.

"We'll talk about it again another time. Think it over."

"I've already thought it over."

I pointed to Bompard who was dozing in a large, deep armchair. "Do you see that fat, bald man over there?"

"Yes."

"When I first came to Paris some years ago, he was a gifted and ambitious young man. At that time I was nothing but an ignorant savage and he tried to make a fool of me. Well, look what I've made of him."

"Nothing you do could ever surprise me."

"I didn't tell you that to surprise you, but only to make you think."

At that moment I saw the Count de Saint-Ange leaving the salon. He was walking unsteadily, like a drunken man.

"Bompard!" I called out.

Bompard started. I like to watch him waking up. He would find himself back among the realities of his life, he would find me there waiting for him, and then he would remember that until the very hour of his death he would faithfully continue to find me there at each awakening.

"Let's follow him," I said.

"What's it all about?" Bompard asked.

"He has to pay me twenty thousand crowns tomorrow. And he hasn't got them. I wonder if he'll be stupid enough to kill himself."

"Of course," said Bompard. "There's nothing else he can do."

Following Saint-Ange we crossed the courtyard of the residence.

"How in the name of God can that still amuse you?" Bompard asked. "Haven't you seen enough corpses in five hundred years?"

"He might board a ship for India, go begging in the streets; he might even try to kill me. Then again he might continue to live out his days in Paris, peaceably and dishonored."

"He won't do any of those things," Bompard said.

I shrugged my shoulders. "No doubt you're right. They all do the same thing."

Saint-Ange went into the gardens of the Royal Palace and slowly walked along the colonnades. I hid myself behind a pillar; I enjoyed watching flies, spiders, the convulsions of frogs, the merciless death struggles of scarabs. But what I liked above all was to witness the combat of a man against himself. Nothing was forcing him to kill himself. If he did not want to die, he had only to decide: "I will not kill myself."

A shot rang out and then I heard a soft thud. I walked over to the body and felt the same disappointment as always. While they were alive, their deaths were events I watched for with great curiosity. But when I looked down upon their corpses, it seemed to me that they had never existed. Their deaths were nothing.

We left the gardens. "Do you know the meanest trick you could play on me?" I said to Bompard.

"No."

"To shoot yourself in the head. Doesn't the prospect tempt you?"

"It would make you too happy," he replied.

"On the contrary. I'd be greatly disappointed." I slapped him amiably on the shoulder. "Fortunately, you're too much of a coward. You'll stay with me a long time—until you die in your bed."

Something awakened in his eyes. "Are you certain you'll never die?"

"Poor Bompard! Yes, I'm afraid for your sake that I shall never die. Nor shall I ever burn those papers you worry so much about. Bompard, my friend, you'll never be delivered of me." The light that had glowed for a moment in his eyes faded. "Never," I repeated. "That's a word the meaning of which no one knows, not even you."

He did not answer.

"Let's go home and do some work," I said.

"Are you going to stay up all night again?" he asked.

"Certainly."

"But I want to sleep."

"Oh, well! You shall sleep, then," I said, smiling.

Tormenting him hardly ever entertained me any more. I had ruined his life, but he had grown to accept it, and now he slept soundly through the nights. He slept and he forgot. The worst disasters never kept him from stretching out in his bed and falling asleep. Saint-Ange had trembled in anguish, but now he was dead, he had escaped me. For them there was always a way of escaping. But for me, on this earth to which I was eternally bound, happiness was worth no more or less than unhappiness, hate was as insipid as love. There was nothing they could do for me.

The carriage brought us back to the house and I went directly to my laboratory; I should never have left it. Only there, far from human life, was I sometimes able to forget myself.

Many astonishing discoveries had been made during my long absence from Europe. Upon landing on the old continent, I had learned to my amazement that the earth, which I had always believed stood motionless in the middle of the heavens, actually turned both on its own axis and around the sun. Some of the most mysterious phenomena—lightning, rainbows, the tides—had been fully explained. It had been proven that air had weight and the method of weighing it was now well known. The earth had shrunk, but the universe had grown larger; the sky was now peopled with new stars that astronomers had brought into human view with their improved telescopes. Due to the microscope, an invisible world had been revealed. In nature's breast hitherto unknown forces had been brought to light and were gradually being tamed and harnessed. But the men who had made these discoveries displayed a profound stupidity in being so proud of them, for they would never know history's last word in the matter; they would all be dead before that distant time. But I . . . I would profit from their efforts, I would *know*. The day when science finally reached its ultimate conclusions, I would be there. They had labored for me. I looked at the flasks, the beakers, at all the idle apparatus. I picked up a glass slide; it was there, perfectly calm in my fingers, a piece of glass no different than all the other pieces of glass I had seen and touched during the five hundred years of my life. All the objects around me were silent, inert, as they had always been, and yet I had only to rub this piece of matter to make unknown forces rise to its surface. Within that seemingly calm object, obscure powers were waiting to be unleashed. In the very air I breathed, the earth I trod upon, mysteries constantly throbbed. A whole invisible world, stranger and more unpredictable than the images of my dreams, was hiding within this old universe of which I had grown so weary. Inside the four walls surrounding me, I felt freer than in the adventureless streets, than on the infinite plains of America. One day, all the forms, all the worn-out colors of the world would burst apart; one day I would pierce through the immutable sky in which the four seasons were inexorably reflected; one day I would gaze upon the other side of this illusory decor which had always ensnared men's eyes and minds. I could not even imagine what I would see then, but it was enough for me to know that it would be something else, something totally different. Perhaps it would be inaccessible to the eyes, to the ears, to the hands; perhaps then I would be able to forget forever that I had eyes and ears and hands; perhaps I would at last become someone other than myself, *for* myself.

🜨

A dark gray deposit remained in the bottom of the retort. "It failed," Bompard said jeeringly.

"That only proves there are impurities in this carbon," I said. "We'll just have to start all over again."

"But we've already tried it a hundred times," he protested.

I tilted the retort and spread out the ashes on a slide. Were those ashes merely the residue of foreign matter? Or did carbon possess some sort of an indestructible skeleton.

"We'll have to perform the experiment with a diamond," I said.

Bompard shrugged his shoulders skeptically. "How can you burn a diamond?"

In the back of the laboratory, a fire was quietly glowing. Outside, evening was falling. I walked over to a glass door leading to the balcony. The first stars were beginning to pierce through the sky's dark blue; there were still few enough so that they could be counted. Lurking in the dusk, millions upon millions of others were waiting to make their appearance. And behind these, there were still others that remained invisible to our feeble eyes. The same stars always appeared first. For thousands of years the celestial vault had remained unchanged; there had been the same icy twinkling above my head for centuries.

I went back to the table where Bompard had set the microscope. In the salons the habitués were beginning to arrive, women were preening themselves for a ball, laughter would soon ring out in the cabarets. For them, the evening that had just begun was different from all other evenings, unique. I put my eye to the ocular and looked at the gray dust. Then suddenly I felt the violence inside me of that storm wind I knew so well. It rushed through the calm laboratory, swept away the flasks, ripped the roof from above my head, and my life shot up toward the heavens like a flame, like a scream. I felt it in my heart; it burned, it leapt from my chest. I felt it at the tips of my fingers—a desire to break, to thrash, to strangle. My hands tightened on the microscope.

"Let's get out of here!" I said.

"You want to go out now?"

"Yes. Come along with me."

"I'd much rather go to sleep."

"You sleep too much," I said. "You're getting fat." I shook my head. "How sad it is to grow old!"

"Oh, I'd just as soon be in my skin as yours," he said.

"That's admirable of you, you know, to face so much misfortune so cheerfully. And yet you were rather ambitious in your youth, weren't you?"

"What strengthens my soul," he said smilingly, "is that I could never possibly be as unhappy as you."

I threw my coat over my shoulders, took my hat and said, "I'm thirsty. Give me something to drink."

Was I really thirsty? There was a painful need gnawing at my whole body, a need that was neither for food, nor for drink, nor for woman. I took the glass that Bompard held out to me and swallowed its contents in one gulp. Grimacing, I set it down on an end table.

"I can understand your predilection for the experimental method," I said. "If a man assured me he was immortal, I would certainly attempt to determine the truth of that statement. But I beg you, *stop spoiling my wine with your arsenic!*"

"You should have died a hundred times over," he said bitterly.

"You'd better resign yourself to it," I said. "I'll *never* die." I smiled at him. I knew perfectly how to imitate their smiles. "Besides, it would be a great loss for you. You haven't a better friend in the whole world than I."

"Nor you than I," he said.

I decided to go to Madame de Montesson's. Why did I feel like seeing their faces again? I knew there was nothing I could expect from them. And yet I could not stand the thought that they were alive under the sky while I was alone in my tomb.

Madame de Montesson was sitting by the fireplace working on her tapestry; her friends formed a circle around her chair. Nothing had changed. Marianne de Sinclair was serving coffee and Richet was looking at her with an oafish expression on his face. They were laughing, talking. No one, during all these weeks, had noticed my absence. Angrily I thought, *But I'll make them notice my presence.*

I went over to Marianne de Sinclair. "Coffee?" she calmly asked.

"No thank you. I don't need your drugs."

"As you like."

They were laughing, talking; they were happy to be together, persuaded that they were living, that they were content. There was no way of convincing them of the contrary.

"Have you thought about our last conversation?" I asked.

"No," she replied, smiling. "I think of you as little as possible."

"I see that you're determined to hate me."

"I'm a very determined person."

"And I'm no less so," I said. "I've heard that your gatherings are extremely interesting. It seems that the most advanced ideas are bandied about at them and that the best minds of the century scorn this venerable salon to group themselves around you . . ."

"Excuse me," she said, "but I have to serve coffee."

"Then I think I'll go have a little chat with Madame de Montesson."

"Whatever you like."

I walked over to the mistress of the house and leaned against her chair. She always welcomed me warmly; my maliciousness amused her. While we were discussing the latest gossip of the court and the city, I caught Marianne de Sinclair looking at me. She immediately turned her eyes away. But it was useless for her to pretend indifference; I knew very well she was worried. I bore no grudge against her, for although she hated me, it was never really I who was hated—or loved. It was a borrowed self for whom I felt only indifference. As for my true self, what feelings could I inspire? Beatrice had said to me one day: neither miserly nor generous, neither courageous nor cowardly, neither evil nor good. In truth, I was no one. I followed Marianne de Sinclair with my eyes as she came and went across the room. There was something in her noble and nonchalant bearing that I liked. Under the feathery cloud that covered her head, a rolling mass of light brown hair could be discerned; blue eyes sparkled in her ardent face. No, I wished her no harm. But I was curious to know what would happen to her calm dignity when faced with adversity.

"There aren't many people here this evening," I said.

Madame de Montesson lifted her head and glanced rapidly around the room. "The weather is bad."

"And I believe the taste for disinterested conversation is waning. People are becoming more and more inflamed with politics . . ."

"Politics will never be discussed under my roof," she said authoritatively.

"You're right," I said. "A salon is a salon and not a club. It seems that Mademoiselle de Sinclair's Saturdays are degenerating into public meetings . . ."

"What Saturdays? What are you talking about?"

"Don't you know about them?" I asked.

She glared at me with her small, penetrating eyes. "You're well aware I know nothing about them. Marianne receives on Saturdays? Since when?"

"Oh, it's been going on for about six months now. I've heard reports that her little gatherings are quite brilliant. Her guests constantly labor at demolishing and reconstructing the social order."

"Ah! the sly little thing!" she said with a small laugh. "Demolish and reconstruct the social order . . . it must be fascinating!"

She leaned over her tapestry again and I took leave of her. Little Richet, who was speaking animatedly to Marianne de Sinclair, walked toward me.

"You've just done a vile thing," he said heatedly.

I smiled. He had a large mouth and round eyes, and despite the obvious sincerity of his anger, his effort to appear dignified only accentuated his naivety. He lent himself to laughter.

"You will answer to me, sir, for that foul act," he said.

I continued to smile. He was trying to provoke me. He did not know I had no honor to defend, no anger to satisfy. And neither was there anything to stop me from slapping him, beating him, throwing him to the ground. I was subject to none of their conventions. If they knew to what degree I was free from them and their inane rules, then they would have been really frightened of me.

"Stop laughing," he half shouted.

He was disconcerted; he hadn't foreseen that it would turn out this way. All the courage and pride he had mustered for the occasion was not enough to bear my smile.

"Are you that anxious to die?" I asked.

"I'm anxious to rid the world of your presence," he replied.

In the heat of his passion, he failed to realize that that death of which he was so defiant might strike *him* rather than me. And yet I had only to speak a word . . .

"Would you care to meet me at five o'clock at the Passy gate? Bring two seconds along." I looked at him steadily and added, "I don't think a doctor will be necessary. I never wound my adversaries. I kill them outright."

"At five o'clock at the Passy gate."

He crossed the room, said a few words to Marianne de Sinclair and walked to the door. Before leaving, he turned around and looked at her, thinking perhaps that it was the last time he would ever see her. A moment before, he had thirty or forty years of life ahead of him. And then suddenly, only one night. When he left I went over to Marianne.

"You take considerable interest in Richet, don't you?" I asked her.

She paused a moment before answering. She wanted to crush me with scorn, but she also wanted to know what I was going to say.

"I take an interest in all my friends," she said. Her voice was icy, but under that mask of indifference I could feel her curiosity throbbing.

"Did he tell you we were going to fight a duel?"

"No."

"I've fought twelve duels in my life, and on each occasion I killed my opponent."

The blood rushed to her cheeks. She could control her handsome body, her facial expressions, the movement of her lips, her voice, but she was unable to prevent herself from blushing. And when she blushed, she seemed very young and very vulnerable.

"You're not going to kill a child?" she said. "He's a mere child!"

"Do you love him?" I abruptly asked her.

"What difference does it make to you?"

"If you love him, I'll take care not to harm him."

She looked at me in anguish; she was searching for the word that would save Richet, trying to avoid the one that might lose him. In a trembling voice, she said, "I don't love him, but I have the most tender affection for him. I beg you to spare him."

"If I spare him, would you consider me as a friend?"

"I would be extremely grateful to you."

"And how would you prove it to me?"

"By treating you as a friend. My door would be open to you every Saturday."

I laughed. "I'm afraid your door will no longer be open to anyone on Saturdays. Madame de Montesson doesn't seem to appreciate your little gatherings very much."

Again she reddened and looked at me in a sort of stupor. "I'm sorry for you," she said. "I'm very sorry for you."

The sadness in her voice was so sincere that I made no attempt at answering her. I stood there without moving, as if nailed to the floor. Was there someone who still existed behind the phantom I had become, someone with a living heart? It seemed to me that it was I, the real I whom those words had struck. Her eyes had pierced through me. Under the costumes, the masks, under that hard armor the centuries had forged around me, I was there; it was I—a pitiable being who found his greatest pleasures in committing shabby acts of malice. It was really I for whom she felt sorry, such as she did not know me, such as I was.

"Listen to me . . ."

She had disappeared. And what, in any event, would I have been able to say to her? What true words could have passed from me to her? One thing was certain: I had had her driven from that house and she felt sorry for me. And all my excuses, like all my challenges, would have never been anything but lies.

I went out the door. Outside, the moonlit night was fresh and beautiful. The streets were deserted; people were settled down for the evening in their salons, in their garrets—at home. Nowhere was I at home; the house in which I lived had never been a home to me. A camping place. This century wasn't my century, and this life of mine which went on interminably, uselessly, wasn't my life. I turned a corner and found myself on a street bordering the river. I saw the apse of the cathedral with its white flying buttresses and its statues which formed a solemn procession descending from the rooftop. The river was flowing cold and black between ivy-tapestried walls. Sunk in the depths of its waters was the round moon. I walked, and as I walked it followed me, in the depths of the water, in the depths of the sky, the hated moon, my companion of five hundred years, chilling everything with its icy look. I leaned against a stone parapet. The church loomed up before me, rigid in the deathly light, and like myself, lonely and inhuman. All those puny men surrounding us would die and we would live on. *One day it too will collapse and there will be nothing where it stood but a mass of ruins. And then one day no trace at all will be left of it, and the moon will be shining in the sky, and I will still be here.*

I continued to follow the river. Perhaps Richet, at that very moment, was looking at the moon and the stars, thinking, "This is the last time I shall ever see them." Perhaps he was thinking of Marianne de Sinclair, remembering each of her smiles and asking himself, "Have I seen her for the last time?" In fear, in hope, he was feverishly awaiting the dawn. If I had been mortal, my heart would also have been beating, that night would have been without equal, the pale glimmer in the sky would have been death motioning to me, waiting for me at the end of the ghostly street. But no, nothing ever happened to me; the duel was a fake. Always the same adventureless, joyless, painless nights. A single night and a single day, repeating themselves throughout eternity.

The sky was beginning to grow white when I arrived at the Passy gate. I sat down at the edge of an embankment. Within me I heard a voice: "I'm sorry for you." She was right. It was a pitiful being who was sitting on that embankment, waiting to commit an absurd murder. Cities had been burned to the ground, armies had slaughtered each other, an empire had been born and collapsed in my hands. And I was there, empty, stupid; I was about to kill another man without risk and without joy. To occupy my time. Was there anyone to feel more sorry for than I?

The last star had just faded when I saw Richet coming toward me. He was walking slowly, looking down at his shoes wet with dew. And suddenly, out of the distant past, a brief moment of my life flashed through my mind, a moment that had happened so long ago I believed it forever buried. I was sixteen. It was a hazy morning and I was astride my horse, a lance in my hand. The armor of the Genoese gleamed in the dawn's faint light, and I was afraid. And because I was afraid, the light was softer, the dew fresher than on any other morning. A voice inside me repeated over and over again: "Be brave." No one before or since ever spoke to me with such fervent affection. And now the voice was stilled, the dawns had lost their freshness; I no longer knew either fear or courage. I stood up. Richet held out a sword to me. Around him morning was being born for the last time; for the last time, the fresh smell of earth was rising in the air. He was ready to die and he held his whole life against his heart.

"No," I said.

He held out the sword to me, but I stood motionless, my hand did not move from my side. No, I was not going to fight. I looked at the two men behind Richet.

"I refuse to fight. Bear witness to it."

"Why?" asked Richet. He had a troubled, disappointed look on his face.

"I don't feel like fighting. I prefer to apologize to you."

"But you're not afraid of me. I know it," he said in astonishment.

"I repeat, I offer you my complete apologies."

He stood planted there before me, disconcerted, his heart overflowing with all his useless courage, useless like my hate, my anger, and my envy. For a moment he was, as I, lost under the sky, cut off from his life, then thrown back into that life, not knowing what to do with

himself. I turned my back to him and strode rapidly toward the road.
In the distance a cock was crowing.

🖋

I dug my cane into the ant hill and shook it from side to side. They
came streaming out, all of them black, all alike, thousands of ants,
thousands of times the same ant. In a remote corner of the grounds
that surrounded my country house, they had spent twenty long years
in building their plump mound, which was so teeming with life that the
grass itself seemed alive. They ran in every direction, even more helter-
skelter than the bubbles that danced over the flames in my retorts.
And yet they seemed to pursue their plans with a stubborn single-
mindedness. Were there among them some who were zealous and some
who were lazy, some giddy-headed, some serious? Or did they all
work with the same stupid ardor? I wished I could have followed them
one by one with my eyes, but no sooner did I pick one out than it
became lost in that monstrous ballet. The only way of distinguishing
them would have been to tie ribbons around their bodies—red, green,
yellow . . .

"Well! Do you think you'll learn their language?" asked Bompard.

I raised my head. It was a lovely June day. The sweet smell of the
linden trees filled the warm air. Bompard, smiling, was holding a rose
in his hand.

"It's my own creation," he said proudly.

"It looks like any other rose to me," I said.

He shrugged his shoulders. "That's because you haven't got eyes to
see with."

He went off. Even since we had withdrawn to Crécy he spent his
leisure in grafting rose bushes. I again looked down at the scurrying
ants, but they no longer held my interest. In the special furnace I had
had built, a diamond was being consumed in the bottom of a golden
crucible. Neither did that interest me. I knew that in a few years every
schoolboy would know the secrets of the elements and compounds; I
had all the time I needed before me to discover them. I lay down on
my back, stretched myself out and looked at the sky. Its blue was no
different for me than for anyone else, the same blue that filled the
skies above Carmona on beautiful spring days. And like everyone else,
I smelled the sweet odor of roses and linden trees. Yet, I would let this

springtime go by without living it. Here, a new rose had just been born; there, the meadows were strewn with the snowy petals of almond trees. And I, a stranger both here and there, would pass through this season of flowers like a dead man.

"Sir!" Again Bompard was standing before me. "There's a lady who would like to speak to you. She's come from Paris by coach and wants to see you personally."

"A lady?" I said, surprised.

I got up, brushed the dirt off my clothes and walked toward the house. *It might kill an hour*, I thought. Seated in a wicker chair in the shade of a tall linden tree, I saw Marianne de Sinclair. She was wearing a linen dress with lilac-colored stripes, and her unpowdered locks of hair fell softly to her shoulders. I bowed to her.

"What a surprise!" I said.

"I hope I'm not disturbing you?"

"Not at all."

I had not forgotten the sound of her voice. *I'm sorry for you.* She had uttered those words, and the phantom I had become was suddenly transformed into a man of flesh and bones. And it was that malicious, guilty man who now stood before her. Was it hate, scorn, or pity that I saw in her eyes? The anguished shame which gripped my heart once again bore witness to the fact that it was I, the real I, at whom she was looking. She turned her head away.

"How pretty these grounds are," she said. "Do you like the country?" A brief silence followed, and then she resumed somewhat haltingly, "I've been wanting to see you for a long time. I wanted to thank you for having spared Richet's life."

Brusquely, I said, "You don't have to thank me. I didn't do it because of you."

"That doesn't matter," she said. "What matters is that you acted generously."

"It wasn't generosity," I said impatiently.

It irritated me that she could have been duped, she too, by that foreign being who, as a result of chance acts, had molded himself around me.

She smiled. "I suppose that whenever you do something worthy, you always find evil motives for it."

"Did you think my motives were good when I told Madame de Montesson about you?" I asked.

"Oh, I don't say that you're not capable of cruelty, too," she said in a calm tone of voice.

Perplexed, I carefully studied her. She looked much younger than when I had last seen her in Madame de Montesson's salon, and she seemed more beautiful, too. What had she come for?

"You don't bear any grudge against me?" I asked.

"No. In fact, you did me a great service," she said gayly. "I wasn't going to spend the rest of my life as a slave to a selfish old woman, and you created the breach."

"Well! So much the better! And to think that I almost felt remorse because of that incident."

"You'd have been wrong. My life is much more interesting now." There was a touch of defiance in her voice.

"Did you come here to offer me absolution?" I asked dryly.

She shook her head. "I came to talk to you about a project . . ."

"A project?"

"For quite a long time now my friends and I have wanted to found an independent university to make up for the insufficiencies of official teaching. We believe the development of the scientific spirit will have a great influence on social and political progress." She cut herself off and held out a notebook to me which had been in her hand. Then, in the same timid manner as she had begun, she said, "All our ideas are set forth in here."

I took the notebook and opened it. It began with a rather long dissertation on the advantages of the experimental method and the moral and political consequences which could be expected to result from its diffusion; next, a curriculum was proposed for the future university; in conclusion, a few pages written in a firm and impassioned tone, announced the advent of a better world. I laid the tract on my knees.

"Did you draft it?"

A slightly embarrassed smile appeared on her face. "Yes," she answered.

"I admire your faith."

"Faith alone isn't enough. We need collaborators and money. A great deal of money."

I laughed. "You came here to ask me for money?"

"Yes. We've opened a subscription list. I hope you'll be the first to make a donation. And we'd be even happier if you would consider accepting a chair in chemistry."

After a few moments of silence, I said, "What gave you the idea to come to me?"

"You're very rich," she answered frankly. "And you're a great scientist. Everyone is talking about the work you've done with carbon."

"But you *know* me. You've reproached me often enough for hating mankind. What made you think I'd agree to help you?"

Her face grew animated, her eyes more brilliant. "On the contrary. I *don't* know you. You might turn me down, but you might accept, too. I decided to take a chance."

"And why should I accept? To make up for the wrong I did you?"

She stiffened. "I told you that you did me no wrong."

"For the pleasure of doing you a favor, then?"

"In the interest of science and humanity."

"I'm not interested in science except insofar as it is inhuman."

"It amazes me how you dare to hate people," she said in a sudden flash of anger. "You're rich, learned, free; you do everything you like, while most of mankind lives in misery and ignorance, enslaved by joyless work. And you never in your life tried to help them. *They* should hate *you*."

Her voice was so full of passion that I felt called upon to defend myself. But how could I tell her the truth?

"At bottom, I think I envy them," I said.

"You?"

"They're alive. For years now, I haven't been able to feel alive."

"Ah! I knew it!" she said in a compassionate tone of voice. "I knew you were very unhappy."

I abruptly stood up. "Come, let's take a walk through the grounds, since you find them so pretty."

"I'd love to."

She took my arm and we strolled alongside the river in which goldfish were lazily swimming.

"Even on such a beautiful day as this, don't you feel alive?"

"No."

With her fingertips she touched one of the roses Bompard had created. "Isn't there anything here you like?" she asked.

I plucked the rose and held it out to her. "I'd like this rose, if you were wearing it."

She smiled, took the flower and deeply breathed in its fragrance.

"It says things to you, doesn't it?" I said. "What does it tell you?"

"That it's wonderful to be alive," she said gayly.

"It tells me nothing. For me things have no voice."

I looked hard at the saffron-colored rose, but there had been too many roses in my life, too many springtimes.

"That's only because you don't know how to listen to them."

We walked for a while in silence. She looked at the trees and flowers. No sooner did she turn her eyes from me than I felt my life abandoning me.

"I'm curious to know what you think of me," I said.

"I used to think very ill of you."

"What made you change your opinion?"

"Your actions toward Richet made me see you in a new light."

I shrugged my shoulders. "That was pure capriciousness."

I felt as if I were deceiving her. I was ashamed. But it was impossible to explain to her . . .

"It would be a mistake, of course, to take me for a good-hearted soul," I said.

She smiled. "I'm not stupid, you know."

"And yet you hope to interest me in the happiness of humanity."

She pushed a pebble along the path with her foot and did not answer.

"Look here," I said. "Do you believe I'll give you that money or don't you? Which way do you bet, yes or no?"

She looked at me gravely. "I don't know," she said. "You're free to do as you please."

For the second time she touched my heart. It was true; I was free. All the centuries through which I had lived rushed forth like moths and died at the edge of that glowing moment which burst out under the blue sky, that moment as new, as unforeseen as if the past had never existed. In that instant I decided to give Marianne an answer that had never before been inscribed in any of the forgotten moments of my life. And it was I, yes, it was I who had decided. I had made the choice between disappointing Marianne or gratifying her.

"Must I decide right now?"

"As you like," she said rather coldly.

I looked at her. Disappointed or gratified, she would walk down the road, pass through the gate, and there would be nothing left for me but to go back and stretch myself out on the grass near the ant hill.

"When will you give me your answer?" she asked.

I paused. I felt like saying "Tomorrow" to be sure of seeing her again. But I did not say it. In her presence, it was I who spoke, who acted—the real I. It would have shamed me to exploit the situation because of a mere whim.

"Right away," I said. "Would you mind waiting for just a moment?"

I returned a few minutes later with a bill of exchange in my hand. When I gave it to Marianne, the blood rushed to her cheeks.

"But it's a fortune!" she exclaimed.

"It's not my whole fortune."

"But it must be a large part . . ."

"Didn't you tell me you needed a great deal of money?"

She looked at the paper, then at my face. "I don't understand," she said.

"You can't understand everything."

Stupefied, she stood motionless before me.

"It's late," I said. "You ought to leave. I don't believe we have anything further to talk about."

"I have one more favor to ask of you," she said slowly.

"But you're insatiable!"

"Neither my friends nor I know much about business. It seems that you're a skillful financier. Help us get our university started."

"Is it in your interest or mine that you ask me that?"

She seemed abashed. "Both," she said.

"More one or more the other?"

She hesitated. She loved life so much that she always had confidence in the effectiveness of truth.

"I believe that the day you decide to get out of yourself, a lot of things will change for you . . ."

"Why do you take so much interest in me?" I asked.

"Can't you understand that it's quite possible for someone to take an interest in you?"

For a moment we stood silently facing each other.

"I'll think it over," I said. "And I'll come and bring you my answer."

"Twelve, rue des Ciseaux. That's where I live now." She held out her hand. "Thank you."

"Twelve, rue des Ciseaux," I repeated. "And it's I who should be thanking you."

She climbed into the carriage and I listened to the sound of the wheels as they rolled off along the road. Then, with both arms I hugged

the trunk of a tall linden tree, pressed my cheek against its rough bark
and thought with desire, with anguish, "Will I again become a living
man?"

ιч

There was a knock at my door. Marianne entered and came over
to my desk.

"Still at work?" she said.

I smiled. "As you see."

"I'm sure you haven't left this room all day long."

"You're right."

"Did you at least eat something?" she asked. I hesitated for a moment
and she said half-angrily, "Naturally you didn't eat. You're going to
ruin your health."

She gave me a worried look and I felt ashamed. Not to eat, not to
sleep; to give of my fortune, of my time did not have the same meaning for her as it did for me. I was, in effect, lying to her.

"If I hadn't come, I'm sure you'd have stayed here all night," she said.

"I get bored when I'm not working."

She broke into a laugh. "Don't make excuses for yourself." With
a firm hand, she pushed away the papers scattered in front of me.
"That's enough of that. Now you must have some dinner."

I glanced regretfully at the desk piled high with papers and folders,
at the drapes covering the windows, at the opaque walls. My Paris
residence had become the center of planning for the future university,
and I felt at ease in this study, with precise tasks before me to execute.
As long as I was here, I had no desire to go elsewhere. It was out of the
question . . .

"Where shall I have dinner?" I asked.

"There are lots of places . . ."

Abruptly, I said, "Come with me."

She hesitated. "But Sophie is waiting for me."

"Let her wait."

She looked at me. There was a trace of a smile on her lips and she
asked coquettishly, "Would that really make you happy?"

I shrugged my shoulders. How could I explain that I sought her
company simply to kill time, that I needed her to live. Words would
betray me; I would say either too much or too little. I wanted to be

sincere with her, but sincerity was a luxury I could no longer afford.

"Of course," I said briefly.

She seemed somewhat disconcerted and then said with assurance, "All right, take me to that new cabaret everyone is talking about. I've been told they have wonderful food."

"Dagorneau's?"

"That's it."

Her eyes sparkled. She always knew where to go, what to do; she always had desires or curiosities to satisfy. Had it been given to me to follow her all through life, I would always have known what to do with myself.

We went down the stairs and I asked, "Shall we walk?"

"Of course," she replied. "It's such a bright, lovely night."

"Ah! So you like the moon!" I said bitterly.

"Don't you?"

"I hate it."

She laughed. "Your feelings are always excessive."

"When all of us are dead, it will still be there, sneering in the heavens."

"I don't envy it," Marianne said. "I'm not afraid of death."

"Really? If you were told that you were going to die in a little while, you mean to say you wouldn't be afraid?"

"Ah! But I want to die when the time is ripe."

She walked with rapid little steps, avidly absorbing the sweetness of the night through her eyes, her ears, through every pore in her body.

"It's remarkable how much you love life," I said.

"Yes, I do love life very much."

"Are there ever times when you're unhappy?"

"Occasionally. But that too is part of living."

"I'd like to ask you one question," I said.

"Ask it."

"Were you ever in love?"

"No," she answered without hesitation.

"And yet you have a passionate nature."

"That's just it," she said. "Other people always seem indifferent, luke-warm. They're not alive . . ."

I felt a small wrench in my heart. "And neither am I alive."

"You told me that once before," she said. "But it's not true, not true

at all. You're excessive in both good and evil! you can't stand medioc-
rity. That's being alive." She looked at me steadily. "At bottom, your
meanness was simply a form of revolt."

"You don't know me," I said dryly.

She reddened and we walked the rest of the way to the cabaret in
silence. A stairway led down to a large vaulted room with smoke-
blackened beams. Waiters wearing brightly colored caps were scurrying
about among the tables around which noisy groups were crowded together. We sat down at a small, round table all the way in the back
and I ordered supper.

After the waiter had placed the hors d'oeuvre and a decanter of pink
wine in front of us, Marianne asked me, "Why do you always get so
angry whenever I suggest that you're capable of good?"

"I feel as if I'm being an imposter."

"Well, isn't it true that you give your time, your money, and your
pains unsparingly to our enterprise?"

"But it doesn't cost me anything," I answered.

"Precisely. That's what I consider true generosity. You give your
all and yet you always feel as if it costs you nothing."

I filled our glasses with the wine. "Have you forgotten already what
I used to be like?"

"No," she replied. "But you've changed."

"One never changes."

"Ah! That I don't believe. If people never changed, all our work
would be for nothing," she said spiritedly. She looked at me thoughtfully. "I'm certain that now you would not be able to divert yourself
by pushing a man to suicide."

"I think that's probably true."

"You see."

She lifted a piece of *paté de foie* to her mouth. When she ate she had
a serious, animal look about her. Despite the graceful reserve of her
gestures, she gave the appearance of a wolf transformed into a woman.
Her teeth shone with a cruel sparkle. How could I explain it to her?
To commit evil no longer amused me. But I had not become any better
for that. *Neither good nor bad, neither miserly nor generous.*

She smiled at me. "I like this place very much. Do you?"

At the other end of the room, a young woman was singing, accompanied by a hurdy-gurdy. In chorus, the audience took up the refrains.
Ordinarily, I hated these loud human clamors, the bursts of laughter,

the voices. But Marianne was smiling and I could not bring myself to hate anything that caused so lovely a smile to appear on her lips.

"Yes, I like it too," I answered.

"But you're not eating," she said reproachfully. "You worked too much; it's ruined your appetite."

"Not in the least."

I pushed a slice of the *paté* onto my plate. All around me, they were eating, drinking, and at their sides were women who were smiling at them. And I too was eating and drinking, and a woman was smiling at me. A sudden gust of heat rose up from my heart, and I thought, *It's almost as if I were one of them.*

"She has a pretty voice," Marianne remarked.

The woman had come over to our table and was gayly singing out the words of her ballad while looking at Marianne. She gave a signal with her hand and everyone began to sing with her. Marianne's clear voice mingled with the others. She leaned toward me.

"Why don't you sing too?"

Something akin to shame made a knot form in my throat. Never before had I sung with them. I looked at them. They were singing and smiling at the women next to them; a fire was burning in their hearts. And a fire had begun to burn in *my* heart; when that fire flamed, both the past and the future were obliterated. Whether death were to come the next day, in a hundred years or never, made no difference. Yes, it was the same flame, the same flame that burned in all of them. *I'm living! I'm one of them!* I thought.

I began to sing along with them.

It's not true, I thought. *I'm not one of them* . . . Half-hidden behind a column, I watched them dancing. Verdier's hand was touching Marianne's and at times their bodies brushed against each other; he was breathing in the fragrant scent of her hair. She was wearing a flaring, blue dress which left bare her delicate shoulders and revealed the cleft of her full, womanly bosom. I wanted to press that fragile body against mine, but I felt paralyzed. *Your flesh is of another kind.* My hands and my lips were granite; I was unable to touch her, I was unable to laugh as they were laughing, with that easy lustfulness. *They* were her kind, and I was a stranger among them. I walked toward the door, but as I was about to leave, Marianne's voice stopped me.

"Where are you going?"

"I'm returning to Crécy," I answered.

"Without saying goodbye to me?"

"I didn't want to bother you."

She looked at me in surprise. "What happened?" she asked. "Why are you leaving so early?"

"You know I'm not the sociable kind."

"But I wanted to speak to you for a few minutes."

"If you like."

We crossed the marble hall and she pushed open the door to the library. The large room was empty. The muted sounds of the violins penetrated through the book-lined walls.

"I wanted to tell you that all of us would be deeply sorry if you really refused to take part in our charity committee. Why don't you want to?" she asked.

"I'd be more of a handicap than a help," I replied.

"But why?"

"I'd do everything wrong," I said. "I'd burn old people instead of building homes for them. I'd set lunatics free and imprison your philosophers in cages."

She shook her head. "I don't understand you. It was only because of you that we were able to found the university. Your inaugural address was magnificent. And yet there are times when you appear convinced that our efforts are useless." I remained silent and she said somewhat impatiently, "What do you *really* believe?"

"Truthfully," I said, "I don't believe in progress."

"Yet it's quite evident that we're closer now to truth and even to justice than ever before."

"Are you so sure that your truth and your justice are worth more than the truths and justices of other centuries?"

"Well, I'm certain you'll agree that science is preferable to ignorance, tolerance to fanaticism, freedom to slavery."

The naive ardor with which she spoke irritated me. It was *their* language she was speaking.

"A man," I said, "once told me that there is only one good: to act according to one's conscience. I think he was right and that all we pretend to do for others is worthless."

"Ah!" she said in a triumphant voice. "And what if my conscience commands me to fight for tolerance, reason, and freedom?"

I shrugged my shoulders. "Then do it," I said. "As for me, my conscience never orders me to do anything."

"If that's the case, why did you help us?"

She looked at me with such obviously sincere anxiety that once again I felt an almost uncontrollable desire to confide myself in her without reserve. Only then would I become truly alive again; only then would I become myself. We would be able to talk without lying. But I suddenly remembered Carlier's tortured face.

"To kill time," I replied.

"That's not true!" she exclaimed.

In her eyes there was gratitude, tenderness, faith. There was nothing I wanted more than to be the person she saw. But my whole being was a lie; every word, every silence, every gesture, even my face lied to her. I could not tell her the truth and I hated deceiving her. The only thing left for me was to leave.

"It *is* true. And now I'm going back to my retorts."

She forced herself to smile. "All of a sudden? Just like that?" She put her hand on the doorknob and asked, "When will we see each other again?"

There was a long silence. She was leaning against the door, very close to me; her bare shoulders were shining in the semidarkness and I smelled the sweet scent of her hair. Her eyes were beckoning to me; just a word, just a gesture, and she would have been mine. But it would all be a lie. Her happiness, her life, our love would be nothing but lies. My kisses would only deceive her.

"I don't believe you need me any more," I said.

Her face suddenly relaxed. "What's bothering you, Fosca? What is it that's gnawing at you? Aren't we friends?"

"But you have so many friends."

She made no attempt to restrain her laughter. "Would you be jealous, by any chance?"

"Why not?" Again I lied; it was not a human jealousy I had in mind.

"That's stupid," she said.

"I'm not made to live in society," I said lightly.

"You're not made to live alone."

Alone. I smelled the odor of the garden around the mound teeming with ants, and once again I felt the taste of death in my mouth. The sky was bare, the plains deserted; suddenly, my heart was empty. And the words I did not want to speak formed on my lips.

"Come with me."

"Come with you?" she said. "For how long?"

I held out my arms. Everything would be a lie. Even the desire that was swelling my heart, and my arms which were holding her mortal body tightly against me, were lies. But I no longer had the strength to fight; I pressed her against me as if I were no different than any other man holding a woman in his arms.

"For a lifetime," I answered. "Could you pass a lifetime beside me?"

"I could pass eternity beside you."

When I returned to Crécy the next morning, the first thing I did was to knock at Bompard's door. He was dunking a piece of buttered bread in a large cup of coffee. He had already taken on the mannerisms of an old man. I sat down in front of him.

"Bompard, I'm going to astound you," I said.

"Go right ahead," he said indifferently.

"I've decided to do something for you, something good."

He did not even lift his head. "Really?"

"Yes. I'm truly sorry about having kept you with me for so long and not letting you take your chances in the world. I heard that the Duke de Frétigny is leaving on a mission to the Russian imperial court and that he's looking for a secretary. A crafty intriguer like you could really do wonders for himself there. I'm going to recommend you warmly and give you a handsome little sum of money so that you can cut a good figure for yourself in Saint Petersburg."

"Ah!" Bompard exclaimed. "You want to get rid of me." There was a contemptible smile on his face.

"Yes," I said. "I'm going to marry Marianne de Sinclair. I don't care to have you around her."

Bompard dunked another piece of bread in his cup. "I'm getting old," he said. "I don't feel much like traveling any more."

A lump formed in my throat and suddenly I realized that I had become vulnerable. "Take care," I warned. "If you turn down my offer, I'll simply tell Marianne the truth and chase you out of here without further ado. It won't be easy for you to find another job."

He could not guess the price I would have paid to keep my secret. And then, he was old and tired.

"It will be very hard for me to leave you," he said. "But I'm counting on your generosity to soften the rigors of exile."

"I hope you'll be happy in Russia and that you'll spend the rest of your days there."

"Oh, I wouldn't want to die without seeing you again."

There was a menacing tone in his voice and I thought, *I have something to fear now, something to defend. I'm in love and I can suffer. At last, I'm a man again!*

※

"I can hear your heart beating," I said to Marianne.

Day was dawning. My head was lying on her bosom which rose and fell with an even rhythm, and I heard her heart beating dully. Every beat drove a stream of blood into her arteries, and then that same moving blood flowed back again to her heart. Somewhere on a silvery beach, waves, snatched up by the moon, rose and fell, beating against a shoal. In the heavens, the earth was rushing toward the sun, the moon toward the earth, in an immense, frozen avalanche.

"Of course it's beating," she said.

It seemed perfectly natural to her that the blood streamed through her veins, that the earth she stood upon was in motion. But I had still not grown used to these strange ideas. I listened carefully . . . the beating of her heart . . . I heard it. Could not the earth's trembling be heard as well?

She gently pushed me away. "Let me get up," she said.

"You have plenty of time. I'm so comfortable . . ."

A ray of light filtered through the drapes. In the semidarkness I could see the silk-padded walls, a dresser covered with knicknacks, puffy petticoats thrown helter-skelter over a chair, a bunch of flowers in a vase. All these things were real; they bore no resemblance to the objects of my dreams. And yet those flowers, those porcelain figures, that iris perfume, were not entirely a part of my life either. It seemed to me as if, bounding through eternity, I had landed in a moment of time which had been laid out for someone else.

"But it's late," Marianne said.

"Do you get bored with me?"

"I get bored from not doing anything," she answered. "I have so many things to do."

I let her up. She was anxious to begin her day. It was natural; time did not have the same value for her as it did for me.

"What are these many things you have to do?" I asked.

"First, the upholsterers are coming to fix up the walls of the little salon." She pulled open the drapes. "You haven't told me what color you prefer."

"I don't know."

"But you must have a preference. Almond green or linden green?"

"Almond green."

"You just picked that one at random," she said, slightly annoyed.

She had set about redecorating the house from top to bottom, and it amazed me to see her taking into lengthy consideration the merits of the design of a tapestry or the shade of a piece of silk. *Is it worth it, going to all that trouble for a mere thirty or forty years?* I thought. It was as if she were preparing herself to settle down for eternity. For a few moments I watched her silently busying herself around the room. She always dressed with great care; she liked clothes and jewels as much as she liked flowers, paintings, books, music, the theater, and politics. I admired the way she gave herself to all things with the same boundless passion. She stopped abruptly in front of the window.

"Where shall we put the bird sanctuary?" she asked. "Next to the big oak tree or under the linden?"

"It might be nice if the brook ran through it," I suggested.

"I think you're right! We'll put it over the brook near the blue cedar." She smiled happily. "You see? You're becoming an excellent adviser."

Almond green or linden green? She was right; if you looked sharply there were hundreds of shades of green and as many of blue; there were more than a thousand varieties of flowers in the meadows, more than a thousand species of butterflies. Every time the sun set behind the hills, the clouds wore different colors. And Marianne herself had so many different faces that I thought I would never know them all.

"Aren't you getting up?" she asked.

"I'm perfectly content just lying here and looking at you."

"My, but you're lazy! And you told me you were going to go back to your experiments with diamonds today."

"Yes, you're right," I said, standing up.

She gave me a worried look. "It seems that if I didn't push you, you'd never set foot in your laboratory. Aren't you curious to know any more if carbon is a pure element or not?"

"Certainly I'm curious. But there's no hurry."

"You always say that. It's funny. I always have the feeling of having so little time before me."

She was brushing her beautiful light-brown hair, hair that would turn white, would fall from her head; and then the skin of her scalp would rot and shrivel and turn to dust. *So little time . . .* We would love each other for thirty years, forty years, and then her coffin would be lowered into a grave precisely like the graves in which Catherina and Beatrice were lying. And once again I would become a shadow. I suddenly took hold of her and pressed her against me.

"You're right," I said. "There's too little time. A love like ours should never end."

She looked at me tenderly, a little surprised by my sudden burst of passion. "It will end only when we reach our ends, won't it?" She passed her fingers through my hair and added, "If you die before me, I'll kill myself."

I held her tighter. "And I promise you I won't outlive you."

I let her go. Suddenly every minute seemed precious. I hastily dressed and hurried down to the laboratory. A hand was turning on the face of a clock; for the first time in centuries, I wanted to stop it. *So little time . . .* Before allowing thirty years to go by, before allowing a year to go by, before tomorrow, her questions had to be answered, for what she did not know today, she would never know. I placed a diamond in a crucible. Would I finally succeed in making it burn? It sparkled, limpid and obstinate, concealing its hard secret somewhere within its transparency. Would I ever discover that secret? Would I discover the secrets of the air, of water, of all the familiar yet mysterious things around me before it was too late? I recalled the old attic with its smell of herbs. The secret was there, hidden in the plants and powders, and I had thought angrily, "Why can't it be discovered *today?*" Petrucchio had passed his life bent over his retorts and he died without knowing. Blood flowed in our veins, the earth was turning, and he did not know it; he would never know it. I felt like turning back the clock and bringing him armfuls of those scientific discoveries of which he dreamed so much. But it was impossible; the door was forever closed. And one day another door would close. Marianne too would sink into the past, and I was powerless to leap ahead into future centuries to find and bring back to her the knowledge for which she was so hungry. There was nothing to be done but wait for time to pass, to submit minute after minute to its fastidious unfolding. The diamond's false transparency fascinated me; I finally turned my eyes away. *I shouldn't waste my time dreaming,* I thought. Thirty years, a year, a day, a mere mortal lifetime. Her hours were counted. My hours were counted.

Seated by the fireside, Sophie was reading *Pygmalion,* and the others, gathered in a group in a corner of the little salon—padded with almond-green silk—were having a discussion about the best system for governing mankind. As if there were a way to govern man! I pushed open the doors to the terrace. Why hadn't Marianne returned yet? Evening had already fallen. Only the black trees, planted in the white snow, could be seen. The garden smelled of coldness, a pure mineral smell which I seemed to be breathing in for the first time. *Do you like the snow?* When I was with her, I liked the snow; she should have been there, next to me. I went back into the salon and glanced peevishly at Sophie who was placidly reading her book. I disliked her calm face, her hearty gaiety, the down-to-earth good sense she always displayed at the slightest provocation. I disliked all of Marianne's friends. But I felt a need to talk to someone.

"Marianne should have been home long ago," I said.

Sophie lifted her head. "She must have been detained in Paris," she said in a matter-of-fact tone of voice.

"Unless she had an accident . . ."

She laughed, revealing her large, white teeth. "What a worrisome nature you have!"

She turned back to her book. They never gave the appearance of having the slightest suspicion that their species was mortal. And yet a blow, a fall—a horse's hoof, a carriage wheel flying off—was enough to break their brittle bones to pieces, to make their hearts stop, to silence them forever. In my heart I felt that sharp bite I knew so well. Sooner or later, it would happen; I would see her dead. *They* could think, "I shall die first. We shall die together," and for them, loneliness would come to an end. Suddenly, I rushed to the door and ran down the steps in front of the house. Muffled by the snow, I had recognized the sound of her carriage.

"You had me terribly worried! What happened?"

She smiled at me and took my arm. Her waist was hardly swollen at all, but her face was drawn, her complexion sallow.

"Why are you so late?" I asked.

"It's nothing," she said. "I felt a little bit sick and I just waited until it went away."

"Sick!"

I looked angrily into her tired eyes. Why had I given in to her? She had wanted a child, and now strange and dangerous alchemies were taking place inside her. I sat her down near the fire.

"That's the last time you're going to Paris."

"What nonsense! I've never been healthier!"

Sophie gave us an inquisitive, knowing look.

"She felt sick," I said.

"That's only normal," Sophie remarked.

"Yes, and it's normal to die, too," I shot back.

With her usual air of quiet competence, she smilingly retorted, "Pregnancy isn't a mortal sickness, you know."

"The doctor said I don't have to begin staying at home until April," Marianne interjected. Two men from the other group walked over to join us, and looking at them cheerfully, she said, "What will become of the Museum if I stop giving my time to it?"

"In any case, they'll soon have to do without you whether you like it or not."

"But by April, Verdier will have completely recovered," Marianne said.

Verdier looked at me and said spiritedly, "If Marianne is tired I'll go back to Paris immediately. These four days in the country have already done me a world of good."

"Don't be insane!" Marianne exclaimed. "You need a good, long rest."

He did not in fact look well. His complexion was livid and there were dark pouches under his eyes.

"Well, then, why don't the both of you take a rest?" I said impatiently.

"In that case, we might just as well close down the university," Verdier replied.

His ironical tone annoyed me. "Why not?" I said. Marianne looked at me reproachfully and I added, "Nothing is so important that you should be willing to ruin your health over it."

"Yes, but if you have to guard it so carefully, being healthy is no longer a good," Verdier remarked.

I looked at them irritably. They formed a solid block against me. Banded together they refused to measure their strength, to count their days; each one refused for himself and for the others as well, and in their common obstinacy they felt as one. My anxiety carried no weight with Marianne. Despite all my love for her, I was not of her kind; any mortal man in the world was closer to her than I.

"What's new in Paris?" Sophie asked in a conciliatory tone.

"It was confirmed to me today that chairs in experimental physics are going to be created throughout France," Marianne replied.

Prouvost's face lit up. "That's the most important thing we've brought about yet," he said.

"Yes, it's a great step forward," Marianne agreed. "Who knows? Things may go faster than we ever dared hope."

Her eyes were beaming brightly; I walked quietly toward the door. I could not bear to hear her speaking so fervently of those days when even her memory would be blotted from the face of the earth. It was perhaps that, more than anything else, that separated me from them so irremediably; their lives stretched out toward a future in which their present efforts would reach fruition. But for me, the future was a hated, unknown time, the time when Marianne would be dead, when our life together would be buried at the bottom of centuries, useless, lost. And *that* time, in turn, was also destined to be buried, lost and useless.

Outside, the night was cold and dry. Thousands of stars were twinkling in the sky—the same stars. I looked up at those motionless bodies which were tugging at each other with opposing forces. The moon was being pulled by the earth, the earth by the sun. Was the sun being pulled? By what unknown stars? And was it not possible that its flight compensated somehow for the earth's and that in reality our planet was frozen in the middle of the heavens? How could it be known? Would it be known some day in the future? And would it ever be known why masses attract each other? Attraction . . . a handy word that served to explain all. But was it any more than a word? Did we really know more than the alchemists of Carmona? We had brought to light certain facts of which the alchemists were ignorant and we had classified them in an orderly manner. But had we penetrated a single inch further into the mysterious heart of things? Was the word Force any clearer than the word Virtue? Or Attraction clearer than Soul? And when it was said that Electricity was the cause of those phenomena which resulted from rubbing amber or glass, were we any better informed than when God was postulated as the cause of the world?

I lowered my eyes to earth. The light beaming from the windows of the salon cast itself over the white lawn, and on the other side of those windows, near the fireplace, they were talking, talking of that future time when nothing would be left of them but dust. All around them stretched the infinite sky, limitless eternity, but one day there would be an end for them, and that, I believe, is why it was so easy for them to live. In their tightly sealed arks they fearlessly sailed from night to night; they sailed together. Slowly, I walked toward the house. For me there was no shelter, no future, no present. Despite my love for Marianne, I was forever excluded.

◥

"Little snail, little snail, show me your horns," chanted Henriette in a singsong tone. She had filled her pail with snails and was taking them one by one and sticking their suction-cup bellies against a tree trunk. Jacques was circling around the linden tree, trying to repeat the simple refrain; Marianne followed him with a worried eye.

"Don't you think Sophie is right? It seems to me that his left leg is a little twisted," she said.

"Take him to a doctor."

"I did, but he didn't notice anything."

She anxiously examined his chubby little legs. Both children were pictures of health, but she could never stop worrying about them. Would they be handsome enough, healthy enough, intelligent, happy? I felt guilty about not being able to share her worries. I liked the children because Marianne had carried them inside her, but they were not really my children. I once had a son, a son of my own; he died at the age of twenty. Now, not a trace of his bones remained in the earth.

"Will you buy a snail from me?"

I stroked Henriette's cheek. She had my high forehead, my nose, a hard, precise little air about her. She bore no resemblance to her mother.

"This one is certainly hardy enough," Marianne said. She carefully studied the little face, as if to decipher the child's future. "Do you think she'll be pretty?"

"Yes, of course."

No doubt she would soon be a pretty, young woman. And then she would grow old, become ugly and toothless, and one day I would learn of her death.

"Which one do you like better?" Marianne asked.

"I don't know. I like both of them equally."

I smiled at her and she slipped her hand in mine. It was a beautiful day. The birds were singing in the sanctuary and wasps were buzzing about among the ivy. I was holding Marianne's hand in mine, but I was lying to her. I loved her, but I did not share her joys, her troubles, her anguish; I did not love what she loved. Next to me, she was alone, and she was unaware of it.

"Well now!" she said, "I wonder who that could be. Were you expecting someone today?"

Bells were tinkling along the avenue, a carriage passed through the gate and a man stepped out. He was an old man, rather heavy and well dressed; he appeared to have difficulty walking. He came toward us with a smile on his large face. It was Bompard.

"What are you doing here?" I asked in a surprised voice which ill-concealed my anger.

"I just got back from Russia last week," he answered, still smiling. "Introduce me."

"This is Bompard," I said to Marianne. "You must have noticed him at Madame de Montesson's some years ago."

"Yes, I remember." She studied him with curiosity, and after he sat down, she said, "So you've just returned from Russia. Is it a nice country?"

"It's cold," he replied bitterly.

They began to speak of St. Petersburg, but I stopped listening. The blood had risen from my heart to my throat, from my throat to my head. I was suffocating. I was blinded for the first time in years by that black glare which I knew to be fear.

"What's wrong?" Marianne asked.

"The sun's given me a headache."

She peered at me with a surprised, worried look. "Would you like to take a rest?" she said.

"No, it'll go away." I stood up. "Come," I said to Bompard, "I'll show you around the grounds. Excuse us for a moment, Marianne."

She nodded her head. But she followed us with puzzled eyes. I had never kept any secrets from her.

"Your wife is charming," Bompard said. "I'd like to know her better and speak to her of you."

"Be careful, Bompard," I said menacingly. "I can still take revenge on you. Remember?"

"It seems to me that today you would stand to lose a great deal if you rashly resorted to any misplaced violence."

"I take it you want money. How much?"

"You're truly very happy, aren't you?" Bompard said.

"Don't worry yourself about my happiness. How much do you want?"

"Happiness is never too expensive. I want fifty thousand pounds a year."

"Thirty thousand," I said.

"Fifty thousand. Take it or leave it."

My heart was pounding violently in my chest. This time I was not playing to lose, but to win; I was not cheating. My love was real, and a real menace was hanging over me. I had to keep Bompard from suspecting the true extent of his power or he would have rapidly ruined me with his demands. I did not want Marianne to be reduced to a life of poverty.

"I'll leave it," I said. "Go speak to Marianne. After a while, she'll pardon me for my lie, and you'll have gained nothing."

He hesitated. "Forty thousand."

"Thirty thousand. Take it or leave it."

"I'll take it," he said.

"You'll have the money tomorrow. And now get out of here."

"I'm going."

Wiping my sweaty hands, I watched him go off. I felt as if I had just gambled for my life.

"What did he want?" Marianne asked.

"Money."

"Why weren't you more cordial?"

"He brings back bad memories."

"Is that why you were so moved when you saw him?"

"Yes."

She examined me suspiciously. "It's funny," she said, "but it almost seemed as if he frightened you."

"You're imagining things. Why should I be frightened of him?"

"Maybe there's something between you two that I don't know about."

"I've already explained to you that he's a man whom I once caused great harm. I'm extremely sorry about it now."

"Is that all?" she said.

"Of course." I drew her close to me. "What are you worrying about? Did I ever keep any secrets from you?"

She lightly touched my brow. "Ah! If only I could read your thoughts," she said. "I'm jealous of anything that goes on in your head that doesn't concern me, and of your whole past. Why, I hardly know anything at all about it."

"I told you everything."

"You told me, but I don't *know* it." She held me tightly.

"I was terribly unhappy," I said. "I was a dead man. You gave me happiness and life."

I suddenly broke off. Words were forming on my lips. I had a passionate desire to stop lying to her, to lay bare the whole truth before her. It seemed to me that then, if she still loved me as an immortal, I would really be saved, together with my whole past and my hopeless future.

"Yes?" she said.

Her eyes were questioning me. She felt that I had something else to tell her. But I remembered other eyes—Carlier's, Beatrice's, Antonio's—and I was afraid of seeing the change that would come over hers.

"I love you," I said. "Isn't that enough?"

I smiled and her worried face relaxed. Confidently, she smiled back at me.

"Yes, that's enough for me," she said.

I gently pressed my lips against her mouth, those lips she believed perishable, like her own. And I silently prayed: "Oh, God in Heaven, please, please don't ever let her discover my treachery!"

※

Fifteen years went by. Bompard had asked me several times for rather large sums of money, which I gave him. But for some time now, I heard nothing further from him. We were living happily. That evening, Marianne had put on a black taffeta gown with red stripes. Standing in front of her mirror she carefully studied herself. I still found her very beautiful. Abruptly, she turned around.

"How young you look!" she exclaimed.

Little by little, I had whitened my hair, I wore glasses, I did everything possible to create the illusion of an elderly man. But I could not disguise my face.

"You look young, too," I said with a smile. "You don't notice it when people you love grow old."

"That's true," she said. She leaned over a bouquet of chrysanthemums and began plucking the faded petals. "I'm really sorry about having to go to that ball with Henriette. It's an evening lost. I like our evenings together so much . . ."

"There'll be others," I said.

"But this one will be lost," she said with a sigh. She opened one of the drawers of her dressing table and took out a few rings which she slipped on her fingers. "Jacques liked this ring so much. Do you remember?" she asked, showing me a heavy silver band in which a blue stone was embedded.

"Yes, I remember," I answered. But in truth, I did not remember; I remembered almost nothing about him.

"He was always so sad whenever we went to Paris without him. He was so sensitive, so much more than Henriette."

She remained silent for a moment; her face was turned toward the window. Outside it was raining, a fine autumn rain. Above the half-barren trees, the sky was cottony. Marianne walked cheerfully toward me and put her hands on my shoulders.

"Tell me what you're going to do, so that when I think of you I'll have the right picture in my mind."

"I'm going down to the laboratory and work until I feel sleepy. And you?"

"We'll have a few things at the buffet table and then I'll be bored to death until the ball ends at one o'clock."

"Are you ready, Mother," Henriette asked as she entered the room.

She was slender and well-shaped like her mother, and she had her blue eyes. But her forehead was a little too high, her nose too hard—the Fosca nose. She was wearing a dress covered with little bouquets; it did not go well with the strong features of her face. She held out her brow to me.

"Goodbye, father. Are you going to be bored without us?"

"I'm afraid so," I replied.

Laughingly, she kissed me. "I'll have fun enough for two."

"Till tomorrow morning," Marianne said. She gently stroked my face and murmured, "Think of me."

I leaned against the window, watched them climb into their carriage and followed it with my eyes until it reached the first turn in the avenue. I felt lost. It was useless; no matter what I did, I remained a stranger in this house. It seemed that I had come here only yesterday and would have to leave tomorrow. I could never feel at home anywhere. I opened a drawer of the dressing table. Inside it, there was a little chest which contained a lock of Jacques' hair, a miniature picture of his face, some dried flowers. In another box, Marianne had stored souvenirs of Henriette's childhood—a first tooth, a page of writing, a bit of embroidery. I closed the drawer. I envied Marianne for owning so many treasures.

I went down to the laboratory; it was empty. The sound of my steps on the white tiles echoed dolefully in the room. Around me, the flasks, test tubes, and retorts had a stubborn, hostile look. I went over to the microscope. Marianne had spread a fine golden powder on one of the slides. I knew it would make her happy if I were able to give her an exact description of it. But as for me, I no longer had any illusions— I would never break through the crusty surface of the apparent world. Even with the aid of microscopes and telescopes, it was still only with my *eyes* that I saw things; objects existed for us only because they were visible, tangible, prudently situated in space and time amid other objects. Even if we were to fly to the moon, or go down to the bottom of oceans, we would still be men in the heart of a human world. As for those mysterious realities which revealed themselves to our senses— forces, planets, molecules, waves—they were hidden by words and protected by the yawning gap of our ignorance. Never would nature deliver up to us her secrets; she had no secrets. We were the ones who invented questions and then formulated the answers to them; in the bottoms of our retorts we would never discover anything but our own thoughts, thoughts that might in the course of centuries multiply, become more complex, be formed into vaster and more subtle systems. But never would these thoughts be capable of tearing me from myself. I put my eye to the microscope; everything would always pass through my eyes, through my thoughts. Never would anything be *something else*, never would I be someone else.

It was close to midnight when, surprised, I heard the tinkling of bells, the sound of an approaching carriage. The wet earth sloshed under the horses' hoofs. With a torch in my hand, I went to the front door. Marianne sprang from the carriage; she was alone.

"What brings you home so early?" I asked.

She walked past me without kissing me, without even looking at me. I followed her into the library. She went over to the fire; she appeared to be shivering.

"Are you cold?" I asked, touching her hand.

She quickly recoiled. "No."

"What's wrong?"

She turned her face toward me. Under her black hood, she was very pale. She looked at me as if she were seeing me for the first time. I had seen that expression in other eyes. It was horror.

"What's wrong," I repeated. But I knew.

"Is it true?" she asked.

"What are you talking about?"

"What Bompard told me, is it true?"

"You saw Bompard? Where?"

"A messenger brought a letter to the house. I went to his flat. I found him there sitting in a chair, paralyzed. He told me he wanted to take his revenge on you before dying." She spoke haltingly. Her eyes glared at me with hostility. She drew close. "He's right," she said. "Not a wrinkle on your face." She held out her hand and touched my hair. "It's been dyed, hasn't it?"

"What did he tell you?"

"Everything. Carmona, Charles V . . . It seems incredible. Is it true?"

"It's true," I said, dejectedly.

"True!" She recoiled a step and stared at me with wild, frightened eyes.

"Don't look at me like that, Marianne. I'm not a ghost."

"A ghost would be less of a stranger to me than you," she said slowly.

"Marianne! We love each other," I said in desperation. "Nothing can bring a love like ours to ruin. What does the past matter? Or the future? What Bompard told you changes absolutely nothing between us."

"Everything is changed, forever." She fell into a chair and hid her face in her hands. "Ah! I'd rather you were dead!"

I kneeled down in front of her and spread her hands apart. "Look at me," I said. "Don't you know me? It's I, your husband, the same man you were with earlier this evening."

"Why did you hide the truth from me?" she said vehemently.

"If I hadn't, would you have loved me?"

"Never!"

"Why not?" I asked. "Do you believe I'm accursed? Is there a demon inside me?"

"I gave myself to you completely," she said. "And I believed you had given yourself completely to me, in life as well as in death. And you were only *lending* yourself to me for a few scant years." A sob choked her voice. "Just another woman among millions. One day you won't even remember my name. And it will still be you. It will be *you* and no one else." She stood up. "No! No! It's not possible!" she cried out.

"Darling, listen to me. You know I belong to you alone. I've never belonged to anyone else like this, and I never will again."

I took her in my arms and she abandoned herself to me with a sort of indifference. She looked deathly tired.

"Listen," I said. "Listen to me!" She nodded her head. "You know that before I met you I was dead. It was you who brought me to life. And when you'll have left me, I'll become a phantom again."

"You weren't dead," she said, tearing herself away from me. "And you'll never really be a phantom. Never for a moment were you like me, like everyone else. Everything was false."

"You could never make a mortal man suffer more than I'm suffering right now," I said. "None of them could ever have loved you like I love you."

"Everything was false," she repeated. "Your suffering is of a different kind than mine, and you love me from the depths of another world. You're lost to me, lost."

"No," I said. "We've just found each other, because now we'll live in truth."

"There can be no truth between you and me."

"My love is true."

"What is your love?" she said scornfully. "When two mortal beings love each other, that love molds them together body and soul; it's their very substance. But for you, it's . . . it's an accident." She pressed her hand against her brow. "Oh, God! How alone I am!"

"I'm alone, too," I said.

For a long moment we sat side by side without speaking. Tears were trickling down her cheeks.

"Have you tried to understand what my lot in life is?" I asked.

"Yes," she answered. She looked at me and her face twisted and shuddered in horror. "It's terrible."

"Don't you want to help me?"

"Help you?" She shrugged her shoulders. "I can help you for ten or twenty years. But what's that?"

"You can give me strength for centuries."

"And after that? Another woman will come to your help." Passionately, she added, "All I want is to stop loving you."

"Forgive me," I said. "Please forgive me. I had no right to force so unhappy a destiny on you."

Tears formed in my eyes. She threw herself into my arms and began to sob desperately.

"And I can't even hope for another destiny," she said.

🖋

I pushed open the gate to the meadow, walked a short distance and sat down in the shade of a red beech tree. Cows were grazing on the sun-drenched grass; it was very hot. With my fingers, I cracked the empty shell of a beechnut. I had just spent several hours bent over a microscope and it was pleasurable simply sitting there and looking at the ground with my unaided eyes. Marianne was waiting for me by the linden tree, or in the cool salon with its lowered blinds, but I felt better away from her. When we were separated, we could imagine ourselves joining each other again.

A cow stopped beside a tree and rubbed its head against the trunk. I imagined for a moment that I was that cow; I felt a rough caress against my cheek, and inside my belly it was dark green and warm; the world was a huge meadow which I consumed with my mouth, with my eyes. If only the illusion could have continued through eternity. Why wasn't I able to lie eternally under that beech tree without moving, never having any desires?

The cow was now standing directly in front of me, staring at me with its large eyes circled by red lashes. Its stomach swollen with fresh grass, it calmly contemplated that mysterious being which was there and which seemed to serve no purpose. It stared at me and yet it did not see me; it was imprisoned in its ruminant universe. And I in turn looked at the cow, at the glaring sky, the poplars, the golden grass. And what did I see in it all? I was imprisoned in my own human universe, imprisoned forever.

I stretched myself out on my back and gazed at the sky. Never would I pass through to the other side of that sky. Prisoner of my own being, I was forever condemned to see nothing around me but the walls of a dungeon. I looked again at the meadow. The cow was lying down and chewing its cud; a cuckoo sang out twice and its calm call, which called to nothing, was swallowed up by the silence. I stood up and walked toward the house.

Marianne was in her boudoir, seated near the open window. She smiled at me—a mechanical smile from which life had withdrawn.

"Did your work go well?"

"I began another experiment today. You should have come to help me. You're getting lazy."

"We're not in such a hurry any more, are we?" she said. "You have all the time in the world." Her mouth twisted slightly. "I'm tired."

"Don't you feel any better?"

"Still the same."

She had been complaining of pains in her stomach. She had grown very thin and her skin had yellowed. *Ten years, twenty years . . .* Now I was counting the years, and sometimes I caught myself thinking, "Quickly! Let it happen quickly!" From the day she had discovered my secret, death had set in upon her.

"What am I going to tell Henriette?" she said after a moment.

"Haven't you decided yet?"

"No, not yet. I've been pondering over it day and night. It's such a serious thing, you know."

"Does she love this man?"

"If she loved him, she wouldn't ask my advice. But she might be happier with him than with Louis . . ."

"Perhaps," I said.

"If she had another kind of life, she'd certainly be very different, don't you think?"

"No doubt of it."

We had already gone through the same conversation more than twenty times, and because of my love for Marianne I truly wanted to take an interest in the affair. But what earthly difference could it make. Whether Henriette stayed with her husband or went with her lover, she would still be Henriette.

"Except that if she leaves him, Louis will keep the child. What kind of life would that child have?" Marianne looked at me. As of late a crotchety, worried look often appeared on her face. "Will you take care of her?" she asked.

"We'll take care of her together," I replied.

She shrugged her shoulders. "You know very well I won't be here much longer." She reached out the window and plucked a cluster of small, blue flowers from a climbing vine. "Actually, it should give me a feeling of security to know that you'll still be here, that you'll always be here. Did it make the others feel secure?"

"Which others?"

"Catherina, Beatrice."

"Beatrice never loved me," I said. "And Catherina must have believed that God would hear her pleas and allow me to join her in heaven one day."

"Did she tell you that?"

"I don't know. But I'm sure she must have thought it."

"You don't know? You don't remember?"

"No," I answered.

"Do you remember anything she ever said?"

"Yes, a few things."

"And her voice? Can you recall her voice?"

"No," I admitted. I touched Marianne's hand. "I never loved her the way I love you."

"Oh, I know you'll forget me. And it's probably better that way. They must weigh heavily upon you, all those memories." She placed the flowers in her lap and twisted the petals with her thin fingers.

"You'll live in my heart longer than you'd have lived in the heart of any mortal man," I said.

"No," she retorted. "If you were mortal, I'd go on living in you until the end of the world, because your death would be the end of the world for me. But instead, I'm going to die in a world that will never end."

I remained silent. There was nothing I could say.

"What will you do afterwards?" she asked.

"I'll try to want what you would have wanted, to act as you would have acted."

"Try to stay a man among men," she said. "There's no other salvation for you."

"I'll try," I promised. "I don't hate people any more, you know. In fact I like them now because they belong to the same species as you."

"Help them. Put your experience at their service."

"I will."

She often spoke to me about my unhappy future, but she could not prevent herself from picturing it with her mortal heart.

"Promise me," she said. A little of her old fervor glowed in her eyes.

"I promise."

A buzzing wasp alit on the cluster of blue flowers; in the distance, a cow mooed softly.

"This may be my last summer," Marianne said.

"Don't say such things."

"In any case, there will come a summer that will be my last." She shook her head. "I don't envy you. But don't envy me either."

We remained seated by the window for a long while, unable to help each other, more apart than if one of us had been dead, no longer capable of acting in consort or even, almost, of speaking together. And yet we loved each other desperately.

"Carry me over to the window," Marianne said. "I'd like to see the sun set one last time."

"It will tire you out."

"Please. For the last time."

I pulled off the covers and lifted her in my arms. She had grown so thin that she weighed no more than a child. She drew apart the drapes covering the window.

"Yes," she said in a voice that seemed to come from far off. "I remember. It was always so beautiful." She let the drapes fall back into place. "For you, everything will continue to exist," she said with a sob.

I laid her down again in her bed. Her face was yellow and shriveled; her hair was cut short—its weight had tired her—and her head had become so small that it reminded me of those shrunken heads scattered over the grounds of the Indian village.

"So many things will happen," she said. "Great things. And I won't be here to see them."

"You can still hold out for a very long time. The doctor said your heart was in perfect condition."

"Don't lie," she said in a sudden burst of anger. "You've lied enough to me! I know it's over. I'm going, and I'm going alone. And you,

you'll stay here without me, forever." She began to weep uncontrollably. "Alone! You're letting me leave the world alone!"

I took her hand and squeezed it tightly. Oh God, how I wanted to be able to say to her: "I'll die with you. They'll bury us in the same grave. We've lived out our lives and now nothing more exists."

"Tomorrow the sun will set and I'll be nowhere," she said. "There'll be only my body. And one day, when my coffin is opened, there will be nothing left but a few handfuls of dust. Even the bones will be gone! And for you, everything will go on as if I'd never existed."

"I'll live with you, through you . . ."

"You'll live without me," she said. "And one day, you'll forget me completely." In a half-choked voice, she added, "Ah, it's not fair!"

"I only wish I could die with you."

"But you can't."

Sweat was running down her face; her hands were cold and moist. "If only I were able to say to myself: 'He'll join me again in ten years, twenty years,' it wouldn't be half so terrible to die. But no! Never! You're leaving me forever."

"I'll think of you always," I said.

But she seemed not to hear me. Worn out, she fell back on her pillow and muttered, "I hate you."

"Marianne, don't you know how much I love you?"

She shook her head. "I know everything. I hate you."

She closed her eyes and in less than a minute seemed to have fallen asleep. But in her sleep she moaned deeply, alarmingly. Henriette came in and sat down next to me; she was a tall woman with hard features.

"Her breathing is slowing down," she remarked.

"Yes, it's the end."

Marianne's fingers stiffened, her mouth sagged at the sides in a grimace of suffering, disgust, and reproachfulness. Then she gave one last sigh and her whole body grew slack.

"How peacefully she died," Henriette said.

Marianne was interred two days later. Her tomb stood in the middle of the cemetery, stones among stones, and she took up no more space under the infinite sky than the precise length and breadth and height of that cheerless tomb. When the ceremony had ended, they went off, leaving Marianne, her tomb and her death behind them. Alone now, I sat down on a slab of stone. It was not Marianne who was stretched out in the tomb; it was the body of an old woman with a heart full of bitterness. Marianne, with her smiles, her hopes, her kisses, her tenderness, was standing on the edge of the past. I still saw her, I could still speak to her, smile at her, and I felt her eyes upon me, those eyes that had made me a man among men. In a moment the door would close forever. I tried desperately to stop it from closing; I had to remain perfectly still, to see nothing, to hear nothing, to renounce the world of the present. I lay down on the ground, closed my eyes and exerting every ounce of strength at my command I kept the door open, stopped the present from being born so that the past could continue to exist.

It lasted a day, a night, and a few hours into the next day. And then suddenly I started. Although nothing had actually happened, I could now distinctly hear the buzzing of bees among the cemetery's flowers; in the distance, a cow mooed. I heard it. In the depths of my being, I felt a dull blow. It was done. The door had closed. No one would ever pass through it again. I stretched out my benumbed legs and raised myself on my elbows. *What am I going to do now?* I thought. *Will I get up and continue to live?* Catherina was dead, and Antonio, Beatrice, Carlier—everyone I ever loved was dead, and I went on living. I was there, the same for centuries. My heart might beat a moment in pity, revolt, distress, but soon I forgot. I dug my fingers into the ground and said aloud in despair, "I don't want to go on." A mortal man could have refused to continue on his way, could have made his rebellion eternal, could have, in a word, killed himself. But I . . . I was a slave to life, to that life which dragged me inexorably toward indifference and forgetfulness. It was useless to resist. I got up and slowly took the road back to the house.

When I entered the garden I looked up and saw that half the sky was covered with heavy, black clouds and the other half was a calm blue. One side of the house seemed gray, while the façade was a hard, glaring white. The grass appeared yellow. From time to time a heavy storm wind bent the trees and bushes; then everything stood still again. Marianne used to like storms. Would it be possible to make her live through me? I sat down under the linden tree, her favorite place. I watched the violently changing shadows, the raw white of the façade; I breathed in the odor of magnolias. But the light and the shadows and the smells did not speak to me. That day was not mine; it remained in suspension, demanding that it be lived by Marianne. But she was not there to live it and I was unable to substitute for her. With Marianne's death, an entire world had foundered, a world that would never again emerge in the light. Now, all the flowers began to look alike, the sky's varied shades became indistinguishable, and the days were destined to have but a single color—the color of indifference.

☙

A maid opened the door of the inn, looked at Regina and Fosca with a suspicious eye and threw a bucketful of water into the street. The clacking of a Venetian blind came from the second floor.

"Maybe they'll give us some coffee," Regina said.

They went inside. On hands and knees, a woman was washing the floor of the dining room with a large, heavy rag. Regina and Fosca sat down at one of the oilcloth-covered tables.

"Could you give us something to drink?" Regina asked.

The woman raised her head, twisted the wet rag over a bucket of dirty water and then, abruptly, her face broke into a smile.

"I can give you some coffee with milk."

"Make it good and hot," Regina said. She turned her eyes back to Fosca. "So, only two centuries ago you were still capable of loving."

"Yes, only two centuries ago."

"And of course you forgot her immediately, didn't you?"

"Not immediately," Fosca said. "I lived under her eyes for quite a stretch of time. I cared after Henriette's daughter, watched her grow up, get married, die. She left a little boy, Armand, and I cared after him, too. Henriette died when the boy was fifteen. She was a hard, selfish old woman and she hated me because she knew my secret.

"But did you think often of Marianne?"

"The world in which I lived was her world, the people were her kind. In working for them, I was working for her. That helped me pass almost fifty years. I did a good deal of research in physics and chemistry."

"But all that didn't keep her from dying," Regina said.

"Was there any way to keep her from dying?"

"No, there was surely no way."

The maid placed a coffee pot, a pitcher of milk and two large bowls on the table—pink bowls decorated with blue butterflies. "They're the same bowls I used to eat from when I was a child," Regina thought. It was a mechanical thought; the words had already lost their meaning.

She no longer had a childhood, a future; for her, too, light, colors, odors, were gone from the world. Fosca filled her bowl and she brought it to her lips. The sharp burning in her mouth, in her throat—*that* she could still feel. She drank avidly.

"The story is almost over," Fosca said.

"Finish it," she said. "Let's get finished with it."

BOOK V

Somewhere in the maze of corridors a drum began beating and everyone turned his face toward the door. There were tears in Brennand's eyes; Spinelle pressed his lips together and his Adam's apple bobbed convulsively up and down in his thin neck. Armand plunged his hand in a pocket of his coat; his face was deathly pale under the short, semicircular beard which formed a ring around it from temple to temple. The windows were closed, but the shouts rising from the square could be plainly heard. They were shouting, "Down with the Bourbons! Long live the Republic! Long live La Fayette!" It was very hot. Beads of sweat gathered on Armand's brow, but I knew that an icy shiver was running down his spine. Now, after all the hundreds of years, I knew them, understood them, could read their thoughts. I felt the coldness of the metal in his damp hand, the coldness of the iron balcony against my own hand. They were shouting, "Long live Antonio Fosca! Long live Carmona!" A church was burning in the night; victory blazed up to the sky and the black ashes of defeat fell back upon my heart. The air tasted of lies. My hand tightened around the balustrade and I thought, "Is there nothing a man can do?" And *his* hand tightened around the butt of a revolver and he was thinking, "I can do something." He was ready to die to convince himself of it.

Suddenly the drum stopped beating. There was a sound of steps and a man appeared in the doorway. He was smiling, but he was pale, as pale as Armand. Under the tricolored sash across his chest, his heart was beating heavily; his mouth was dry. La Fayette was walking alongside him. Armand slowly withdrew his hand from his pocket. I grabbed his wrist.

"Forget it," I said. "I took out the bullets."

A thunderous roar filled the hall—the roar of the sea, the wind, of volcanos. The man passed before us. I tightly held Armand's wrist and it grew limp in my hand. I relieved him of the revolver. He looked at me and his cheeks became slightly flushed.

"You've betrayed us," he said.

He walked to the door and ran down the stairs. I ran after him. In the square they were waving tricolored flags and some were still shouting, "Long live the Republic!" But most of them were now silent, hesitant, waiting. They were fixedly watching the windows of the City Hall. Armand took a few steps and grabbed hold of a lamppost, like a drunken man. His legs were trembling. He was weeping. He was weeping because he had been defeated and because his life had been saved. He was lying on a bed with a hole in his belly; he was the victor and he was dead. He was smiling. Suddenly a great clamor arose from the crowd. "Long live La Fayette! Long live the duke of Orleans!" Armand lifted his head and saw the general and the duke, draped in the folds of a tricolored flag, embracing each other on the balcony of the City Hall.

"They won," Armand said. In his voice there was no anger, only a great weariness. "You had no right to do that. It was our only chance."

"It would have been a useless suicide," I said dryly. "What's the duke? Nothing. His death wouldn't change a thing. The bourgeois have made up their minds to snatch this revolution away from us, and they'll do it because the country isn't ripe yet for the Republic."

"Listen to them!" Armand said. "They let themselves be maneuvered like children. Won't anyone ever open their eyes for them?"

"You're a child yourself," I said, putting my hand on his shoulder. "Do you think three days of violence are enough to educate a people?"

"They wanted freedom," Armand said. "They gave their blood for it."

"They gave their blood, but do they know why? They themselves don't know what they really want."

We had reached the banks of the Seine. Armand was walking beside me, his head lowered, wearily dragging his feet.

"Just yesterday, victory was still in our hands," he said.

"No. You would never have been victorious because you were never able to exploit your successes. You weren't ready."

A white surplice, swollen with water, was floating down the river with the current. Tied up alongside the quay was a boat flying a black flag. Men were carrying stretchers which they set down on the bank of the river and the smell rose up toward the silent crowd leaning over the parapet of the bridge. The smell of Rivella, of the Roman squares, of fields of battle, the smell of victories and defeats, so flat after the red burst of blood. They piled the bodies on the boat and covered them with straw.

"Then they died for nothing," Armand said.

I looked at the sun-colored straw under which human flesh, crawling with maggots, was fermenting. They had died for humanity, liberty, progress, happiness, had died for Carmona, for the Empire, for a future that wasn't theirs, died because they always ended by dying, died for nothing. But I did not utter the words that came to my lips; I had learned to speak *their* language.

"They died for the revolution of tomorrow," I said. "During these three days, the people discovered their power. They still don't know how to use it, but tomorrow they will know. They'll know if only you devote your energy to making preparations for the future instead of seeking a useless martyrdom."

"You're right," he said. "It's not martyrs the Republic needs." He leaned against the parapet for a moment longer, his eyes fixed on the funeral boat, and then he turned around. "I think I'll go over to the newspaper."

"I'll go with you," I said.

We walked away from the river. At the corner of the street a man was sticking a poster against a wall. Printed in large, black letters it read, *The Duke of Orleans Is Not a Bourbon. He Is a Valois.* Further on, posted on a wooden fence, we saw the shredded Republican manifesto.

"And there's nothing we can do!" Armand exclaimed. "And yesterday we could have done everything!"

"Patience," I said. "You have your whole life before you."

"Yes, thanks to you." He gave me a forced smile. "How did you guess?"

"I saw you loading your revolver. It's not very difficult to read your thoughts."

As we crossed the street, Armand studied me with a perplexed look on his face. "I often wonder why you look after me with so much concern," he said.

"I've already told you. I loved your mother very much, and you've become dear to me because of her."

He remained silent, but as we passed in front of a bullet-starred shop window, he stopped me. "Did you ever notice that we look alike?" he asked.

I looked at the two reflections—the immutable visage that had been mine for centuries and the inexperienced, young face with its long, black hair, its ring of beard, its ardent eyes. We had the same nose, the nose of the Foscas.

"What do you have on your mind?" I asked.

He paused. "I'll tell you some other time."

We arrived in front of the building in which the *Progress* was published. On the sidewalk was a mob of men dressed in tatters who took turns at heaving their shoulders against the closed door. They were shouting: "Shoot the Republicans!"

"The idiots!" Armand exclaimed.

"Let's go in the back door," I said.

We circled the block of houses and knocked at the rear door. A small window opened, then the door.

"Come in quick," Voiron said. His shirt was open and his chest was damp with sweat. He was holding a rifle in his hand. "Try to make Garnier leave. They'll kill him."

Armand bounded up the stairs. Garnier, surrounded by a group of young people, was sitting on the edge of a table in the editorial room. They were unarmed. From the ground floor, bloodthirsty yells and a dull pounding could be heard.

"What are you waiting for?" Armand said. "Get out of here by the back door."

"No," Garnier said firmly. "I want to be here to greet them."

He was afraid. I could see it in the corners of his mouth and in his half-clenched fists.

"The Republic doesn't need martyrs," Armand said. "Don't let yourself be murdered."

"I don't want them to smash my presses and burn my papers. I'll wait for them."

His voice was firm, his eyes cold. But I sensed the fear that was in him. Were he not afraid, he would no doubt have agreed to leave.

"I'm not stopping anyone else from leaving," he haughtily added.

"That's not true," I said. "You know very well that these young people here won't leave you."

He looked around him and seemed to be wavering. But at that very moment, there was a loud crash, followed by the sound of a wild rush on the stairway. "Death to the Republicans!" they shouted. The glass door flew open and they stormed into the room with their bayonets thrust forward. They looked half drunk.

"What do you want?" Garnier asked in a calm, dry tone of voice.

They hesitated and then one of them cried out, "We want your dirty Republican hide!"

As the man sprang forward, I threw myself in front of Garnier. The bayonet struck me full in the chest.

"Are you murderers?" Garnier cried out.

His voice came to me from far off. I could feel the blood soaking my shirt and there seemed to be a fog surrounding me. *Maybe this time I'll die. Maybe it will finally be over!* And then I found myself lying on a table with a white cloth wrapped around my chest. Garnier was still speaking and the men were withdrawing toward the door.

"Don't move," Armand said to me. "I'll get a doctor."

"It won't be necessary," I said. "The bayonet hit a bone and stopped dead. There's nothing wrong with me."

Out in the street, under the windows, they were still shouting, "Shoot the Republicans!" But the men who had burst into the room now turned heels and went down the stairs. I got up, buttoned my shirt and put on my coat.

"You saved my life," Garnier said.

"Don't thank me before you know what life has in store for you."

Yes, I saved you, I thought, *and now you'll have to go on living for years with your fear-ridden heart.*

"I'm going home to rest," I said.

Armand came with me. For a few moments we walked along in silence, and then he said, "That stab would have killed anyone else."

"The bayonet struck a bone . . ."

"No normal man," he interrupted, "could get up and walk away after being wounded like that." He grabbed hold of my wrist. "Tell me the truth."

"What truth?"

"Why do you watch over me? Why do we look alike? Why didn't you die when the bayonet went right through you?" He spoke in a feverish voice and his fingers tightened about my arm. "I've suspected it for a long time . . ."

"I don't know what you're talking about."

"Ever since my childhood I've known that among my ancestors

there's a man who will never die. And ever since my childhood I've wanted to meet him."

"Your mother spoke to me of that legend," I said. "Does it really seem credible to you?"

"I've always believed it," he said. "And I always thought that we'd be able to do great things together if he had any liking for me."

His eyes gleamed and he looked at me fervently, hopefully. Charles had turned his head away; his lower lip had sagged loosely, his eyes had seemed dead under their drooping lids. And I had promised, "We'll do great things!"

I remained silent and Armand said impatiently, "Is it a secret? Why all the mystery?"

"You believe me immortal and you can still look at me without horror?"

"Why should I be horrified?"

A smile lit up his face. He suddenly seemed very young and something stirred in my heart. It was a tasteless thing, very old and a little musty. Spouting fountains were singing in a garden.

"It's you, isn't it?" he said.

"Yes."

"Then the future is ours!" he said. "Thank you for having saved my life!"

"Don't be so happy about it. It's dangerous for mortal men to live by my side. Their lives suddenly seem too short, their undertakings useless."

"I realize I have only a normal man's life before me," he said. "Your presence doesn't change that at all." He looked at me as if he were seeing me for the first time, and he was already avidly seeking to profit from the extraordinary opportunity that had just opened before him. "What things you must have seen! Did you take part in the big Revolution?"

"Yes."

"You'll tell me about it sometime," he said.

"I didn't play a very big role in it."

"Oh," he said, looking at me disappointedly.

"Well, here I am," I said abruptly as we arrived at the door to my house.

"Would you mind if I came up with you for a moment?"

"I never mind anything."

We went upstairs and I opened the door to the library. Inside an oval frame, Marianne was smiling; she was wearing a blue gown which left her young shoulders bare.

"That's your mother's grandmother," I said. "She was my wife."

"She was very beautiful," Armand said politely. His eyes circled the room. "Did you read all those books?"

"Most of them."

"You must be a great scientist."

"I lost all interest in science a long time ago."

I looked at Marianne and I felt a strong desire to speak to her. She had been dead many years, but for Armand she began to exist only that very day. Could she come to life again in his ardent young heart?

"She had faith in science," I said. "Like you, she believed in progress, reason, freedom. She was passionately devoted to the happiness of humanity."

"Don't you believe in all that?" he asked.

"Of course. But for her, it was something else again. She was so alive; everything she touched came to life—flowers, ideas . . ."

"Women are often more largehearted, more spirited than we men," Armand said.

I drew the drapes and lit a lamp. What was Marianne to him? A dead person among millions of others. She was smiling, but her smile was frozen in the middle of an oval portrait. Never would she be born again.

"Why aren't you interested in science any more?" Armand asked. He was staggering from fatigue, his eyelids were twitching, but he was determined not to leave before finding a way to profit from me.

"It's no help to man in discovering a way to escape from himself," I said.

"But is it necessary for man to escape from himself?"

"For you, I'm sure it's not necessary." I looked at him and abruptly added, "You ought to get some rest. You look completely worn out."

"I haven't slept much in the last three days," he said with an apologetic smile.

"It's a trying experience to die and come to life again all in the same day," I said. "Lie down on the couch and go to sleep."

He threw himself on the divan. "I'll take a little nap," he said.

I stood beside the couch. Evening was falling. Outside, the clamor of festivities was drifting through the dusky air, but in my study, with the drapes drawn over tightly closed windows, no other sound could be heard but Armand's light breathing. He had already fallen asleep. For the first time in four days, he was delivered of fear, of hope. He was sleeping, and now it was I who had awakened to feel the weight in my heart of that long day, that dreary day which was slowly dying on the other side of the windows. Pergola's deserted squares, Florence's glittering, inaccessible domes, the flat taste of wine on a balcony in Carmona . . . And I had also known triumphant rapture, Malatesta's hearty laughter, Antonio's smile as he lay dying, Carlier looking at the yellow river and sneering, "I made it." And I, ripping open my shirt with both hands, choking with life. And in my breast there had also been hope, the red sun in a cloudy sky, the blue line of hills far out on the plains, sails disappearing on the horizon, snatched up by the earth's invisible curvature. I leaned over Armand and looked at his young face with its black stubble of a beard. What was he dreaming of? He was sleeping, as Tancredo, Antonio, Charles, and Carlier had slept. They all looked alike, and yet for each of them life had a unique taste, a taste that none of the others, that no one else in the world, had ever known. And their lives would never begin again, be born in some-one else; in each of them it was complete, completely new. He wasn't dreaming of Pergola's squares, nor of the great yellow river. He had his own dreams and I could not rob him of even the smallest particle of them. Never would I be able to escape from myself, to slip inside one of them and live his life. I could try to serve him, but I would never see through his eyes, feel with his heart. Behind me, I would forever drag the red sun, the winding, muddy river, the hateful solitude of Pergola. My past. I walked away from Armand; I could hope for no more from him than from any of the others.

⚔

The smoke made a bluish ring in the yellow air, then the ring stretched, became deformed, finally broke. Somewhere, on a silvery beach, the shadow of a palm tree was creeping toward a white rock. I wished I were lying on that beach. Every time I forced myself to speak their language I felt empty and tired.

"Regarding the printing and publication of written matter, *flagrante delicto* exists only when the call to revolt is actually in the process of being printed in a place known in advance to the authorities. Not a single one of the writers arrested on a warrant within the past month was actually caught in *flagrante delicto*."

In the next room, Armand was reading my article aloud and the others were listening attentively. From time to time they applauded in approval. They applauded, but if I had pushed open the door, their faces would have frozen up. No matter that I worked with them every night and wrote what they wanted me to write, I still remained a stranger to them.

"I say that when an innocent man is taken from his home, when he is held for weeks in a dungeon under an illegal accusation, when you dare to condemn him only because despair and anger tore a bitter word from him against your magistrates, I say then that you trample upon the sacred rights the French people bought so dearly with their blood."

As I listened to those words I had written being read aloud, I thought, "Marianne would be pleased with me." But already, I no longer recognized them. There was nothing in me but silence.

"Now there's an article that will create a stir!" Garnier said. He came over to my writing table and looked at me. His mouth twisted nervously; he wanted to speak a few friendly words. Of all of them, he was the only one who wasn't afraid of me, but somehow, we had never been able to converse together.

"There'll be a trial," he finally said. "But we'll win it."

The door flew open and Spinelle burst into the room. His cheeks were rosy and in his curly hair there was coldness and night. He threw his scarf on a chair.

"There was a riot at Ivry," he said. "The workers smashed the spinning machines and troops were called in. They made a bayonet charge."

He spoke so rapidly that he stuttered. He was not concerned with the workers, or the smashed machines, or the spilled blood; he was happy because he had important news for his newspaper.

"Was anyone killed?" Garnier asked.

"Three deaths and several wounded."

"Three deaths . . ."

Garnier's face was tense. He, too, was far from Ivry, far from the outcries and stabbings. He was picturing the heavy, black letters of the headline: TROOPS CHARGE WORKERS WITH BAYONETS. He was already weighing the first words of the article.

"Smashed the machines!" Armand exclaimed. "Don't they know that's idiotic? We'll have to explain to them . . ."

"What's the difference?" Garnier said. "What counts is that there

was a riot." He turned toward Spinelle. "I'm going down to the com-
posing room. Come along with me."

They left and Armand sat down in a chair facing me. He thought for
a while and then finally said, "Garnier is wrong. These riots serve no
purpose at all. You were right when you explained to me that the
people have to be educated first." He shrugged his shoulders. "To
think that they've gone as far as breaking up machines!"

I did not answer. He did not expect any answer. He gave me a
perplexed look and I had no idea what thoughts he was reading on my
face.

"What makes things difficult is that they're suspicious of us," he
said. "Evening courses, public meetings, pamphlets! That's not the way
we'll reach them. Our words just go in one ear and out the other."
There was a sharp note of urgency in his voice and it was aimed at me.

I smiled. "Well, what do you expect me to do about it?"

"To control them you have to live among them, work with them,
fight by their sides. You have to be one of them."

"You want me to become a laborer?"

"Yes," he replied. "You could accomplish a tremendous amount."

He gazed at me avidly and I felt a certain sense of security under
his gaze. A force to be exploited, nothing more. I inspired neither horror
nor friendship in him; he made use of me, and that was all.

"It would be a great sacrifice to ask of a mortal man. But for you, I
don't imagine ten or fifteen years counts very much."

"As a matter of fact," I said, "it counts very little."

His face lit up. "Then you agree to do it?"

"I'll try," I said.

"Oh, it won't be difficult. If you try, you'll surely succeed."

"I'll try," I repeated.

I was lying on the ground near the ant hill, and she had come, and
I had gotten up, and she said to me, "Be a man among men." I could
still hear her voice as I looked around at them. "They're men," I said
to myself. "And I'm here, working with them." But in the shop, where
the light was growing dimmer with the coming of night, as I brushed
the damp rolls of paper with red, yellow, and blue paints, I could not
choke off that other voice which was saying to me, "But what *are* men?
What can they do for me?" Under our feet the whirring machines
made the floor tremble, the trembling of restless, stagnant time.

"Is there much more to go?" asked the child.

Standing on his stool, he was wearily grinding colors in a mortar. I could feel his benumbed legs, his bent back, his head, so empty, so heavy, tugging him toward the floor.

"Are you tired?"

He did not even answer.

"Rest a moment," I said.

He sat down on the topmost step of the stool and closed his eyes. Since early morning we had been swabbing rolls of paper with brushes dripping with liquid colors; since early morning we had been standing there in the same dim light, with the same smell of paint, and the even, rhythmic whirring of the machines. Always, always . . . Since morning, since the first days of the world, always boredom, weariness, the trembling of time. The looms were humming, always, always, through the streets of Carmona, through the streets of Gand where the weavers' shuttles wove in and out, in and out. Houses were blazing, voices were raised up in song amid crackling flames, blood mingled with violet gutter water, and the machines purred obstinately, always, always. Hands were dipping brushes in red creamy paint and stroking the brushes against paper. The child's head was bent over his chest; he was sleeping. For them living was merely not dying. What was the good of struggling for them? They would soon be delivered in any case; they would die, each in his turn. Far off in another world the shadow of a palm tree was creeping toward a stone, the sea was beating against the shore. I felt like going out that door and trying to become a stone among stones.

The child opened his eyes. "Didn't the bell ring?"

"It will ring in five minutes."

He smiled and I avidly shut that smile away in my heart. And because of that light in his face, it all seemed changed—the whirring of the machines, the smell of the paint, everything. Time was no longer a slack, stagnant sheet of water; there were now hopes and sorrows on earth, hates and loves. In the end there was always death, but first they lived. Neither ants nor stones, but men. Through that smile, Marianne again appeared to me: "Believe in them, stay with them, remain a man." I put my hand on the child's head. How much longer would I still be able to hear her voice? And when their smiles and their tears no longer found an echo in me, what would become of me?

"It's all over," I said.

The man remained seated on the edge of his chair. With a dumb-founded look on his face, he stared at the blue mask lying on the pillow. A woman had died and another on the sixth floor had been saved. It might just as easily have been the other way around. As for me, it made no difference; but for the man it was *this* woman, his wife, who was dead.

I left the room. At the beginning of the epidemic I had offered my services and since then I spent my nights applying vesicatories and leeches to infected bodies. They wanted to be cured and I was trying to cure them. I was trying to help them and not ask myself questions.

The street was deserted, but to the right a noisy metallic rattling could be heard. It was an artillery wagon jolting along a sidestreet; they had been put into use to cart away coffins. It was said that the jolts often ripped apart the board, and the bodies burst open on the cobblestones, splattering the street with their entrails. Through narrow pink streets, on mattresses and planks, men were carrying white bodies covered with black spots which they threw pell-mell into hastily dug pits. All those who were able to flee were fleeing; by foot, horse and mule, they went through the posterns; in coaches, carts and buggies, they galloped through the gates of Paris. The peers of France, the rich bourgeois, the officials, the deputies, all the wealthy were fleeing, and those who were sentenced to die danced away the nights in abandoned palaces. It was morning; they were listening to the prophetic voice of the tall, dark monk who was preaching in the square. The poor were unable to flee; they remained in the infested city, sprawled on their beds, cold as stones or burning with fever, blue masks on their faces, on their faces black masks, their bodies covered with dark blotches. In the morning, the bodies were lined up along the walls and the smell of death rose heavily toward the blue sky. Under the gray sky, the half dead were being carried to hospitals; the doors closed quietly on their death pangs. In vain did their relatives and friends stand watch at the gates to gather up their last sighs.

I pushed open the door. Armand was sitting on the edge of the bed and Garnier was standing next to a table on which a candle was burning.

"Why did you come?" I asked. "You're just tempting death. Don't you have any confidence in me?"

"We weren't going to let him die alone," Armand said.

Garnier remained silent. He stood there with both hands in his pockets, looking fixedly at the body lying on the bed. I leaned over Spinelle. His shrunken skin was stretched taut over his bones. The outlines of a death's head could be seen forming under his blue parchment face. His mouth was white and beads of cold sweat covered his forehead. I took hold of his wrist; it was cold and clammy. His pulse had almost stopped beating.

"Can't anything be done?" Armand asked.

"I tried everything."

"He looks like a corpse already."

"Twenty years old," Garnier said. "And he loved life so much . . ."

In despair both of them looked at the shrivelled face. For them, that life which was about to be snuffed out was unique, Spinelle's life, Spinelle who had just turned twenty and who was their friend, unique as each of the golden spots that danced in the air among the rows of cypresses. I had looked at Beatrice and had asked myself, "Is she no different than those ephemeral insects?" I loved her then, and she did seem different; but now I no longer loved her, and her death was of no more importance to me than an insect's.

"If he just holds out until morning, he can still save himself," I said.

I slipped my hands under the sheets and began slowly, then vigorously rubbing his icy body. I stretched him out on my coat and my hands kneaded his young muscles. For the second time, I brought him into the world and he left the world with a hole in his belly. I brought him corn and smoked meat and he shot himself in the head because he was dying of hunger. I rubbed him for a long while and under my fingers a little heat began to rise toward his heart.

"He might hold out," I said.

Outside, people were running past the window. At the corner of the street was an emergency station, identified by a red lantern. They were running there to ask for help. Then there was silence again.

"You ought to get out of here," I said. "You can't do him any good."

"We've got to stay," Armand said. "I'd like to have my friends beside me when I die."

He looked tenderly at Spinelle and I knew he did not fear death. I turned toward Garnier. That man intrigued me. There was no tenderness in his eyes, only fear.

"Don't be fools! The chances of contagion are enormous."

His mouth twisted slightly and once again it seemed to me that he wanted to speak to me. But he was walled in upon himself; he was almost never seen to smile and no one ever knew what he was thinking. Suddenly, he walked to the window and opened it.

"What's going on?"

A great clamor was rising from the street. Every night fires were lit at all the intersections of Paris in the hope that they would purify the atmosphere. By the light of the flames, we saw a mob of men and women dressed in rags pulling a cart through the square. They were shouting, "Death to the oppressors!"

"It's the ragpickers," said Garnier.

An ordinance had been put into effect making it mandatory that filth and garbage be removed during the night, before the ragpickers had a chance to gather their pitiable harvest. Reduced to misery, they cried out hatefully, "Death to the oppressors!" They cried out, "Son of the devil!" and they spat on the ground.

Garnier closed the window.

"If only we had leaders," Armand said. "The people are ripe for a revolution."

"For a riot, at most," Garnier said.

"We could easily change a riot into a full-scale revolution."

"No, we're too divided."

With their foreheads pressed against the window they were dreaming of riots, of murders. I looked at them and did not understand. At times it seemed to me that men attached a ridiculous price to a life that death would ultimately destroy: why had they looked so despondently at Spinelle? And at other times they seemed all too willing to run the risk of obliterating themselves forever: why did they stay in that infested room when there was absolutely nothing they could do for their friend? Why were they planning bloody riots?

"Armand," a voice murmured. Spinelle had opened his eyes and his eyeballs, lost in the depths of hollow sockets, seemed to have melted. But they were living eyes, they saw.

"Am I going to die?"

"No," Armand said. "Try to sleep. You're going to be all right." Spinelle's eyelids closed and Armand turned toward me. "Is it true? Will he be all right?"

I took Spinelle's hand. It was no longer cold. His pulse was beginning to beat faster.

"If he lives through the night," I said, "he'll be out of danger. And right now, it looks to me as if he'll see morning."

Dawn was already approaching. A large black van passed by under the windows. From house to house coffins were being collected and piled in the van under funeral drapes. Along the hilly street with its pinkish cobblestones, carts stopped in front of one house after the next, and bodies were piled up under canvas coverings. Armand was sitting in a chair; he had closed his eyes and was sleeping. Garnier was still standing, leaning against a wall, his face closed to the world. At the intersection the fire was dying out and the ragpickers had dispersed. For several minutes the square remained empty, and then a janitor appeared at his door. He inspected the cobblestones with a suspicious air. It was said that chunks of meat and strange pill-like objects, deposited by mysterious hands, were sometimes found on the streets. There were people, it was rumored, who poisoned the fountains and the meats in butcher shops; a vast conspiracy was supposedly menacing the populace. The rumor was spread that I had made a pact with the devil and they spat at my feet in disgust.

"He lived through the night," Garnier murmured.

"Yes."

A little blood now appeared in Spinelle's cheeks; his hand was warm and his pulse was beating steadily.

"He's all right," I said.

Armand opened his eyes. "All right?"

"It's almost certain."

Armand and Garnier looked at each other. I turned my eyes away. With that look, they shared the joy that had just burst in their hearts. It was in those triumphant exchanges that they found both the strength to confront death and reasons for living. Why had I felt compelled to turn my eyes away? I called Spinelle's face to my aid. He was twenty, he loved life. I remembered his shining eyes, his young, stuttering voice. I had saved him, had swam through the icy lake, had brought him back to shore and carried him in my arms. I had gone in search of an Indian village, and laughing with joy, he devoured the corn and meat I had brought back. A hole in his belly, a hole in his temple. What would this one die of? There wasn't a spark of joy in my heart.

🖤

"Well?" Garnier said.

In the editorial room of the *Progress*, the members of the Central Committee and the section chiefs of the Society for the Rights of Man had gathered around old Broussaud. All of them were looking at me anxiously.

"Well, I didn't have any luck with the Society of Gauls or its organizational committee," I said. "The only one I was able to get anywhere with was the Friends of the People. They seem to be in favor of an insurrection, but they haven't reached any firm decision yet."

"How can they possibly decide anything without knowing what we decide?" Armand said. "And how can we make any decisions without them?"

After a brief silence, Garnier said, "*We* have to make the decision."

"Since we're not having much success in coordinating our efforts," old Broussaud said slowly, "we'd do better to abstain from making any rash decisions. Under present conditions, it would be impossible to set off a full-scale revolution."

"Who knows?" Armand said.

"Even if the insurrection turned out to be only a riot, it wouldn't be useless," said Garnier. "Every time there's a revolt, the people become more and more aware of their strength, and the chasm that separates them from the ruling class becomes deeper and deeper."

A buzz spread through the room. "There might be a lot of blood spilled," said a voice. "Spilling blood won't get us anywhere," said another.

For a moment they argued noisily. His voice lowered, Armand asked me, "What do you think?"

"I have no opinion in the matter."

"But you have a world of experience," he said. "You ought to have *some* opinion."

I shook my head. How could I have given them advice? Did I know what value they placed on life and death? It was for them to decide. Why live, if living is merely not dying? But to die in order to save one's life, is not that the greatest dupery of all? In any event, it wasn't for me to choose for them.

"There's no doubt that there will be incidents," Armand said. "If you don't want to start an insurrection, then at least let's make preparations in case one breaks out."

"That's right," Garnier said. "Let's not start anything ourselves, but let's be ready, and if the people begin to march, we'll march with them."

"I'm afraid they won't begin to march without first calculating their chances of success," Broussaud said.

"In any case, the Republican party has to stand behind them."

"On the contrary . . ."

Again voices were raised. They were speaking loudly and their eyes were shining, their voices trembling. On the other side of those walls there were, at this very minute, millions of men who were speaking with the same trembling voices, the same shining eyes. And while they were speaking, the insurrection, the Republic, France, the future of the whole world was there, in their hands. At least that's what they believed. They held humanity's destiny pressed against their hearts. Half the city was seething around the catafalque in which the remains of General Lamarque were lying, and no one was thinking of the general.

None of us slept that night. We were at work establishing communications between the various groups along the boulevards. If the insurrection turned out to be successful, we would have to try our best to persuade La Fayette to accept leadership, for he alone, by the prestige of his name, was able to rally the masses. Garnier entrusted Armand with negotiating, in case of success, with the principal Republican leaders. As for himself, having assembled a group of men at the Austerlitz bridge, he intended to stir the citizens of the Saint-Marceau district to revolt.

"But you should be the one to carry on negotiations," said Armand. "Your voice carries more weight than mine. And Fosca, who's a lot closer than we are to the workers, can hold the Austerlitz bridge."

"No," Garnier said. "I've done enough talking in my life. This time I'm going to fight."

"And if you got yourself killed, that would be smart, wouldn't it?" Spinelle said. "What will happen to the paper?"

"It will get along all right without me."

"Armand is right," I said. "I know the workers of Saint-Marceau. Let me go there and lead them."

A thin smile appeared on Garnier's face. "You saved my life once," he said. "That's enough."

I looked at his nervous mouth, at the creases on either side of it, at that tormented face with its hard, somewhat shifty eyes. He was gazing at the horizon beyond which the serpentine river was hidden; green

tufts were waving in the breeze atop tall reeds, and alligators were
sleeping in the warm mud. "I've got to feel that I'm alive, even if I have
to die trying," he said.

At ten o'clock the next morning, all the members of the Society
for the Rights of Man and the Friends of the People, as well as the
medical and law students, were gathered in the Place Louis XV. The
students of the polytechnical school were missing; the word was passed
around that they had been confined to their quarters. Green branches
and banners and tricolored flags fluttered above their heads; everyone
was holding some kind of insignia in his hand, and some were carrying
arms. The sky was dark. It was drizzling. But the bloody fires of hope
were burning in their hearts. Something was going to happen, they were
going to make it happen. They believed it. They believed that they
were capable of doing something, and with their hands gripping the
butts of revolvers, they were ready to die to prove it to themselves,
ready to give their lives to prove that those lives weighed heavily on
earth.

Six young men were pulling the hearse and La Fayette was holding
the cordons of the canopy. Two battalions of ten thousand municipal
guards were following behind. The government had stationed guards
all along the route, but this huge show of force, far from setting the
people's minds at ease, only made the danger of a disturbance seem more
imminent. Men and women were jammed together on the sidewalks, at
windows, in trees, on rooftops. Italian, German and Polish flags,
reminders of the tyrannies the French government had been unwilling
to fight against, hung from balconies. As the procession moved along,
the marchers sang revolutionary hymns. Armand was singing, and so
was Spinelle whom I had saved from cholera. The sight of the dragoons
filled their hearts with anger and they ripped branches from trees and
picked up stones to serve as arms. We had arrived at a street leading to
the Place Vendôme and the young men who were pulling the hearse,
instead of continuing along the predetermined route, turned off and
circled the monument. Someone behind me cried out, "Where are they
leading us?" and a voice answered, "To the Republic!" *They're being
led to a riot, to death*, I thought. What, after all, did the Republic mean
to them? They were preparing to fight, but none of them knew what
was really at stake. They were certain only that it was something very
important, for they were going to pay for it with their blood. "What's
Rivella?" I had said. But it was not really Rivella that Antonio had

coveted; he had wanted a victory. He died for that victory and he died contented. They gave their lives to prove to themselves that they were living men and not ants, or flies, or blocks of stone. *We won't let ourselves be turned into stones.* And the stakes blazed, and they were singing, and Marianne was saying: "Be a man among men." But what was the use? I could march beside them, but I couldn't risk my life with theirs.

When we reached the Place de la Bastille, we saw the polytechnical students, heads bare and clothes in disarray, running toward us. They had managed to get out despite the confinement. The crowd began to cry out, "Long live the engineers! Long live the Republic!" and the band in front of the catafalque struck up the *Marseillaise.* A rumor was being spread that an officer of the twelfth regiment had just told some of the students that he was a Republican, and from mouth to mouth the word was circulated among the marchers: "The troops are with us."

The procession drew to a halt at the Austerlitz bridge. A platform had been erected, and La Fayette climbed up on it to give his speech. He spoke of General Lamarque whom we were bringing to his last resting place. Others spoke after him. But no one was concerned with these speeches nor with the general who was lying dead in his coffin.

"Garnier should be over there, at the other end of the bridge," Armand said. He searched the area with his eyes, but it was impossible to pick out a face from among the milling crowd.

"Something's going to happen now," said Spinelle.

Everyone was waiting, waiting for something, not knowing exactly what. Suddenly, a man on horseback, dressed in black and carrying a red flag on top of which was a Liberty hat, rode through the crowd. There was an immediate uproar; people looked at each other and voices cried out, "No red flags!"

"It's a trick, a betrayal," said Spinelle, stammering in anger. "They want to intimidate the people."

"Do you think so?"

"Yes," Armand said. "The troops and the municipal guards are afraid of the red flag. And the crowd can feel it."

We waited a moment longer, and then Armand said abruptly, "Nothing's going to happen here. Go find Garnier and tell him to give the signal himself. I'll be at the *National.* I'm going to try to get the Republican leaders together."

I made my way through the crowd and found Garnier at the place we had marked on the map during the night. A rifle was slung over his shoulder. The streets behind him were filled with somber-faced men, many of whom were carrying rifles.

"Everything's ready," I said. "The people are ripe for a riot. But Armand asks that you give the signal."

"All right."

I silently watched him. Like every other day, like every night, he was afraid, I knew it, afraid of the death that would sweep down upon him in spite of himself and reduce him to dust.

"The dragoons!"

Their shining helmets and bayonets could be seen above the black mass of the crowd; they were streaming out onto Quai Morland and riding in columns toward the bridge. "They're charging us!" Garnier cried out. He grabbed his rifle and fired. No sooner had he done so than shooting burst out all around him and a loud clamor filled the air: "To the barricades! To arms!"

Barricades were hastily thrown up. Men with guns rushed forth from every neighboring street. Followed by a veritable army, Garnier headed for the barracks on Rue Popincourt. We rushed the building, and the soldiers ceded to us after offering only token resistance. We took twelve hundred rifles and handed them out to the insurgents. Garnier then led them to the cloister of Saint-Merri which they set about transforming into a stronghold.

"Tell Armand that we're holding the whole district," Garnier said. "And that we'll hold it as long as we have to."

Everywhere, people were erecting barricades. Men were cutting down trees and laying them across streets; others were dragging iron beds, tables and chairs from houses. Women and children were carrying cobblestones which they had dug out of the ground with their hands. Everyone was singing. Around joyous fires the peasants of Ingolstadt were singing.

I found Armand in the building of the *National*. His eyes were beaming with joy. The insurgents were holding half the city and they had attacked and taken most of the barracks and magazines. The government had decided to bring the troops out against them, but they weren't at all sure that the troops were loyal. The Republican leaders were about to name a provisional government with La Fayette at its head, and the national guard was counted on to rally to its former chief.

"Tomorrow the Republic will be proclaimed," Armand said. His voice was alive with excitement.

They loaded me down with food and ammunition which I was to take to the cloister of Saint-Merri for Garnier and his men. Bullets were whistling through the streets. People tried to stop me at every corner: "Don't go that way! There's a barricade!" they shouted. I ran on. A bullet tore through my hat, another struck me in the shoulder. I continued to run. The sky fled by above my head and the earth bounded under my horse's hoofs. I was running; I was delivered of the past and the future, delivered of myself and that bitter taste of boredom in my mouth. Something existed that had never before existed—that frenzied city, swollen with blood and hope; its heart was beating in my breast. Suddenly I thought, "I'm alive!" and then immediately after I said to myself, "It may be the last time."

Garnier was sitting among his men behind a pile of bricks, tree trunks, furniture, cobblestones, and sacks of cement. Atop that hastily constructed wall they had stuck green branches. They were busily occupied making cartridges, using as wadding shreds from their shirts and pieces of signs they had ripped from walls. All of them were bare from the waist up.

"I've brought along some cartridges," I said.

Shouting joyfully, they grabbed the boxes from my hands. Garnier looked at me in surprise.

"How did you get through?" he asked.

"I got through. Let it go at that."

He pressed his lips together. He envied me. I wanted to say to him, "No, you're wrong to envy me. Neither courage nor cowardice are permitted me." But it wasn't the moment to speak of me or of him.

"The provisional government will be proclaimed sometime tonight," I said. "You're asked to hold until morning. The whole of Paris will rise up if the insurrection doesn't falter."

"We'll hold."

"Are you having much trouble?"

"The troops attacked twice. We pushed them back both times."

"Many dead?"

"I haven't counted."

I remained seated beside him for a moment. He was tearing pieces of white cloth between his teeth and with an absorbed look on his face he stuffed them into cardboard shells. He wasn't very adroit with his hands and it was obvious that he had no desire to be sitting there making cartridges. He wanted to speak to me, I knew it. But when I got up, we hadn't exchanged a word.

"Tell them we'll hold through the night."

"I'll tell them."

Again I hugged walls, hid under porches, ran through barrages of bullets. When I got to the building of the *National*, I was dripping with sweat and my shirt was soaked with blood. I thought of Armand's smile and the way his eyes would light up with joy when I told him that Garnier was stoutly holding the district.

"I saw Garnier. They'll hold."

But no smile appeared on Armand's face. He was standing in front of the door to the office. Standing in front of the fortress, Carlier stared vacantly into space. He was sitting in the canoe, staring at the yellow river which flowed from north to south. I knew that look.

"What happened?" I asked.

"They don't want the Republic."

"Who?"

"The Republican leaders don't want the Republic."

His face was so full of despair that for a moment I thought it might awaken an echo in me, a remembrance. But I remained empty and dry.

"Why?"

"They're afraid."

"Carrel doesn't want to risk it," said Spinelle. "He claims the people can't do anything against one loyal regiment." His voice was choked up. "And the troops would come over to our side if only Carrel would speak out."

"They're not afraid of a defeat," Armand said. "They're afraid of a victory, afraid of the people. They call themselves Republicans, but the republic they want wouldn't be any different than this stinking monarchy. They prefer even Louis-Philippe to the kind of regime we want to establish."

"Is it really hopeless?" I asked.

"We talked for more than two hours. Everything's lost. With La Fayette, with the municipal troops, we could have won. But we can't fight along against the armies that are marching on Paris."

"Well, what are you going to do?"

After a brief silence Spinelle said, "We still hold half of Paris."

"We hold exactly nothing," Armand said. "Our cause hasn't even got any leaders. It . . . it disavows itself. All those people who are getting themselves killed, are getting killed for nothing. The only thing we can do now is stop the massacre."

"I'll go tell Garnier to lay down his arms immediately," Spinelle said.

"Fosca will go. He knows his way around better than you."

It was six o'clock in the evening; night was falling. At every corner there were municipal guards and soldiers. Fresh regiments had just arrived and they were savagely attacking the barricades. Bodies were sprawled out in the streets, and men were carrying the wounded on stretchers. There were red puddles on the sidewalks and cobblestones. The insurrection was beginning to weaken; the people had not heard a word of hope for hours. They no longer knew why they were fighting. Many of the streets which the insurgents had held only a short while before were now teeming with red uniforms. I saw from afar that the barricade defended by Garnier was still standing; I ran toward it through a hail of bullets which came whistling past my ears from all directions. Garnier was leaning against the sacks of cement; bloody bandages were wrapped around his bare shoulder and his face was black with gunpowder.

"Any news?"

"They couldn't reach an agreement," I said.

"I knew it," he said indifferently.

The calmness with which he took the news astonished me; he was almost smiling.

"The troops aren't going to come over to our side. There's no hope left of winning. Armand asks that you stop the bloodshed."

"Stop the bloodshed?" This time he laughed openly. "Look at us."

I looked. There were only a handful of men left around Garnier. Their faces were black and bloody; all of them were wounded. Bare-chested bodies were stretched out against the walls; their eyes had been closed and their hands crossed on their chests.

"Would you happen to have a clean handkerchief?"

I pulled a handkerchief from my pocket. Garnier took it and wiped his sooty hands and face.

"Thanks." His eyes fell upon me and he suddenly seemed surprised to see me there. "You're wounded!"

"Just a few scratches."

We remained silent for a moment and then I said, "You're going to get yourself killed for nothing."

He shrugged his shoulders. "Does anyone ever get killed for *something?* Is there anything that's worth a life?"

"Ah! So that's the way you think," I said.

"Don't you?"

I paused. I had developed the habit of never saying what I really thought. "It seems to me that useful results are sometimes achieved."

"Do you think so?" Garnier asked. He was silent for a moment, and then something suddenly unloosed itself in him. "Suppose the negotiations had been successful? Do you believe our victory would have ultimately proven itself useful? Have you ever thought of the tasks the Republic would have had to accomplish? Refound society, moderate the party, satisfy the people, bring the rich under our subjection, and conquer the whole of Europe because all the other nations would immediately band together against us. All that to face, and we're only a small minority. And we lack political experience in the bargain. In fact it might very well be a stroke of luck for the Republic that it *didn't* triumph today."

I looked at him in surprise. I had often said these very same things to myself, but I never imagined that any of them had ever entertained such ideas.

"Then what made you start this insurrection?" I asked.

"We don't have to count on the future to give a meaning to our acts. If that were the case, all action would be impossible. We have to carry on our fight the way we decided to carry it on. That's all."

I had kept the gates of Carmona closed and I counted on nothing.

"I've done a lot of thinking about that," he said with a dry smile.

"Then you've chosen to die out of hopelessness, is that right?"

"I've never felt that things were hopeless because I've never hoped for anything."

"Is it possible to live without hope?"

"Yes, if you believe in something with absolute certainty."

"As for me, I believe in nothing," I said.

"For me, just being a man is the greatest thing possible."

"A man among men."

"Yes, that's enough. That's well worth living for—and dying for."

"Are you sure your comrades think the same way you do?" I asked.

"Try asking them to surrender!" he said. "Too much blood has been spilled. Now we have to fight it out to the end."

"But they don't know that nothing came of the negotiations."

"Go ahead and tell them if you like," he said in an angry voice. "What do they care? What do I care about their deliberations, their decisions and counter-decisions? We swore we'd defend the district and we'll defend it, that's all."

"This fighting here at the barricades is only one part of your battle. To finish it, you have to go on living."

He stood up, leaned against the fragile rampart and looked down the deserted street. "Maybe I don't have enough patience," he said.

"You don't have patience," I shot back rapidly, "because you're afraid of death."

"That may be true," he admitted.

Suddenly he seemed far from me. His eyes were glued to the street through which death would soon come charging, a death he had chosen. The stakes were blazing, the wind was scattering the ashes of the two Augustinian monks. *There is only one good: to act according to one's conscience.* Stretched out on his bed, Antonio was smiling. They were neither insane nor bloated with pride; I understood them now. They were men who wanted to fulfill their destinies as men by choosing their own lives and deaths: free men.

Garnier fell at the next charge. By morning, the insurrection had been crushed.

❧

Armand was sitting on the edge of my bed and I felt the weight of his hand on my shoulder. He was leaning toward me. His face had grown thin.

"Tell me about it," he said. His upper lip was swollen and there was a blue bruise on his temple.

"Is it true they took you to the tribunal by force?" I asked.

"Yes, but I'll tell you about that later. First tell me what happened to you."

A yellow lamp was hanging from the ceiling; I watched it swing back and forth. The dormitory was empty, but the sounds of clinking glasses, of laughter, of festive voices could be heard coming from another room; the guards were giving a banquet for the workers. Soon the prisoners would straggle back to the dormitory, half-drunk with food, drink, friendship and laughter. They would barricade themselves behind their beds, engage in a mock revolutionary battle and, for their evening prayer, would kneel down and sing the *Marseillaise*. I had grown used to these rites, and I felt comfortable and contented lying on my bed, looking at the yellow lamp hanging from the ceiling, swinging back and forth. Why stir up the past?

"It's always the same," I said.

"What do you mean?"

I closed my eyes. With much effort I plunged into that long, confused night which stretched out endlessly behind me. Blood, fire, tears, songs. They had ridden into the city at a gallop, had thrown flaming torches into the houses. Their horses had shattered children's skulls, crushed women's breasts. Blood was on their hoofs and a dog was howling at death.

"Women's throats are slit open, children's heads are smashed against stone walls. The cobblestones turn red, and where there were once living beings, there are only dead bodies."

"But what happened on the thirteenth of April at Rue Transnonain?" Armand asked impatiently. "That's what I want to know."

Rue Transnonain, the 13th of April. Why that remembrance rather than another? Was the past less dead after three months than after four hundred years?

"We went out into the street," I said. "We were told that Thiers himself had announced on the rostrum that the insurrection at Lyons had been triumphant. We raised barricades. Everyone was singing."

They had gathered together on the square. They raced through the streets shouting, "Death to the son of the devil!" They were singing.

"And then?" Armand asked.

"The troops attacked in the morning. They swept right through the barricades and went into the building. They killed everyone they could lay their hands on." I shrugged my shoulders. "I told you. It's always the same."

We both remained silent for a moment and then Armand said, "How is it you didn't realize it was a trap? Thiers knew on the evening of the twelfth that the insurrection had been put down in Lyons. And when he set off the riot, all the leaders had already been arrested. I was arrested . . ."

"We didn't know that until afterwards."

"But you have lots of experience. You should have felt the danger and stopped them."

"They wanted to go down to the street; I went down with them."

Armand gave his shoulders an impatient shrug. "You should be leading rather than obeying them."

"But I can't look upon things the same way they do," I said. He looked at me irritably and I continued, "I can do whatever they ask me to do. But how can I decide for them? How can I possibly know what they believe to be good or bad for themselves?"

Antonio had died with a smile on his face at the age of twenty; Garnier was avidly watching his death as it turned the corner of the street; and Beatrice was bending a fleshy, mournful face over her manuscripts. They alone were the judges.

"Do you believe they wanted that massacre?" Armand bitingly asked.

"Is it so great an evil?" I said.

The dead were dead, the living alive. The prisoners did not hate their prison; they were delivered of their dreary work, could finally laugh, rest, chat. Before dying, they had sung . . .

"I'm afraid these months in prison have tired you out," Armand said.

I looked at his pale face. "Aren't you tired?" I asked.

"Just the contrary."

There was so much passion in his voice that it pierced through the calm haze behind which I had taken shelter. Abruptly, I got out of bed and paced back and forth for a few moments.

"The organization lost all its leaders, didn't it? That's like cutting a head off a body."

"Yes. It's our own fault. You don't engage in conspiracies right out in the open. It was a lesson we had to learn, a lesson that will serve us well one day."

"When?" I asked. "They're going to sentence you to ten to twenty years."

"In twenty years I'll only be forty-four."

I silently looked at him for a moment and then said, "I envy you."

"Why?"

"Because one day you'll die. You'll never become like me."

"Ah! If only I didn't have to die!" he said.

"Yes, that's what I used to say."

I squeezed the greenish bottle in my hand and I thought, "The things I'll be able to do!" With rapid little steps, Marianne scurried about the room. "I've so little time ahead," she said. I looked down at Armand and for the first time it occurred to me that he was our child.

"I'll get you out of here," I said.

"How?"

"There are only two guards in the court at night. They're armed, but someone who's not afraid of bullets can attract their attention and give an agile man enough time to scale the wall."

Armand shook his head. "I don't want to escape now. We're counting a great deal on the repercussions our trial will have."

"But they might separate us from one day to the next," I said. "And it would be an extraordinary stroke of luck if they ever put us together again. You should jump at the chance."

"No, I have to stay," he insisted.

I shrugged my shoulders. "You too!"

"Me too? What do you mean?"

"Like Garnier, you've decided to become a martyr."

"Garnier chose a useless death and he was wrong about that. But I believe there's nowhere else I can do as much useful work as right here."

Armand looked around him at the large, empty dormitory. In another room, seated around a table laden with food and drink, they were laughing heartily and singing drinking songs.

"I was told that here at Sainte-Pélagie they were very easy on the prisoners. Is there any truth in that?"

"Yes, it's true. The bourgeois even have their own private rooms. This dormitory is only for the workers."

"Well then!" he said. "Do you realize what a wonderful opportunity this is to make contacts, to talk things over, to plan, to thrash out our differences? Before I leave here, a united front *must* be formed."

"But ten or twenty years of imprisonment, doesn't the prospect frighten you?"

He gave a short laugh, a laugh that failed to light up his face. "That's another question."

On the plains the Genoese could be seen scurrying about their red tents. The dusty road was deserted. I turned my eyes away; it was not for me to ask myself questions. I, I kept Carmona's gates closed . . . I had been that man and now I no longer understood him.

"What makes you think that a man must prefer the cause he happens to be serving for the moment to his own destiny?" I asked.

He reflected. "I can't make any distinction between the two."

"Yes," I said.

I kept the gates closed and I said to myself: "Carmona will be the equal of Florence." I had no other future.

"I remember."

"You remember?" he asked, perplexed.

"I was once your age . . . a very long time ago. I believed then that the cause I was serving and my own destiny were one."

A glimmer of curiosity shone in his calm eyes. "And you don't any more?"

"Not entirely."

"And yet your fate should be completely bound to humanity's since you'll last as long as humanity."

"And perhaps even *out*last it," I said. I shrugged my shoulders. "You're right. This prison life has tired me out. It will pass."

"I'm sure it will pass," he said. "And then you'll see how much good we'll accomplish."

There were two opposing tendencies in the Republican party. One group was in favor of maintaining the privileges of the bourgeoisie: they demanded liberty, but they demanded it only for themselves. They desired political reforms only, and repulsed all suggestions for social reforms. If there were to be social laws passed, they wanted them to be nothing but new forms of repression. Armand and his friends, on the other hand, held that liberty could not be the appanage of a single class, and that only the advent of socialism would allow the workers to become free. Nothing compromised the success of the revolution more seriously than this division, and it therefore did not surprise me that Armand sought so passionately to form a united front. I admired his perseverance. In just a few days he had transformed the prison into a political club. From morning till evening and through a large part of the night, discussions took place in the rooms and dormitories. Although they never led anywhere, Armand never became discouraged. In the meanwhile, the guards would grab hold of him and his comrades several times each week and drag them by force through the corridors of the prison to the tribunal; their heads would sometimes strike the stone floor or the steps of a stairway. But each time they would come back smiling. "We didn't talk," they would say. One evening, however, when he entered his room where I had been waiting for him, I saw that same look on his face as I had seen in front of the *National*. He sat down and for a long moment remained silent. Finally he said: "The men from Lyons talked."

"Is that so serious?"

"They destroyed the whole effect of our silence." He sunk his head in his hands. When he looked up at me again, his face had hardened, but his voice trembled. "We mustn't delude ourselves. The trial is going to drag on and on, and it won't have the effect we had hoped for."

"Do you remember what I once proposed?" I asked.

"Yes." He stood up and nervously paced back and forth in the room. "I don't want to leave alone."

"You can't all escape."

"Why not?"

Before three days had gone by, Armand had found a way of escaping from Sainte-Pélagie with his comrades. Opposite the door which gave out onto the courtyard was another door leading to a small cellar. Workers who were making repairs in the prison told Armand that this cellar extended under a neighboring garden. He decided we would try to dig our way out into the garden. There was a guard stationed in front of the door; some of the prisoners were to occupy his attention by playing ball in the courtyard while the others were digging. The noise of the repair work would cover the sounds of our improvised picks and shovels. In six days a hole was dug almost to the surface of the garden. Only a thin layer of earth separated us from the light. Spinelle, who had escaped the April 13th roundup, was to come during the night with a few other men and bring ladders to help us get over the walls of the garden. Twenty-four of the prisoners were planning to escape and seek refuge in England. But one of us, giving up all hope of making his way to freedom, had to detain the guard while he was making his rounds.

"I'll do it," I said.

"No, we'll draw lots," Armand said.

"What's twenty years of prison to me?"

"That's not the question."

"I know what you're thinking," I said. "You think I can be of greater service to you than any of the others. Well, you're wrong."

"You've already been of great service to us."

"But there's no guarantee that I'll continue to be. Leave me here. I'm satisfied staying here; I feel at ease in this place."

We were sitting in his room facing each other, and he looked at me more attentively than at any time during the past four years. That day, he believed it useful to try to understand me.

"What's the reason for all this apathy?"

I laughed. "It came upon me little by little. Six hundred years . . . Do you know how many days that makes?"

He did not so much as smile. "Even if I live for six hundred years, I'll still go on fighting. Do you think there's less to do on earth today than in other times?"

"*Is* there something to do on earth?"

This time he laughed. "It seems so to me, at least."

"Tell me," I said, "what makes you want freedom so much?"

"I like to see the sun shining," he said in a fiery voice. "I like rivers and the sea. How can anyone sit back and allow those magnificent forces that are in man to be choked off?"

"And what would he do with them?"

"What's the difference? He'll do whatever he likes with them. But first he has to be delivered." He leaned toward me. "Men want to be free. Don't you hear their voices?"

I could hear her voice: "Stay a man." They had the same faith in their eyes. I put my hand on Armand's shoulder.

"This evening I can hear you," I said. "That's why I say: accept my offer. This may be the last evening. Every evening may be the last. Tonight I want to serve you, but tomorrow, perhaps, I might not have anything to offer you any more."

Armand looked at me intensely and a cloud passed over his face. He suddenly seemed to have discovered something which he had never before suspected and which frightened him a little.

"I accept," he said.

彭

Lying on my back, lying on the frozen mud, on the wooden deck, on the beach of silvery sand, I stared at the stone ceiling, felt the gray walls around me, around me the sea, the plains, and the horizon's gray walls. Years had gone by; after centuries, years as long as centuries, as short as hours. I stared at the ceiling and I called out, "Marianne." She had said, "You'll forget me," but against the hours and centuries I fought to keep her alive in me. I stared at the ceiling and occasionally, for a brief instant, an image of her formed in the depths of my eyes, always the same image: the blue gown, the bare shoulders, that portrait which did not look like her. I tried again. Something stirred in me. It was almost a smile. It lasted as long as a flash of lightning, and then it quickly faded. What was the use? Embalmed in my heart, in the depths of that freezing cellar, she was as dead as in her tomb. I closed my eyes, but even in my dreams I could no longer escape. The fogs, the phantoms, the adventures, the metamorphoses all had that stale, stagnant taste—the taste of my saliva, the taste of my thoughts.

Behind me the door creaked. A hand touched my shoulder and their voices came to me from very far off. *It had to happen,* I thought. They touched my bare shoulder and they said: "Come with us," and the shadow of the palm tree vanished. After fifty years, or one day, or one hour, it always ended by happening. "The carriage is waiting, sir." I had to open my eyes. There were several men around me who were saying that I was free.

I followed them through the corridor and I did everything they ordered to me to do. I signed papers, I took a package which they authoritatively put in my hands. And then they led me to a door which closed behind me. It was drizzling. The tide was low; as far as the eye could reach, only gray sand could be seen around the island. I was free.

I put one foot forward, then the other. To go where? In the swamp, the rushes spit drops of water with a raucous murmur, and I continued on, step after step, toward the horizon which retreated with each step. I put my foot on an embankment and gazed at the horizon. And then, a few feet away, I saw him, holding out his hand and smiling. He was no longer a young man. With his broad shoulders and heavy beard, he looked as old as I. "I came to get you," he said.

His warm, hard hands tightened around mine. On the other side of the river a fire was burning, a fire was burning in Marianne's eyes. Armand took me by the arm. He spoke, and his voice was a quick, clear fire. I followed him, putting one foot forward and then the other, thinking, *Will it begin again then? Will it always go on? Always go on beginning again, day after day, forever, forever?*

I followed him along a road; there were always roads, roads which led nowhere. And then we climbed into a coach. Armand continued speaking. Ten years had passed, a large slice of his life. He was telling me his story and I was listening. The words still had meaning—always the same meaning, the same words. Horses were galloping, outside it was snowing; it was winter. Four seasons, seven colors. The stuffy air smelled of old leather. Even the odors, I knew them all. People were getting out of the carriage and others were climbing in. It had been a long time since I had seen so many faces, so many noses, mouths, so many pairs of eyes. Armand was speaking. He was telling me about England, the amnesty, the return to France, his efforts to obtain a pardon for me and his joy when at last it was granted.

"I had been hoping for a long time that you would escape," he said. "It wouldn't have been difficult for you."

"I didn't try," I said.

"Oh!"

He looked at me and then he turned his eyes away. He began to speak to me again without asking me questions. He was living in Paris in a small apartment with Spinelle and a woman he had met in England. He was counting on my living with them, too. I acquiesced.

"Is she your wife?" I asked.

"No, just a friend," he quickly replied.

We arrived in Paris after traveling all night. It was early morning, the streets were covered with snow. That too was an old scene. Marianne had liked the snow, and suddenly she seemed at once closer to me and more lost than when I lay gazing at the ceiling in my dungeon. There was a place for her in this winter morning, and that place was empty.

We climbed up a stairway. Nothing had changed in ten years, in five centuries; there were always ceilings above their heads, and around them, beds, tables, chairs, paper on the walls, olive green or almond green. And between those walls, they went on living, waiting to die, caressing their mortal dreams. In barns, there were cows with their warm green stomachs, their large, bland eyes in which dreams of hay and green meadows were reflected into infinity.

"Fosca!"

Spinelle squeezed my hand in his and grinned broadly at me. He was the same as ever. His features had hardened only very slightly. And also, after that long night, I found Armand's face the same as I had always known it. It seemed to me that I had left them only the day before.

"This is Laura," Armand said.

She had a serious expression on her face. She looked at me and, without smiling, held out her hard, nervous, tiny hand. She was not very young. She had a slender waist, large, dark eyes and an olive complexion. Her hair fell in black curls to her shoulders which were covered by a shawl with long fringes.

"You must be hungry," she said.

She had placed large bowls of coffee and a plate of buttered toast on the table. They ate, and Armand and Spinelle spoke animatedly. They both seemed very happy to be with me again. I took only a few swallows of coffee. I had lost the habit of eating in prison. I tried to answer their questions and to smile, but it seemed to me as if my heart were buried under cold lava.

"In a few days there's going to be a banquet in your honor," Armand said.

"A banquet?"

"The leaders of the principal workers' organizations are going to be there. You're one of our heroes . . . The thirteenth of April uprising, ten years of confinement . . . You can't imagine the weight your name carries today."

"No, I hadn't the remotest suspicion," I said.

"You must be surprised by this idea of ours to give a banquet for you," Spinelle said. I shook my head and he continued authoritatively, "I'll explain it to you."

He still spoke in the same voluble, stuttering manner. He explained to me that the tactic of fomenting insurrections had been abandoned. Violence was to be reserved for the day when the revolution would really be unleashed. In the meantime, what they were trying to do was to unite all the workers in one vast union. The exiles who had been in London learned the importance of a united workers' association. Banquets were to serve as occasions for manifesting this solidarity; they were to be repeated throughout France. He spoke for a long while. From time to time he turned toward Laura as if to ask her approbation, and she nodded her head in approval.

"I see," I said when he finished.

There was a brief silence. I felt I wasn't saying the words or making the gestures that they expected of me. But I was incapable of inventing them.

Laura stood up. "Don't you want to rest awhile?" she asked. "I'm sure the journey must have been very tiring."

"Yes, I'd like to get some sleep. I used to sleep a lot there."

"I'll show you to your room."

I followed her. She opened a door and said, "It's not a very beautiful room, but if you like it here, it would make us very happy."

"I'm sure I'll like it."

She closed the door and I stretched myself out on the bed. There was a clean, pressed suit and fresh linens on a chair. Shelves were filled with books. Outside, voices and the sound of steps could be heard. At times a cart passed by. It was Paris, it was the world. I was free, free between the earth and the sky and the gray walls of the horizon. In the Faubourg Saint-Antoine machines were humming, always, always. Children were being born in hospitals, old people were dying. Behind the snow-heavy clouds, the sun was red. Somewhere a young man was looking at that sun and something was bursting in his heart. I held my hand against my heart. It was beating, always, always, and the sea was beating against the shore, always, always. It was beginning again, it was going on, and it would go on beginning again, always, always.

Night had long since fallen when someone knocked at my door. It was Laura. She was holding a lamp in her hand.

"Do you want me to bring you your dinner here?"

"No, don't bother. I'm not hungry."

She put down the lamp and came over to the bed. "Perhaps you didn't want to leave prison," she said.

She had a soft, rather husky voice. I raised myself to my elbows. A woman. Like the seasons, the hours, the colors, they were the same as always—their hearts beating under warm flesh, their fresh teeth, their eyes constantly in quest of life, the smell of their tears.

"We thought we were doing the right thing," she said.

"But you did do the right thing . . ."

"It's hard to tell." She looked at my face, at my hands, and she murmured, "Armand told me . . ."

"He told you?"

I got out of bed, glanced in the mirror and walked over to the window. I pressed my brow against the glass pane. The street lamps were lit. In their homes, families were gathered around tables. For centuries and centuries, eating, sleeping . . .

"I imagine it's tiring to begin living again," she said.

I turned toward her and said something I had said long before, "Don't worry about me."

"I worry about everything and everyone," she said. "That's how I'm made." She walked to the door. "You mustn't hold it against us."

"I assure you, I don't hold it against you. I only hope I'll still be able to be useful to you."

"But can't anyone be useful to *you?*" she asked.

"I strongly advise you not to try it," I answered.

※

"It's going to be a terrific manifestation!" Spinelle exclaimed.

His foot was propped on a chair and he was energetically brushing an already sparkling shoe. Laura was leaning over a table, pressing a shirt.

"I know of nothing more depressing than those banquets," she murmered.

"They serve a purpose," Armand said.

"I'd like to think so," she said.

Armand was going through a pile of papers stacked on the marble mantel of the fireplace, in which a thin fire was burning.

"You know more or less what you have to say, don't you?" he asked.

"More or less," I answered without enthusiasm.

"It's a shame I can't speak in your place," said Spinelle. "I feel inspired tonight."

Laura smiled. "You're always inspired."

He spun around and said spiritedly: "Wasn't my last speech good?"

"That's what I say. Your speeches are always magnificent."

In the fireplace, a log broke and collapsed, Spinelle began violently brushing his other shoe, Laura was sliding the iron back and forth over the white shirt, Armand was reading and the pendulum of the big clock was swinging peacefully to and fro: tick-tock, tick-tock. I heard it, I smelled the odor of the hot cloth, I saw the flowers that Laura had arranged in vases; Marianne had once told me what they were called. I saw each piece of furniture in the room and the yellow stripes of the wallpaper. I noticed every quiver in their faces, every inflection in their voices. I even heard the words they did not utter. They spoke gayly to each other, worked together, and each of them would have given his life for the other. And yet a drama was unfolding between them. They always managed to create dramas in their lives: Spinelle loved Laura, but she wasn't in love with him; she loved Armand, or at least she regretted no longer loving him; and Armand dreamed of women who were far away or who did not love him. I turned my back to Eliana and looked at Beatrice, thinking, "Why must it be Antonio whom she looks at with eyes like that?" Laura's hand moved back and forth above the smooth cloth, a tiny hand the color of dull ivory. Why didn't Armand love her? She loved him, she was there—a woman, a living being. And the others were nothing more than women, they too. And why did Laura refuse to love Spinelle? Was there so much of a difference between Armand and him? One was dark brown and the other auburn, one was serious and the other gay. But both of them had those eyes that saw, those lips that moved, those hands that gestured . . .

All of them had those same eyes, those same lips, those same hands. There were at least a hundred of them in the hall. The table was laden with bottles and food. And it was I at whom their eyes were looking. Some of them knew me. They slapped my back, shook my hand and laughingly remarked, "You haven't changed a bit." At Spinelle's bedside they had looked at each other and their hearts burst with joy. I had envied them. Now it was I at whom they were looking, but their looks slid off me. In my heart, not a spark. Buried under the cold lava, under the ashes, the old volcano was deader than the craters of the moon.

I sat down beside them. They ate and drank and I ate and drank with them. Marianne was smiling at them. A woman was singing and everyone took up the refrain. *You have to sing, too.* And I had sung. One after the other they arose and drank toasts to my health. They recalled incidents out of the past: Garnier's death, Rue Transnonain, Sainte-Pélagie, and those ten years I had lived in the underground dungeons of Mont Saint-Michel. With those words that fell from mortal lips, they created a radiant legend which stirred them even more than songs. Their voices trembled with emotion, and in the women's eyes there were tears. The dead were dead, and from that dead past the living made a burning present. The living were alive.

They also spoke of the future, of progress, of humanity. Armand arose and spoke. He said that if only the workers would unite, if only they wanted it strongly enough, they would become the masters of the machines to which they were now enslaved. Those very machines would become the instruments of their deliverance, of their happiness. He conjured up images of a time when swift trains speeding along steel rails would break down the barriers raised by the selfish protectionism of nations. The world would then become an immense market place which would generously provide mankind with all its needs. His voice filled the hall. They stopped eating, stopped drinking. They listened. With wide eyes, they looked beyond the walls of the hall and saw golden fruits, streams of milk and honey. Marianne was looking through the frost-rimmed window. In her belly she felt the warm, heavy weight of the future, and she was smiling. Screaming women threw themselves to their knees, ripped their clothes, and men trampled upon them. On the squares, in the back rooms of shops, in the open countryside, prophets were preaching—a time would come when justice would prevail, a time of happiness. When her turn came, Laura stood up. In her ardent, husky voice, she too spoke of the future. Blood was flowing, houses burning, shouts and songs ripped through the air, and in the green meadows of the future snowy white sheep were peacefully grazing. The time would come . . . I listened to their heavy breathing. Well, here it was! The time had come, the future was *now*—the future of the burned martyrs, of the decapitated peasants, of the ardent-voiced orators, the future that Marianne had hoped so desperately to see. The future was these joyless days metered by the humming of machines; it was the physical exhaustion of children, it was prisons, hovels, weariness, hunger, boredom . . .

"It's your turn," Armand whispered to me.

I stood up, I wanted to obey him. *Stay a man.* I leaned my hands on the table and I began: "I'm very happy to be among you again . . ."

And my voice dried up in my throat. I was *not* among them. That future which for them was pure and smooth, and as inaccessible as the sky's azure, would for me become a present through which I would have to live day after day, in boredom and weariness. 1944. I would read that date on a calendar while other men would be gazing ahead with astonished eyes at the year 2044, the year 2144 . . . Stay a man. But she had also said to me: "We don't live in the same world. You look at me from the depths of another age."

Two hours later, when I was alone with Armand, I said to him, "I'm sorry."

He put his hand on my shoulder. "There's nothing to be sorry about. Your silence had a more gripping effect than a long speech."

I shook my head. "I'm sorry because I realized I could no longer work with you."

"Why not?"

"Let's just say I'm tired."

"That doesn't mean anything to me," he said impatiently. "What's the real reason?"

"What good would it do you if I told you?"

Somewhat irritably, he shrugged his shoulders. "Are you afraid of convincing me of something? That's being a little too scrupulous."

"Oh, I have no doubt you're capable of resisting even the devil or God," I said.

"Then tell me your real reasons." He looked at me and smiled. "Maybe *I'll* convince *you*."

I looked at the flowers in the vases, at the yellow stripes on the wall, at the pendulum swinging back and forth with the same even rhythm.

"I don't believe in the future," I said.

"There will be a future, that at least is certain."

"But all of you speak of it as if it were going to be a paradise. There won't be any paradises, and that's equally certain."

"Of course not." He studied me, seemed to be searching my face to find the words that might win me over. "Paradise for us is simply the moment when the dreams we dream today are finally realized. We're well aware that after that other men will have new needs, new desires, will make new demands."

"How can you have any desires at all, knowing that man will never be satisfied?"

He smiled at me coldly. "Don't you know what it's like to have desires?"

"Yes, I've had desires," I said. "I know." I paused a moment and then went on, "But it's not simply a question of desires. You're fighting for *others*. You want *others* to be happy."

"We're fighting together, for us," he said. He continued studying me attentively. "You always use the term 'man' and you look at people through the eyes of an outsider. If I were God, then it might very well be that I wouldn't find any reason to do this or that for them. But I'm one of them. With them, for them, I want certain things and not others. And I want them today."

"I once wanted Carmona to be free," I said. "And because I saved her from being subjugated by Florence and Genoa, she was lost along with Florence and Genoa. You want the Republic, freedom. Well, what makes you so sure that if you succeed, your successes won't lead eventually to the worst tyrannies? If one lives long enough, one sees that every victory sooner or later turns to defeat."

My tone no doubt irritated him, for he said sharply, "I've had a little smattering of history. You're not teaching me anything. Everything that's ever done finally ends by being undone. I realize that. And from the hour you're born you begin to die. But between birth and death there's life." His voice softened. "I suppose the big difference between us is that a human destiny—for you, an ephemeral human destiny—isn't very important in your eyes."

"That's correct," I said.

"You're already far off in the future," he said. "And you look upon these moments as if they were part of the past. And all past enterprises appear derisive when they're seen only as dead, embalmed, and buried. That Carmona was great and free for two hundred years doesn't move you much today. But you know very well what Carmona meant to those who loved her. I don't believe you were wrong in defending her against Genoa."

The fountains were singing, a white doublet shone against the dark yews and Antonio was saying, "Carmona is my country . . ."

"Then why did you say that Garnier was wrong in defending the cloister of Saint-Merri to the bitter end?"

"It was an act without tomorrow," Armand said. He reflected a moment. "In my opinion, we should concern ourselves only with that part of the future on which we have a hold. But we should try our best to enlarge our hold on it as much as possible."

"You're doing exactly what you reproached me for doing. You're looking down upon Garnier's action without participating in it."

"Perhaps," Armand said. "Perhaps I haven't the right to pass judgment on him."

"You admit," I said after a short silence, "that you're working for only a limited future."

"A limited future, a limited life—that's our lot as men. And it's enough," he said. "If I knew that in fifty years it would be against the law to employ children in factories, against the law for men to work more than ten hours a day, if I knew that the people would choose their own representatives, that the press would be free, I would be completely satisfied." Again his eyes fell upon me. "You find the workers' conditions abominable. Well, think of those workers you know personally, only of them. Don't you want to help change their lot in life?"

"One day I saw a child smile," I said. "It seemed very important to me then that that child be able to smile sometimes. Yes, there are moments when I'm touched." I looked at him. "But there are also moments when everything is obliterated."

He stood up and put his hand on my shoulder. "And if everything were obliterated for good, what would become of you?"

"I don't know," I answered.

The flowers, the pendulum, the wallpaper with its yellow stripes . . . if I left those things, where would I go? If I stopped submissively obeying them, what would I do?

"You have to live in the present, Fosca," he said in a pressing tone of voice. "With us, for us. And it will also be for you. The present has to become important to you."

"But words dry up in my throat," I said. "Desires dry up in my heart and gestures at the tips of my fingers."

In his eyes, I again noticed that precise, practical look I knew so well.

"At least allow us to make use of you. There's so much prestige attached to your name, to your person. Attend the banquets, come to the meetings, go with Laura on a tour of the provinces."

I remained silent.

"Will you do it?"

"What reason would I have to refuse?" I said to him.

"Only two francs a month," Laura was saying, "and all the mill workers would be protected against sickness and lay-offs, against the miseries of old age. You could even stop work for several days whenever you think it necessary to go on strike."

Dull and weary, they listened to her speaking. Hardly a handful of men were there. It was the same in every city. They were too worn out by their daily work to find the strength to wish for any other future but their evening meal and sleep, restful sleep. And their wives were afraid.

"Who would handle all that money?" one of them asked.

"You'll elect a committee which will give you an accounting every month."

"That would be a very powerful committee."

"You'll watch what it spends."

"Who'll watch?"

"Everyone who comes to the meetings."

"It would be a lot of money," one of the men repeated.

They would willingly have sacrificed two francs every month, but they were wary of the obscure power the relief fund would represent in the hands of one of their own. They were afraid of creating new masters over themselves. In her hoarse, ardent voice, Laura pleaded with them, but their faces remained closed.

"They're suspicious of us," she said to me with a sigh as we were leaving the meeting hall.

"They're even suspicious of themselves."

"Yes," she said. "And it isn't really surprising—they've never known anything but their own weakness."

She pulled her shawl around her shoulders. The air was mild but it was drizzling. Ever since we had arrived in Rouen, it had not stopped raining or drizzling.

"I've caught a cold," she said.

"Come and have a hot grog before you go back to your room."

Her shawl was very thin, her shoes soaked up water. When she sat down in the leather chair, I noticed the heavy bags under her eyes, her red nose. She could have been sitting peacefully by a fireside, sleeping through long nights, could have been beautiful, elegant, and no doubt loved. But she went from city to city, ate badly, slept little, neglecting her appearance, wearing out her shoes and her strength. For what profit?

"You tire yourself out too much," I said.

She shrugged her shoulders and remained silent.

"You ought to pay more attention to yourself."

"One can't pay attention to oneself," she replied.

There was a note of regret in her voice. Armand paid very little attention to her and Spinelle paid her the wrong kind of attention. He irritated her. And I, I followed her through the cities of France, hardly ever speaking to her.

"I admire Armand," she said. "He has so much inner strength; he never has any doubts."

"Do you have doubts?"

She put down her glass. The fuming alcohol had brought a little blood to her sallow cheeks.

"They don't want to hear what we just told them. Sometimes I wonder if it wouldn't be better to let them live and die in peace."

"And what would you do then?"

A smile crossed her face. "I'd go back and live in the warm countries.

That's where I was born. I'd stretch myself out in a hammock and forget everything."

"Well, why not do it?" I said.

"I can't," she replied. "Because I wouldn't really be able to forget. There's too much misery, too much suffering in the world. I'll never be able to just sit back and accept it."

"Even if you were happy?"

"I wouldn't be happy."

In a yellow mirror opposite us, I saw her face, her damp locks of hair under her black hat, her velvety eyes in her weary face.

"In spite of everything, we're doing useful work, aren't we?" she asked.

"Of course."

She looked at me and shrugged her shoulders. "Why don't you ever say what you're thinking?"

"Because I never think anything," I answered.

"That's not true."

"I assure you, I'm incapable of holding an opinion."

"Why?"

"Let's not talk about me," I said.

"On the contrary."

"Words don't have the same meaning for you as they do for me."

"I know. One day I heard you say to Armand that you didn't belong to this world." She looked at my hands and then raised her eyes to my face. "But it isn't true," she said. "Here you are, sitting next to me. We're talking together. You're a man, a man with a strange destiny, but a man of this world."

Her voice had an urgent tone—a caress and an appeal. Very far off, in the darkest depths, under the cold ashes and the hardened lava, something trembled. The rough bark of a tree against my cheek, a lilac-colored dress disappearing down a path.

"If you want," she said, "I can be your friend."

"You don't understand. No one can understand who I am, what I am."

"Explain it to me."

I shook my head. "You'd better go to bed."

"I don't feel like going to bed."

Like a well-behaved child, her hands were resting on the table, but her nails were scratching the marble. Alone beside me, alone among her comrades, alone in the world, with all that weight of suffering she loaded upon her shoulders.

"You're not happy," she said.

"No."

"Well!" she exclaimed with a sudden burst of ardor. "You see! It's perfectly plain that you too belong to the world of men—people can feel sorry for you, can love you . . ."

Laughing, she breathed in the fragrant scent of the roses and the flowering linden trees. *I knew you were unhappy.* And I hugged the tree trunk in my arms. Would I become a living man again? Under the cold lava, a warm vapor was trembling. She had loved me for a long time. I knew it.

"One day you'll be dead and I'll forget you," I said. "Doesn't that make friendship impossible?"

"No," she replied. "Even if you forget me, our friendship will have existed. The future could never affect it." She raised her eyes; a look of tenderness flooded her face. "That whole future in which you'll forget me, that past in which I didn't exist, I accept them, they're a part of you. It's you, the real you, who are sitting here together with that future and that past. I've often thought about it and I'd say to my-self that time could never separate us if only . . ." her voice choked up and she finished quickly, "if only you were my friend."

I held out my hand. Because of the strength of her love, despite the past, despite the future, I once more found myself completely present, completely alive for the first time in centuries. I was there, a man loved by a woman, a man with a strange destiny, but a man of this world. I touched her fingers. Only a word and that dead crust would have caved in, the fiery lava of life would have begun flowing again, the world would once more have had a face. There would have been expectations, joys, tears.

"Let me love you," she said very softly.

A few days, a few years, and then she would be lying on a bed with a shriveled face. Colors would all become jumbled together, indis-tinguishable, the sky would fade, odors would freeze up. *You'll forget me.* Her face was frozen in the middle of the oval painting. There weren't even words any longer with which to say: "She's not here." *Where* was she not? I could see no emptiness around me.

"No," I said. "It's useless. Everything is useless."

"Is it because I mean nothing to you?"

I looked at her. She knew I was immortal, had weighed the meaning of that word, and still she loved me. She was able to love an immortal man. Were I still capable of using human words, I would have said, "Of all the women I've ever known, you're the most generous, the most passionate, you're the noblest and the purest." But those words meant nothing to me. Laura was already dead. I withdrew my hand from hers.

"Nothing. You couldn't understand."

She sank back into the leather chair and stared at her reflection in the mirror. She was alone, she was weary. She would grow old, alone and weary, without receiving anything in exchange for the gifts she lavished and which were not even sought from her, fighting for them, without them, against them, doubting them and doubting herself. In my heart, something still trembled—pity. I could have torn her from her present life; there was still enough left of my former wealth to take her to the warm countries. She would stretch herself out in a hammock in the shade of a palm tree and I would tell her I loved her.

"Laura."

She smiled timidly. There was still a little hope in her eyes. And Beatrice was bending her fleshy face over the red and gold manuscript. "I want to make you happy," I had said. And I had lost her more surely than I had lost Antonio. She was smiling. But what reason did I have to prefer her smiles to her tears? There was nothing I could give her. Because I wanted nothing for myself *with* them, there was nothing I could want *for* them. I would have had to love her. I did not love her. I wanted nothing.

"Go back to your room," I said. "It's late."

Among the rows of cypresses, golden dots rose and fell as if they were being pulled by invisible strings, rose, fell, rose again. Drops of water squirted up and fell back to earth. Always the same foam and always different. And the ants came and went, thousands of ants, thousands of times the same ant. They came and went in the offices of the *Reform*. They walked over to the window, walked away from it, slapped each other on the shoulders, sat down, got up and talked without stopping. The rain was beating heavily against the windows, seven colors, four seasons; and all of them talked at once: "Is it the Revolution? . . . For the revolution to be successful we must . . ." The good of Italy, the good of Carmona, the security of the Empire. They were talking, their hands tightened around the handles of their swords, around the butts of revolvers, ready to die to convince themselves of it.

"I'd like to see what's happening," Laura said. "Would you care to come with me, Fosca?"

"Yes, why not?"

The street was teeming with people. An oblique rain was pounding the pavement, the roofs. A few umbrellas were open above their heads, but for the most part they walked unconcerned through the wet night. *Le jour de gloire est arrivé*. They were singing and waving flags and torches. Every house was lit up, lamps and paper lanterns were hanging on all the walls, at the intersections blazing fires were waging a battle against the wind and water. *Aux armes, citoyens!* They were singing. Festive shouts, clamors of death, canticles rising from taverns together with the sounds of brawls. The day of justice had arrived. "To arms!" They streamed out onto the streets, danced around joyous fires, waved flaming torches. Always the same foam and always different. "Down with Guizot!" they were shouting. There was a strange smile on Laura's lips. She was looking at something in the distance that I could not see. Sitting in the canoe in the middle of the calm waters, he was gazing off into the distance at the invisible mouth of the river which emptied into the Pacific. The Pacific?

"Don't go that way!"

A woman hidden in a doorway motioned us to turn back. In front of us, the street was deserted. Suddenly a shot rang out. Everyone stopped dead in his tracks. Laura grabbed my arm and pulled me through the hesitant crowd.

"Is this prudent?" I said.

"I want to know what's happening."

The first one we saw was a man in shirtsleeves. His face was flat against the ground and his arms were outstretched as if he were trying to grip the cobblestones to prevent himself from slipping into death. The second one was looking up at the sky with wide open eyes. There were some who were still writhing in the last pangs of death. From the intersecting streets came men bearing stretchers, their torches lighting up the red cobblestones on which the dead and wounded were sprawled out, cobblestones strewn with umbrellas, canes, hats, crushed lanterns and shredded flags. The squares of Rome were red. In the gutters, dogs were fighting over nauseating pink and white things, and another dog was howling into the night at death, women and children turned toward the moon faces mutilated by horses' hoofs, and flies were buzzing around bodies lying on the hard ground surrounded by bamboo huts, and a low moaning rose from the dust which soldiers had trampled upon. Not to die for twenty years or sixty years, and then finally, inexorably, to die.

"To the Bastille!"

There was a crowd now on the square. They had stopped a wagon and were piling the dead bodies into it. "To the Bastille!" they shouted. "Revenge! They're killing innocent people!" Laura's face was completely white. Her fingers tightened around my arm. "This is it," she murmured. "It's the Revolution." The alarm began ringing as the wagon got under way. "To the Bastille! Revenge!" The dead were still warm, the blood on the cobblestones still wet. A few moments before, they were alive and now they were dead, dead forever. And the living continued to live, as if they would never have to die. Inside them, they were carrying submissive corpses through their lives. The alarm was ringing, and from every street streamed bands of people waving flags and carrying torches which cast a fiery red glow on the wet cobblestones. The procession grew from minute to minute, the boulevard was submerged under a black sea, the immense human sea, erect, intact, the same as ever, always the same. There had been plagues, cholera, famine, the stakes, massacres, wars, revolutions, and still it was there, the human sea, indestructible. The dead were in the earth, the living on the earth, the same foam . . . They were marching, marching toward the Bastille, toward the Revolution, toward the future. Tyranny was about to be vanquished, and soon there would be no more poverty, no more classes, no more frontiers, no more wars, no more murders. Justice, fraternity, and liberty would reign, reason would soon govern the world, *my* reason. A white sail was vanishing on the horizon, men were going to conquer leisure and prosperity, they would rip the earth's riches from her bowels, construct huge, bright cities. I swept away forests, cleared brushlands, roads streaked across the green, yellow and blue globe which I held in my hands, the sun flooded the new Jerusalem where men in white robes exchanged peaceful greetings. They danced around joyful fires, trampled upon screeching women in dark back rooms. Seated in perfumed boudoirs, they spoke through their mortal mouths with measured voices, low voices, high voices. "Revenge!" they were shouting. There, at the end of the boulevard, a red and gold paradise opened to them, a paradise in which happiness had the coppery sparkle of anger. It was toward that paradise that they were marching. Each step brought them closer to it. As for me, I walked over the flat plains where rushes spit drops of water as I trod upon them. I advanced step after step toward the horizon which retreated with each step, the horizon on which the same sun went down every evening.

"Long live the *Reform!*"

They had stopped under the windows of the newspaper. Armand appeared on the balcony, he gripped the iron balustrade in his hands, he cried out words. In the distance a church was burning, flares cast a blood-red glow on the statues in the main square. "Long live Antonio Fosca!" Perched atop roofs and in trees, they shouted, "Long live Luther!" And glasses clinked together. Carlo Malatesta was laughing and life was burning; it was burning in Carmona, in Worms, in Gand, in Münster, in Paris, right here, at this very minute, in the hearts of living men, mortal men. And I trod over the flat plains, tested the frozen ground with my foot, blind, an outsider, dead as the cypresses without flowers, without winters or summers, springs or autumns.

They began marching again, and inside me I called out: "Marianne!" She would have had eyes to see and ears to hear, her heart would have beat faster. For her, too, the future would have flamed in the black streets—liberty, fraternity. I closed my eyes and she appeared to me, appeared to me as she really was, as I had for so long lost her, in her dress with the pink and black stripes, with her locks of hair carefully arranged, with her calm smile. "Marianne." I saw her. Horrified, she drew close to me and held me tightly. She hated disorder, violence, shouting. She would have turned away from those dishevelled women, would have stopped her ears to shut out that savage uproar. It was of a reasonable revolution she had dreamed. "Marianne." I tried to think. If she were living now, she would be different, she would know these people, would love them, would become used to the smell of gunpowder and death. I looked at Laura. Her hair was wet and in disarray, she was holding her shawl tightly around her shoulders and her eyes were beaming. She was Laura; she was not Marianne. To remain here at my side, Marianne would have had to stop being herself. She was frozen in the depths of the past, in her times, and I was no longer able to call her to me, not even her image.

I raised my eyes, looked at the moonless sky, the illuminated façades, the trees, and around me the crowd of people, her fellow creatures. And I realized then that the last bond which attached me to the world had just been broken. It was no longer Marianne's world and I could no longer contemplate it through her eyes. The image of her face was now snuffed out completely, forever, and in my heart, even the beating of her heart had stopped. *You'll* forget me. It was not I who had forgotten her. She had slipped out of the world, had slipped out of me who would never leave this world and yet who did not belong to it. No trace under the sky, neither on the waters nor on the earth, no trace in any heart. No emptiness, no absence, everything was full. The same foam and always different, forever the same, forever different.

They were marching. They had almost reached the Bastille. The procession was a huge, turbulent river. They came from every street, from the boulevards, from the depths of time; through the streets of Carmona, the streets of Gand, of Valladolid, of Münster, on the roads of Germany, Flanders, Italy, France, by foot, on horses, in tunics, in shirtsleeves, in flowing white robes, or protected by coats of mail, they came, the peasants, the workers, the bourgeoisie, the vagabonds, in hope, in anger, in hate, in joy, their eyes fixed on the paradise of the future, they came, leaving behind them a wake of sweat and blood, their feet torn by the rocks on the roads, they came step after step and with each step the horizon retreated a step, the horizon on which the same sun went down every evening; tomorrow, in a hundred years, in twenty centuries, they would still be marching, the same foam and always different, and the horizon would continue to retreat before them, day after day, always, always, trampling over the black plains for centuries and centuries as they had trampled over them for centuries and centuries.

But in the evening, I threw my pack on the frozen ground, I lit a fire, I stretched myself out; I stretched myself out only to set off again the next day. And thus, sometimes, they stopped, they shouted, they fired their guns in the air; a woman standing on the mounting of a cannon was singing the *Marseillaise*. "Long live the Republic!" The king had just abdicated, they believed they were holding their victory in their hands, they were holding goblets filled with wine in their hands, they were laughing, Catherina was smiling, Malatesta was laughing, Pergola's walls crumbled amid joyous shouting, the domes of Florence sparkled in the sun, the cathedral bells were sounding the victory. Carmona was saved, peace was proclaimed. Armand came out on the balcony; on a huge streamer they had painted in big letters: LONG LIVE THE REPUBLIC! They hung it up over the windows and threw down fistfulls of leaflets on which words of faith and hope were written. "Long live the Republic!" shouted the crowd. "Long live Carmona!" and Carmona was lost, it was war, we turned our backs to Florence which we had been unable to enter; with sunken hearts, we left deserted Pergola; the peasants of Ingolstadt twisted in agony in fires they had lit . . . I felt Armand's hand on my shoulder.

"I know what you're thinking," he said.

For a moment we stood side by side, motionless, watching the frenzied mob. With their tomahawks they struck at the tall, red stake and they let out savage cries; they danced, they shattered the heads of babies against walls, flares lit up the night, they threw torches into the palace, the cobblestones were blood-red, embroidered banners fluttered at windows, hanging from balconies, from lampposts, dead bodies were swinging slowly to and fro, cries of horror, cries of joy, songs of death, canticles of peace, the sound of clinking glasses, the sound of arms, the moans and laughter rising together toward the sky. And then silence closed in again; on the well-scoured squares, women came to fetch their daily water, they cradled babies in their arms, the spinning machines began to hum again and the weavers' shuttles wove in and out, in and out, the dead were dead, the living alive, Carmona was stagnating on her rock, motionless, like a giant mushroom, boredom hung heavily in the sky and crushed the earth until the time when a new fire would begin to roar. A new voice, always the same voice and always different, burst out into the night: "Long live the Republic!" Standing on the mounting of a cannon a woman was singing.

"Tomorrow we'll have to fight again," Armand said. "But today we're victorious. Whatever may happen, this is a real victory."

"Yes."

I looked at him. I looked at Spinelle and Laura. Today. The word had a meaning for them. For them, there was a past, a future. There was a present. In the middle of the river that was flowing—from north to south? or east to west?—he was smiling. *I like this time of day.* Isabella was walking slowly about in the garden, the sun was playing on the beautiful, polished furniture, and with a smile he was stroking his silky beard; in the center of the square stood the stakes around which a crowd had gathered, and they advanced, singing; they were pressing their whole pasts against their hearts. The people had shouted,

"Down with the Republic!" and he had wept; and because he had wept, because he was smiling now, his victory was a real victory. The future could do nothing to destroy it. He knew that the next day he would have to begin wanting again, refusing again, fighting again. The next day he would begin again, but *this* day he was the victor. They looked at each other, laughed together, spoke to each other. They were the victors. And because they looked at each other and spoke to each other, they knew they were neither gnats, nor ants, nor stones, but men. And they knew too that it was important to be alive, to be victorious. They had risked, had given their lives to convince themselves of it, and they were convinced. There was no other truth for them.

I walked toward the door. I could not risk my life, could not smile at them; there was never a flame in my heart nor tears in my eyes. A man of nowhere, without a past, without a future, without a present. I wanted nothing, I was no one. I advanced step after step toward the horizon which retreated with each step; drops of water squirted up and fell to earth again, each instant destroyed the next, the last. My hands were forever empty: An outsider, a dead man. They were men, they were alive. I . . . I was not one of them. I had nothing to hope for. I went out the door.

EPILOGUE

For the first time since Fosca began telling his story, his voice trembled. He lowered his head. His hands were spread out on the oilcloth with the blue bowl between them. He looked at them as if he did not recognize them. He moved his right index finger, then the left, and then his hands were still again. Regina turned her eyes away. It was broad daylight. Peasants were sitting around tables, eating soup and drinking white wine. In the world of men, a new day had begun. On the other side of the windows, the sky was blue.

"And on the other side of the door, was there still something?" Regina asked.

"Yes. The square of the City Hall, Paris. And then a road which led off into the country, a woods, thickets, sleep. I slept sixty years. When they awakened me, the world was the same as ever. I said to them: 'I slept sixty years.' And they put me in the asylum. I wasn't unhappy there."

"Don't go so fast," Regina said.

She stared at the door, thinking, *When he's finished, I'll have to go out that door, and on the other side of it there will still be something. I won't be able to go to sleep, and I won't have the courage to die.*

"There's nothing more to tell," Fosca said. "Every day the sun rose and set. I went to the asylum and I came out. There were wars, after each war, peace, and after the peace, another war. Men are born every day and others die."

"Stop it," she said. "Stop it!"

She held her hands against her mouth. A feeling of anguish went from her throat to her heart to her stomach. She wanted to scream.

A moment later, she asked, "What are you going to do now?"

Fosca looked around him, and suddenly a perplexed, mournful expression appeared on his face. "I don't know," he said.

"Sleep?"

"No, I can't sleep any more." He lowered his voice. "I have nightmares."

343

"You? Nightmares?"

"I dream that there are no more men," he said. "They're all dead. The earth is white. The moon is still in the sky and it lights up an earth that's completely white. I'm alone with the mouse." He was speaking very softly and he had the look of a very old man.

"What mouse?"

"The little accursed mouse. There will be no more men and the mouse will go on turning around in circles through eternity. It was I who condemned it. That was my greatest crime."

"It doesn't know," Regina said.

"Precisely. It doesn't know, and it goes on spinning in circles. And then one day there will be nothing but that mouse and I on the surface of the earth."

"And I under the earth," Regina said.

She pressed her lips together. A scream rose from her stomach to her heart, from her heart to her throat. In her head, a great, burning light was vibrating, more blinding than the night. She had to stop herself from screaming. And yet if she screamed, it seemed to her that something would happen. Perhaps that painful trembling would freeze up, perhaps the light would go out.

"I'm going to leave now," Fosca said.

"Where are you going?"

"Anywhere. It doesn't matter."

"Then why go?"

"There's a desire to move in my legs," he said. "I have to take advantage of those desires."

He walked toward the door and she followed him.

"And me?" she asked.

"Oh, you." He shrugged his shoulders. "It will come to an end."

He went down the two steps in front of the door and with long strides walked along the road which led out of the village. He was walking very rapidly, as if in the distance, beyond the horizon, something was waiting for him—a world entombed under a glass dome, without men, without life, white and bare. She went down the two steps. *Let him go!* she said to herself. *Let him disappear forever!* She watched him striding down the road, and for a moment it seemed to her that the sorcery with which he had stripped her of her being was leaving with him. He disappeared at the first bend. She took a step and stopped, nailed to the spot. He had disappeared, but she remained the same as he had made her—a blade of grass, a gnat, an ant, a bit of foam. She looked around her; perhaps there was a way out. Furtive as the beating of an eyelid, something lightly grazed her heart; it was not even a hope, and even that quickly vanished. She was too tired. She pressed her hands against her mouth, bent her head forward. She was defeated. In horror, in terror, she accepted the metamorphosis—gnat, foam, ant, until death. *And it's only the beginning*, she thought. She stood motionless, as if it were possible to play tricks with time, possible to stop it from following its course. But her hands stiffened against her quivering lips.

When the bells began to sound the hour she let out the first scream.

ABOUT THE AUTHOR

SIMONE de BEAUVOIR was born in Paris in 1908. After studying in a religious institution, she attended the Sorbonne where she received her agrégation in philosophy in 1929. She taught for several years in lycées in Marseilles, Rouen, and Paris, but left teaching for a writer's life in 1942. From that time on, she devoted her life to writing and lecturing, and as a novelist, dramatist, and philosopher became probably the most distinguished woman writer in contemporary France. She gained great attention in the United States upon publication of *The Second Sex*, a monumental work on what it means to be a woman. Among her many novels, *The Mandarins* won France's highest honor, the Prix Goncourt. Simone de Beauvoir died in 1986.